Avaland

AMY CROUCHER ROSE

ISBN - 978-1-5272-2283-0

Printed in the United Kingdom

Cover design and layout by www.spiffingcovers.com

To Phil,

Best wishes.

[illegible]

I dedicate this book to Tyler, Joshua, Joseph, Mandy, Barry, Danielle and Ben.

Avaland liveth upon earth,
Midst water, fire and air
Thy Merlin's Isle of Apples
Where Magick folk shall fare.

CHAPTER ONE

THE IMPOSSIBLE DAY

Mr and Mrs Crump ran a very tight ship, to strict routine and deadline. Every point in every day was precisely planned and always ran as scheduled. So when the residents of the cottage awoke one grey midwinter's morning, they were unprepared because today was going to be far from ordinary.

Walter Crump was retired. He spent most of his time tending to his allotment. His masterpiece was the giant cabbage, an invention he believed could one day feed the world. On a typical morning you would find him wandering up and down his plot, stroking his grey beard and talking to his vegetables from behind his fine silver spectacles.

The teenagers in the village found this highly amusing and would taunt and tease him. 'IT MAKES THEM GROW BETTER!' he would shout angrily, waving his walking stick.

Walter wasn't easily intimidated; after all, he had fought in two wars. If at any point there was any disturbance, he would quickly stamp it out. He knew what they thought of him. *Lost my marbles, they reckon!* Though he didn't show it much, anything unforeseen like this made Walter upset and angry, because he was a man that thrived on routine.

Blonde-bobbed Aphra Crump, however, was much more down to earth than her ever-so-slightly eccentric husband, though she did mirror his eccentricities in her cooking. She would spend hours muddying the kitchen inventing new foods, for competitions, that most people would never dream of putting together in case they got food poisoning. But somehow she almost always managed to pull it off and was quite famous for it within the local community.

That morning Aphra awoke to find her husband had already left the house. She breezed through her usual morning activities quite effortlessly, receiving a six-digit cheque refund in the post which made a nice change from the usual bills that came through the letter box. Even the weather was turning out to be promising.

Polishing her favourite picture of the Queen on the mantelpiece, and leaving their pebble-dash cottage, she pouted in the rear-view mirror, adjusting her curls. Turning right at the sign on the corner of Hoddinott's Bluff she could honestly say she had never felt happier.

Her husband, however, could not say the same; he was having an extremely bad morning; and had never felt so unlucky.

Lately some of the youths in the village (probably as a result of his grumpy ways) had been moving some of his prized inventions around in the middle of the night, causing him much stress and fury to recover them. His van was now full of them, because they had been placed around the village in precarious places by a bunch of these youths.

'Wait until I get my hands on 'em!' he cursed to himself, huffing and puffing with anger.

By lunchtime he had already had words with plenty of teenagers, just in case they knew the culprits, who had vanished. *Good job too*, he thought, *as they would have gotten a piece of my mind!*

He found the last of his giant cabbages in elderly Mrs Perkins' chimney spout, much to her inconvenience, which she expressed eagerly.

Mrs Perkins cringed with utter disgust, wittering on about pigeon poo in his toupee before slamming the door on him.

Walter quickly ran over to the restroom in The Old Rasping's pub, removing the hairpiece to scrub it with soap. But it didn't matter how hard he scrubbed, it just wouldn't come out and now to make matters worse the soap had caused his toupee to go frizzy and stand up on end.

Slamming it onto his head, ducking behind pillars and hiding behind newspapers, he tried to get to his van as quickly as he could without being spotted.

But when he arrived he realised the van was gone.

Looking up the busy street, he caught a glimpse of it on the back end of a tow truck, cabbages and all. It just didn't matter what he did, nothing was going to go right for him today. He felt like slamming his toupee onto the ground in fury!

'Good afternoon!' greeted Constable Bone. 'Strange day it's turning out to be, isn't it?'

'How do you mean?' grunted Walter, preoccupied with his own thoughts.

The officer tried not to stare at the fluffy mass on top of his head, which only aggravated Walter further.

'Everywhere I turn there is another problem to deal with,' insisted the policeman. 'Not enough officers to deal with 'em. Poor Amery Moon, the greengrocer, has been driving around all day trying to outrun a cloud. Says it's been following him. It tried to strike him twice with lightning, apparently!'

Walter looked around, noticing for the first time that he wasn't the only person having a spot of trouble.

'Better dash!' said the officer, sidetracking hurriedly to rescue an elderly gentleman from a gang of rebellious ducks. 'Good to see you, Walter!'

Squinting to get a better look, he hadn't realised how much he needed his glasses until now. Pulling them out of his top pocket, he looked on, astonished as scenes of devastation unfolded all around him; indeed, something very odd was going on. He had been completely blinded to the situation unfolding, so preoccupied with finding his creations that he hadn't noticed what had been taking place all around him.

Walter (a superstitious man) decided to get back to the van sharpish. 'Oh, excuse me,' he said moving out of the way of a man with each of his hands superglued to the side of his head.

'That's OK,' the man replied, tripping over a cat on a skateboard.

Picking up his feet, Walter sprinted down the path to the corner of the street, where two men were running in the opposite direction.

Open-mouthed and paralysed with fear, a slight delay saw him plunging over a hedge to escape from an oncoming bull, making an emergency landing on a woman planting a conifer tree.

'Sorry,' he hastily shouted out behind him, hurtling like a secret operative over her gate.

Back on the main road, he found a moment to bend over and breathe, resting his hands on his hips and turning his head sideways.

The view ahead showed him what must have been causing all of the trouble: a roadblock and an overturned truck that had lost most of its livestock.

But something had riled them.

Sheep were bumping their heads into car side doors, leaving dents and passengers with no choice but to wait for help to arrive.

Cars were backed up the street as far as the eye could see.

Abandoning the retrieval of his van, he jumped onto a bus that was headed in the opposite direction but got stuck in a traffic jam that did not move for ten minutes before it broke down. Deciding it would be quicker to cut through the park, he stepped off, narrowly avoiding being knocked over by a man who had lost control of his bicycle because he was being chased by a swarm of bees.

The equally bemused fellow behind him, who had also decided to get off early, wasn't as fortunate; he did get hit by the bike and landed in a nearby bush where a little dog called Timmy did his business on him.

'WHAT ON EARTH IS GOING ON?' Walter bellowed, more to himself than anyone else. He had never seen anything like it in his life.

Then he remembered something: a shortcut through the park. But the moment he'd reached it, he instantly regretted the decision; the ground had become a minefield of recently laid eggs and what appeared to be sleepwalking chickens.

Those who had entered the park were finding it difficult to escape, falling on slimy shells and struggling back to their feet.

But Walter didn't falter. It was too late to turn back now. If he could make it across an enemy trench, he could do anything.

Never have you seen a man of that age run with such vitality.

The teenagers that had got him into this trouble in the first place could not take their eyes off him as he skated decadently through the air. A scruffy-haired boy attempted to copy his technique, pratfalling straight to his buttocks.

Amazingly, Walter arrived on the other side completely unscathed, dusting down his trousers and giving himself a nod of self-approval before taking a more direct route through the hedge.

He arrived home dishevelled and anxious, deciding to shut the curtains, lock all of the doors and telephone immediately for his wife to return home.

Checking out of the curtains every few moments or so, he sat in darkness under the windowsill until he heard her car turn the corner and she finally arrived up the driveway, confused about why her husband had insisted she come home so early.

He spent the rest of the evening telling her about his day and what he thought about it. She spent the rest of the day telling him she thought he was mad and should throw that darn toupee in the bin because he looked better without it anyway.

But to put his mind to rest, she agreed to stay indoors with him until the morning and that is exactly what they did.

#

Ice droplets fell from the sky; over time they became thicker then heavier until inches of snow rested over the whole village.

The woods at the bottom of the cul-de-sac started to stir. The trees swayed in all directions, creating an odd sort of rippling effect. A collision in the foliage caused the loud crack of several tree trunks, and a burst of wind blew through Hoddinott's Bluff.

But this was not an ordinary wind; it behaved unusually, as though an invisible force was driving it.

It was searching for something.

It knocked over a plant pot and scared away the neighbour's cat before it seemed to find what it was looking for: an open cloakroom window, which Walter had forgotten to close.

Normally wind would disappear, but this travelled through the house, almost knocking a vase from a sideboard in the hallway, before pushing open the bedroom door.

Snoring happily, his grey moustache tickling his top lip, Walter was muttering to himself, but Aphra appeared to be having a nightmare.

The wind hit them both square in the chest, causing them to jolt upright. Still fast asleep, their heads flopped to their sides like marionettes, each stumbled over to the wardrobe, getting dressed in the nearest clothes to hand.

The sun was just starting to rise by the time they got outside, and they made their way down the crunchy snow-covered path towards the entrance to Hoddinott Woods.

Ashen-faced, Aphra clasped the arm of her much taller husband and Mr Crump broke into an odd hypnotic smile.

The morning air was icy cold and he was wearing a pair of slippers and Bermuda shorts, but today it seemed like a fantastic idea to go for a walk, even if it was still snowing and only five o'clock in the morning.

Mr Curtis, who was also up because he had an early meeting, was peering out of the curtains with a look of utter bewilderment on his face.

Walter waved at him, wearing a puzzled expression.

'GOOD MORNING!' he shouted loudly.

Mr Curtis had always thought the Crumps were strange and this just confirmed his suspicions about them.

'Totally mad!' he said to his wife, closing the curtains behind him.

But then this was unusual behaviour even for the Crumps, who rarely left the house when it was snowing at all.

Vapour poured from their mouths with every breath as it hit the cold air. They were now deeper in the woods than they had ever been before. Icicles hung from branches over a nearby river that was completely frozen and morning dew had highlighted all of the spider webs.

Walter had fallen over several times but it wasn't until they were completely off the gravel path that they both came to their senses.

As though waking from a dream, a feeling of being lost overcame them.

Walter (who did not like surprises) spent the next few minutes yelling and cursing.

'I TOLD YOU, APHRA! DIDN'T I SAY SOMETHING STRANGE WAS GOING ON? IT'S BEEN IMPOSSIBLE FROM THE MOMENT I LEFT THE HOUSE YESTERDAY!'

As Walter continued to moan, Aphra's heart sank with a feeling of déjà vu. Hadn't she just dreamt this?

'AND WHAT ON EARTH AM I WEARING?' Walter yelled to his wife.

Walter took his wife's arm protectively as a flash of white light consumed the air around them.

Staring with bated breath, they beheld an old oak that was alight, every branch with candles.

Beneath lay a small child, covered with cuts and bruises.

'Is she alive?' asked Walter urgently, as Aphra reached out to cuddle her in.

She was surprisingly warm and started to stir. Aphra gave a sigh of relief, noticing a lump of crystal had fallen to the ground from her long silk dress.

Walter bent down to pick it up, holding it out for Aphra to see. The sparkling pyramid began to glow to the touch.

'What is it?' Aphra asked, mesmerised.

But Walter had no explanation. Leaning forward, he removed his dressing gown to put it around the child. This was the first time that Walter had ever been lost for words.

The child was now awake and staring up at them helplessly, with luminescent blue eyes. The little girl looked around, panicked. She screamed, frightened.

Aphra spoke to her softly so as not to alarm her. 'It's OK, you are safe now.'

'Mummy!" the little girl sobbed wildly.

Aphra became overpowered with emotion, catching her husband's eye. 'I had a dream,' she whispered. 'I know what happened to them.' But she did not further explain, deciding now to be the incorrect moment. 'Her mother desires us to give her a home.'

Walter thought for a moment, mumbling to himself before shaking his head. 'Then we shall do as has been asked of us – we will raise the girl as though she were our own.'

The exhausted child rested her bruised face against Aphra's chest and closed her eyes.

Stroking her thick blonde hair, Aphra kissed her head, a tear falling down her cheek. 'It's OK, you're safe now.'

Husband and wife stared at each other. 'We must be careful,' Aphra informed him. 'They are still looking for her.'

Walter picked up a fallen branch to deter attackers and, with their footprints covered by the falling snow behind them, together they navigated their way cautiously back to the cottage.

CHAPTER TWO

The Baffling Bazaar

A scattering of white sifted across the crisp lawn, dusting the frosty wisteria that clambered the cottage walls. Insects scurried into their tiny houses to take shelter from the cold.

Not a soul remained but one: a pair of piercing blue eyes surveying the scene from inside the window. Ten years had passed since the day Aphra and Walter had found the child in Hoddinott Woods but now she was sixteen and had recently left school.

With long blonde hair cascading over her shoulders, she yawned and stretched, revealing a twisted gold bracelet that named the girl as Charlotte. The young woman scratched her wrist in yet another attempt to remove the band, but she already knew her attempt would be futile, because it had been tried without success many times.

She often wondered how it was possible for the bracelet to grow but not be removed.

The first try had seen Walter failing to break it with a pair of secateurs that shattered in his hand without even leaving a mark.

They had even taken it to a jeweller's. The goldsmith had been left mystified at the strength of the gold, something he had never come across before in an item of such delicacy.

As much as it annoyed her, she knew she was going to have to be patient; after all, she didn't really have a choice.

Smoke billowed from one of the six chimneys as steam vented from the large kitchen window – which was open because Aphra was cooking.

Skipping down the stairs to breakfast, Charlotte tripped over the cat, a usual morning occurrence because the cat was greedy and constantly wanted to be fed.

Wisteria Cottage had yet to change since the day she'd arrived. The same drab wallpaper hung on the walls and old-fashioned fabrics, mostly crochet, were scattered about on the sofa and random chairs. It was very homely, and the almost-always-lit fire made it rather cosy.

The kitchen also held a stone fireplace; it could easily fit a grown man inside of it. The chimney was full of soot because it was lit frequently and Walter hadn't quite gotten around to cleaning it yet.

A dozen or so chairs stood around a large pine table, and most of the walls were covered with dried flowers, herbs or bunches of garlic.

Aphra stood on the tips of her toes to give her a kiss. 'Remember we have the village fayre this afternoon, dear.'

Charlotte swallowed her bit of toast. 'But it's snowing; doesn't that mean it's cancelled?'

'Of course not,' Aphra replied with a giggle. 'It's the Baffling Bazaar, the snow makes it even better.'

The fact that it was snowing in September at all was unusual, but then unusual had come to be Charlotte's middle name. Her bright blue eyes made her look quite unhuman at times and it was quite common for strangers to stop and stare.

Though it wasn't just Charlotte's appearance that was strange. Inexplicable things had been happening to her for as long as she could remember.

Only yesterday she had somehow subconsciously set all of the cats in the neighbourhood on to petrified, cat-phobic Mrs Curtis, who lived next door, after she heard her suggest to the postman that Aphra was probably a witch.

Charlotte had learned to live with peculiar events like these, never really believing that they were anything to do with her. After all, she was just a normal girl. Right? Having little memory of the day she had arrived in Hoddinott's Bluff, Aphra and Walter had never attempted to hide the truth, even if she didn't quite believe it. Though these events had sometimes proved useful, they were probably the reason that she had never made any real friends and suffered at the hands of bullies for most of her life.

Aphra was more practical than orderly when it came to the housekeeping because she (like her husband) was an inventor, not a cleaner, as she reminded him regularly.

As she shovelled the contents of the pan onto her favourite royal wedding plates, Walter picked up his second newspaper from the small pile on the table.

It headlined: *BLACK PANTHER SPOTTED*.

Pouring hot water into the teapot, Aphra tried to disguise a tear by dabbing her eye with the corner of her tea towel.

'All grown up,' she said, pretending to snivel. 'And I haven't aged a day.'

Walter peered up from behind the page he was reading and rolled his eyes.

'When's you next karate tournament?' he barked at Charlotte. Walter took the matter with extreme seriousness.

Aphra looked at the calendar besides the fridge. 'It's tomorrow afternoon. Gosh, that's come around quickly.'

'Have you been practising your roundhouse properly?' he demanded, folding up the newspaper and throwing it on the table.

'Yes,' Charlotte audaciously replied. 'I practise, each leg twenty times per day.'

'Good,' he said. 'Hopefully you'll do better than last time.'

It was hardly Charlotte's fault. The last tournament she'd entered, she had been paired with a girl twice her size and nerves had got the better of her. But even though she wasn't as good as she'd like to be, she enjoyed her karate lessons even if she didn't much like the tournaments that Walter insisted she enter for self-protection purposes.

Charlotte didn't need reminding that she wasn't very good at karate yet, but the important thing was she hadn't given up. Even if Walter was a bit pushy, she knew he only had her best interests at heart.

Now she had left school, she had a lot of time on her hands. She only worked at weekends at the moment, a part-time job in a local burger bar; she was waiting for more hours so had decided to make herself useful by helping Aphra prepare for the district Baffling Bazaar, a contest she entered every leap year.

Some of the creations for this year's event were her most innovative yet and among some of her oddest.

Walter had also been preparing something special. He had spent many more hours than usual at his allotment, but the reason remained top secret. Aphra and Charlotte had already sneaked up for a peek, but been shooed away with Walter's hosepipe – something he looked like he'd had a lot of practice with.

Charlotte was used to attending odd events, though she hadn't always competed in them. Walter and she had spent many days out together whilst Aphra was working, none of which she could say she had particularly enjoyed. They had visited art galleries, museums and local historical places of interest. They tended to stay away from fun places like funfairs or bowling alleys, because Walter didn't like going anywhere unpredictable, although she could remember getting excited about a trip to the cinema that turned out to be a thirty-year-old documentary on whales.

Charlotte specifically remembered the only thing she'd enjoyed about that day was the popcorn.

Outside the window was a mound of Walter's giant cabbages.

'Caught the little blighters trying to steal 'em again,' he complained, looking frustrated. 'And the day before an important competition, so I dug 'em up and brought 'em here! Aphra's not happy about her crumpled begonias,' he grumbled.

Walter liked to moan, and it was normally about Aphra's cooking.

Aphra packed the last of the cakes into boxes and they loaded the car. Walter shook his head as his wife handed over a tub of something to Mrs Curtis, who was trying to rush to her porch without being spotted.

'Trying to inflict your cooking on the neighbours again, eh?' said Walter. 'Cucumber cake! Whoever heard of such a thing?'

They spent the next twenty minutes defrosting the vehicles, which Charlotte was grateful for because the snow had made her dress wet and she was allowed to go and change into her much more comfortable jeans.

Giving her a disapproving tut, Aphra pulled back the front seat to allow Charlotte to climb into the back of her racing green Mini.

'Wipe your face, you have dirt on it!' she complained, a little annoyed that Charlotte had managed to find a way out of the outfit she had picked for her.

'Don't forget the dillybag dear!' she then called to Walter, who was locking the front door.

'Phah.' Walter waved his hand.

Then the two vehicles made their way off to the Baffling Bazaar, Walter impatiently at the rear.

Going like the clappers, they finally arrived.

Double gates opened out on to a grey manor house. Its extravagant gardens led to a field that was filled with hundreds of cars. As they drove around the gatherers, Charlotte checked out some of the competition.

There were many peculiar stands here and it made for most odd viewing. One had thousands of colourful scented candles and smelled of joss sticks; next to it was a stall that sold crystals of all shapes; another played 1920's music and a miniature pantomime Punch and Judy was performing.

They pulled up next to a tent draped in flowing silk; a fortune teller was standing outside, wearing a purple turban with a diamond in the centre of his forehead. He was hanging a sign up that said:

Magnificent Nick

For all your soothsaying needs.

Charlotte and Aphra stopped and began to lay out trays of sherbet strudel, cucumber cake, pickled egg tarts, hogfish pie and aniseed apple crumble. Then Charlotte filled plastic cups with liquorice lemonade and parsnip tea.

Groups gathered around the stall, which surprisingly was very popular; people seemed perplexed by the strangeness of it all.

Walter's stall was also doing very well. Crowds flocked around his giant cabbages, square pumpkins, melons and other vegetables, quite baffled and amused. Charlotte even saw him talking to a news reporter and having his photograph taken, which he looked very uncomfortable with, his smile looking more like a constipated gaze.

'Surpassed yourself yet again, my dear, I dare say you'll make the paper this year!' said the mayor, shaking Aphra's hand and smiling merrily as a photographer took their picture. 'Do tell me, Aphra, what do you put in this hogfish pie?' he said, picking up several and handing them to Charlotte across the counter. 'I must say it's quite up to the mark.'

Charlotte wrapped the pies and put them in a paper carrier bag for the mayor, who then gave her five pound coins.

'Splendid!' the mayor beamed, giving his portly belly a tap. 'You must give your recipes to my wife!'

Mayor Quigley gave Aphra a playful wink and his wife forced a strained smile.

'Can you pass me Mrs Perkins' seaweed snaps, dear?' Aphra asked. 'They're in my glovebox.'

Aphra's car was situated at the back of the stall, so Charlotte went to it and took a small labelled bag from the dashboard. She was about to turn to come back when she felt an urge to look up.

Watching her from the bushes was a palomino horse, the same white stallion she had been seeing all her life. Once again it appeared that nobody else had noticed it was there.

To most people this wouldn't be strange at all, but to Charlotte mysteriousness shrouded this creature.

The first time the horse had appeared was her seventh birthday, at her fancy dress party. Its white snout had poked out of a bush, knocking off her top hat, which landed on the iron-clad table. It had been such a shock, even her favourite teddy bear had appeared to jump.

Lately she had been seeing this horse at least once a month, but every time she approached it simply disappeared.

From the tent came a loud cough that made her turn around.

'I haven't got all day, you know!' complained Mrs Perkins, holding out her hand, demanding her dried fishy sweets.

'Oh yes, sorry,' said Charlotte, passing them to her and looking back up at the horse, but once again it was nowhere to be seen.

'Thought you'd come by car instead of broomstick today, did you?' came a voice from behind that Charlotte recognised at once to be her next-door neighbour's daughter Beatrice Curtis.

Beatrice was the same age as Charlotte and had been in the same year at school. From a young age she had made it her personal ambition to make Charlotte's life as miserable as possible. Unfortunately, the month since leaving school had done nothing for her manners and she was just as much a bully now as she was then.

'I didn't think this would be your sort of thing, Beatrice?' replied Charlotte confidently. 'Have you run out of people to look down your nose at in the village?'

Beatrice smiled sarcastically. 'I thought I'd come and check out all you freaks at this pile of shit they hold every four years, though I can't say I'm surprised to see you and your weirdo family here!'

Her comments were totally outrageous, completely unjustified – the Baffling Bazaar attracted people from all over England, and not all of them were completely weird.

OK, most of them were, but not all of them.

Beatrice was soon joined by her equally charming best friend and lookalike, Constance.

'What are you talking to abnormal people for?' she spat, looking Charlotte up and down like she was something she had just scraped from the bottom of her shoe.

'We know what your granny is,' Constance continued. 'She's the Over Wallop Witch! She filled the village pond with poisonous frogs last Halloween!'

'... and she gave all the first-born boys chicken pox on their birthdays last year!'

Charlotte laughed to suggest the idea of Aphra being a witch was ridiculous. 'That was an accident!' she teased.

'Daddy wants us to move, but we can't sell our house because nobody wants to live next door to you!'

The two lipstick-smothered girls crossed their arms and tilted their heads to one side sarcastically.

Charlotte exhaled with annoyance. These two were exhausting sometimes.

It hadn't gone unnoticed that there had been a 'For Sale' sign outside the Curtis residence for a while but somehow Charlotte found it very difficult to believe that the Crumps were the reason they couldn't sell their house; it was probably much more likely to do with the fact it was grossly overpriced.

'Nobody likes you,' taunted Beatrice. 'Nobody likes any of you, so just do us all a favour and get lost!'

That was it, Charlotte had had enough now, especially with Aphra so close by, so she (kind of on purpose) held out her finger and told them to 'GO AWAY.'

'AHH!' the two lipstick-smothered teenagers screamed. 'SHE'S HEXED US!' And within moments they had turned the icy corner and were out of sight.

#

The next afternoon, the cuckoo clock struck a quarter past two.

Charlotte stood nervously by the driveway waiting for Walter.

'Come on then,' he ushered, picking up her gym bag and carrying it out of the back door before slamming it into the back of his three-wheeled van.

Aphra wasn't coming today; she didn't like watching the contests because they made her nervous. 'Good luck, dear,' she shouted from the window. 'You know, I was thinking; next week we could do some more girly things. You could always come along to the Over Wallop Knitting Club with me this Thursday?'

'I like karate,' said Charlotte defensively, absolutely certain that she did not fancy sitting around a table knitting with Aphra's strange witchy friends. After all, she didn't even like it when they came to the house.

Once she had said goodbye, Charlotte sat in the front seat of Walter's chugging van, the rickety engine misfired.

'Right, shall we go then?' he said, stalling it by accident, then starting it back up again.

A turn of the steering wheel and they were on their way.

Charlotte didn't like Walter's driving. He drove far too fast – they had avoided a number of high-scale accidents over the years – but the benefit to his atrocious driving was that they always arrived sooner.

As they were pulling up to the industrial estate, a tweed-capped man pasted a red sign to a billboard, labelling the entrance.

'How's your left side kick coming along?' said Walter, knowing this to be one of Charlotte's weakest moves.

'Alright,' she lied suspiciously, because she hadn't practised it at all.

It was busy inside; about half the rows of seats had been filled, mostly with parents and relatives that had come to cheer them on. As they approached the front bench, Walter tried to spot the best place to get a clear view of the ring.

Charlotte joined the other contestants, all young females similar in age to her.

Walter took out a white towel and water bottle and handed them over. 'Good luck,' he said, patting her on the arm, then wandered off to find a seat.

Charlotte recognised a hard-faced blonde who had also fallen victim to bullies at the same school she had, Tracey Stimpson. Tracey gave her a nod from behind narrow eyes, a motion Charlotte understood.

'You got me into a load of trouble yesterday,' said a squeaky voice from behind, that Charlotte recognised straight away. 'I'm going to kick your arse in there.'

'Oh, Beatrice, if you knew anything about martial arts at all, you would know that is not how it works.'

Just behind Beatrice was her magnet, Constance, looking obviously wary. She didn't say a thing to defend her friend.

A middle-aged man came out carrying a clipboard. 'First up, Constance and Charlotte.'

Stepping into the arena, both girls stood barefoot on the spongey mat, directly opposite one another.

Together they bowed, and Constance leapt in suddenly with a front kick to the chest, but Charlotte had a knack for anticipating things and was able to move out of the way, then slip Constance's other foot out from under her.

The crowd cheered, and Charlotte could see Walter jumping on the bench, whistling loudly.

The two attempted a second round, a deflected roundhouse that went in Charlotte's favour.

The final round saw Constance kicked clean off the mat, almost landing on Beatrice's lap.

The ref held up Charlotte's arm for all to see. 'Red wins!' he declared in unbiased settlement.

Walking back to the benches, Charlotte and Constance watched the next fight, which was between Beatrice and a much taller red-headed girl.

Beatrice was a lot stronger than Charlotte remembered, with a few moves she had yet to encounter herself. Looking rather like a sumo wrestler with worms, her unrelenting throws saw the round over surprisingly quickly. In this case, the girl's height had been at a disadvantage to Beatrice's sheer aggressive bodyweight.

Tracey also did surprisingly well; she seemed to have the best technique, a sharp and smooth extension of limbs and a good knowledge of how the body bends to manipulation. It was obvious to Charlotte that she was the one to watch, and she secretly hoped she didn't have to face her.

The TV screen along the back wall showed Walter dropping his half-eaten cheese sandwiches on the floor. Then a profile of each of the contenders in their current positions.

Charlotte had made it into the quarter finals; to get into the semis she would have to deal with the wrath of Beatrice.

She saw the hook-mouthed smirks the Curtis parents were trying to hide, openly hoping that their daughter would indeed 'kick Charlotte's arse'.

But not today. Yes, Beatrice was twice as big as her, but she wasn't as fast and that would be her weakness on this occasion.

In the ring, Beatrice was, to say the least, unpredictable and if Charlotte was being honest, she had put up a rather good fight. Unfortunately for her, though, she was losing and the more apparent this became to her, the sloppier she became.

Before long Charlotte was able to get some punches between those loose blocks, and the points quickly began to mount up until there was an update on the screen.

Red Wins! said the strip of writing.

Beatrice was seething, red with anger, and ran over to shout at the judge, but Charlotte was filled with satisfaction.

Maybe she was getting stronger after all.

The Curtis's ashamedly led their daughter out of the dojo with disappointment in their faces, turning then tutting towards Charlotte as they walked out.

The opportunity to rest before the next fight was just what she needed, not counting Walter trying to force-feed her cheese sandwiches. 'Just the water, thanks,' she said, taking the bottle.

Twenty minutes later she found herself in the ring again. She had been paired with a girl she had never seen before, equal in size but obviously way more skilled.

Charlotte was out of her depth, having been tripped to the ground twice now. A kick off the mat signalled the end of the competition for her, still earning a rather noble fourth prize.

Tracey Stimpson won the trophy, which was rather lovely to see. It was clearly a big moment for her to have finally outdone the bullies that had made her life a misery for years.

Charlotte and Walter hung around for a little while, talking to some of the other contestants and their families, but had to get back for tea.

After a surprisingly smooth drive home, Walter threw his keys onto the kitchen table. Aphra came scurrying into the kitchen, carrying a basket of herbs from the garden, to tend to the hotpot on the stove.

Walter sat down to rest at the top of the table, reading the latest edition of *Flourish and Sprout*, a monthly subscription of his. (It had a bald-headed gentleman on the front cover shaking hands with the prime minister at an allotment.)

'That could be you in a year!' Aphra joked, giving Charlotte a wink.

He gave Aphra a sarcastic grunt from behind the pages as she sliced crusty bread and put it on the table. He then stared proudly at a newspaper cutting he'd tucked under a magnet on the fridge door. (Walter holding a bunch of square tomatoes.)

Rolling up his magazine, he tapped Charlotte on the head and they all sat down to enjoy bowls of stew.

'How'd it go at the tournament, dear?' asked Aphra, holding out the medal a little away from her face because she was long-sighted. She gave it a nod of approval before handing it back.

Aphra had always disapproved of her martial arts training, but was recently coming around to the idea. Charlotte argued that it was a necessary component for protecting herself. She had received the bog flush too many times growing up, and she certainly wasn't going to let anything like that happen to her as an adult.

'That Curtis girl next door is in a lot of trouble, apparently,' resumed Aphra, scraping her chair across the floor as she joined them. 'She fell in the first prize cake at the Bazaar; the mayor got covered in it. He's furious, apparently, said it was an attempt to make a mockery of the whole event… here on page two!'

Charlotte felt her head sinking towards the table. Hopefully the pointing of her finger was just a coincidence.

'I gave poor Penelope the rest of my batch of chicken cheesecakes to take the strain off her. She's a very proud woman, I had to practically demand that she take them.'

Walter and Aphra were starting to have a rather in-depth conversation about activities between the postman and Flora, a thirty-something woman that lived across the street, when there was a knock at the door.

Having been just about to take a mouthful of food, Walter spilled the contents of his spoon down his front.

'Who could it possibly be at this hour?' he protested, marching down the hall, but when he opened the door there was nobody there.

Walter's cap fell as he scratched his head, coming back to the table. His bottom had barely reached the chair when there was a second knock, this time coming from the back door.

Flying from his seat across the kitchen, Walter flung it open. 'Ah ha!' but again there was nobody there. 'Ruddy hooligans,' he mumbled, picking up his walking stick from the corner and treading on the cat, who let out an almighty squeal.

Walter practically had kittens when both doors started knocking at the same time.

He was just about to run out and strike someone when he stopped because the lights began to flicker.

The knocking grew louder and faster until it was so fast it didn't sound like knocking at all, but one great almighty hum. Then the floor began to shake and plates fell from the dresser, smashing to their feet. Snow began to burst through the fireplace, filling the kitchen with a blizzard.

Walter's eyes widened as he clutched the worktop, holding on for dear life. 'Aphra!' he recalled, reflecting on the moment of Charlotte's arrival. 'The pyramid!'

Charlotte stood stunned, shaking with cold and lost for something to say as a white light flew down the chimney breast and flooded the entire room.

CHAPTER THREE

THE PHANTOM CARRIAGE

Charlotte was lying awake inside a forest. Leaves fell over her face, drifting to the ground in one final moment of death.

Sitting up, the path ahead was difficult to see, lit only by the glimmering of light coming from her palm. Glistening in her clutches was a crystal pyramid, but she had no idea how it had got there.

Holding it up to see, she noticed a tall thick stone nearby that had been embedded into the earth. She withdrew from the ground to read the writing that had been chiselled into the rocky surface.

It read: *Here lies Avaland.*

Looking around did nothing to reassure her; she had no idea where she was or how she had got there. Her instinct was telling her to keep walking straight, but ahead was forest and she didn't want to go that way. Wading through the undergrowth, she questioned whether her instincts were playing tricks on her.

Then, from nowhere, orbs of light lit her path, providing her with some security in the darkness, but they also brought her unwanted attention.

Howls echoed from the shadows, but she had no choice other than to persevere.

Charlotte held out the pyramid to see a little clearer. 'Who's there?' she shouted bravely. But the glow began to fade, as though the pyramid was conscious and didn't want to be seen.

Darkness was closing in, and the snarls drew closer, forcing her to her knees. She cowered, back against a young elm.

The crunching of undergrowth told her she was no longer alone. Pushing the pyramid into her pocket and grasping a fallen branch instead, she stepped out to stare upon the face of her attacker.

A ravenous wolf with ferocious blood-stained teeth.

Charlotte knew she didn't stand a chance, but if this was her time to die, she would do it fighting.

An unexpected arrival, a winged horse, came charging from the sky.

Protectively it stampeded across the ground and leapt into the air again, frightening away the mad dog.

Then the horse leant its head towards the ground. Charlotte took this as an indication to climb hurriedly. Because she'd seen the horse before, she trusted it and her instinct had never led her wrong before.

The orbs followed alongside and, wasting no time, the majestic creature spread its wings and bounded unrelentingly into the sky. Almost knocked back by the brawny branches of an old oak, Charlotte took hold of the stallion's mane and pulled herself in for protection.

Seconds later they levelled out, giving her the opportunity to open her eyes. Holding on, she watched the far-reaching feathers rise then descend by her side, revealing a better view of the forest beneath.

The air was icy cold, and the height and speed they were going made it feel like it was piercing the skin. The moonlight shone down on them, making them twinkle like the stars.

Finally they started to descend, lowering to the tops of the trees. Cantering to the ground, the elegant grace of symmetrical hooves slowed to a stop. Tucking its wings neatly into its back, the horse allowed Charlotte to descend, and she did so most inelegantly, falling to the ground with pins and needles in her arms.

At that moment, she noticed chatter nearby. Wiping down her dirty jeans, she parted a small section of foliage to get a better view.

A small group of people were holding flaming torches nearby, but on closer inspection some of them didn't appear to be human at all. Turning back to her protector, still shaken with cold and fear, burning dread took over as her worst fear was realised; she was alone. Once again the horse had vanished.

Steadying herself, Charlotte made her way out of the hedge. She concluded there was nowhere to go but forward.

Taking care to blend into the crowd, she walked behind the gatherers, looking for someone who appeared to be friendly that could help. The boy she noticed first was by far the largest there, almost twice as tall as anyone else. He was a mighty boy, sporting a smart shirt and a pair of thick-framed specs, looking to be a Werewolf because his face was covered in hair. He was talking to another boy, this one much smaller, whose stiff posture suggested he was trying not to show the young Werewolf that his incisors in fact intimidated him.

A group of girls were sparring with one another, displaying gymnastic skills as they playfully engaged in combat. Each had a different coloured glittery fleck on the side of their face. They had caught the attention of a lad nearby. He displayed his ability with a sword then posed fiercely, exposing a perfect set of white teeth.

Everybody started clapping. He seemed to be very popular.

Then Charlotte noticed someone staring intently. More modest-looking than his friend, he tilted his head to one side to consider her for a moment. With brown bouncy hair and khaki eyes that could make any girl weak at the knees, he became quite attractive to Charlotte, who had never had any interest in boys until now.

His sword was by his side because he appeared to have no interest in showing off.

'Hello,' said a tall and thin green man. 'I'm Frugal the Hobgoblin.'

'I'm lost,' she replied. 'I wonder if you might tell me where I could find a telephone box?'

Frugal stroked his chin, appearing to consider her unusual name. 'I don't know what that is,' he replied, 'but the Carriage will be here soon, they will know.'

'Thanks,' she said, relaxing a little. 'I've never met a Hobgoblin before.'

Frugal smiled kindly. 'It's good luck to meet a Hobgoblin, miss. According to my dad, Hobgoblins make good Guardians, because we are more magic than most.'

Frugal held out his hand.

A flame appeared inside his palm, which he froze, instantly turning it to crystal. He then gave it to Charlotte. 'A gift,' he said.

Charlotte started to feel a little more at ease now she'd

made a friend. ‘Thank you,’ she acknowledged. ‘Is everyone here magic, then?’

‘Not everyone. Most here are Gladiators, all masters of their craft.’

‘What’s a Gladiator?’ she asked, taking note of the vast number of them.

‘They are trained to fight, most of the time with weapons.’

Charlotte felt scorned by about fifty pairs of eyes; her attempt to blend in had been unsuccessful, and some of the girls had started to whisper.

‘Are you magic?’ Frugal asked, looking her over for some form of protection.

‘I’m not really sure. I suppose I never believed it was possible until now.’

Their conversation was stopped short because from nowhere a cloud of fog appeared.

Soon the sound of hooves approached them.

Encircled completely by the fog, she could barely see beyond the tip of her nose but she could hear that horses had halted somewhere nearby. When the mist cleared, a long black horse-drawn carriage stood valiantly beside them all.

The wood was carved with magnificent detail; gargoyles stood in each of its corners. Twelve hefty black stallions, all with red eyes, pulled ferociously at the reins, almost knocking off one of the two men who sat on top; a scruffy fellow with long dark curls wore a top hat. Charlotte assumed these must be the drivers. Next to him sat a bald-headed gentleman, who smiled menacingly, revealing several gold teeth.

The door to the coach creaked open and a stern-looking woman with hair pinned to the back of her head stepped out.

‘Ira Demsky!’ greeted the woman. ‘And this here is the

Phantom Carriage, giving you safe passage this evening.' Drawing out a large book bound with leather, she called out a list of names from its pages.

One by one the people strolled into the carriage. It was a long list and the time seemed to drag before finally only Charlotte and Frugal were left. 'See you later, Lost!' He waved, climbing inside.

The thought of being alone again terrified her, so with some uneasiness Charlotte approached the severe-looking female.

'Name?' snapped Ira. She dragged her finger down the page, but soon pursed her lips together before curling them into a smile.

'Charlotte Crump, you made it after all.' Slamming the book shut, she snapped her fingers. 'Beaver, Mouse! Luggage!'

Ira shot them both a cold glance as they dropped several cases to the ground. She then looked at her watch to indicate that time was hurried.

Charlotte followed her up the steps, and the door slammed shut behind them.

'I think there might have been some kind of mistake,' insisted Charlotte. 'You see, I'm lost and I'm looking for a telephone box …'

Ira turned abruptly and stared. 'This coach is for Guardians only, not for people looking for telephone boxes. My dear, once there was a boy I found as a stowaway in one of the luggage compartments; he has been a Gladiator for twelve years. You did not stumble upon us this evening by mistake. Now …' Ira dusted down Charlotte's jumper '… you have been invited to become a Legendary Guardian of Avaland – I suggest that you accept that invitation. If not, then I'm sure we have a few moments for you to make your exit before we leave.'

And with a swish of the cloak she was gone.

Charlotte stood in shock, her mind racing with a thousand questions.

She didn't really have much of a choice; even if she did want to leave, she wasn't going back into that forest alone. Knowing full well she'd rather be here with Frugal than outside, Charlotte proceeded to the seating area; except there was no seating area to proceed to.

Clapping her hands over her face, she gasped as she found herself standing inside a large drawing room with two lit fireplaces. Chandeliers swung from the ceiling and wax dripped from candelabras that flooded the drab peeling wallpaper with candlelight.

Scattered about was every type of chair you could imagine. Clusters of Gladiators had since planted their bottoms into the much more comfortable sitting position, and others were sitting alone, looking as nervous as she felt, but most were standing in groups.

Deciding to walk over to the least crowded part of the room, she spotted Frugal swinging his legs back and forth in a big comfortable armchair.

Flames roared inside one of the fireplaces, supplying the room with a pleasant blast of warm air. For a moment, it reminded her of being at home. That was the first time she had thought of Aphra and Walter and her heart sank as she wondered if they were OK.

With a crack of the whip to the dirt path, the carriage shook violently.

'I saved you a chair,' said Frugal, wiggling about, trying

to find the most comfortable spot.

'Thank you,' she said. 'How did you know I was coming?'

'You were in the right place at the right time; a coincidence like that could only be destiny.'

She could kind of relate to what he meant, if you believed in that sort of thing. 'By the way my name's Charlotte, not Lost.'

Frugal swung his legs backwards and forwards rather like an overexcited child before enthusing about his own inauguration.

'I have wanted to be a Guardian of Avaland my whole life!' he said with wide eyes. 'Have you?'

'I'd never even heard of one until a minute ago,' she informed him. 'I'm not from here, you see.'

'Where are you from, then?' he asked, most confused. 'You're not one of those savage women, are you?'

'No,' she replied, unsure of what he meant. 'I'm from England.'

'I don't know where that is,' he declared, proceeding to take out a brown paper bag filled with sweets and shoving them under her nose.

Charlotte gracefully declined.

'Since I was very small, my brothers Fuzz and Fungus would tease me. They told me that I would never get an invitation, but I knew I would, as long as I kept working on my craft. Then lo and behold, a scroll came, just like it did for my dad when he was my age. My dad and I are the only ones to become Guardians in our family – in our whole village, even.'

'Good for you, Frugal!' acknowledged Charlotte, who could see how much this invitation meant to him.

The points of his ears turned pink with bashful pride.

'May I borrow this seat?' said a confident voice. Charlotte looked up to see a girl whose hair had a tinge of blue in it. As she sat down Charlotte noticed she was holding a cerulean sceptre. Frugal leant over, giving the girl a shock.

'You're a Blue Hag, aren't you?' he said, invading her personal space.

Charlotte felt a little shocked, though she was sure Frugal was not trying to sound rude.

'I'm Mandy,' said the girl, shaking her hand.

'That's right,' Frugal continued, clicking his fingers. 'I saw your photograph in the *Fairytale Press* last week, you're the daughter of Nicholas Zain.'

The girl gave him a shocked and awkward smile.

'What's the *Fairytale Press*?' asked Charlotte

'It's a newspaper. My father is a famous historian; he has been studying some of the wizard Merlin's most controversial work, but it's brought the family a little unwanted attention.'

'Who's Merlin?'

The girl giggled, though it was well intentioned. 'I take it you're not from around here.'

'She's from England,' Frugal revealed.

The Phantom Carriage was moving at full speed now and its passengers were growing more excited by the minute.

'So, where are we going?' questioned Charlotte, mindful of asking too many questions.

'To where all the Guardians of Avaland live,' answered Mandy. 'The Coliseum.' Her sceptre gave a little spark of excitement as she said this. 'But first we need to see Arafolle.'

Charlotte had no idea who that was, but luckily Mandy gave a little more information.

'He's a ghoul, centuries old.'

'My dad said Arafolle was attacked with some kind of bewitched dagger,' Frugal told them.

'I'm reading this book at the moment.' Mandy reached into her bag and pulled out a copy of *Ghosts and Ghouls* by Frederick the Wise, then started flicking through the pages until she'd found the one with the bookmark.

'There's a section about Arafolle in here – it describes how his body was absorbed into the tree he died against, and he apparently became conscious with that tree as his body.'

'So was he an oracle before he died, then?' asked Frugal curiously.

'Yes. He was on his way to warn the Pixie Queen about the looming Goblin war and was killed before he could give them the message; that's why Feign Forest is always in the season of autumn, because it's in mourning for the massacre that took place that day.'

'I always thought ghouls were bad but maybe they're not,' Frugal decided, peering over Mandy's shoulder at the page she was referring to.

The Carriage rode on. They were soon accompanied by the sound of howling wolves.

'We must be close!' reported Mandy. 'They always send the wolves to protect the Carriage in moonlight.'

The stagecoach thrashed around violently; Charlotte would have felt quite apprehensive had there not been so much chatter on board. Then it slowed. Ira stepped into the room and the chatter subsided.

'I now ask for silence as you make your way to the Oracle. This is essential for fear of drawing too much unwanted attention. The forest is a dangerous place, especially at night.'

Ira didn't have to tell Charlotte; she knew full well how dangerous it was and she wasn't going to take any chances.

As instructed, everyone fell silent and gathered into a single line. When the coach stopped, they followed Ira down the steps.

The forest was murky at twilight. The moon was full and the sky was clear. Charlotte would barely have been able to see had the trees not been lit with candles. She instinctively felt danger lurking in the shadows.

They crossed a bridge that was hidden by fog. Peering out over the side, she noticed the river beneath was completely frozen.

Singing was coming from a fountain, and the further they walked the louder it became.

This was like no music she had ever heard; it was as strange as it was beautiful. People broke from the line to touch the water flowing inside the fountain; some poured it on themselves, some drank it and one even filled up his silver tankard.

'That's Apollo's Fountain,' whispered Mandy. 'The water is healing.'

Coming to a valley, a series of roots formed steps in the dirt, leading down to a very old tree. Just like the roots had formed stairs, they had also formed seats sticking out of the ground; but others found somewhere to sit among the branches. Charlotte, Frugal and Mandy sat together at the back and the candles in the great tree lit of their own accord.

Charlotte got a fright when the bark started to move and a pair of eyes, a nose and a mouth appeared. The tree groaned, stretching its branches like it had just woken from a long sleep.

'BUNFUDDERS, CLOPSNOFFS!' the tree snorted sleepily, taking a few moments to come to his senses before staring out at the new faces. 'IS IT THAT TIME OF YEAR ALREADY?' said the tree, before rolling into a well-prepared speech. 'FOR THOSE OF YOU THAT ARE UNAWARE, I AM ARAFOLLE. THESE ARE DIFFICULT TIMES: THE SHADOWS IN THE NORTH EXTINGUISH THE HEARTS OF THOSE WHOM WE DEFEND IN THESE DOMINIONS. BUT TOGETHER, WE WILL STAND AND FIGHT. WE WILL BRING JUSTICE TO THESE LANDS. FOR THE FUTURE OF THIS WORLD DEPENDS ON EACH AND EVERY ONE OF US.'

Arafolle paused for effect.

'STEP FORTH BY NAME TO RECEIVE YOUR TALISMAN. LOKI ALACTO.'

A silver-haired girl with a wolf-like face stood up and tottered down the dirt track before pulling a cheeky face at her friends.

'YOUR TALISMAN IS AMBER.'

The girl turned and did a cartwheel, pulling a necklace out of the fountain, which she put around her neck.

'Show-off!' said Frugal simply, in a tone that would suggest he didn't like her.

Arafolle opened his mouth and the girl stepped inside before disappearing.

'LAURAUS BALTHAZAR,' called the tree.

The boy that had been staring at Charlotte was standing coolly against the back wall when his name was called. He collected his talisman without fuss.

'JET,' said Arafolle.

From the fountain, Lauraus collected a ring with a black

stone, albeit with some hesitation; it appeared that he saw something in the water that startled him. He also continued to Arafolle's mouth before disappearing.

'SINOPE BLATIO.'

A short blonde-haired girl jumped up, turning her gold glittery face to one side. She ran comfortably down the valley to Arafolle to pick up her talisman.

'TIGER'S EYE,' announced the tree.

'LONDON CARRICK.'

The crowd cheered as the boy who had been standing next to Lauraus marched down to the tree.

'YOUR TALISMAN IS ALSO JET.'

London got a round of applause as he collected his talisman, before turning and bowing.

'CHARLOTTE CRUMP.'

Standing up, her insides doing somersaults, she tried not to trip over her own feet as she took her place beneath the great Oracle.

She was sure he was going to send her back into the forest. But he didn't. Instead, he said:

'QUARTZ CLEAR.'

The onlookers gasped and started whispering amongst themselves.

Walking slowly to the fountain, she stared at the reflection in the water, but was surprised to see that it wasn't herself staring back at her. The reflection belonged to a woman with long red hair, pale skin and bottle-green eyes.

The female was handing her a flower, a white rose.

Charlotte reached into the water and took it, but the rose coiled around her bracelet like a snake, digging its thorns into the skin around her forearm and drawing a little blood before turning to diamond.

She did not feel any different wearing the talisman as she walked back to Arafolle.

The remaining few looked stunned.

Giving her a wink, Arafolle opened his mouth and Charlotte stepped inside onto a cobbled path; she had been instantly transported to another place. Lit brightly in the distance was the most magnificent building Charlotte had ever set eyes on. It had thousands of arches and stained-glass windows lit by torches. Charlotte had never seen anything quite like it in her life.

In front of her stood a giant semicircle made of gold. A navy phoenix flapped its wings, encircling the place, dripping thick liquid to the ground.

For a moment she stood there wondering what to do.

'You need to sign it,' came a voice from behind.

Much to her surprise, the boy who had taken such an interest in her was leaning against a flickering lamp post with his arms folded; he must have been waiting for her to arrive.

Charlotte tried to remember his name. Larry? Laurence? No, Lauraus; that was right.

Reaching out, she took the bird by its inky beak; she yelped as it tried to peck her. Regaining her cool she signed her name into the gold archway.

It shimmered before sinking inward and disappearing.

She was closely followed by Lauraus who practically strangled the bird in an attempt to show it who was boss. He also signed his name into the wall, Charlotte noted how his signature was very neat and elaborate.

Charlotte felt nervous; why was he following her?

'I hope you don't mind my asking,' he said, scrutinising

her bracelet, 'but I can see you've been placed in Quartz Clear and I wonder to whom you might be related?'

'I'm an orphan,' she told him. 'Why? What is Quartz Clear?'

'Quartz Clear is a very rare grouping. It is considered to be the VIP of all of the Talisman groups – not even kings or queens can get into it, only those that are due to change the course of history in some way.'

Charlotte silently wondered how that could be when she hadn't been aware of Avaland's existence an hour ago.

'Arafolle must see something about your destiny that is important,' he added. 'A psychic told me that I was going to meet a beautiful woman that would change my life this year, but I didn't believe it until now.'

Charlotte needed to put him in his place and quickly.

'Look, you're good looking and everything but trust me, I'm really not that type of girl.'

He laughed. 'Good, I'm not that type of guy either.'

Lauraus continued to follow her across the lawns to where all the others were standing. He seemed to like the fact that Charlotte wasn't falling over herself for him, even if she was bordering on being a little rude.

Lauraus turned his head away with guilt as Sinope glared at him menacingly, giving Charlotte a look of contempt.

'Who's this?' she barked. 'Have you found my replacement already?'

But Lauraus ignored her. It appeared to Charlotte that the two of them knew each other well, and were not on good terms.

Frugal came skipping across the lawn towards Charlotte. Some of the others sniggered but Charlotte didn't care. She was pleased to see him.

Everyone fell silent once again and Frugal turned an even paler shade of green.

Ira Demsky stood on the topmost step. Two bolted iron doors opened slowly, allowing an official-looking gentleman to stand beside her. Wearing a navy tailored suit, his hair was slicked to the side of his head. He was closely followed by a fellow half his height who was carrying a clipboard and feather quill.

As the gentleman spoke, the miniature man scribbled notes on the clipboard's rolled-back parchment.

'Welcome,' he said proudly. 'I am Orobus Pluto … and this magnificent building you see before you is the Coliseum. Home to those of you that wish to make it such. Some of you will be better informed about the proposal that has been put to you. But for those of you that are unaware, some of the greatest that have ever lived have abided behind these walls.

'The Coliseum is the most important grounds the world's magical arts has ever seen, and in which the fiercest Gladiators reside. Those that occupy this place pledge their lives to the citizens of Avaland every day, and the same will be true for each of you. In return you will be given one of the most fulfilling jobs one could ever hope to seek. To become a Guardian of Avaland.'

Everyone clapped in awe at this man's seemingly spellbinding speech. Which, by the smile on Orobus Pluto's face, was gratefully received.

'Please make your way through the atrium, into the canteen.'

'Oh good, I'm starving!' said Frugal, rubbing his rumbling pot belly.

They all went inside, and Orobus gave each of them a nod and smile to greet them.

The atrium was filled with paintings and suits of armour, some of which were too large to fit any human. A grand spiral staircase, wide enough to fit fifty men alongside each other, ringed the atrium's circumference. Different colours poured through the stained-glass windows.

Nothing could have prepared her for the magnificence of this place. Its tall ceilings gave a real feeling of presence, like generations of history lay deep within the walls. A statue stood valiantly in the centre of the room with water cascading down its side to a pool filled with glimmering stones.

'That's Jupiter,' said Frugal captivated. 'He's the Roman king of the spirits.'

Flags of every colour hung above them, one to represent each race, uniting in the centre of the ceiling at a plaque called the Seal of Avaland.

After visiting the canteen, Charlotte and Frugal took seats next to Mandy in the centre of the room. She was sitting beside another bronze sculpture, this time of a young male with curly locks squeezing grapes into a glass. Underneath was the inscription *Bacchus, spirit of wine*.

Six others also sat at this table. One of whom, a fuzzy haired Giant, introduced himself as Grendel. He almost trod on Frugal.

'Sorry,' he said, grabbing a handful of sausages. 'Mmm, mint and dragon liver, my favourite.'

'I'm Loki,' greeted a yellow-eyed girl, the first to have presented herself to Arafolle. 'I'm half wolf.'

'Did you hear that, Lomax?' interrupted another girl,

straightening her fringe in the reflection of her spoon. 'That girl's just like us.'

'I'm not exactly half wolf, am I, Valentine? I'm a Werewolf; it's a bit different.'

'I'm a shape shifter too,' Valentine told the group. 'A black panther ... it has its uses.'

Charlotte was starting to feel more out of place with each passing second, so she decided to divert her attention to the food. Frugal gulped a plate of fried eggs down in one. He then patted his bloated belly and burped.

'I've got a thing for eggs,' he said to a repulsed Goblin sitting next to him. 'I only normally eat goose eggs because they are the only birds that live in our village, so it's good to try something new.'

A wide-nosed, dirty-haired boy (who didn't introduce himself) stared blankly over to the next table.

'I see one of the princes is here,' he said expressionlessly.

Charlotte realised that he was talking about Lauraus.

'I was told that he didn't want to come to the Coliseum, but his father forced him,' said the Goblin in an attempt to discredit him.

Frugal stood up defiantly, knocking the table and wobbling the plates. 'Nonsense!' he complained angrily. 'Lauraus Balthazar is a good man, like each of his brothers!'

'How many brothers does he have?' asked Charlotte curiously.

Valentine smirked.

'Two,' answered Mandy. 'He is the second eldest – his elder brother, Saul, coaches Ludus.'

'That London's a bit of a dish, isn't he?' giggled Loki, staring over at his friend.

'He is an exceptional marksman,' said Mandy. 'Among the best I have ever seen.'

'Lauraus is exceptionally talented too!' defended Frugal. 'Just much more modest.'

'I heard his younger brother, Ilex, is a seer,' said Valentine.

'I heard that too,' Mandy replied earnestly.

'What's a seer?' asked Charlotte.

'It's someone that can see into the future,' said Frugal, 'but I thought only family and close friends were aware of it.'

'Do you know him or something?' interrogated Valentine, breaking the subject.

'I spent a lot of time at the palace when I was growing up – Lauraus and I would play. My father and our king are friends.'

The Goblin grimaced contemptuously. 'I have no king!' he said furiously. 'Goblins will not be ruled by any other being than a Goblin'

'... and that in itself is a very dangerous task,' muttered Lomax under his breath. 'Wasn't the last Goblin king killed?'

'Like I said... I have no king.' The Goblin gave Lomax a malicious and cold narrow smile that sent shivers down Charlotte's spine, but Lomax did not appear at all intimidated.

Frugal had now moved up several inches and decided not to talk to the Goblin any more, a decision Charlotte couldn't help noticing was shared among the group.

The prince's friend slipped backwards on his chair after swinging it back on two legs in an attempt to look cool causing a few snorts and giggles.

'Look, balcony boxes!' he said trying to evade the stares, which appeared to work because everyone looked up. Inside they were filled with some perilous-looking faces, much older than those gathered about the round tables.

Sitting next to Orobus was a man with the lower body of a horse and further down a woman glistened. They looked like they were discussing something important.

Charlotte became fixated upon a blonde sitting at the other end of the table to Orobus. Pale and disinterested in the conversation, she seemed detached from the rest of the assembly.

As the woman moved the food around her plate with her fork, for some reason Charlotte became aware of what she was thinking.

How would I find it anyway? There must be hundreds to go through. The consequences if I fail. The woman shuddered. Resting her head in her hands, she turned to look at Orobus, as though she'd thought of a solution to her problem.

Outside, the clock chimed nine times, shaking the tables.

The doors swung back, allowing the newcomers into the canteen for pudding. Once again, the selection was vast. Charlotte helped herself to a chocolate sponge cake with cream, then stared back up at the table, but the woman had gone.

Orobus Pluto stood and cleared his throat, ushering silence in the room. 'In front of you are the keys to your sleeping quarters. Look for the lock that matches your key. You are dismissed.'

Charlotte and Frugal left the table. Thankfully Frugal seemed to know where he was going because she had no idea. A suit of armour bowed to them as they re-entered the atrium, keys in hand, en route to their beds.

Frugal slid past her on the polished floor.

'That's a lot of stairs!' she said, looking up at the

meandering red-carpeted staircase.

'You don't have to climb them, silly,' he said, propping his bottom onto one of the banisters, which pulled him upwards. 'The banisters are enchanted.'

A reluctant Charlotte sat on one of the handrails. As she did so, it gave a little jolt from underneath. She didn't like this at all, but luckily, they only had to go up one floor.

They found themselves in a corridor with three arched doorways. Each was made of a different material: gold, silver and bronze.

'Which one should we go through?' she asked.

'The clue is in the key.' Frugal opened his hand, revealing a blue key with silver scratches, then asked her what she had.

Charlotte had been given a long elaborate copper key with purple rust.

'That means we're in different corridors,' he advised. 'Just go through the bronze doorway until you find the lock that matches your key. If it's the right one, the door will open.'

Frugal rushed off with his silver key, spinning on the spot with one final piece of information for her. 'Breakfast starts at six, I'll meet you in the corridor after we've met our Talisman groups. See you tomorrow!'

Then Charlotte was alone. She headed towards the bronze door, looking up at the ceiling. As she went, she took a moment to appreciate the incredible works of art above her head; paintings of clouds and spirits stared down at her, some of whom she recognised from the hall. Charlotte tried to take in this masterpiece but people were coming and she was hurried along by the crowd.

The bronze door creaked open, and a cheerful looking man squeezed through the gap wearing a star-and-moon-covered hat. 'Good evening,' he chirped.

Through the doorway, the corridor was carpeted in scarlet and portraits hung on the walls. Examining each of the locks, she looked for her own; each was ever so slightly different from the next. Staring at some of the paintings on the wall, she stopped first to analyse a tall woman dressed in an indigo wrap. Underneath, a plaque read:

Betty Brockhurst

1935–1981

Sacrificed her arm to save a family of Unicorns

Next to this was a one-eyed man glaring scarily out of his portrait. With a hand upon the dagger in the scabbard to his side, this man looked quite alarming. His plaque said,

Gorse the Cyclops

1953–

Awarded for bravery in the face of oncoming danger

Even though she was fascinated, Charlotte felt out of place; she knew she did not have any of the attributes the others seemed to possess. But for now she needed to sleep, and her room couldn't be that far because she was nearing the end of the passageway.

At that moment, London started walking from the opposite direction. He smiled at her, giving her a flirtatious wink as he passed, making her feel uncomfortable.

Finally finding the lock that matched her key she clambered inside in relief, closing the door behind her.

When she turned she was met with shock, because she was back inside her old bedroom at Wisteria Cottage. Even the candle wax she had spilt on her desk the night before was still there.

She opened the door again to get her bearings and the

corridor was still on the other side.

Feeling disorientated, the first thing she did was look for a piece of paper and her fountain pen. Lying on the bed, she wrote a long letter to the Crumps explaining everything that had happened and knew that tomorrow she would have to find a way to get it to them.

It had been such a long day, and she struggled to keep her eyes open. She didn't notice ink dripping from the quill onto the bed sheet beneath and spreading through the fibres. The urge to fall asleep was too strong.

Finally giving in, exhaustion overcame her and she did not wake until morning.

CHAPTER FOUR

The Labyrinth

Charlotte had never really believed in magic, but for the first time in her life she was sitting on the bed, wishing for a miracle.

Aware that it was far more likely that she'd been dreaming than consorting with Hobgoblins inside a Coliseum, she tried to pluck up the courage to push down the door handle. Unable to stand the knots in her stomach a moment longer, Charlotte took a deep breath and forced it open with a bit of a kick.

A friendly gnome passed nervously down the hall with the hoover. 'Morning,' he gasped, having just made it out of the way in time. Charlotte was unable to apologise because she was trying to control a semi-audible scream coming from the pit of her stomach with hysterical excitement.

Getting dressed quickly, she spotted a dark purple booklet on her dressing table.

A meet and greet had been arranged for this morning with her Talisman group, Quartz Clear, in the hall at 9 am. Flicking through the pages, she read out loud a short note on the first page.

Dear Charlotte,

Please find enclosed a map of the grounds and surrounding areas. Your personal timetable has been designed to maximise the result of your training.

Any questions can be directed to your team leader.

May I wish you the best with your placement opportunity.

Yours sincerely,

Orobus Pluto

Charlotte inspected a map on the back page. It showed every floor with meticulous detail. The floors she had already visited were exactly as they appeared in real life, down to the last troll-sized suit of armour. Presented with some restriction were the courts, then the vaults were underneath what Charlotte knew was the ground floor of the atrium.

Looking at her watch, Charlotte realised she was running late. Putting the letter she'd written to Aphra and Walter in her bag, it was time to leave the familiarity of her bedroom.

Hurrying down to the atrium, Charlotte thought of them both at home, wondering where on earth she'd disappeared to; and with some urgency approached the front desk.

Behind it was a stern-looking woman talking to a very hairy girl. The girl was asking for a temperature report on Geyser Lake; the bag slumped over her shoulder looked to be carrying her swimming costume.

Once at the front of the queue, Charlotte placed her letter on the counter and pushed it towards the receptionist with the tips of her fingers.

'Can I help you?' droned the receptionist in an unhelpful tone.

'I urgently need to post this letter to my relatives in England.'

The woman stared at her as though she were stupid.

'Why don't you just send a scroll?' she stated in a condescending way.

'I don't know how to do that,' admitted Charlotte with some hesitation. 'I'm not from here.'

'There is one postbox, located near the front gate. Mailing a scroll from inside the grounds is free.'

'Great,' said Charlotte, and she made her way outside, aware of the fact that she was going to be late for her meeting with her Talisman group. But this was important and she felt that she needed to make it a priority.

The weather was dismal. Grey clouds filled the sky and it was starting to drizzle; Charlotte had forgotten her coat so ran across the lawn, trying not to slip on the muddy grass.

There she found a gold postbox that looked as though it was in need of a bit of a clean. The next collection was in five minutes' time.

Charlotte posted the letter then headed back, but something cast a shadow on the floor as it dived from the sky, making her jump. The ground shook as it landed. Charlotte could not believe what she was seeing.

Just ahead of her, blocking her path, was a fire-breathing dragon, panting with exhaustion. Covered in scales, it was at least five times taller than her and almost as wide as it was high. A skinny man dressed in a brown racer jacket and goggles surfed coolly down the scaly beast's tail. With a bag slumped over his shoulder that appeared to be empty, he opened the postbox to collect the mail. He turned to the dragon, delighted, and started to do a celebratory dance.

'We got one!' he cheered, swinging his knees back and forth. 'Knuckles, look, we got a letter.'

The dragon belched, scorching a patch of grass very close to where Charlotte was standing.

'CAREFUL, KNUCKLES!' the man shouted furiously. 'Sorry,' he then said, spinning to Charlotte. 'Dragons are a bit of a health and safety risk, especially this old brute,' laughed the fellow as he buffed the beast's snout with perfectly aimed saliva. 'Are you trying to get through?' he quizzed guiltily. 'Knuckles, budge your great behind, will you?'

'That's OK,' Charlotte sighed, accepting his admission of responsibility.

As she dusted herself down, the chap flung out his arm to introduce himself. 'Monty Huck,' he said, shaking her hand profusely. 'Is this your letter?'

Charlotte nodded; she was still trying to put out her singed jumper.

'England, eh?' he then said, wiping his cold running nose with his glove. 'Well I can't deny it's going to be a bit of a challenge … but we are the folks for the job. I will deliver your letter personally myself.'

Monty bowed, then tucked the letter into his jacket. 'See you later, miss.'

Monty ran up the dragon's spine, positioning his goggles over his eyes and shot out his arm to indicate the beast take flight. They then flew off into the distance, almost hitting the clock tower.

Twenty minutes to get breakfast, Charlotte thought nervously, about to meet her Talisman group in the hall for the first time.

She couldn't help feeling a little bit startled as she entered what could only be described as a room full of monsters. A brawl broke out between a man and a Troll on the other side of the room; cheering ensued. Light lit dust particles as it shimmered through the stained-glass windows, drawing attention to two suits of armour that were battling one another. If she hadn't known these creatures were good-natured, she would have lost her bottle and run.

Looking around at each of the tables, she tried not to stare at anyone in particular, glancing instead at the exquisite stone discs, looking for her own. A pink stone called kunzite was the first polished centrepiece she could make out. Then there was jade, amethyst … and a turquoise stone called lapis lazuli.

By day the hall looked very different. Charlotte became drawn to the names carved into the stone walls and floors, digging her fingers into the crevices, some of which must have been carved many centuries before. But one began to stand out for a reason she could not understand, because it looked no different to the others; it was like she had seen it before.

Kristoffer Enoch 1776

Touching the surface of the rock, Charlotte put her palm over the carved letters. She felt the urge to shut her eyes, and a face met her view.

Troubled, Kristoffer hid his weary eyes behind his long dark hair, making it quite obvious he didn't want to be seen. Someone dropped a goblet outside the now empty hall, making him jump, and sweat gathered on his lined forehead, which he wiped away with a dirty cuff covered in soot.

'Are you lost, my dear?' came a voice from behind, waking her from a daydream. 'He was forty-three when he died, a great tragedy when you think of what he achieved so young.'

Charlotte turned around again to a full hall. Standing before her was a tall red-headed gentleman wearing a dark green waistcoat. Clipped to his pocket was a stopwatch on a long chain and he wore a very tall green hat. The man beamed down at her with dimples in his cheeks.

'Abacus Creedy,' he greeted in a strong Irish accent. 'Top of the morning to yer.'

'Charlotte Crump,' she said, putting the vision to the back of her mind.

'Right ye be. Seein' as though everybody else is sat with their teams, come … let me introduce yer.' He led Charlotte to a less crowded table in the corner of the room.

She noticed Frugal pulling different coloured handkerchiefs from his nose, and Emerald group were clapping with laughter in their eyes; as she passed he waved then pointed at the double doors to indicate that he would meet her there when they were finished.

'Good morning, Antonious,' acknowledged Abacus, greeting a wolf-eyed man eating a bloody raw steak with his bare hands. The man said nothing, only glared upwards menacingly.

'Don't worry about him!' said a pretty albino with a short haircut. 'It was a full moon last night.'

Slamming his fists on the table, the man got up and left irritably.

'Antonious Draconi is a right miserable git sometimes!' joked another man, who was much older and complete with a light blue wizard's cloak. 'Bloody good Guardian, though! … Get it! … Bloody!' The man laughed at his own joke.

'Ahh, this is my good friend Magnus Fillius,' said Abacus.

'Descendant of Merlin,' Magnus said proudly, removing his hat with a bow.

'I don't know who that is,' Charlotte apprised them, unintentionally making everyone laugh. Magnus went bright pink with embarrassment.

Abacus hit him on the head with a rolled-up newspaper. Magnus snatched it back and threw it across the room, accidentally hitting a Cyclops on the back of the head. The Cyclops turned around and scowled at Charlotte, mistaking her for the aggressor.

'I'm Topaz,' said the albino. 'We are all good friends here; different, but we work well together.'

'Sir Gualish Knight is missing, o' course; he is away on business,' said Abacus in a well-versed fashion.

Then Magnus asked the question Charlotte had been dreading.

'So, what are you then … Gladiator or Sorceress?'

The albino's pointy ears perked up with interest.

'I'm a Sorceress, I think, but I'm not very good yet.'

Magnus's expression turned from one of intrigue to utter disappointment, and suddenly his bowl of porridge became more interesting to him.

'"Yet" being the operative word,' added Abacus. 'Not all that arrive here possess the skills they eventually hold. I'm sure a trip to the armoury is all ye need; I will see to it that an appointment is made for you right away.'

Charlotte smiled enthusiastically; these were words she'd longed to hear.

'What talisman did Arafolle give you?' asked Topaz, moving the subject on. 'Mine's this crystal.' She pointed to a clear droplet in the centre of her forehead.

Charlotte lifted up her sleeve to show the group the arm bracelet the mysterious red-head had given her.

They all looked at it with shocked faces.

'But how can that be?' gasped Magnus, looking startled.

'What is it?' probed Charlotte, feeling concerned at their reaction.

'We've seen that talisman before,' Abacus told her, looking the most shocked of all.

Magnus got up and left the table. He had a wooden leg and, to Charlotte's amazement, they appeared to be having a conversation.

'That's a bit strange isn't it?' said the wizard. 'Do you think it has anything to do with ...'

'Back from the grave, gives me the heebie jeebies, old boy.'

'How can you get heebie jeebies?' argued Magnus. 'You're made of wood!'

'That's Proteus, his cackling stump,' explained Topaz. 'They're best friends.'

'Right, first lesson,' said Abacus, taking the stool next to Charlotte. 'Being a good Guardian takes a huge strain on your body, so you are going to need a good breakfast.'

Charlotte helped herself to the fried food on the table. Topaz gave her some privacy whilst she ate, stealing one of Magnus's discarded newspapers and becoming engaged in its pages.

'We'll make a great Guardian of you yet!' Abacus winked.

#

That went off to a good start, she thought as she left the hall a few moments later to meet with Frugal; she was late, so rushed through the crowd.

'There's that new girl that got put into Quartz Clear!' One of a small group of girls her own age pointed.

'I wonder what she is?' whispered the tartan-dressed lass.

'I bet she's really powerful,' murmured another.

The truth was, the most supernatural thing about Charlotte was the crystal pyramid in her pocket and it worried her that people had such high expectations.

The atrium was an ideal meeting place and this morning it had been chosen by many. Eventually she spotted Frugal; he was showing Mandy how to ward off Vampires with a garlic chicken, much to the amusement of passers-by.

'Whereabouts is the Labyrinth anyway?' asked Mandy, adjusting her afro. 'We need to go up one floor,' instructed Charlotte, having already studied the map before she'd left. 'Come on, we should be there by now.'

Frugal put the garlic chicken in his bag for later and clucked behind as they climbed the stairs.

The banisters revealed more windows made up of stained glass, and some were highly detailed in their message. They appeared to be telling a story. A Troll under a bridge, in a village of Gnomes, its residents unable to pass.

'They give clues to whereabouts support is needed,' Mandy told them. 'I'm sure someone's looking into it already.'

'How did it go?' asked Mandy, and Charlotte shrugged her shoulders.

'OK, I suppose' recalled Charlotte, relieved her Talisman group seemed to like her. 'But I think they were expecting someone with more experience.'

'My group asked me to give them a demonstration,' said Frugal proudly. 'Colonel Fortesque has really been there, you know? So I don't fink he was expecting me to turn his bushy eyebrows into caterpillars … gave him quite a shock.' Frugal did an impression of a caterpillar with his index finger. 'They said they were looking forward to working with me.'

'That's great!' congratulated Mandy, nudging her head in Charlotte's direction, hinting to him to be quiet in case he upset her. Charlotte knew Quartz Clear had not been quite so excited about her arrival.

The others were waiting, valorous in their demeanour as they waited for their guide.

Lauraus was looking particularly striking as he stood with his friend London, focusing his gaze on the Labyrinth doors though they could hardly be seen for all the plants and foliage that covered them. In front of them was a building made of stone, with many windows.

'They are fire exits,' Mandy informed Charlotte, taking a place beside her.

Ivy slithered across the walls and bugs skimmed the foliage only to be snatched and devoured by weeds. Everything here was a little disorienting. Beneath her feet was a polished mahogany floor leading to a temple that looked like it belonged in the middle of a desert. The doors opened of their own accord, revealing a pale blonde man with a narrow face who flew out towards them with one swoop. Landing on the floor, he tucked his wings behind his back and addressed them.

'Welcome to the Labyrinth,' he said. 'I am Erebus Quarus. One cannot be harmed here,' declared the Birdman. 'The Labyrinth's only purpose is to educate you, and you will not be able to move on until each task is complete. Once you have been deemed confident, you will graduate to full Guardian status and join your Talisman groups on real missions.'

'We should go together,' Mandy whispered softly, looking keen to get going. Charlotte got the same impression from everyone as Frugal gave her a thumbs up.

'First you will be required to complete a set of tasks, followed by a team-building exercise; after that you will begin.'

Erebus held out a large coin between his thumb and index finger. 'You will be collecting these, one for each of the elements.' The coin spun, changing from platinum to bronze, gold then silver. Each coin face revealing the words *Magnum Opus.*

'A clue will be given as to their whereabouts, usually by scroll, and at the end of each task a door will appear to bring you back to the Coliseum to rest before the next attempt; that is unless, of course, the tests overlap. Before graduation you will be required to sit a written examination. To prepare you will have full use of library resources, and of course any other member of staff willing to lend you a friendly ear.'

Erebus walked over to the building's doors and unlocked them with a wave of his feathered hand; they then flew open of their own accord.

'When you are ready you may begin,' he said.

London and Lauraus were the first to lead, charging in ahead of everyone else, their swords already drawn. Then a group of girls followed, Sinope at the front. Next, Grendel the Giant trundled into the Labyrinth with hefty strides.

'Come on, let's go,' instructed Mandy as the three friends hurried inside.

The door behind disappeared and darkness consumed the air around them. Frugal lit the torches on the walls with a flaming hand, and the darkness was replaced by candlelight.

Inside, those that had entered before them were no longer around. Neither were they joined inside the tunnel by anybody following them. Water dripped from the mud ceiling, their surroundings appearing not that dissimilar to a cave. There was a small light coming from the distance, so they followed it.

The light became bigger and more prominent the further they travelled until eventually they opened out on to a raised rocky platform, level to the tops of the highest trees.

Music filled the air; it was the same heavenly song Charlotte had heard at Apollo's Fountain. But they were nowhere near there and she wondered how that could be.

The view before her was potent in colour, a sight to behold and a pleasure to the eye.

'Look,' said Frugal. 'The tunnel; it's gone.'

Indeed it had; behind them now was nothing but a steep drop and it was clear to them that there was only one way down.

Charlotte searched through her satchel for something that would help her; Mandy was tugging on a piece of rope that had a four-pronged hook on the end, so she did the same.

'It's a grapple,' advised Frugal, securing the clasp into a crevice in the rock and giving it a tug to make sure it was secure. 'Where do you think we are?' he then asked, ready to descend.

'Well, I don't want us to get too excited,' disclosed Mandy, 'but I think we are in the Wirral.'

Frugal looked like he might burst with excitement and became much more interested in his surroundings.

'What's the Wirral?' Charlotte asked after a second unsuccessful attempt to fasten her grapple.

'It's where the Fairies live,' squeaked Frugal in a blaze of pyrotechnics.

'Obviously it's not the real thing because we're inside the Labyrinth,' Mandy said, 'but it's as close as any of us are ever going to get to it.'

'A moment to treasure,' said Frugal overwhelmed, immediately steadying himself, hoping nobody noticed.

'No one ever comes here,' clarified Mandy, 'because it's impossible – well, unless you're invited of course.'

It must have been clear that Charlotte hadn't understood, because Mandy went on to explain further. 'Everything has a frequency.'

Frugal already looked confused and lost interest. He started tugging on Charlotte's rope to make sure she had attached it properly. (Which she hadn't.)

'… and our brains are designed to tune in to our surroundings. Avaland is a different frequency range to, for example, your world, Charlotte … which is why most of us are invisible to humans.'

'We have to step into their range and show them that we are there,' sniggered Frugal. 'For the most part they confuse us with ghosts.'

Frugal looked suspiciously like he'd tried this before, and was having some kind of amusing flashback.

'The same goes for this place,' continued Mandy. 'The Wirral has a much higher frequency range then even Avaland, because Fairies are ethereal … if this is the Wirral, then we're very lucky.'

Mandy looked exhausted and Frugal appeared to be glad she had finished telling her little story.

'Can we go now?' he groaned, leaping backwards with his rope. Charlotte and Mandy followed.

It took a few attempts to build up her confidence and it didn't help when they were engulfed by pink blossom halfway down being blown in the wind from a nearby tree.

Finally they reached the bottom and the ground illuminated where they stood, as they walked a trail of footsteps faded over time. Flowers delicately retracted their petals as they passed, revealing a valley that was adorned in fruit trees. A red squirrel groomed its bushy tail on a trunk that was twisted with fungi.

'I don't ever want to leave,' gushed Frugal, sitting on a funny looking snail that was glowing red, having puffed out all of its tentacles. Lifting his bottom, he picked it up between his fingers, then flicked it into his mouth and started to chew. 'Hmm, they're really rather good.'

A dozen orbs of light ignited around them.

'What are they?' Charlotte asked, recognising them straight away from the moment she'd first arrived at the Avaland milestone.

'They're Fairies,' Frugal said, looking a little shamefaced he'd been caught eating the snail.

'I've seen them before,' Charlotte told them.

Frugal and Mandy were looking at each other in disbelief when a scroll appeared, falling onto the ground.

The Hobgoblin then picked it up and unravelled it, dropping a second piece of parchment from between his fingers.

'It's a map,' Charlotte identified, handing it to Mandy to explore further. Frugal then read the scroll out loud.

Welcome to the Wirral.

A set of tasks have been compiled at random; until they are complete, the exit will not appear. Please note that you are able to abort the tasks at any time by pressing your talisman, but by forfeiting the task you risk redistribution of team members.

The exercises may be completed in any order but the sequence specified is recommended.

Number one: collect the Jade Grimmelkin.

Mandy pointed to the map where a green housecat had been positioned in the middle of the lake.

At the completion of today's task, the Grimmelkin will lead you to the exit; this amulet will continue to be used for future training events.

Number two: set up camp using equipment provided in your survival kit only. A campfire must be lit by hand and it is noted that one team member should be nominated for this task whilst the others proceed to the first.

Any injuries must be treated as per instruction; further information can be found inside your first aid handbook. All incidents are to be logged and reported to the register in reception.

Frugal looked up to indicate that he had finished reading.

'Come on, we're wasting time,' said Mandy, having analysed the map for directions. 'It's this way.'

'What's a Grimmelkin anyway?' queried Charlotte, looking at the chart over Mandy's shoulder.

'It can be any kind of small animal,' she informed her, 'and normally it's made of some sort of precious stone, but in this case, it's made of jade.'

The chart clearly showed the image of a green cat in the middle of a lagoon but gave no clue how to collect it safely. Even though it looked to be a small distance on the map, the distance they had to travel was vast, but the scenery more than made up for the length of time it took to get there.

They followed a winding path to a side river through the trees. Eventually crossing a bridge over a large stagnant pond, Mandy pointed out, 'There it is.'

A statue was glowing at the bottom of the water.

Frugal looked worried. 'It looks too easy,' he said.

'What do you mean?' said Mandy hesitantly, rolling the map and putting it into her back pocket.

'I mean something's going to happen when you get in the water.'

Charlotte knew he was right, but Mandy did not seem to share his concern.

'We have only a few hours of daylight left,' she said, hinting at him to set up camp.

'But—' Frugal tried to argue.

'Just go, we'll be fine,' Mandy assured him confidently.

Frugal slowly wandered over to a spot quite nearby and began to pull all manner of things from his satchel.

'Who's going in?' Mandy asked, touching the water with the tips of her fingers. 'Damn, it's cold,' she then warned. 'Quite a lot of the lakes are warm in Avaland, especially near the Coliseum because they are heated by volcanic energy underneath the rock.'

Mandy started to remove her clothes but Charlotte intervened. 'It's OK, I'll go. If something happens, at least you will be able to help me with magic.'

Stripping down to her pants and T-shirt, she cast aside her clothes and stepped into the water. The second it hit her skin she regretted volunteering. A few moments later she was swimming. Her whole body seemed to go into shock and it took a lot of focus to push against the cold.

Luckily Charlotte had always been quite a good swimmer. The Crumps had pressed her to take swimming lessons since she was four, so she was able to dive under the water without fuss. Holding her breath, she swam to the bottom, searching amongst the reeds.

She had come up for air a few times before she saw an emerald hue.

'Do you see it?' shouted Mandy supportively, kneeling down from the bridge.

'Yeah, I've found it,' Charlotte panted, gasping for air.

'Pass it to me on the bridge!' she said. 'I'll wait here.'

Another deep breath and Charlotte submerged herself again, this time deeper than before.

She managed to pick up the Grimmelkin quickly; she struggled to the surface because it was surprisingly heavy but somehow she managed to pass it to Mandy on the bridge.

Charlotte had almost climbed out of the water when something grabbed her around the ankles and pulled her back in.

Reeds were dragging her to the bottom and now, to make matters worse, the river surface had completely frozen over. Charlotte was trapped and running out of air. Trying not to panic, she watched as Mandy attempted to break through the ice with her sceptre but even if she did break through they would never reach her in time.

She was going to have to forfeit the task.

'Frugal!' shouted out Mandy. 'You need to melt a hole in the ice!'

Running over he waved his palms, pulling her out quickly and snapping the reeds in two. Cold pierced her like a hundred knives as she lay immobile, shivering on the surface. Frugal covered her with a silver blanket and Charlotte lost consciousness for a few moments.

Startled, Charlotte opened her eyes.

Cold sweat ran down her body as she realised that a miscalculation had been made. More than a few moments had passed by, because it was dark outside the tent. A camp fire roared menacingly close by, but she realised that the flames had been enchanted not to be dangerous. Frugal must have finished setting up camp, but he was nowhere to be seen.

For that matter neither was Mandy, and she wondered where they might be; surely they hadn't left her in the Labyrinth alone. She dropped the silver blanket that wrapped her to find herself dry and properly clothed.

White orbs surrounded the tent, seemingly keeping a watch on her. Now knowing them to be Fairies, she reached out to touch one of the lights but it moved away.

Charlotte got a fright when she noticed a figure walking towards her on the water's surface. She recognised her long red hair, and the woman's eyes bulged oddly just as they had inside the fountain when Charlotte had been handed her talisman.

The woman spoke softly through pale narrow lips. Her voice was chilling and ghost-like, but Charlotte did not fear.

'I have come to warn you,' said the angelic figure, a ray of panic in her speech.

'Warn me of what?' questioned Charlotte, dumbfounded in mystery.

'You are not safe here,' she cautiously advised. 'You must not bring the Obelisk into the Labyrinth unconcealed because it opens a portal.'

'I don't understand what that means?' worried Charlotte innocently, searching for danger. 'Who are you?' she asked, curious as to why this female kept appearing to her.

'I am many things,' the woman replied, 'but there is no time for an explanation; I can only buy you some time but when you wake you must run.'

'Run from who?'

But the woman did not reply.

Ringing filled Charlotte's ears. Washing around in the water beneath her feet was a poster, and the answer to her question.

WANTED

MIZALDUS

DEAD OR ALIVE

Beneath was a photograph of a psychopathic-looking woman; her face was dirty, and her hair was long and brown. Somehow, strangely, Charlotte recognised her, but the face she remembered was much kinder than the one in the picture.

'WAKE UP!' screeched the Lady of the Lake threateningly, her face becoming distorted. 'WAKE UP!' she said again, but this time the voice was not hers, it was Frugal's.

Charlotte's vision was instantly restored.

She was standing in the same place, looking out on to the lake, where crows were squawking, encircling rising black smoke. The white lady had disappeared but the water bubbled where she'd stood. Frugal and Mandy screamed instructions to each other in slow motion.

Charlotte realised she'd been in a trance.

'There's something wrong with the lake,' yelled Mandy, directing her staff at the target, ready to attack.

The Grimmelkin was hissing on the ground at Mandy's side, its back arched up on end.

'We must fight it,' ordered Frugal, holding out both his palms as they sparked with nerves.

'No, we must run,' Charlotte told them.

Both friends looked at her with utter bewilderment.

'Are you mad?' jeered Frugal. 'We've almost completed the assignment.'

'This isn't part of the task,' Charlotte insisted. 'Please trust me, there is no time to explain.'

Stalling for a moment, Mandy and Frugal were at first a little reluctant to walk away so easily, but both individually came to the conclusion that she would not ask them to run if it was not absolutely necessary.

'Lead us to the exit, Grimmelkin,' commanded Mandy and the jade feline turned and ran across the bridge, where a gold ornate frame was waiting for them. They all followed quickly, and had barely reached the bridge when the woman from the poster burst out of the lake.

She looked more menacing in the flesh than in the photograph. Mizaldus had murder in her eyes as she insistently pursued them.

Mandy was first through the door, the Grimmelkin by her side. Afterwards came Frugal, but he checked to see where Charlotte was and established that she'd fallen behind, so waited.

'What do you want?' Charlotte raged, edging backwards across the timber; but the woman did not speak, only advanced on her faster.

Frugal's eyes enlarged with terror when he spotted the twisted face of Mizaldus. Protectively grabbing Charlotte's arm, he pulled her backwards through the door with only moments to spare. They landed together on the hard, polished mahogany floor, the entrance to the Labyrinth in front of them.

'Why did we have to run?' snapped Mandy, looking irritated that she had been forced to forfeit the task early.

'It was Mizaldus,' Frugal said, getting to his feet with a face full of worry. 'Mizaldus is inside the Labyrinth.'

CHAPTER FIVE

A Centaur's Warning

With research on her mind, Charlotte thrust open the steely doors to the library.

A flash of lightning struck outside the window, from which hung the longest pair of curtains she had ever seen. The fabric dragged across the recently varnished floorboards, which creaked as she strolled inside.

This was unlike any library she had ever seen. The sheer scale of it made her wonder if she was going to find what she was looking for at all. She was overcome by the grandiose scale; bookcases were stacked tall to the ceiling with five levels. The clatter of moving ladders being drawn to their desired locations made her mind feel clouded. The room was filled with nothing but the haunting whispers of residual ghosts.

Pulling down as many potentially relevant titles as she could carry, Charlotte stacked them all on one of the tables to examine them further. The titles she had chosen so far were:

An Avalonian Guidebook for Nincompoops

Villains, Myths and Legends

Predictions and Prophecies

And on the top of the pile was: *Key Cultures and Customs.*

Choosing the book that was most applicable to what she was looking for – *Examining Tradition and Artefact* – Charlotte skimmed the index page looking for anything to do with an Obelisk, the name the mysterious Lady of the Lake had given the prism.

Nothing.

This time Charlotte examined all of them for local folklore and mythologies. She couldn't find anything to do with that either. Abandoning the pile, she took to the shelves, leaving a trail of chaos behind. Some of the books had been too high to get back on the shelves and were sticking out of places they didn't belong.

Deciding to take a rest, Charlotte sat back in one of the armchairs, and listened to the raging storm outside. The wind was whistling against the glass, blowing dust out of the drapes. Beginning to lose faith, she sighed; two hours had passed and there was no time to start again.

The clock tower chimed eight times, indicating she had reached the end of her allotted schedule.

Charlotte approached the librarian's desk feeling somewhat disappointed. She couldn't honestly say that her trip to the library had gone very well at all, having trawled through stacks of parchment only to find a few titles that may be helpful. Taking out her library card, Charlotte handed over the small pile in her palms.

A single black hardback on the librarian's trolley, waiting to be put back on the shelf, caught her attention; it must have been recently returned.

'I wonder if I might look at that?' she asked, picking it up and smoothing the imprinted leather on the front cover. *The Lies and Lunacy of Kristoffer Enoch.*

'That is no problem,' agreed the pretty Russian, pressing her date stamp to the desk.

This was the same man Charlotte had envisaged carving his name into the wall. Recognising the significance of this, the compelling urge to pick it up was inevitable.

Examining the inside, Charlotte considered the name of the person to borrow it last. *Lone Wolf* had been stamped onto the frontmost page. Everybody had a library nickname, probably for the very reason it made them difficult to identify.

One of the pages had been folded over in the top right corner so Charlotte flicked straight to it. To her amazement, there it was; a picture of the Obelisk, but a different colour to her own.

'Can you tell me who borrowed this last?' she enquired, receiving back an insolent glance.

'That is against policy,' rasped the librarian. Of course, Charlotte knew this to be true, but there was no harm in asking.

The librarian stamped the book's inner cover: *Black Swan.* Charlotte politely expressed her gratitude with a 'thanks' and left.

Impatiently reopening the book whilst she was walking, she misjudged where she was going and sauntered straight into the rear end of a Centaur. As she dropped the pile to the floor, the Centaur turned and gave her a look of disgust.

'I'm sorry, I wasn't looking where I was going …'

'Do you think it wise, girl, to be carrying an artefact like that around so carelessly?'

Charlotte froze, overcome with shock; how did he know she had the Obelisk?

'That's right,' he gloated. 'There are those that can sense its presence, and I can tell you now, an object like that does not belong in the pocket of a teenager. You need to conceal it like the others.'

'The others – you mean there is more than one?'

'Don't play naïve with me, girl, I know what you lot get up to and I will be sure to put a stop to it just as soon as I can; that much you can be sure of.'

The door behind them opened. It was Lauraus.

'Is everything OK?' he interrupted, picking up the mess on the ground.

'Ahh, another one! Should you not be with your betrothed, Lauraus Balthazar?'

'The betrothal is broken and legally acknowledged by the king.'

'Yes, well, we shall see,' smirked the spitting stallion. Giving them both a look of contempt, the Centaur turned on his hooves and trotted away.

'Who was that?' Charlotte trembled, concerned to be making more foes than friends of late.

'Zavantus Lavlock,' Lauraus declared. 'Centaurs are rare at the Coliseum; that particular one is considered to be an outcast even by his own kind.'

'I don't think he likes me.'

'Don't worry about it!' laughed Lauraus. 'He doesn't like anyone.'

'Why was he made an outcast by his people?' Charlotte asked curiously, trying not to sound nosey.

'Because his father was a human.'

While that information took a moment to digest, Lauraus squinted at the book she had just been reading.

'That is an interesting choice you have there,' he reflected casually. 'Is there any particular reason you have chosen it?'

'I saw it on the librarian's trolley on the way out,' she justified herself nervously. 'I just thought it looked like an interesting read.'

Charlotte didn't know why she hadn't told him the truth about her vision, and by the look on his face he could tell she was lying. He considered her for a moment, looking straight into her eyes.

'I have an appointment in the armoury now,' she revealed, looking at her watch, which confirmed that she was five minutes late.

Picking up her pace, she ran through the corridor, making an effort to be more careful this time. Looking over her shoulder, she saw that the prince's eyes were still smouldering. They didn't say goodbye, just stared at each other as they always did.

One more floor up was the armoury, the largest of all the places visited so far. Only able to guess as to its capacity, she imagined being able to fit twenty Wisteria Cottages inside.

The room was brightly lit, with burgundy wallpaper. A gold vaulted ceiling first drew Charlotte's attention to a gilded recess in a wall designed specifically for the storage of weapons. Equally positioned around the room were suits of armour, most of which did not appear to be for humans. Fanned out across the walls were an array of weapons, some in glass cases and others on neatly constructed shelving.

In the centre of the room were mats of royal blue. Gladiators engaged in combat, though not against each other; the opposition would attack as great plumes of smoke disguised in the ghostly form of a rival opponent. Charlotte quickly spotted London Carrick wielding a sword against one of these veils and she couldn't help feeling a little impressed with his ability.

Known as a bit of a ladies' man, the handsome celebrity seemed to delight much more in combat than in the attention of the usual females that paraded around him. He was clearly a very accomplished swordsman.

Recognising the aggressor, the mythological snake-haired temptress Medusa cowered to her knees in a decapitated mist and let out the almighty scream of defeat, causing everyone to turn around and look.

Charlotte ushered herself to the front desk where a Gnome was waiting, signing important documents. Scratching his long warty nose, he became impatient with her staring and Charlotte quickly addressed him, realising that she was being rude.

'I have an appointment with the Gnome Gamelyn,' she explained. 'I'm sorry I'm late.' Giving him a friendly smile, Charlotte attempted to reverse some of her reaction to their meeting.

The grumpy Gnome dismissed it without acknowledgement. 'Leave your things on the desk and follow me,' he vacantly barked, leading her down a set of stone steps, through a tunnel to a room made entirely of stone.

The Gnome shook his head as he shut the door behind him.

Through a door on the other side of the room came Gamelyn, who she was able to identify because he was wearing a small imprinted bronze badge. He was equally as small and hairy but much friendlier-looking than the Gnome that had led her here. He pushed his tiny glasses closer to his eyes as he inspected her further.

'Charlotte Crump, I presume.'

'Yes, that's right,' she said, trying not to feel awkward as he circled, giving her a once-over.

'You are unusually tall and your eyes are rare in colour,' he said, prodding her with a stick. 'Tell me about your ancestry?'

'I don't have one,' she revealed. 'I am an orphan.'

'Hmm … Interesting,' he said, dipping his tail into an ink pot and jotting something down in his notebook. 'Are you a Gladiator, my dear?'

'No,' she replied ashamedly. 'That's why I'm here; I already know I'm going to struggle inside the Labyrinth … I can't defend myself like the others. I'm worried that someone's made a mistake and I am not supposed to be here.'

To her surprise the Gnome did not seem to partake in her concerns.

'That is nonsense, my dear; nobody has ever been called by the Coliseum that did not belong here.' Gamelyn gave her a warm reassuring smile, then clicked his fingers, commanding a ladder to walk across the room. He climbed it and patted her on the arm. 'Believe me when I say that you possess something remarkable … We just have to find out what it is.'

Gamelyn took a tape measure from his pocket and measured her forehead. 'Do you possess any skill that would be considered out of the ordinary?' he asked.

'How do you mean?'

'I mean has anything strange ever happened to you?' Gamelyn descended the ladder, awaiting an answer.

'A few things,' she said, thinking back to her childhood. 'I can sense things that others can't. Sometimes when I touch an object, I can see its history, and there have been times in the past when I have made things happen but I don't know how I have done it.'

'Telepathy,' he proposed, looking pleased. 'It sounds as though you have much to do in order to develop your skill; I recommend you visit the armoury for at least two hours every day.'

'But how will I defend myself inside the Labyrinth? I have no defence from attack.'

'When you have developed your abilities, you will be better equipped to protect yourself than many of the others, and in time you will use this skill to safeguard the people. But no one else can do it; you will have to find your own way. But I can help … and I will … every day.'

Gamelyn rummaged through a cabinet on the back wall that held a number of small wooden drawers. He took something and placed it in her hand. 'In the meantime I want you to take this.'

In her palm was a small black pebble; very similar to something you would pick up on a beach.

'This will help you,' he said. 'Use its energy to manifest whatever magic you can form. Once you learn to conjure on request, you will be able to start learning to control your ability.'

If he was right and she was a Sorceress, then she was willing to give anything a try.

Gamelyn went back to look through the drawers for a second time.

'What if you're wrong? About me being telepathic, I mean.'

'Then it would be a first, my dear … There is a simple way to test the theory, of course.'

'What's that?' she said, speculating as to what kind of magical gadget he was going to pull from the drawers.

'You could tell me what your favourite colour is?'

'How is that going to help me establish whether or not I can perform telepathy?' she grumbled.

Gamelyn turned to face her. 'Because I am not speaking to you with my lips, my dear,' he said, his mouth tightly sealed and wearing a blank expression.

Charlotte was taken aback; now she was starting to believe him.

'Homework!' asserted Gamelyn, giving her a candle. 'I want you to light it using only your mind, but you must remember you are limited by your own expectations; you must believe you can light the candle, otherwise it will be impossible.'

On the way out he handed her a leather satchel with lots of pockets inside. 'Everything you need will be in there – I suggest you take some time to familiarise yourself with its contents.'

#

On returning to her room, Charlotte got to work straight away, instantly recognising that the stone had given her some new ability.

She spent several hours trying to light the candle, eventually setting her curtains on fire. Pleased with her progress, she laid on her bed opening the library's copy of *The Lies and Lunacy of Kristoffer Enoch.*

> *Kristoffer Enoch was born in Paris on the 4th January 1756. He was a small child. Upon moving to Avaland after his mother developed*

the plague, his father, a well-respected royal blacksmith, had secured him an apprenticeship in journalism when he received his scroll inviting him to the Coliseum.

Working on many high-profile cases, Kristoffer made many friends and allies, but soon before his fortieth birthday concerns about his mental health were detected. His dismissal from the Coliseum was an inevitable consequence.

At one time liked and respected by many, Kristoffer continued working as a historian, claiming to uncover the mysteries of the controversial secret society The Last Seven. The long-awaited acknowledgement he thought he deserved was never received and his autobiography was withdrawn from publication due to inaccurate findings presented as truth.

Suddenly there was a loud crack from inside her bedroom fireplace.

Frugal had sent a scroll: *Meet me in the atrium at seven thirty, bring your jacket because it's been raining.*

Charlotte shut the book on her bed and looked at the clock; there was still well over an hour until then. Taking the Obelisk from her bedside table, she looked into the glass with speculation. Without really knowing why, Charlotte held the stone to her lips and joked quietly, 'Is anybody there?'

She almost fell from her bed as the crystal began to glow brightly back in response.

She grabbed a coat, feeling alarmed; the door slammed behind her as she scaled the stairway.

Charlotte had to ask herself whether someone was trapped inside. Coming to the conclusion that a little advice might help, the decision to talk to someone older gave her little reassurance. Not really knowing who to trust, the decision to approach Quartz Clear on the matter finally seemed like the best idea.

She remembered that Topaz had mentioned the location of headquarters. The tower at the end of the atrium was accessed by a spiral staircase made entirely of stone, with no barrier to prevent your fall. Charlotte carefully clambered along the inside, a fear of heights taking over a desire to inspect each fiery oil painting.

The doorways were covered with canvas, on which flames seemed to glimmer, representing each of the Talisman groups. Dread overcame her as she considered the possibility of Quartz Clear being at the top of the tower. But the feeling of relief replaced it when she realised her own Talisman group was about halfway.

She gave the doorframe a tap, and Antonious popped his ghostly head out of the canvas a few seconds later.

'Are you coming, then?' he grumbled.

Stepping into a small domelike room made entirely of quartz, Charlotte noted that the benches were made out of the same material as the walls.

Abacus and Topaz let out a small cheer, pleased that she'd found the way. Magnus was trying to sew up a dirty old rug and saluted in a small show of welcome.

'You're keen,' jabbered Topaz, in high spirits 'Only been here a week and you want to come out on the job with us already.'

Abacus cheerfully interjected, 'And of course we would love to take you, but I'm afraid it's against regulations.'

Charlotte was not at all bothered by his intervention; if anything she felt relief, appreciating that it was a little too soon.

The right moment for bringing up the Obelisk didn't arise, as it appeared that the group were keen to get underway with today's patrol.

'We'll show you the ropes before we head out if you like, give you an idea of what you're aspiring to.'

'What are we dealing with today?' Topaz winked, directing Antonious to start.

'Minos has escaped the caves of Caladonia and is wreaking havoc all over the city.'

'He's escaped again!' hooted Magnus, having now finished sewing up his magic carpet.

As Antonious began to speak again, the table in the centre of the room lit up and projected the scene from a bird's-eye perspective.

'The town's people have been told to lock themselves indoors and there are four units out trying to find him.'

'Who's Minos?' enquired Charlotte, eyeing the scene.

'Minos is a Minotaur,' said Abacus. 'An unfriendly beast! He was placed inside the caves not only to protect the public, but for his own protection as well. He was being sought by hunters; a fine trophy to any one of them. The Coliseum would not stand back and let that happen.'

'Except he escapes every couple of months and we have to go back and put him in there again,' complained Magnus. 'It's a complete shambles.'

'So what's the plan?' buzzed Topaz, clasping together her palms.

'Ruby, Jade and Amethyst are stationed in three quadrants of the city; we are to take over from Flint, who are due to end their shift once we arrive but they have agreed to stay on longer to assist if necessary.' Antonious pointed to some castle ruins with a maestro's baton. 'I suggest we start in the south, doing door-to-door searches whilst sweeping the city. When we do reprimand him, I have been briefed of the existing plan to sedate him and move him back to the caves. This assignment will be carried out by Emerald group.'

'Sounds like a plan,' said Topaz, setting forth from the bench. 'Shall we?'

Abacus took his broomstick that was leaning up against the wall and all four Guardians clasped their talismans.

'So there you go, Charlotte,' concluded Abacus. 'Don't worry 'bout it, you'll soon get a piece of the action.'

As they disappeared before her eyes, Charlotte was left alone in the room. Seven-thirty had arrived, and it was only a short walk to meet Frugal.

They decided to get hot chocolate and the Hobgoblin had somehow gotten hold of marshmallows to roast over the lake of lava. The ground was dry enough to sit on, and the rising heat made it warm, somewhat like a heated blanket.

'So the talismans transport you,' she corroborated, taking a brown melted s'more from the roasting stick.

'The Labyrinth too,' he mumbled, his mouth full of oozing sugar. 'Instead of getting hurt, you are transported back to the doors.'

Lanterns floated overhead, sent from an unknown location in the vicinity.

'They must be getting ready for Halloween,' Frugal mysteriously stated. 'Anyway, I've been meaning to ask you – how did you get on in the armoury today?'

Reflecting on the day's events, Charlotte pointed out that she'd been able to manifest magic on request for the first time. 'But it's still in its very early stages,' she pondered, deciding not to mention the incident with her curtains.

After a lengthy description, Frugal swished around the remainder of his cocoa. 'I reckon you might have some sort of dormant ability, you know? Everybody here has been training for years, it just seems odd that you could get put into Quartz Clear when you don't even know how to hold a sword.'

If Frugal was trying to make her feel better, he was failing miserably. But Charlotte was able to respond; that question had already been answered for her today.

'They invited me because I'm a telepath,' she defended herself. 'But telepathy isn't going to protect me in dangerous situations, so I'm going to have to learn to fight if I want to survive inside the Labyrinth.'

Frugal agreed. 'Then the armoury would be the obvious place to start,' he said.

Checking no one else was around, she pulled the Obelisk from her pocket and Frugal's eyes lit up. 'It might not just be the telepathy they are picking up on.'

'Where did you get that?' he burst, hooking his eyes in awe.

'It brought me here. I'm trying to find out what it is.'

'You should put it away before someone sees it,' he decreed, trying to block it from view with the bag of marshmallows.

'Why? What is it?' she asked, concerned that he'd reacted that way.

'The Last Seven is a secret organisation,' he said. 'They have warrants for their arrest; you could get in a lot of trouble for having that in your possession.'

Charlotte's heart sank. If the Obelisk was going to make her a criminal, she wasn't sure she wanted it.

'Why are the Last Seven wanted?' she asked, trying to disguise the sadness in her voice.

'Murder!' he said. 'All lies, of course, just an excuse to get hold of the stones for themselves. You see … there are those that wish to abuse their positions of power. Look … I'm not going to say anything to anyone, in fact … I'm in line for an Obelisk myself, but you mustn't tell anyone else you have this.'

Charlotte profusely agreed, watching him throw his polystyrene cup onto the lava, where it went up in flames.

'I mean … look what they did to poor Kristoffer Enoch.'

'I think someone's trapped inside,' she recited uneasily.

'Listen …' said Frugal. 'Here's not a good place to talk about it, but I know one of the bearers. I'm not allowed to tell you who it is, because it's against the law, but with your consent I could ask them to present themselves.'

Charlotte agreed. Frugal looked uncomfortably like he wanted to change the subject, so she didn't ask any more questions.

Both of them jumped as they were alerted to shouting nearby, Charlotte unintentionally zoning in to the voice. She realised it was Orobus Pluto.

Running his hat through his fingers to shape it, he expressed his frustrations to a much older grey-haired gentleman.

'I cannot believe there are no clues!' he raged. 'What I want to know is how they got into my office. There are forty-five different enchantments on the lock of my door … forty-five! Even if nothing was taken, that doesn't mean they didn't get what they were looking for! There is an enemy among us,' he said, finally alerted to Charlotte's eye contact.

She quickly looked away, pushing the Obelisk further into her pocket.

'What is it?' asked Frugal, aware that she had just picked up on something important.

'It sounds like Orobus Pluto's office was broken into,' she said in astonishment.

'I don't think anything like this has ever happened before,' Frugal said, withdrawing his bottom from the stone and pushing on towards the entrance, Charlotte wandering unobtrusively behind.

'But why would anyone want to break into his office?' he probed, goose pimples spurting up on his arms and neck. 'My skin does that when I get a funny feeling about something; it happens to all Hobgoblins.'

Charlotte giggled.

'That's what he's trying to work out,' she said, countering the vibe. 'And he seems very angry about it.'

Frugal examined the situation methodically. It took him a while to come to a decision. 'If there is an enemy among us, then no news is not necessarily good news,' he finally said.

'How do you mean?' she pressed, leaving no stone unturned.

'It means they found what they were looking for.'

He waved away any other possible explanation, but Charlotte couldn't help feeling something was wrong. Becoming inundated with a negative feeling, she shut her eyes in an attempt to use her gift to find out more, but was unsuccessful.

She did conjure some sort of magic, though. They watched as the floating jack-o'-lanterns broke free of their bonds and the orange balls of light flew up into the sky, disappearing into broken clouds until only the moonlight was shining down on them.

CHAPTER SIX

The Dagger of Thor

Rain saturated the grass beneath Charlotte's muddy boots as Mandy led her away from the Coliseum. Mandy then pointed to an overgrown path that looked like it hadn't been visited for a number of years.

'That's Maisie's Woods,' she eventually revealed. 'Nobody ever comes to this place.'

Pulling back overgrown weeds Mandy released a rusty gate that barely swung aside.

Squeezing through, Mandy argued with the reasoning. 'They think the local Pixie folk are cursed,' she said. 'A load of cobblers if you ask me.'

Looking irritable, it became apparent there was something she wanted to share. Wiping a welling eye with her sleeve, Mandy held open the entrance.

'They are the victims of a lie, built to justify the cruelty. I'm starting a campaign as soon as I graduate but until then it will have to be an eye for an eye.'

Was Charlotte sensing a desire for revenge in her words?

Feeling relieved she'd hidden the Obelisk in the bottom of her wardrobe, the last thing Charlotte needed right now was trouble; one wrong move and she could get arrested for being a member of the Last Seven. An organisation she had yet to meet.

Underneath the canopy it was very different, and it took Charlotte entirely by surprise. The weeping canvas was dropping a fine layer of glitter, which lit up the foliage like Christmas trees. Trunks thrived majestically, bearing jewel-encrusted crowns that shook in the prevailing breeze. Fallen sparkles perished before they hit ground; the fluorescing overtones appeared to be composed of magical properties.

This was the stuff of fairy tales, and Charlotte had to pinch herself to check that she was actually awake.

Half expecting Mandy to have scheduled them in for a bit of protesting, Charlotte would have been happy to exhibit some action for the cause, but she appeared to have been mistaken.

'I thought it would be fun to collect our polypus pearls ourselves rather than go to the apothecary like everybody else.'

Mandy must have been responding to a scroll sent to all of the newcomers the previous morning. They had been advised to have these polypus pearls in their possession at all times, and that they should be considered part of their uniform. Mandy had remembered a newspaper article discussing how these deterrents were supposed to be quite easy to collect and gave a stronger resistance that way; they were a necessary safeguarding component, repelling against most monsters.

That was the part that worried Charlotte the most, the bit about monsters, so she couldn't be blamed for questioning their safety as they left the protection of the grounds entirely.

But Mandy had insisted they were safe because she had bought a spray can of face-fungus repellent, whatever that was supposed to be.

'Here, put these on,' she said, throwing Charlotte a pair of thick-rimmed spectacles. 'They're called gig lamps. With these we'll be able to spot trouble from a hundred yards away.'

Charlotte didn't want to offend Mandy by telling her the glasses dulled her senses and that they would be safer without them, especially when Mandy had put so much thought into organising it all, so she went along. Putting them onto her face, feeling a bit silly, she could only hope that Lauraus was not out here collecting his polypus pearls too.

'Can you see anything?' asked Mandy, holding out her can of repellent, ready to attack.

'No …' Charlotte said truthfully. 'I can see bugger all. Arghhh!' Panic-stricken, Charlotte stepped back into Mandy, who drenched a forward-facing shrub with mould.

'Oh … it's OK,' said Charlotte, breathing a sigh of relief. 'It's a squirrel.'

'You nearly gave me a heart attack,' complained Mandy, snatching away the glasses. 'Here, you take the spray.'

'What's in that stuff anyway?' Charlotte whined, holding the can as far away from her as she could. 'It stinks of rotten eggs.'

They left behind the weeping plant. Its leaves curled inward before shrivelling to powder and scattering to the ground.

Determined to reach wherever they were going in one piece, Charlotte let Mandy take the lead. Looking like she'd had a lot of practice with the glasses, Mandy navigated the way with a map and compass.

Journeying on, the trail became denser until the trees were growing so close together they had to squash through the gaps.

'There it is,' directed Mandy, drawing Charlotte's attention to a carelessly built road.

As they reached it, they noticed there were horse and cart tracks imprinted in the mud.

'The poachers have already been,' Mandy then agonised, worried about the scene that lay ahead.

The unremitting downpour made it difficult to see; had it not been for the lateral branches, Charlotte may not have noticed the looming cliff face at all.

Tiny cries flittered around them as Pixies hid behind brushwood, sobbing. It wasn't easy to see the detail, not just due to their speed, but because the weather was abysmal.

Catching a glimpse of tiny fluttering wings, Charlotte spun her head around in time to spot a freckled female with boyish locks, pointed ears and a wider than usual nose. Throwing a miniature handful of dirt in Charlotte's face, this appeared to be one of the more fearless of the clan.

'They think we're poachers,' Mandy snivelled, 'because it's hunting season.'

'Why aren't they flying away?' worried Charlotte, because the Pixies weren't even attempting to escape.

'They're protecting the trees,' agonised Mandy. 'If they leave too suddenly, the tree will die. It takes time to choose a new nest, because they have to prepare it, as well as making sure the old one is ready for life without them. A tree that is abandoned by a Pixie is never the same again; studies have proven that it will be depressed for the rest of its life.'

Charlotte's heart ached with sympathy as she listened to the miniscule heartbeats panicking whilst attempting to hide their children.

'Don't the poachers let them go once their dust has been harvested?'

Realising how insensitive her question had been the moment she asked it, Charlotte tried to help Mandy from plummeting to her knees.

'We're too late!' She broke down crying in her arms. 'I wanted to reach them first this year.'

Taking the bag from her shoulder, Mandy took a handful of tiny brown worms and threw them as far as she could in an attempt to seal up the poachers' way through.

'What are those?' Charlotte asked, feeling a little nauseous at the thought of them being in Mandy's bag the whole time.

'Knapweed seeds,' she said. 'Except these have had a large dose of steroids.'

Burrowing beneath the soil, the larvae pushed stalks from the ground, sprouting very quickly. They began to stretch and twist with life.

With the last handful, Mandy ensured the safety of the nest. Anybody that came with the intention of hunting now was going to get a shock. In the last few minutes, the knapweed had taken on a life of its own, coiling around trees with the intention of apprehending anything that came close enough. Charlotte and Mandy were going to have to get out of there, and fast; the weeds were growing out of control.

Mandy turned and lunged onto one of the Pixie trees.

One of the vines failed to grab Charlotte's foot, because she'd leapt out of the way in time. But she'd misjudged the distance and landed a lot further down than anticipated, cutting her bottom lip.

Mandy climbed down to reach her. 'Are you OK?' she asked.

'Yeah, I'm fine. It was the knapweed.'

The Pixies raised their arms, certain that Mandy had only been trying to help, but weren't so sure about the choice of knapweed seeds.

'Hopefully that will slow them down a bit,' grinned Mandy, pleased with her efforts. 'Well … until I graduate and can do things the proper way.'

Mandy's mood seemed to have lightened now she knew the Pixies were safe from further harm. 'Come on! We'd better go; you might mistake one of the Pixies for a monster,' she joked.

'It had really big teeth,' protested Charlotte, referring to the squirrel. 'It must have been chewing on a nut or something.'

They walked on once again, but this time they didn't have to go far.

'Can you hear that?' squeaked Mandy with excitement. 'We're here, we made it to the River of Colours.'

They ran downstream after the current, to a place where toads chanted in brassy discord. The stream got larger, opening out on to a pebble bay with a narrow tumbling waterfall. Beneath the plummet was a pool of blue that penetrated the water so deeply it could have been the ocean, hues of flaxen gold and balefire red faded, disappearing gradually into the ripples as the shingles surged.

So much beauty couldn't be accidental.

'The Pixie magic doesn't just affect the trees,' counselled Mandy. 'Hopefully it will give a little something extra to the pearls.'

Charlotte scanned the backdrop for a way down.

Stripping down to her underwear, Mandy put her clothes into her backpack, threw it onto the bank, then dived headfirst into the lake.

Poking her head out of the water, Mandy invited Charlotte in. 'Come on!' she shouted up as raindrops fell onto her skin from the sky.

Charlotte did the same then threw her bag onto the embankment and jumped in much less elegantly than Mandy.

The water was warm, which was the last sensation she had been expecting. Wiping the spray from her eyes, a lungful of air was all Mandy needed before disappearing under the water.

Picking something up from the riverbed, she resurfaced carrying a pink opalescent shell.

'Clamping clams,' Mandy gasped, panting a little. 'They love these waters.'

'So are these going to help us inside the Labyrinth?' Charlotte inspected the shell's exterior battle scars.

'It's not the shells that are the repellent.' Mandy split the husk, revealing inside a pink pearl. 'It's their contents.' Discarding the casing, she swam to the shore and wrapped herself in a towel.

Charlotte hadn't brought a towel, but then she hadn't realised she was going swimming.

'It's OK, you can use mine,' said Mandy.

Feeling a bit of a fish out of water, Charlotte took a deep breath in and dived underneath the surface; it was even warmer the further down you went. Because she was a strong swimmer, she was able to spend some time scanning the river bed for the mollusc that stood out to her the most.

There were lots of clamping clams to choose from; they shrieked, snapping their bevelled mouths as she passed. They were aware they were being hunted and were trying to ward her off. Charlotte decided to go for one that was different.

Attempting to pull a lighter coloured grey from the side of a rock, she noticed seaweed still attached. Removing it was trickier than it looked, but, eventually succeeding, she swam to the surface.

Underwear sodden, Charlotte trembled onto the shore, passing her catch to Mandy so she could dry herself.

'I wouldn't bother!' Mandy teased. 'It's not like it's going to make any difference. Here, take my vest and jacket.'

Charlotte put back on the clothes in her rucksack, but was still freezing. They needed to get on with things and quickly, as the rain showed no sign of relenting.

Mandy studied the clam, recognising the seaweed meant that it must have once lived in the sea.

'Wow! Those ones are really rare,' Mandy assessed, looking a little jealous that she had not found it first.

Taking out one of her knives, Charlotte wedged it into the slit. The clam effortlessly opened, giving up its treasure: a perfect black pearl.

'We might as well do it here.' Mandy pulled a needle and thread from her bag. She pierced the pearl, and the two ends of the cotton bound together by themselves.

'Won't the thread snap?' asked Charlotte as Mandy put the band around her neck.

'The thread is everlasting; it's unbreakable.'

Next Charlotte pierced her pearl; it glistened like the midnight sky as she put it on.

'Are there mermaids here?' she then questioned, surrendering to an anxious feeling clenching from inside. There had been a noticeboard in the atrium warning against this very thing, how certain creatures could venture into unexpected places.

'The water is too warm. Mermaids are cold-blooded and generally found in salt water. Besides, I doubt they would be interested in us anyway; they are only really attracted to men.'

Charlotte was now certain her senses were alerting her to a threat coming their way.

Realising it was unlikely to be mermaids that she had been picking up on, the hairs on the back of her neck stood up on end as the acute sixth sense Charlotte had come to rely on was alerting her to somebody undesirable nearby.

Mandy noticed Charlotte's expression change. 'What is it?' she acknowledged, concerned that her friend's extrasensory perception had picked up on something.

'There's someone here.'

A rustle came from the bushes, sounding like panicked footsteps. Someone cloaked and hooded was running away.

Luckily the two girls hadn't been seen.

'Who was that?' shot Mandy nervously, lowering to her knees out of sight.

'I don't know, but they looked suspiciously like they were up to something.' Charlotte pulled herself up to the waterside to peer through a hole in the thorns.

'What are you doing?' Mandy protested in a whisper. 'Come back!'

'I just want to get a better look.' Charlotte then held her index finger over her lips to tell her to be quiet.

Mandy looked nervous, but Charlotte's precognition had taken over, and something was telling her this was important.

A little distance ahead was a woman. As she took down her hood, Charlotte recognised her as Sarah Sanctamoni, a member of the Jet Talisman group.

Pulling out a whip, she tried to ward off a tall masked stranger advancing on her in a hostile way. Sanctamoni seemed unmoved by his aggressive body language, but remained on guard, ready to attack at a moment's notice.

'It's not the right time,' she argued facing him. 'If I act too soon then I will fail, and I can't. Too much is riding on this.'

The man stopped and surrendered his mask. He was grey and heavily scarred.

'Who are you to question orders?' interrogated the conceding man. 'I have been summoned here to tell you that you must carry out the objective that has been appointed to you; anything less will be considered an act of treason for which the punishment will be severe. These instructions were given to you months ago; the task should be complete by now.'

'There have been complications,' raged Sanctamoni.

'What kind of complications? Unless perhaps your allegiance has changed?'

'You dare to question my loyalty? You are in no position to make such an allegation, Bedweguar.'

'I do not have time for your triviality. Complete your orders or pay the price. I have done what has been asked of me. The message has been delivered,' concluded the man, backing off.

He turned and disappeared towards Feign Forest.

Charlotte and Mandy remained hidden until Sanctamoni had passed. Charlotte wanted to read her mind, but decided not to for fear she might give away her position. She knew she shouldn't be eavesdropping, but Sanctamoni's behaviour was so unusual she couldn't help feeling that something was wrong.

The return journey seemed quicker; it must have been because Mandy took them a different route than before. They could hardly climb a cliff only to get seized by fast-growing knapweed.

Positively soaking from head to foot, Charlotte could not wait to return to her chamber, but on their return it was clear by the mood in the Coliseum that something had happened. The air was sombre, leading Charlotte to believe her intuition had been correct once again.

Patrols were searching the grounds, commanding everybody to check in to their groups immediately. Charlotte and Mandy, who were still wet from collecting polypus pearls, proceeded directly to their Talisman headquarters.

As Charlotte walked through the Quartz Clear entrance, she saw the rest of the group were waiting with some anxiety.

Getting the impression they'd forgotten she was coming, Charlotte stood static amid a puddle of her clothes' creation, because they had got so wet in the rain. 'What's going on?'

'We don't know,' grimaced Topaz, 'but it doesn't look good, does it?'

'Orobus has asked all the team leaders to do a headcount,' answered Abacus. 'He wants to see who's missin'.'

At the sound of two booming taps from the other side, Abacus withdrew from the conversation and hurried to the door. The time had come to deliver his piece of the puzzle. Able to rest easy that everyone was accounted for, he gave his count to the marshal.

'Everyone from Quartz Clear is here, excluding Sir Gualish Knight, who is away on business.'

The bald-headed nobleman glanced inside to confirm he'd been given the correct numbers. He then nodded and wrote it down in his journal before shuffling along to collect the headcount from the next team.

Once the registrar was out of range and she couldn't be heard, Topaz spoke up. 'He didn't trust you,' she suggested. 'Did you not notice him do a recount?'

'It's protocol,' said Abacus, 'but only in extreme situations, which is what's concerning me. Not least because the man collecting the information is one of Orobus Pluto's best and most trusted advisers; it's rare for him to ever get involved in things this hands-on. I think he was chosen for his photographic memory.'

When the headcounts were finished, the regiments congregated on the steps outside. Orobus Pluto was standing at the bottom, ready to make an announcement.

He looked up to address them.

'There has been a theft from inside the vaults,' he said. 'If anybody has experienced anything strange, or has any information leading up to this event, please report this to your team leader. A list of missing staff has been taken and we will be beginning our enquiries shortly. Carry on as usual.'

The crowd cleared away, but those that had something to report stayed behind, including Charlotte and Mandy. The rest of Quartz Clear thought this was strange, so lingered around.

'Abacus, I have something to report,' Charlotte disclosed, feeling a bundle of nerves.

'Cut to the onions of ye, I have to open the door now.'

'Sanctamoni is in some kind of trouble; I saw her being threatened by a strange man in the woods.'

Antonious stormed from his seat in a pit of rage. 'Where is she?' he demanded, with intensity in his eyes.

'She was near the River of Colours.'

He launched himself towards the door, but a pair of frizzy ginger forearms reached out and took him by the scruff of the neck. Charlotte was surprised to see how strong Abacus was.

'You are not to leave this room, do you hear me? That is an order. I will not have you being caught up in all of this.'

Antonious looked helpless; for the first time he'd lost the hard edge Charlotte was used to seeing.

'Come with me Charlotte!' Abacus ordered, with no show of emotion, sealing up the door behind them to remind Antonious of his last instruction.

Abacus led her down the stairs to a room filled with filing cabinets that mirrored a mottled green glow. Charlotte took a seat at a round table. Abacus stood behind her, an action that was replicated by the others already present.

Mandy was also there with her team leader, an enigmatic brunette wearing dangling moon-shaped earrings. Charlotte had yet to be introduced, but now was hardly the time.

A tall gentleman with a goatee spoke first. 'Your grace, I present to you Icarus Parnell from Silver group.'

Icarus was a small man with a receding hairline. 'I saw a young lady, running from the vaults, your excellency.'

Orobus Pluto exhaled noisily, rising to his feet with intrigue. 'Did you recognise the woman?' he puffed impatiently.

'Yes, I did,' the timid man affirmed. 'I recognised her straight away as Sanctamoni from Jet group.'

'It was indeed Sanctamoni!' agreed another man, with crooked teeth and sideburns. 'I saw her too! She dropped a chandelier on me. That ruddy crop is a menace of a thing. I was unable to stop her as she made her escape, because I was rendered unconscious, forced to sneak out of the sanatorium to attend council, my lord.'

With each passing moment it became clearer that Sanctamoni was in a lot of trouble. Charlotte needed to say something to defuse the attack on her integrity.

Orobus tutted and shook his head. It seemed he had now made up his mind as to who was the guilty party, even though the evidence was, in Charlotte's mind, still inconclusive.

'Does anybody here have any information as to Miss Sanctamoni's current whereabouts?'

Charlotte stood and Abacus introduced her. She did not speak to Orobus formally as the others did. 'Mandy Zain and I overheard an argument in Maisie's Woods. It was between Sanctamoni and someone called Bedweguar.'

Orobus gave Mandy a quick glance, but did not ask her to confirm if this was true. 'It cannot be!' he said, fraught with an inner disagreement of some kind.

'He was threatening her, sir, ordering her to finish a job of some kind, though I sensed she was in danger. I didn't get the impression that the orders were coming from him.'

'Sensed?' enquired Orobus, looking to Abacus for an explanation.

'We believe Miss Crump to be a telepath; she is in her first year of training at the moment.'

'You are telepathic, they say,' Orobus paused to think for a moment; when he spoke next he looked as though he had some use for her. 'Abacus, I would like Quartz Clear to accompany me on an urgent mission to locate Miss Sarah Sanctamoni.'

Orobus then spoke to Charlotte directly. 'That is a very rare skill you possess, my dear. It will prove most useful here.'

'Sir, Charlotte's skill has not developed yet, it may take some time before we can use it reliably.'

'Still, she is the only one of her kind since Nelphinie; we must see that we do everything we can to help her develop that skill, even if those qualities are presently limited.'

Orobus dismissed the rest of the group and Abacus touched his talisman, summoning the rest of Quartz Clear, who arrived straight away.

'I request your presence today,' Orobus said. 'I want to locate Sarah Sanctamoni for questioning in relation to the theft of the Dagger of Thor. We are to meet at the River of Colours.'

'Sir, may I request that Antonious Draconi be dismissed from this mission?' pleaded Abacus.

'You can't do that!' shouted Antonious viciously. 'I have more of a right to be here than any of you.'

'I'm afraid I agree with Antonious,' said Orobus 'Besides, she is more likely to come quietly if you are with us!' And just like that, the matter was closed.

'Run along then, Charlotte' said Magnus, sounding a little patronising.

'Charlotte Crump will be leading the way,' Orobus corrected him.

'But she's underage, sir.'

'I am aware of that, thank you, Magnus.'

Even though she wasn't looking at him, Charlotte could feel Antonious staring. He had a lot of questions for her.

Noticing how cold she looked, Antonious took off his jacket and flung it over her shoulders.

'Charlotte!' came Orobus Pluto's voice, cutting short her churning thoughts. 'I said, are you ready?'

'Yes,' she lied, wishing she didn't have to be involved.

Topaz pointed towards her talisman to indicate that she needed to grasp it like the rest of them. The moment her fingers touched the stone, a black hole appeared beside her and she felt herself being drawn unwillingly inside.

From the void, Charlotte morphed to a cylindrical vortex and on into the abyss. Blurry-eyed, she reached out for Orobus Pluto's office but her hand hit a bubble, making her realise that she was trapped alone inside. Cast down the channel against her will, different circles appeared, but her route had been set and she could not access those that were not meant for her.

Eventually finding the right exit, Charlotte popped out of the other side, landing flat on her face. Nobody came to her aid. This was her first example of a Guardian's professionalism on the job. They surrounded Charlotte and Orobus in a circular formation, weapons at the ready, in case they were attacked.

Once the dizziness subsided, she realised she was back by the River of Colours.

Antonious had since turned into a wild grey wolf and was growling, ready to attack. Magnus was holding out his wand and Abacus clapped his hands together, making a red orb appear between his palms. Scanning the surroundings for danger, they tried to make sure they were alone. Topaz was first to lower her weapon – a perfectly drawn bow and arrow.

'Show me where the argument took place,' ordered Orobus in an imperious way, as though enjoying the hunt.

Swamped by the oversized jacket, Charlotte led them to the riverbank, the place where she had seen the argument occur. Growling at a patch on the ground, Antonious led the others over to investigate. Topaz, Magnus and Abacus kept watch as Orobus practically grazed his nose on the ground, inspecting it closely with his eye glass.

'Blood,' insisted Orobus, sniffing it, his pupils dilated. 'It looks as though she's been injured, probably by the Dagger.'

Taking a handkerchief and holding it over his mouth, he then asked Charlotte what she had seen. His mind seemed cold, noticeably more methodical than sympathetic.

'I see a trail,' Charlotte predicted, but she didn't want to follow it; she knew this path led to death. Sanctamoni's face appeared in her thoughts and it was an agonising sight. Opening out her hands in front of her she saw that they were covered in blood.

'She is frightened.' Charlotte turned her head away and the wild dog by her side faintly whined. They walked silently for some time before she had the courage to speak again.

'She's here,' Charlotte said, bowing her head to avoid the consuming stench of sadness.

Taking a panoramic view of their surroundings, the others all stopped and spread out.

'The Dagger! Is it here?' Orobus strategically questioned. 'Be careful not to touch it.'

'No,' said Abacus, responding to the order, albeit a little impatient with Orobus's lack of compassion.

Behind a tree lay a blonde lifeless body, her skin bone-white and drawn, and her lips peacock blue. Antonious then let out a strong and almighty roar that sent shivers down Charlotte's spine, as he changed from a wolf back into a man. He picked Sanctamoni up into his arms, her long grey coat dragging on the ground behind her.

Watching him bow his head into the shell of the woman he loved, Charlotte was overcome with regret, but it wasn't her own.

Abacus came to comfort her, putting his arm around her as she sobbed. But he could not shield her from the grief Antonious was feeling.

CHAPTER SEVEN

Hallows' Eve

Not for the first time this week, the bottom of the shower was Charlotte's hiding place of choice.

But she couldn't wash away the feeling of sadness that consumed her. No amount of sobbing was going to bring Sanctamoni back, and she was going to have to get used to the seriousness of the job she had agreed to.

The events leading up to Sanctamoni's death heralded a warning; it was only a matter of time before her own life was going to be on the line. She needed the ability to defend herself, and with this realisation, everything changed. Numbed by the expectation to get results, fused with the emotional impact of seeing a dead body for the first time, something awakened inside. Passion ignited within, melting away her worries.

Everything she had ever been through was preparing her for this purpose, and she had never felt more ready for a challenge. Night and day, Charlotte trained hard and didn't give up. Every moment from that point was regimented and focused. Yielding high hopes, having never broken a promise to anybody, she had no intention of breaking one to herself.

Within two weeks there had been a noticeable improvement in her ability.

Focused with clear intention, Charlotte revisited the armoury. Thirsty for combat, she entered with no particular destination in mind, only the note to find herself a weapon. Exploring the walls, she saw there were many a fine armament to choose from.

But Charlotte knew looking wasn't enough; her clairvoyance need be her only guide. Stroking each with the tips of her fingers, she hoped to entice some kind of energetic response. Kneeling on the blood red carpet, Charlotte opened the drawer to a cabinet containing dozens of silver balls. The tiny canons seemed of no obvious purpose to her, so she dropped them back inside.

Shutting her eyes as she stood, gratification came quickly as she realised the deterrent she had been seeking was nearby.

Angelic singing came from the air, soft yet loud enough to beguile. A gleam of sunlight caught her eye. Reflecting high upon a shelf was the very thing she had been compelled to seek.

Borrowing Gamelyn's ladder for a moment, she climbed, running her hand over the edge.

A silver box was just within her grasp.

As she swept aside the grime, the container startled her, bursting into song and reflecting light into her eyes. She had heard this music twice before. Delicately lifting the lid, she saw the purple velvet encased six black knives. The handles were encrusted with metallic stones.

Taking out the largest, she inspected it, surprised at how comfortable it felt to hold.

Instinctively Charlotte knew what to do.

Underneath the velvet lining were straps that had been neatly rolled, ready to be bound to the body. Attaching two to her arms and thighs, Charlotte traversed confidently to the mat. As she stood astride, ready to fight, a burst of smoke came from the ground, selecting the shape of a lion.

Encircling each other, neither took their eyes off the other; then without warning the smoking lion attacked. Reality seemed to slow down for a moment, and somehow her senses seemed magnified; but she knew what to do.

Reaching down to her thighs, she commanded the knives into her hands without touching them, then pointed the daggers to the creature and let go. Filled with some kind of power, they struck the heart of the fearless feline, exploding it to blue fire. Then they reappeared back inside the straps on her thighs.

She looked up towards the doors where Gamelyn was staring at her, open mouthed. He had been talking to London and Lauraus; the two boys looked impressed.

Joining them a few moments later, Charlotte hoped she wasn't in trouble for removing the daggers. 'I'm sorry, I shouldn't have taken these without asking.'

'Nonsense, you can take whatever you like from this chamber if you feel that it will help. I'm just surprised, that's all.'

Charlotte gave him the befuddled raise of one eyebrow.

'Well, it's never been done before. No one has ever been both a Sorceress and a Gladiator, and … the knives?'

'What about them?' As Charlotte questioned every little vibe she was picking up on, Gamelyn took one of the blades from her armband and held it up to his ear, giving it a little shake.

'They belonged to somebody famous; placed on that shelf so that they could only be chosen by the one who went looking for them. Rumoured to have been the property of the spirit Athene herself, they have been hidden on that shelf for centuries.' Gamelyn looked at her oddly, lifting his questioning fingers to his chin. 'How did you find them, my dear?'

Charlotte took the dagger from him and put it back aside her arm. 'I heard them singing.'

Taken aback, Gamelyn shot up insistently straight, growing at least an inch. 'The knives don't sing,' he said.

'Well, that's how I found them,' she corrected him. 'It's the same music that I heard at the Wirral and Apollo's Fountain.'

Though he knew her well enough to trust her words, he gave a look that would suggest otherwise, then commanded her back to the mat where a crowd gathered around.

#

Antonious was missing from lunch in the hall that day.

It was obvious why, but Topaz confirmed it with a mouth full of bread and butter pudding. 'He's been given absence of leave, and probably for a while.'

If his reaction to Sanctamoni's death had been anything to go by, Antonious had been carrying around a hidden affection for her, and now that she was gone he was exhausted with guilt. It was very quiet at the table without him, even with all the chatter and chinking cutlery.

Charlotte could only hope he was OK.

Topaz flew up from her chair, appearing puzzled. 'What are you doing here, Abacus? I thought you were on guard duty this afternoon.'

Abacus trundled over to the table, looking rather cross. He was holding a letter. 'I just bumped into Monty Huck and his dragon by the clock tower, and he asked me to deliver this to Charlotte.'

'What's that smell?' blasted Topaz, flapping at his smoking jacket.

'I wasn't joking when I said I bumped into him; well, it was that blithering beast of his, actually. Dratted thing set my favourite pair of slacks on fire! Handmade, from a little Irish village I visit every year for one jug of stout on my birthday.'

Charlotte doubted that he was being completely honest about the quantity of stout he liked to consume, but then that was none of her business.

Hoping he wasn't cross, she gratefully took the letter, recognising Aphra's handwriting at once. Charlotte's heart pounded. 'Thank you,' she said, leaving the table.

Barely able to contain her excitement, she settled on the banister. The rising staircase gave enough privacy to open the envelope.

Hello our darling girl,

Thank you for writing to us, we have been extremely worried. Poor Walter has refurbished half the house with the anxiety of it all.

We are glad to hear you are doing well. Avaland sounds like a remarkable place, it's called Avalon here in England. Did you know its folklore overspills even into our own world? There are some interesting stories to tell from an English perspective, maybe we could compare notes when we see you.

We do hope that will be soon.

Love always and forever,

Aphra and Walter.

On the other side of the page, a small note had been scribbled:

PS: The silly old goat got a fright when the dragon landed in the garden. Slid on his bottom all the way to the porch, funniest thing I've seen all year. Thanks for that, I needed a laugh. Luckily none of the neighbours saw.

Relief filled her from within. She felt so much better for receiving a letter; her spirits had been completely renewed. Of course, they had no idea she had been involved in the recovering of a dead body and she didn't intend to worry them.

Letting herself into her chamber, she put the letter onto her desk beside a drawstring bag full of coins. Stupidly, she hadn't even considered the fact that she was going to be earning any money, and became quite excited about being paid for something she was prepared to do for nothing.

Charlotte remembered Frugal telling her his room wasn't far, and he'd hung a coat hanger on the handle so they could find it. Now seemed like a better time than any, and within minutes she was back in the passage, roaming the royal blue carpet inside the silver corridor.

As she rapped with her knuckles, there was some clattering about inside before the door slowly opened and Frugal's nose popped out.

'Phew,' he sighed in relief. 'I thought you were Erebus Quarus for a second, apparently he's found out that I've been sneaking live snacks from the Labyrinth and wants to talk to me.'

Frugal stepped aside to let her through. 'I thought it was only us that knew about that?'

'What's-her-name from Crimson group saw me sneaking out grubs. It's a disaster, I could be dismissed.'

'Can't you just say you haven't been?'

'Yeah, I thought of that, but Hobgoblins' ears turn pink when we don't tell the truth, so he'd know right away.'

Surprised to see that Frugal's room was much larger than hers, Charlotte felt kind of jealous. It was dark green throughout, and he'd been fortunate to acquire furniture that had been streaked with gold. Frugal lay back on his four-poster bed, legs crossed, enjoying it all.

They were starting to discuss the prospect of spending some of these unusual coins when there was another knock; it was Mandy.

'The copper ones are Trollstones,' she explained, emptying hers onto the bed. 'Ten of those make one of the crescent-shaped silver coins; those are called Moonstones.'

Charlotte rolled the unusual moon-shaped coin between her thumb and index finger.

'Five Moonstones make one Sunstone, which is the big gold coin I'm holding. But most people call these Rubies.'

Charlotte examined the largest flat round piece. 'So, this big gold coin is a Ruby?'

'Yes, that's right! Or a Sunstone, but don't worry too much, you'll get the hang of it.'

Sidetracking her curiosity to Frugal, Mandy impatiently cleared her throat. 'What are you doing?'

Lying on his stomach, the hyperactive Hobgoblin rocked his legs back and forth whilst scribbling notes onto parchment.

'My brothers Fuzz and Fungus had an idea over the summer about starting a family business, and I've had a brainwave, so I'm doing some research.' Lifting up the paper, he showed them scribbled footnotes and colour-keyed diagrams.

'As Loose as a Goose, it's called! Anyway, if I don't graduate I'm going to need a backup plan.'

'I'm sorry, but there is no way you are not going to graduate!' guaranteed Mandy with certainty. 'You're one of the most gifted people in our year, probably even the whole Coliseum.'

At that point in time, Charlotte doubted anyone thought the same about her, but she didn't care about that right now; she was too busy listening to what Frugal had to say.

'It's a chimney cleaning company,' he proclaimed unrolling a second piece of parchment. It was neatly filled with an array of sporadic summaries, statistics and points of detail.

Charlotte found his modesty endearing; he had been put down so much over the years that he had no idea how brilliant he was. 'Walter forgets to clean our chimney all the time. I think it's a great idea.'

Frugal scribbled the name *Walter*, then *Charlotte* in brackets onto the paper; next to it he wrote *VIP discount*.

Mandy was getting irritable. She knew full well Frugal didn't need a backup plan. Even though her approach was brash, the confidence she had in him shone through.

'Come on, let's go shopping,' she said, patting him on the back.

Wrapping up warm, they left Frugal's room in their full winter attire. Once they were outside, a trio of skeletons holding candles tailed them to the gate. When they were through it went dark, so Frugal lit a lantern. They were not alone; faster Guardians overtook them, following the winding path to a nearby town.

Daydreaming, Frugal watched ghostly steam evaporate into the air. It was coming from a river flowing alongside them. 'The water is heated by the volcano. It never erupts, because they enrich the grounds with enchantments to stop it blowing.'

Mandy interrupted with a more textbook explanation. 'The renewed energy excretes an unlimited source of magic.' Looking at her watch, she then verified the time. 'Everyone is meeting in the tavern at eight; we don't have long. I think we should split up when we get there.'

'Why are the shops open so late?' questioned Charlotte. 'The shops in England are usually shut at night.'

'They're only open 'cause its Hallows' Eve,' said Frugal. 'A few never close but you wanna avoid those ones, 'cause they're usually for Vampires.'

Taken aback, Charlotte was surprised to hear that Vampires were real. She certainly didn't want to cross paths with one of them.

'... but, strictly speaking, they're not allowed to hunt in Avaland.'

His words gave her little reassurance as they edged the hilltop, which opened out on to a Victorian-style village lit by street lamps. The old-fashioned street was filled with an array of shops where odd sorts hurried about.

They joined the impatient crowd, and chaos developed as a diverse set of bodies collided on the pebbledash pavement. Charlotte almost trod on a spider the size of a house cat, with legs extended to each side. Giving out a little shriek, the spider held out one of his legs and air-punched towards her.

'Shopping spiders!' she gasped, leaping away quite horrified.

'They're actually OK,' Frugal assured her. 'Spiders have got a bad name but they're really clever. My dad lost a game of chess to one once. Accused it of cheating at the time but then he's always been a sore loser.'

Mandy was humming along with a circle of singing pumpkins impaled to stakes. 'Listen!' she wailed. 'I love this song … haven't heard it since I was a child.'

Hoist the skull and crossbones

I'll crush your bones with stolen gemstones

Don't try to flee … I'll hoist you up with water weed

'Nice song.' Charlotte smiled. If this was Avaland's version of a nursery rhyme then she was definitely a long way from home.

A barrage of vegetables had been carved most peculiarly and left proudly out on view. Candles had been melted and also placed in random places, flooding the darkened alley with light. This, Charlotte assumed, made it easier for the stall keepers to pour hot cocoa. Folk had gathered around these pockets of light in cheerful celebration, dipping toffee apples into their cups so as not to break their teeth.

As they left the alley, a group of cheering boys crowded around an old toyshop called the Jester, which had a creaky sign swinging in the wind. Moving miniature soldiers appeared to be having a battle in the window; smoke billowed from their cannons, much to the annoyance of the shopkeeper, who was trying to clear the mess with a broom.

'Me and Mandy want to go to different places and we have to be at the Shrieking Mermaid in half an hour, so I reckon we should do what she suggested,' said Frugal.

'We can't leave her by herself, Frugal, she's never been to Prince Street before.'

'It's OK, I'll be fine,' Charlotte told them. 'I can see the pub from here, and I'm not planning on going too far anyway.'

'See, I told you she'd be fine,' groused Frugal, giving her a double thumbs up and wandering down the street.

'Well, as long as you're OK,' said Mandy. 'I won't be long because I've come for something in particular. It was in a magazine so was easy to place an order. If you need me I'll be in that shop over there, The Old Bookcase; you see it?' Mandy smiled then walked away, leaving Charlotte unaccompanied in the street.

Dodging an oncoming Troll, she came to a shop that caught her attention: Briony Picket's Bud to Bloom – Indoor Shrubbery and Garden. By the looks of it they sold plants. It was Walter's birthday soon; perhaps she could get Monty to deliver something for him.

When she was within reach of the door, a delighted elderly gentleman came skipping outside; he was squeezing a pot with bell-shaped flowers that chimed with motion. Something like that would make the perfect present.

Hurrying in out of the cold, she removed her gloves and tried to warm her hands by squeezing them together.

Now she could see why that fellow had been in such high spirits. Charlotte wasn't much of a gardener, but this was something quite enchanting. A peacock bush with blinking flowers watched as she passed. Snake-like weeds slithered across the walls. One was hidden away in the corner of the shop with a caution sign because it smelt like rotten eggs and was letting out gassy belches.

Recognising the plant she had first seen outside, she

read the sign naming it: *Forewarn Horn. From the very edges of Avaland.*

A cheerful lady with curly hair wearing a furry jumper came to greet her.

'Briony Picket,' beamed the woman, shaking Charlotte's hand, grinning from ear to ear before continuing. 'Proprietor, and over there wrestling with the knapweed is my husband Basil.'

The woman pointed to a short fellow wearing a tweed cap who had been grabbed by the ankles and was currently being shaken up and down.

'Don't worry, he can easily cut his way out with a sharp blade,' the woman whispered reassuringly. 'They don't like being pruned much,' she whispered. 'I see you're interested in the Forewarn Horn; these particular breeds come from beyond the boundaries of man. Tricky one to get, actually, because it resides by the only known Irish Waterfall in existence.'

'What's an Irish Waterfall?' asked Charlotte.

'You know? Where the water flows backwards,' she told her as though that cleared the matter up entirely. 'The Leprechauns didn't like us taking cuttings; poor Oswald the collector had pustulating boils for a month.'

'Leprechauns?' Charlotte questioned, surprised to hear of their existence.

'Yes, dear, they use this plant to guard their territory; it warns them when someone is approaching by blowing its trumpets.'

Though the forewarn horn was impressive, Charlotte was interested in another. The plant that had apprehended Briony's husband looked to be much more suitable for Walter's needs. The next person to step foot on his allotment without his permission could very well end up in the same position as Basil, and Charlotte was certain he would like this for his birthday.

'I sell miniature versions over there on the table for two Rubies.'

Taking one to the counter, Charlotte handed over two large gold coins.

'Thank you, dear. Instruction pamphlets are on the table beside the door.' Then Briony rushed to the back of the store; her husband had been dropped on his head from a considerable height and was groaning.

The next shop to take her interest was directly opposite. Pimpernel Potions, Ailments for All; it looked to be an apothecary.

The bell chimed above the door, notifying the keeper that somebody had entered. Inside it was dark and dimly lit with candles. Charlotte could hear the brewing of potions; the sound of bubbling liquid was coming from the next room.

The curtain was only half drawn, giving her the glimpse of a Warlock's back; his long white hair swayed as he turned the pages of an oversized hardback in front of him.

Clattering glass and pouring liquids echoed from the walls, where stacked potion bottles had been filled with fluids of every colour. Textures varied from thick goop to runny consistencies. Limpied, Caldrops and Toadflax to name a few. Some bottles had been provided with screw caps to stop the breathing contents from escaping.

Crystal dials were laid out inside a glass cabinet; these Charlotte recognised as ready-made spells. One was padlocked inside a see-through jar and been tied several times with a chain. *Verto*, said the label. *Transformation for thirty minutes. Licence holders only.*

Charlotte's eyes continued to wander around this dark gloomy room.

But the thing that caught her attention most of all was a thick silver liquid with bolts of electricity, flashing blue in the corner.

Invisus. Invisibility Serum. Effects last for up to four hours dependent on body mass.

Mesmerised, she picked up a bottle and approached the counter, catching the end of a conversation London was having with a sallow-faced man with greasy black hair.

'I came in here yesterday and purchased this bottle because I've been under a lot of stress lately and seem to be, er ...' London removed his hat, and as he did so a clump of missing hair was revealed on the top of his head. 'Well, I tried to apply it to my head, twice as recommended!' he complained, pointing to the label on the bottle then removing his glove. 'My head is balder and now look at my hands!' London wiggled his hairy fingers at the shopkeeper.

The shopkeeper stared at him blankly. 'You were supposed to wear gloves.'

'Well, I need this rectified straight away,' he ordered. 'I have a photoshoot at the weekend.'

The shopkeeper then drifted off to the back of the store before returning with a small bottle of green gunge. 'Apply this as per the instructions on the back of the bottle.'

London was unexpectedly joined by a female Elf, dressed in her very best furry hat. His hands shot off the counter and the half-used bottle instantly vanished. It became obvious he hadn't wanted his female friend to see it.

London turned with shock to see Charlotte had heard the entire conversation, then gave her a regretful look. He put his glove on behind his back and threw some money on the desk before making his exit.

Charlotte paid the shopkeeper four Rubies. He did not speak to her, nor directly acknowledge that she was there. As he soundlessly slid the coins into a ringing till, Charlotte couldn't get out of there quick enough.

As she crossed the busy street, it came to her; every day must be like Halloween in Avaland.

Not a moment too soon, she was reunited with Mandy and Frugal. Charlotte showed them the plant she had bought for Walter, Frugal lifted up a giant-sized bag of Halloween candy and Mandy had managed to collect the book she had reserved on ethereal regulation. Charlotte assumed this was to help in her pursuit of changing the laws surrounding the illegal Pixie trade.

The room would have been dark and gloomy had there not been so many lanterns hanging from the walls; instead it emitted a warm glow, amplified by burning fireplaces.

Tables and chairs filled every inch of the terracotta-tiled floor, but all were taken, so barrels were being used as backup seating. Staircases ascended to the rafters, which were difficult to tell apart from the beams, and posters hung on the grainy walls.

'Look,' screeched Frugal, pointing towards an advertisement that had been pinned up in front of them.

Barely recognisable behind the brilliant white teeth was London, intensely posing; he was promoting a toothpaste called Mega Teeth.

'The Elders have made him very famous,' said Mandy, checking out another flyer only a short distance away. This one was much larger; he was wearing nothing but tailored fur underpants, with an apple in his mouth.

In Charlotte's opinion, Maudlin Merryweather's Dress Wear had a lot to answer for. 'But why?' she asked, confused as to why London would agree to such a thing.

'Other than some people will do anything for money?' frowned Mandy. 'Maybe it's because he's the youngest man to ever be knighted. You see, he and Lauraus aren't just best friends … they're second cousins too.'

Charlotte felt sorry for him; some of the males in the tavern were laughing at his expense by doing impressions of him with their toffee apples.

Abacus almost didn't notice them as he passed.

'Oh, there you are, I didn't expect it to be this packed in here,' he said, a tray of drinks in hand. 'Luckily I reserved a table a week ago. Follow me, I'll lead you to the table.'

Squeezing through the crowd, Charlotte noticed Magnus waiting nervously at the bar.

'Yoo hoo!' came a voice from the entrance.

'Oh, watch out … here comes trouble,' said Frugal, watching Ira shuffle inside.

'Go on, then,' croaked Proteus. 'Tell her you love her.'

Magnus crossed his legs to prevent the wooden peg from disclosing anything else.

'What did he say?' interjected Ira, trying to prompt Magnus into admitting how he really felt.

'He said … tell her you love her … most recent thesis, yes, that's right.' Magnus was a terrible liar, but he had thought of a great comeback. 'Excellent theory, by the way, and the line of argument was right on the money.'

Ira's eyes lit up; he had obviously said all the right things.

'I didn't know you were into the consumption of entrails,' she said, delighted.

Magnus's face dropped; he had clearly not read her last thesis at all.

'The benefits far outweigh the risks,' she continued. 'We're not getting any younger, are we, hey?'

Magnus turned his head, quite horrified, and Ira pulled a sneaky smile.

'She's winding him up,' marked Frugal. 'I like this woman.'

'Here you go, Charlotte,' said Abacus, pulling out a chair. 'I thought you could sit next to me.'

There was one empty seat at the table; this must have originally been meant for Antonious.

'Would you mind if I invite Ira to join us?' requested Magnus, leading his perfect match to the table.

'Why, o' course,' said Abacus. 'The more the merrier.'

It was obvious that Magnus had indulged in one too many glasses of sherry, because he was recounting his stories of the battlefield in an attempt to impress.

Before long came hot plates, cold meats and more bottles of mead. Topaz approached the table with a man who could only have been Frugal's father, because the resemblance was striking.

'Dad!' said Frugal, running over and giving him a hug. 'You made it.'

'Of course I did,' replied the wizened Hobgoblin, removing his cap and shaking everybody's hand. 'You didn't think I'd miss seeing my youngest boy on Hallows' Eve, did you? Besides, it gives me a chance to catch up with my old friends.'

'Hey, watch who you're calling old,' joked Magnus, dropping a little sherry onto the tablecloth.

'But where are Fuzz and Fungus, aren't they coming too?' Frugal grabbed the almost finished bottle from Magnus and poured his dad what was left of it.

'They've gone to see the Pumpkin Smashers. Your mum apologises she can't be here, but she insisted they need a chaperone; we all know what teenage boys are like.'

'So, Knave, how's the retirement going?' chortled Abacus, his favourite bottle of stout in hand.

'It's rather boring, actually.'

Frugal hit his father's arm playfully.

'But it's nice to spend more time with the wife and kids.' Knave picked up his half glass of sherry. 'Why, you must be coming up for retirement soon, my good man?'

Abacus paused awkwardly, pressing the bottle towards his lips. 'Not for another five years. Honestly, I can't imagine what I'm gonna do, I have no wife to keep me busy … or children. Can't think of anything worse than being outta the forces.'

'You don't need children, Abacus,' reassured Topaz, giving him a nudge. 'You have all of us to look after!'

'I do indeed.' He chuckled, his cheeks like cherries.

Knave filled his plate with cold sliced goose. 'I'm awful sorry to hear about Sarah,' he said. 'How's Antonious taking it all?'

Abacus sighed. 'Not so good. I've never seen him like this before, he's an essential member of our team and I fear he could be off for a while.'

'Is it true that the Dagger of Thor was stolen last month? I haven't seen anything about it in the papers.'

'You wouldn't,' Abacus recounted. 'They only print what they want you to know.'

Topaz glared up anxiously, looking as if she wanted to get something off her mind. 'I don't believe Sarah stole the Dagger,' she said.

Abacus turned to her with a nod of agreement. 'Me neither.'

The rest of the table looked up in shock.

'But that would mean the intelligences were false,' said Ira with noticeably stiff shoulders, uneasy about the whole conversation.

'Not necessarily, but also not totally impossible.'

Magnus implored for a subject change with every facial expression he could muster. But Abacus didn't listen.

'If Sarah Sanctamoni did indeed steal the Dagger that day, then why is it she was inside Maisie's Woods?'

'Probably running!' sneered Ira, utterly convinced of her guilt.

Trying to earn yet more points with his iron lady, Magnus shrewdly nodded. 'Or maybe she was hiding it! Yes, that could've been what happened?'

Then Frugal shot up from the table. 'She could have been giving it to someone.'

'Frugal!' shouted Mandy. 'You're supposed to be on our side!'

'Oh yeah, sorry.'

'Precisely, Frugal,' acknowledged Abacus, prompting Mandy to give him a treacherous glance.

As Frugal quavered looking at the table, Abacus attempted to further explain. 'Take her encounter with Bedweguar for example, why didn't she tell him she had the Dagger? And how was it that she was able to conceal it for all that time? The damn thing has twenty venomous snake heads. You see, my friends, as soon as you raise any investigation into the events as documented; they only seem to make one case. That Sanctamoni is innocent.'

'That's absurd!' argued Ira, looking like she wanted to leave.

'Is it?' countered Abacus. 'Sarah was our friend, and those of us that knew her know she was too honest a woman to do anything like this; all she ever yearned for was the protection of the innocent.'

'What about Mizaldus?' interjected Charlotte, cutting short the conversation as silence befell the surrounding tables. 'I saw her inside the Labyrinth, maybe she wants the Dagger?'

Magnus started to laugh, thankfully stealing her unwanted attention. 'Oh, Charlotte, how many times do I have to tell you ... that wasn't the real Mizaldus you saw inside the Labyrinth, it was an apparition.'

But Charlotte could tell that Abacus didn't agree, neither for that fact did Ira.

'Psst,' came a hiss in her left ear, as chatter continued at the table. 'Dad's hired one of the apartments upstairs. He said I can have a sleepover, if you're up for it. Mandy's coming.'

'Yeah, OK. Cheers, Frugal.'

Frugal stood up and politely bade farewell, the tips of his ears flushing. 'Well, I guess it's time for us to turn in for the night, see you in the morning for a full Scottish, Dad.'

Knave nodded and everybody wished them goodnight.

Oppressive boots followed them up the staircase. When Charlotte turned to see who was behind, she noticed an extra shadow on the wall. Were they being followed by a ghost?

'Oh yeah, don't worry,' said Frugal. 'That's only Gordon, the pub poltergeist. We're staying in his suite tonight. He might throw some things in the middle of the night, but don't take any notice; he can't hurt you. Well, unless something lands on you.'

If Charlotte had known this earlier, she would never have agreed to leave the table, but it was too late now.

On the top floor was a room made entirely of pine. A brick fireplace had two rocking chairs in front of it, each with a pile of neatly folded blankets. Sitting at the breakfast bar, Frugal started the fire with a wave of his hand.

Taking out Walter's plant, Charlotte began to write the gift card. One of the stalks had escaped, so she tied it back into the loosened tag. 'I'm gonna see if Monty can deliver this in the morning.'

'Why don't you just do it now?' said Mandy. 'We'll teach you if you like.'

'Right, come on,' agreed Frugal, wrapping the plant up in one of the threadbare covers and tying it in a knot. Charlotte inserted the information pamphlet before Mandy pulled a small bottle of white glitter from her bag.

'Don't worry, it's Fairy dust,' she said, pouring it into her hand. 'Fairy dust is gifted, not stolen. They contribute a generous amount to prevent further harm to fellow Sylphs.'

Mandy sprinkled sparkles over the moving parcel and afterwards Frugal threw it into the fire.

The misshapen package hovered for a moment before disappearing up the chimney making a popping sound as it took off into the sky.

Mandy then poured some Fairy dust into one of Frugal's discarded toffee wrappers. 'Here, take some.'

Removing her dangling pumpkin earrings in preparation for bed, Mandy yawned. 'I'm surprised you sent him knapweed, but don't worry; I know they spray those with a suppression concoction to prevent them growing over six foot.'

Charlotte curled up beneath a threadbare blanket, as Knave, Magnus and Proteus came trundling into the next room. They were singing a popular Avalonian song called 'Three Crows'.

It took some time to fall asleep because of all the talking, but eventually the noise subsided and she was able to hear nothing but the popping fire.

The shatter of glass forced her eyes open. It must have been the middle of the night because the burning logs had reduced to hot ashes.

Maybe it was Gordon the poltergeist, she thought, getting comfy again.

A second smash roused her entirely, because it was coming from the street below. She shook Frugal. 'Can I ride the donkey now,' he snorted, rolling over and cuddling Mandy's legs.

'Mandy, wake up,' she whispered softly, but Mandy had slipped a night tonic because Frugal's snoring was so loud and the stars were still twinkling above her head.

Charlotte pushed up the sash frame and poked her head out of the dirty window.

A shop across the street was being burgled. One of the square panels had been broken and the catch unlocked from the inside to gain entry. Candlelight flickered inside, telling her the intruder was still there.

Summoning Quartz Clear with a clasp of her palm, she pivoted out of the window and slid down the drainpipe. Approaching the dusty old-fashioned store, she caught a glimpse of the name, bathed in a warm tapered glow.

Elbst & Sons

Antique Specialists throughout the ages

Est. 1563

For a moment she wondered what to do, because Quartz Clear still hadn't arrived. Maybe they were sleeping. Deciding it would at least be a good idea to get a look at the intruder's face, Charlotte crept inside, hiding behind a vintage dressing table. The place was dusty; it must have lain dormant for a number of years.

Not wanting to give herself away, she took a decorative mirror from the tabletop and looked into the reflection.

The thief was examining a photograph on the back wall, removing it with a pocket knife, and eventually stowing it away in their cloak. Charlotte called Quartz Clear again. Why were they taking so long?

Without warning, the figure leapt towards the entrance, pushing her into the wall with a wave of the hand, where a shelf of cut-glass decanters collapsed onto her.

Rendered subdued for long enough to give them a head start, Charlotte chased the burglar down the street. The compulsion to do so was not a conscious choice. From behind it was difficult to tell if they were male or female, but the impostor looked human. Nearing the end of the street, the person turned around.

'It's you!' Charlotte gasped, instantly recognising them; but in that moment she was hit with a cool blast of blue, instantly erasing her memory.

A hand reached out from behind, making her jump.

'What are you doin'?' said Abacus, looking troubled.

'This woman broke into Elbst and Sons,' Charlotte updated him forcefully. 'I am detaining her for you.'

'What woman?' he asked simply.

Charlotte veered her head in confusion, because there was nobody there.

Just then, Magnus arrived on his flying carpet. 'What's going on?' he queried sullenly.

'Who were you chasing?' asked Abacus with authority. 'Your first impression was of a female.'

'I don't know, I think they might have deleted my memory?'

'Charlotte, there was a break-in, but that was two months ago. The thief stole a bottle of Verto from the apothecary by drilling a hole into the wall.'

'I recognised their face,' she told him. 'But the last thing I can remember seeing is blue light.'

Magnus poked his head up with intrigue and Abacus looked fraught with disbelief.

'What is it?' muttered Magnus with intrigue.

'That was the colour of Sanctamoni's lucky ring,' he advised. 'It enabled her to alter the recollections of her adversaries, a rare but most useful gift.'

'That's proof, then,' asserted Magnus firmly. 'She's guilty.'

'No, my friend, this proves her innocence.'

Magnus scratched his head, most puzzled by the decision Abacus had drawn.

'Can't you remember her telling Antonious that her lucky ring was stolen while she slept some months ago? And why would Sanctamoni be stealing a bottle of Verto, only to be seen at the crucial moment?'

'Horsefeathers!' gulped Magnus remorsefully. 'This is an open and shut case of identity theft. Whoever broke into the vaults was pretending to be Sarah to the last finite detail.'

Abacus exhaled noisily, his face full of sorrow. 'She must have been sent into the woods to get her out of the way. She was set up ... then murdered. I'm sorry to break short your celebrations, Charlotte, but I'm going to need you to come with me. We are going to have to inform Orobus Pluto straight away.'

Magnus climbed aboard his magic carpet. 'I'll come with you.'

Charlotte hoped Mandy and Frugal would be OK with the window still open.

'Don't worry about your friends,' said Magnus kindly. 'I will send a scroll.'

CHAPTER EIGHT

The Secret

Whisperers had begun to express concern that an extrasensory Guardian had arrived inside the great walls.

The Talisman group Tiger's Eye discussed the matter quite freely at the adjoining table, concluded by a man with dreadlocks and an eyepatch. 'It is not usual practice to invite people of this nature. Why have them spying about when it is so easy to procure a psychic without all of the hassle?'

To Charlotte's surprise, Sinope had not joined in the debate, but she did have a big smirk on her face.

Since that incident, Charlotte had tried to lay low. People were even unsubtly leaving rooms just in case she read their minds. In fact, they couldn't have made it more obvious if they tried. She felt like spreading a rumour that tin foil hats would protect them, just to lighten her mood.

Of course, Charlotte couldn't really read minds, not intentionally anyway; even if she could, the only one she would be interested in understanding was Orobus Pluto's.

Orobus had declared her last testimony on the matter of Sanctamoni inconclusive, much to Abacus Creedy's outrage.

However, Creedy's vote of confidence on Charlotte's behalf was reassuring to say the least. It would have been easy to bow under the pressure of the powers that be, but he refused to, instead demanding the need for an official enquiry.

Mandy kept chewing off their ears with hourly lessons on ethereal regulation, from the book she had obtained on Prince Street. Frugal had been quite adamant that if he heard another word, he was going to start wearing Ergot Ear Plugs (a parasitic fungus that dulls the senses). But Charlotte gently reminded him that some of what Mandy was telling them could very well come in useful one day.

Life at the Coliseum had grown more arduous with every passing day, but the pressure had bought about a noticeable improvement in Charlotte's ability. Of course, there was always room for improvement, so she'd set her alarm to wake her four hours earlier than usual.

The ringing launched her from the bed with little time to adjust to reality, and Charlotte found herself clumsily shuffling towards the mirror, stubbing her little toe.

Jumping about, swearing, foot in hand, she came to a halt in front of her reflection, removing a Post-it note from her face that had been dribbled on at some point in the night.

This was not the productive start to the day she'd anticipated.

Focusing in on the blurry words, the feeble reminder stated that her favourite twelfth mat was waiting. She preferred this one in particular because it was hidden away in a corner that no one ever used.

At first sight, it appeared she'd been successful in her attempt to avoid the masses. The usually packed hallways were empty; she saw no one as she climbed the stairs two floors. Even the stained-glass windows were empty.

Pushing the door ajar to procure a small gap, she paused, wondering at first if she was in the right place.

Inside it looked darker than a broom cupboard; the moving shadows made it appear drab and uninspiring, and to a certain extent creepy; even – dare she say it – haunted.

Blazing oil lamps gave the room a subtle glow but the light did not appear to be evenly distributed. It was as though portions had just been switched off. At the desk on the left-hand side was Gamelyn's sleeping assistant, completely unaware of the pile of letters he was jiggling with his breath, waiting to be unsealed.

As she pushed the doors entirely open, her hopes were dashed the moment she entered. She had hoped to get some practice in without an audience, but the room was filled with Guardians, some of them very large indeed.

Deciding not to wake the irritable Gnome, she sat on the bench to wait for Gamelyn.

Mat thirteen had given rise to a flock of vampire bats, who were carrying out a bloodthirsty attack on a bald Cyclops, inflicting deep wounds. The task looked damn near impossible to complete but the Cyclops seemed to be OK; he was enjoying the pain.

Hopefully he wouldn't be training there much longer; one oversight on his part and she would be crushed, which was not what she needed the day before she was due to go back inside the Labyrinth.

The clock tower struck five times and Gamelyn stepped out of his office, efficient to the second. The Cyclops picked up his towel and smiled at her before leaving, and his passing brought something to her attention that she hadn't noticed before.

Whilst Gamelyn was fiddling about with some papers on the desk, she walked over to a portrait hanging between two claret curtains. Seated upon his throne was a man wearing a crown, and between his legs was a sword made from the finest silver.

'Excalibur,' said Gamelyn admiringly as he joined her side. 'The man in that painting is King Arthur.'

Charlotte looked at the slim-faced man in ceremonial dress, wearing robes of royal blue. Arthur had a strong jawline, scarred greatly from battle, yet his piercing eyes were strangely familiar.

'That portrait was fashioned a year after he relocated. Apparently, he'd been joined by his wife Guinevere the week before. His adviser Merlin had joined him much earlier than that, of course; without Arthur's protection he was fair game. England was not safe for a wizard then. Most people think it's a legend.' Gamelyn giggled, appearing to find English folk law rather funny. 'King Arthur was one of the greatest men to ever exist. He went on to do great things in Avaland. The sword is still royal property, I expect it lays by the king's side. Of course, Lauraus has an older brother and is not in line for the throne, which is a shame because he is a worthy swordsman.'

'You mean to say that Lauraus is a descendant of King Arthur?'

But Gamelyn did not have a chance to answer.

'My ears are burning,' came a voice that Charlotte recognised at once to be Lauraus himself.

'Ahh, yes, Lauraus, I was just telling young Charlotte here about your interesting lineage.'

'Hmm, so I heard,' said Lauraus, pressing his lips into a half smile. Was she sensing rebellion in him? Something was telling her that he disliked being a prince.

'Ahh, right, well then, on with the lesson I think. Do excuse the darkness – the older Guardians prefer it that way.'

Lauraus leaned against one of the cabinets. Charlotte was mortified. Surely he wasn't going to watch?

'I'm pleased with your progress,' Gamelyn informed her, handing her a bookmark with a date stamp. 'I have had a book sent to your quarters, which I hope you will find most useful. It has some great moves in it I think you will like. Please familiarise yourself and practise before our next appointment.'

'Great!' Charlotte thanked him, most enthralled.

In an attempt to stall their assembly, Charlotte avoided taking her place and instead said what was on her mind. 'Why is it that those vampire bats were able to inflict wounds? I didn't think that was able to happen.'

'Oh, are you talking about Gorse?' Gamelyn said approvingly. 'Gorse is a level six Guardian – you are on stage two – and each level is more grievous than the last. It's up to you how far you want to take it, of course, but sometimes only certain levels are called upon in extreme situations.'

'How many levels are there?' enquired Charlotte with interest.

'Ten,' he promptly replied. 'Though there is only one stage ten here at the Coliseum and that is Orobus Pluto himself.'

Charlotte wondered how that could be, because Orobus was such a small man. He looked more like a dinner party sort of person.

'Looks can be deceiving,' said Gamelyn, picking up on her thoughts. 'You see, Orobus Pluto is a Vampire, a good one of course. He can't be hurt like the others, because technically he is already dead.'

Glancing over, Lauraus stood with his arms folded, waiting for her to start; he had now been joined by London and several of his friends.

Gamelyn was picking up on her nerves. 'Concentrate only on my voice,' he said hypnotically. 'In a moment you will find yourself under attack. Think logically for a solution to the problem that is facing you and this time I don't want you to direct the knives with your thoughts.'

Others started to gather around, wondering what all the fuss was about; she knew they were trying to be supportive, but it was not helping at all.

From nowhere a plume of smoke exploded, taking the ghost-like form of a scorpion the size of a horse. As it tried to pierce her body with its tail, Charlotte took three steps backwards off the mat because fear got the better of her.

'Your mind, Charlotte. Think of a solution to the problem.'

On the second attempt the creature was successful, knocking her from her feet and piercing her through the heart before disappearing. As it did so a strange tingling sensation ran through her entire body. Some of the spectators laughed and Charlotte went red, but Lauraus raised his hand into the air to signal that his friends not do the same. He gazed at her intently, which did nothing to calm her.

'What do you think you did wrong?' asked Gamelyn, most unhelpfully.

'I didn't use my mind,' she joked playfully.

Gamelyn gave her a withering glance. 'In order for you to be successful you must believe you can achieve your goal. See the end result first; visualise it and then you must carry out steps to achieve this. Up!' he said, pulling her from the ground by her forearm.

This time she didn't look at anyone there. Standing on the mat again, she faced the monster confidently.

Taking butterfly candles from her satchel, she encircled the scorpion with them, distracting it for enough time so that she could get behind. As she leapt up onto its tail, the stinger revolved towards her face but missed. Drawing her knife, she savagely cut as the scorpion let out one shrill shriek.

The only way down was to flip over. 'Now you can't hurt anyone,' she concluded, fastening the blade to her skin. She held out her hand for the butterfly candles to return, and the scorpion exploded into a sapphire haze.

A round of applause came swiftly, from all except Lauraus, who stared intensely. 'You did not kill the creature?' affirmed Gamelyn, most interested with her approach.

'Why would I do that?' she reasoned. 'I thought it was our job to protect the innocent. It was just following its instinct.'

'Excellent, Charlotte, now you're thinking like a Guardian. You just earned yourself a place on level three.'

#

Frugal burst out of the theatre doors in frustration; today's instruction had clearly gotten to him.

'How are we supposed to learn every Avalonian law for each culture in nine months?' he bawled pushing aside the double doors irritably.

Mandy had just caught up. The atrium was filled with angry gatherers uttering similar things. 'Frugal, we'll be fine. We'll set a study plan and stick to it; all the other Guardians have had to sit this test. You have to see it from their point of view – if we are going to be regulating the lands we need to understand what's illegal and what's not. If we don't understand the customs of other cultures, how are we supposed to respect them?'

'Yeah, I know, but I can't read or write like the others. They may as well send me home now.'

Charlotte sensed sadness in his voice.

'I'm not going to be able to do it,' he said, snivelling a bit. 'I'm gonna fail.'

'No you're not!' insisted Mandy. 'Because we'll study together.'

'I'm in,' said Charlotte supportively. 'We'll just do it all aloud. They give out practice questions, right?'

'You'd do that for me?' He smiled, trying to hide his welling eyes.

'Of course we would,' said Charlotte faithfully. 'You two are my best friends, and best friends are always there for each other. Besides, I could do with some help too. I'm rubbish at exams.'

'Right, well, that settles it then,' said Mandy, as though she had already worked out the entire timetable in her head on their way to the canteen. This would not normally be allowed. The exception had only been made because they were expected at the Labyrinth doors in an hour's time.

An early meal had been organised which meant they could sit together for a change.

'Any news on an official change of decision about Sanctamoni's guilt?' probed Frugal mashing up his omelette.

Charlotte was upset that she had to tell them her testimony had made little difference. 'Apparently the original decision is being upheld,' she said.

'What? Why?' interrogated Mandy, dropping her baguette into her bowl of stew.

'They said my telepathy isn't developed enough yet and until its accuracy has been tested they are not allowed to accept my testimony as evidence.'

'They weren't saying that when they dragged you into Maisie's Woods to look for Sanctamoni's dead body.'

'You can kind of see what they mean though,' said Mandy, expecting to be challenged. 'I mean, there is a chance you could be wrong. Not to say that Sarah robbed the vaults but, you know … the details.'

Frugal looked outraged that Mandy could say such a thing but didn't argue for the sake of keeping the peace.

'Abacus is fuming, he said there is no way I could have known about her mind-altering ring. He believes everything I told them.'

'And why wouldn't he? You're as upstanding as they come.'

'Thanks, Frugal. There is one thing, though.'

Both Frugal and Mandy stopped eating and stared intently, awaiting some new information.

'I only saw them remove a photograph from the wall.'

'What?' they both said together, apparently deflated by this big new lead.

'Well, Abacus told me whoever broke into that shop punctured a hole through the wall and stole a bottle of Verto from the apothecary. But that's not what I saw; whoever it was stole a photo.'

Both Frugal and Mandy looked up again, apparently interested now.

'They must have done it before you'd turned up,' Mandy insisted, blind to any other state of affairs. 'There's no way of knowing what the picture was of now, not if the photo is gone.'

'Yeah, I know,' she replied, disappointed they hadn't come up with anything more helpful. 'I don't think they intended to take the picture. I think they came across it by accident … and … there's one other thing, my first reaction was to tell Abacus that I saw a woman that I recognised.'

Frugal now dropped his bread, his face filling with dread. 'You don't think it's …'

'Who?' barked Mandy, impatiently wanting to be let in on the secret.

'He thinks it's Mizaldus,' said Charlotte, bringing her up to date.

'That's absurd. For one thing, what would Mizaldus be wanting with a useless old photograph?'

'Yes, but a woman like that would be interested in stealing the Dagger of Thor,' said Charlotte.

'… and we did see her in the Labyrinth,' supported Frugal.

'We were told that wasn't real.'

'Bollocks,' said Frugal. 'They just told us that to calm us down, that was the real Mizaldus alright. Besides, didn't that Lady of the Lake thingy tell you we were in danger … before she actually turned up and whatnot.' Frugal took a bite of a chicken drumstick and spat out the meat. 'Ugh, always dry, why don't they ever serve goose in this place?'

'Frugal, you've got it.'

'Have I?' Frugal looked at his chicken drumstick in confusion before faltering once again. 'Got what?'

'I need to speak with the Lady of the Lake.'

'That's madness!' said Mandy. 'That's even more stupid then the Mizaldus idea – the Lady of the Lake is in the middle of Feign Forest. You could be attacked.'

'Yeah, you're right. But there must be another way around it.'

'Why don't we steal the Phantom Carriage?' laughed Frugal, losing himself in humorous thought.

'Not the Phantom Carriage … but a horse would do nicely.'

'Is she really going to steal a horse?' bellowed Frugal, a lot louder than Charlotte would have liked, because Sinope's friends were sitting at the next table and had heard.

Charlotte retreated her head inwards and whispered, 'I don't need to steal a horse; I already have one.'

#

The Labyrinth doors were already open by the time they'd arrived, and the root-covered walls stirred, aware that someone was passing through. Mandy led the way, taking care not to slide on the recently polished floor, stopping where the parquet converged with grains of sand.

For a moment Charlotte questioned why the doors had been left open at all.

Frugal started to get annoyed. 'What is it?' he grumbled impatiently.

'Someone's trying to play a trick on us,' Mandy realised, holding back Frugal as he passed, in an attempt to prevent him from going inside. 'We got a scroll telling us to go to entrance two …' she said, pulling a piece of folded paper from her back pocket.

'I didn't get one,' said Frugal, most puzzled, and they both looked at Charlotte to see whether she had either.

'I don't know if I did,' she told them. 'I've been in the library since early morning and I haven't been back to my chamber.' She thought it unwise to tell them she had a crush on Lauraus and was trying to accidently on purpose bump into him for the third time this week.

'Why didn't you get a scroll, Frugal?' she said, shaking Lauraus from her mind.

'Well, how am I supposed to know? Maybe whoever arranged it don't like Hobgoblins. Or maybe it's because I overslept and left in a hurry and didn't see it.'

'Look,' gasped Charlotte, darting to the stained-glass window, where creaking vines slithered across the walls. 'Oh, it's only sleet.'

Both Frugal and Mandy looked at her. 'What are you doing?' they said together, baffled.

'I thought it was snowing,' she rejoined, disappointed. 'I love the snow.'

'Are you mad?' booed Frugal. 'I hate the snow, it's too cold and wet.'

Mandy looked more neutral. 'It can be nice sometimes,' she mumbled to herself.

They were joined by Sinope and a group of her friends. Halting briefly, they also lingered to consider the doors for a moment before turning left and gliding to the back beneath a dripping window. Sinope knew they were there but didn't acknowledge them.

'Rude cow!' squealed Frugal.

'Come on,' said Mandy, following Sinope and her friends beneath a leaking hole in the wall, then into a sandy arched corridor.

The end of the archway led to a small wooden door that looked to be a tiny outside toilet. To its side sat an ordinary pot plant shaking off water like a wet dog.

'I bet Grendel had a hard time getting through here,' said Mandy with an air of concern, just about fitting through.

'I bet Grendel walked straight through the double doors,' joked Frugal cynically.

'That's not very nice,' said Mandy, who had reached the other side. 'You nearly walked through them too.'

Charlotte was last through, and it was a bit of a drop to the dirt path. Looking back up at the door, she saw it opened out on to a tree.

'Weird,' said Charlotte, more astounded every day. Dusting down the cobwebs from her trousers, she took a moment to get her bearings.

They had come out into a section of Feign Forest that had been secured with barbed wire fencing for security. Something about this made her nervous. It looked as if someone had been sneaking in or out, because crevices had been dug underneath. A forest of entirely red treetops was swaying in the distance, separated by a field of long grass.

Following the path, Frugal looked nervous. 'I've never seen the banished lands so close up before. My parents have always insisted I never come anywhere near the border. There are stories … those that go there don't ever come back, then there are those that commit a third-degree crime and are never allowed to return.'

None could deny it was a beautiful sight, especially from where they were standing. The trees above had scattered a deluge of fresh leaves, replenishing the ground with a sheet of reds, auburns and muddied browns. The beauty of Feign

Forest was complemented by the striking scarlets from the scene beyond.

As they were joined by the rest of the year, minus a few absent members who Charlotte suspected had gone the wrong way, the weather took a sudden turn for the worse. As they stood side by side like sculptures in a storm, the ground became marshier with each fleeting moment.

The silhouetted figure of a warrior princess rose valiantly from behind a misty brook. Her plaited hair flew out behind her as the buxom woman fluttered towards them, carried by winged sandals.

Settling on the ground, she marched authoritatively across the line, inspecting each of them before speaking.

'For those of you that do not know, I am Gallore Knatterjack,' said the curvaceous temptress, bursting from her garment. 'Lay your weapons by the old oak there – you won't be needing them for this exercise.'

Those that had a weapon cast them aside and Gallore gave each of them a luminous vest to wear. They were finally joined by Grendel, who had figured out where he was going. He was handed the same red vest as Charlotte, and he gave it a confused glance because it was at least five sizes too small.

'This here is the furthest reach of Avaland you could ever hope to seek. For those who don't know, outside the boundary lies danger.'

Charlotte looked up beyond the metal enclosure. She knew something nasty was hiding in the grass, so she shut her eyes to investigate.

Something eight-legged and crawling was scurrying beneath the dugout holes. She opened her eyes with a start.

'There are spiders in the grass!' she mouthed to Mandy.

'It is against the law for Guardians to enter the Banished Lands without prior permission,' the teacher resumed. 'It is our job to protect everything up to this border. There are times we have needed to cross but these instances are very rare indeed. If you have half a brain you will not go there, because evil awaits you on the other side. It would be unwise to come even this close in normal circumstances. Alas, you are completely safe inside the Labyrinth, unless you count being scared to death.' The woman laughed wickedly.

'This is probably the furthest part of Avaland you will ever see, and it will certainly be the farthest you will be travelling during this practical assessment. Make your way to the others that share your coloured vest; this will be your team for today.'

Charlotte and Grendel were teamed with Lomax and Lauraus. Lauraus did not give any hint of his affection for her as both she and Grendel drew nearer. Lomax let out a short-tempered groan of displeasure for having been paired with a Giant.

Gallore flew above the groups, so close you could see her strong hairy legs. The Werewolf bounded quickly aside, for her extra-long toenails were headed straight his way.

'The Labyrinth has been designed not only to test your abilities but your integrity as well. Your teamworking abilities are paramount to the role. We want to see how you solve problems, come to conclusions and whether you can follow orders. If you can't, you may as well leave now because you are not what we are looking for. For you self-professed leaders, I suggest you stay a little closer to the fence. However, those that are nominated by their own team are just and should be obeyed. So, who here can carry out tasks under pressure? We shall see soon enough.'

There was a flash and a rumble of thunder.

'Any questions so far?'

Valentine, the shape-shifting black panther, raised her hand. 'How long does the Labyrinth take to complete?'

Gallore gave her question a callous look of disdain, but answered anyway. 'How long it takes is really down to each of you,' she advised scratching her hairy chin. 'Some take days, some take weeks; I remember one boy took so long in here we had to send out a search party … but he didn't falter, and therefore graduated. If you have been given a harder path, you can still succeed – the true key to success is never giving up. Now, on to the task!'

Gallore looked out to the grass, and Charlotte caught her speaking with her mind: *Not much longer, my pretties.*

None of the others realised that there was a nasty surprise in store for them and Charlotte tried to warn as many as possible.

'First you must nominate a leader,' said Gallore, standing back to observe.

Most of the teams were arguing over who was going to lead. Sinope had bullied her way into the role with Green group. Gallore walked past and gave Grendel's vest a confused glance, but he just looked pleased to have been able to get it on – minus the rips, which he hid by tucking in his arms.

A few moments later and Lauraus had been nominated the leader. One intense current of air swayed the trees, blowing leaves all about the place as another flash lit up the sky. With it came an almighty laugh from Gallore Knatterjack, making some of the girls a bit scared.

Lomax glanced up at the only member of the group that was larger than him. 'Well, this is going to be interesting,' he assumed crossly. 'Don't you tread on me, mate!'

Gallore finally introduced the task, letting her winged sandals carry her down to eye level. 'Flags are scattered all around this part of the forest, ten per team in total. You need only find them then retrieve them. The first team across the finish line wins. You may start.' As Gallore Knatterjack clapped her hands, the sky opened up from drizzle to torrential rain.

Everyone scattered about in confusion looking for their flags, screaming plans to each other as they went, but Lauraus prepared them in a quick-thinking huddle.

'There are probably giant tarantulas in the grasses,' he warned. 'The pregnant ones are supposed to have a particularly nasty bite so be careful – our foot soldiers have had issues here before.'

Spiders were bad enough, but biting spiders were Charlotte's worst nightmare. Had Lauraus not been standing right in front of her, she would have forfeited the challenge there and then, but, not wanting to look like a coward, she carried on.

'We need to fan out. You guys take the top and me and Charlotte will take the bottom.'

Lauraus was lingering. The clenching of sharp teeth told her Lomax was getting impatient.

'Charlotte, can you see any of them?' asked Lauraus, utilising the skills among them to overcome the task.

Gallore hovered over them to see why they hadn't left yet, but looked impressed when she saw how they were working as a team.

'Four are in the treetops, another four on the right, one is buried, and another inside the tree trunk … be careful, Grendel, there's a pregnant spider in there.'

Gallore looked impressed; she gave Charlotte a nod of approval before flying to the railing.

'Got that, guys?' Lauraus confirmed, before taking Charlotte's hand and pulling her out of the huddle. 'Be careful,' he shouted back. 'I've heard Gallore Knatterjack likes to play tricks on newcomers.'

And off they went. That was the thing with Werewolves, they were very fast, and in the blink of an eye Lomax had collected one flag already. Charlotte heard a loud yelp; Grendel must have just been bitten.

'Well done, Grendel mate,' cheered Lomax, coming round to him.

'There are two flags to the right,' shouted Charlotte efficiently, whilst looking behind her. 'Both are hidden in the same tree.'

Lauraus was also very fast, surfing the mud then manoeuvring a forward roll over a fallen tree trunk. 'Where are we going?'

Charlotte closed her eyes. Precognition was taking a little longer this time; the last flag was well hidden.

Along the ground scuttled hundreds of spiders heading straight towards them, but only those small enough could get through the railings. The larger ones started to burrow. Lomax and Grendel had collected all eight of their flags and ran off speedily towards the finish line but neither crossed; instead, they displayed a heroic attempt to protect their friends, kicking as many of the largest spiders as they could back over the fence.

'I think it's in a bog,' shouted Charlotte, running around the tree Lauraus had just catapulted himself over.

They came to a small bubbling bog that smelled terrible. It was surrounded by marshland and there were stepping stones enabling them to cross. 'Come on,' he said, taking her hand.

In the centre was the flag, flapping with the wind. She could hear shouting coming from the distance as other team members were being bitten, and started to feel glad they were away from the crowd.

'Here will do,' he said, pushing her in. 'The mud will protect us.'

After screeching, Charlotte giggled with shock then flung a handful of mud in his face. Some went in his mouth, which in her mind was proof he liked her; she was sure she wouldn't have gotten away with that if he hadn't.

Because she was the closest, Charlotte extended her arm until the tips of her fingers were drawing in the prize. The moment it detached, a dozen hairy stones floated to the surface and little hairy brown monsters shot out of the mud, baring warty faces.

'It's OK, they're Boglins. They can't hurt you, they just stink.'

Even though they were supposed to be harmless, their ugly screwed-up faces were growling and their breath smelt even worse than the mud.

Lauraus picked her up and heroically carried her out. It seemed they were now immune; spiders were scuttling past them, oblivious to the fact they were there. The moment they got a whiff of the mud, they retreated in the opposite direction.

Neck and neck with Green group, they ran towards the finish line, joining Lomax and Grendel, then the four teammates crossed the finish line together.

'Red group wins,' announced Gallore as the remaining spiders retreated to the ground.

One very brave and stupid boy kicked the spider next to him, only to have his buttocks bitten.

'That's enough!' shouted Gallore, sending the spiders away.

They celebrated with a group hug that left Sinope seething. She gave Charlotte a look of pure hatred, making her feel uneasy. Lauraus spotted this and went over to talk to Sinope, but before he reached her she had walked off.

'Go on, then! Off to the Roman baths with you. Go and soothe those nibbles.' Gallore laughed again but this time she sounded a lot more psychopathic.

'I think she's a bit mad, you know,' said Frugal, carrying multicoloured spotty eggs. Charlotte wasn't so sure it was a good idea, but didn't say anything. 'A little snack for later,' he said, hushed, putting them into his pockets.

The group looked very sore and tired. Some were too exhausted to climb, and sat on the atrium banisters for the first time.

'That's it, then; the next time we come here we will be in the Labyrinth properly,' said Valentine, joining Lomax, her best friend, with some excitement to get upstairs.

'I haven't been to the baths yet,' said Mandy with intrigue.

'I've been there three times already,' interjected Frugal. 'Last time I saw Sinope shouting at Lauraus.'

'I heard they are not betrothed any more,' said Mandy. 'They don't get on so they've called it off. It's been off for a while now, apparently.'

Charlotte had not yet admitted her feelings about Lauraus to Mandy or Frugal, but she was sure they suspected. Her quick subject change made them even more suspicious. 'So, I read that the Gladiators go there to soothe their aches and pains after complicated missions.'

Both friends looked at each other sceptically, because she never usually spoke in that tone. Frugal didn't bother to respond but Mandy humoured her and answered the question. 'The water is healing, the same as Apollo's Fountain, but a slightly different form of magic.'

'Is that why the fountain sings? Because the water is enchanted?' asked Charlotte.

Frugal appeared to be surprised because he was staring open mouthed. 'It doesn't sing,' he said.

For a moment she wondered why nobody else was hearing the same. Mandy cut in on the conversation before she had a chance to question it. 'Honestly, Charlotte, you stink so bad. You need to wash off some of that mud before you get in.'

'Look,' argued Charlotte playfully, 'I might be a bit smelly but I didn't get bitten, did I?'

Mandy looked at the throbbing bite on her arm. 'I suppose so,' she said.

'I don't know what you two are going on about,' said Frugal. 'All you've got to do is tickle them under the chin, then they tuck their heads in.'

'Now you tell me!' barked Mandy, the most annoyed Charlotte had ever seen her.

The eighth floor opened out to a wet stone floor and the sound of a harp, except the strings were along the side of the wall and being strung by falling water. Gargoyles looked down on them, dripping with condensation which hit the cool ice doors. As they opened, fog flew out, colliding with her breath.

Inside, glass covered the entire circumference of the baths in a single dome; windows were misted with iridescent steam ascending from the kaleidoscopic slick rising from the hot spring. The rising water collected at the top then flowed through a duct to the foot of the baths, at times rising to their ankles. The air glittered gold around her. It was quite remarkable, and she had never seen anything like this before; she was really starting to appreciate the chance she had been given here and was not going to waste it.

Taking a look at some of the statues. Some of them seemed strangely familiar. The mighty Jupiter gazed upon her through his long wavy hair; he had gritted teeth behind his beard in a display of rage, and hell had no fury like the stone lightning bolt clasped between his fingers. To the side sat his fearless queen, with piercing eyes that were intimidating yet beautiful. Charlotte saw intellect and wisdom in her stare.

A Gnome came to the changing room carrying a fresh basket of replenished vanilla-scented towels, and put them in the corner away from the wet.

Taking one, she held it up and smelt it, the softness brushing up against her cheek.

'Here, take one of these,' said Mandy, throwing her a black full-length bathing costume. 'It's all available in an unlimited amount.'

'See you in there,' sang Frugal, running off towards the male changing rooms trunks in hand.

Once changed, Charlotte followed people into the baths. There were long steps leading down into the warm water, but that didn't matter to Frugal, who just ran and jumped, drenching everyone before they got in.

An ice sculpture of the young wine god Bacchus was melting, the water dripping into, then cascading, from his goblet. The pool itself was filled with bubbles, but this was no ordinary pool; different valleys filled with plants meandered inside it like a maze. There looked to be a lot of hiding places, and areas you could sit on your own and collect your thoughts.

With this being her intention, Charlotte dived under the water and set off on her own to explore.

Coming up for air, she rested besides a statue of the child spirit Cupid, his golden bow and arrow pointing down at her. It was so relaxing in here and the scratches and bruises she had collected had almost disappeared.

She swam around, exploring the many tunnels and pockets where you could sit and reflect, crossing paths with many Guardians who politely greeted her. Finding a vacated seat beneath the shimmering water, she rested her eyes and cleared her mind entirely, living in this soothing moment.

When she opened them again there was a one-eyed, hairy-nosed Cyclops sitting next to her, and he gave her a bit of a fright.

To Charlotte's surprise, he spoke. 'I'm Gorse,' he greeted her, holding out one very large hairy hand. 'I knew your mother.'

Charlotte felt shocked; she hadn't anticipated that at all. The pit of her stomach ached. 'I don't have a mother; I'm an orphan,' she politely corrected him.

'Oh, I'm sorry,' he said. 'I just assumed what with you being in Quartz Clear and looking so alike that you were the daughter of Nelphinie.'

Charlotte looked at him in disbelief; nobody had said anything like this to her before.

'We were friends, you see, Nelphinie and I, good friends. Before she died, that is.' Gorse's face filled with sadness.

'Did I see you inside the armoury yesterday?' she wondered, eventually recognising him.

'Yes, that's right,' said the gentle giant. 'Those vampire bat bites are taking a while to heal.'

Gorse looked a bit uncomfortable with what he was about to say. 'I hope you don't presume me to be rude, but may I ask you on what day you were born?'

'I don't have a birthday, well not a proper one anyway. The people I live with gave me the same birthday as the Queen of England.'

'You have a queen in England?'

'Yes, we do, we are very lucky.'

'So, you don't have a birthday?' Gorse eyed her suspiciously, this seemed to be the confirmation he needed. 'Well, I'd better be off. Nice to meet you, Charlotte.'

It wasn't until he had been gone for a few moments that she realised that she hadn't told him her name.

A little ahead in the distance, there was a rocky waterfall. It looked interesting so she swam over. Gliding through the rippling curtain of water, she realised it was a cave dimly lit with jar-trapped fireflies. She had just turned around to go back when none other than Lauraus entered the waterfall.

At first Charlotte didn't know where to look instead of at his half-naked body. She tried to ignore the sweat dripping down his chest and the cute goose pimples on his arms.

She blushed, then tried to think of something to say. 'Do you know where Frugal and Mandy are?'

'Frugal's on the diving board but I haven't seen Mandy anywhere.' Lauraus smiled from the corner of his mouth; he must have suspected that she was feeling nervous.

Under the thin veil of water, he pulled her in until their bodies were touching, and, taking her breath away, he kissed her.

It was softly at first, then became more passionate, making her lose track of time. Even though they had never kissed before, he felt familiar to her; like they were the same in some way, equals. Her surroundings didn't matter any more; nothing mattered other than this moment. The build-up had been immense and she had been waiting for a long time.

When they did eventually break apart they both giggled at each other and he wrapped his arms around her caringly and kissed her on the forehead.

Then Frugal came steaming in, ruining the moment entirely.

'We've got to go,' he insisted immediately. 'You know those eggs I collected? Well, they've hatched and now they're crawling round the pool biting people.'

Charlotte bit her bottom lip. 'Oh, Frugal, no.'

Lauraus laughed as Frugal grabbed the back of her bathing costume and pulled her out from under the waterfall. She didn't have time to say goodbye to Lauraus, as she was now being drawn into a different section towards the exit.

'Where's Mandy?' she asked, looking around.

'She's already got out, I think I might have embarrassed her.'

The Roman baths were almost empty now, and after a quick costume change they got out as quickly as they could without being spotted.

Rushing down the staircase, Charlotte tried not to trip. 'Excuse me, coming through!' shouted Frugal.

Once they had reached the chambers, he darted off towards his room. 'Right, see you later.'

'Was there actually any point in you making me leave?' shouted out Charlotte, but Frugal didn't answer; he had already bound through the silver doors.

Charlotte had a lot to think about as she made her way back to her room. That kiss had been the best moment of her life so far but it had been combined with the reflection of sadness when Gorse had asked about her mother.

She sat on her bed staring at the wall. What if Nelphinie was her mother?

Knowing she should have felt happy, she didn't at all; it just brought back the loss she had felt in her life.

The book Gamelyn had delivered was on her desk. It was bound with tan leather and tied up with string, embossed with the title *Kunai Master.* Inside were techniques for throwing knives; the further she flicked to the back of the book, the more complex these moves became until they were eventually paired with other martial arts.

Martial arts had always been a passion of hers, so she was looking forward to reading it and would have started straight away had it not been for the blue jewellery box sitting beside the place she'd just picked the book up from.

Dropping the book onto the desk, she picked up the case and opened the lid. Inside was a blue marble. A swirling storm was contained within, creating pictures from the clouded distortions. Mesmerised, she looked at the detail, which revealed the flying horse she'd come to know.

Her heart began to thump quickly. Feeling weak, she dropped it to the carpet and everything went white.

#

Falling into clouds, Charlotte began to fly, lowering to the trees then beneath the leaves. A rumble of thunder saw heavy rainfall; the woods were consumed by a darkness lit only by lightning bolts approaching from the distance.

The stony road beneath her feet made it difficult to walk, but she could not slow down. Control of her body had long since left her. She was a motionless soul in a prisoner's body, void of free will.

The canopy gave rise to shadows, lanterns lit by candles and voices coming from afar. Stepping out of the bushes was a grey wolf, eyes like daggers in the moonlight. As it changed to a handsome male, Charlotte had to take a second look; the resemblance to Lauraus was uncanny. 'Antonious,' she called out to him. But he did not hear her. Behind him from the bushes came another who she recognised to be her good friend Abacus Creedy.

Abacus held up his lantern, which showed him to have the face of a much younger man than the one she currently knew. Antonious too. He couldn't have been much older than she was now. But a shadow of the past, one that could not feel her presence.

Charlotte touched his cold unscarred face, but he couldn't feel her skin.

'Where's Nelphinie gone again?' shouted Abacus with worry, looking over his shoulder.

A slim brunette came from the bushes. 'I can feel pain

and sorrow nearby,' she said, dashing down a muddy bank and out of sight.

Antonious retransformed to wolf then took off after her scent, following the muddy tracks, Abacus following closely behind.

Sliding down the silhouetted riverbank, Charlotte followed behind the distant bobbing of Abacus Creedy's lantern.

When she caught up, she saw a woman, who must be Nelphinie, lying on the ground across the body of a wounded horse. The skin on one side of its face and body was badly torn, and a name tag around its neck named the mount Medwin. Nelphinie cried out as though she could feel the pain of the creature which seemed close to death. Leaves had been left trailing where the poor horse had been dragged behind what looked like a carriage, and left to die. The penetrating crying was overwhelming to hear; it made Charlotte shed a tear. Now able to feel the pain, she collapsed to a heap on the ground with only enough energy to lift her neck.

Comforted by Nelphinie, tears fell from its eyes, a silver skin growing over the wounds to bind the blood. Brilliant white soaked the creature in light, obscuring the view. When the light disappeared, so had Medwin.

Nelphinie looked around; whatever she had done it was clear this had not been her intention. Antonious helped her protectively from the floor, and she collapsed into his arms; whatever it was she had attempted to do had left her weak. Distressed, Nelphinie had shared some kind of connection with this creature, but her attempt to help had failed, so it was time to move on.

As he ushered her away, a light appeared among the trees.

Abacus lifted both his palms defensively, Antonious pulling a weak Nelphinie behind his back for protection. But Nelphinie pushed him gently aside and approached the light like an old friend.

Bursting from the trees came a winged Pegasus enveloped by light; elated to meet its saviour, it shook the feathers on its wings and rubbed its pink nose affectionately on her face.

Darkness fell once more. The only company was the thumping of her own heart. Something was wrong.

She needed to wake up.

Shaking her arm with her hand, 'Wake up!' Charlotte said, pinching her own skin.

Then came screams in the darkness, high pitched and deadly; distorted skull faces surrounding her entirely.

Charlotte's forearm ripped open. The excruciating pain had caused an injury, but it was too dark to see it.

A white face screamed towards her, howling into the air before running off into the darkness again, then another and more until she fell to the ground in a pool of her own blood. Unable to escape, Charlotte lay still, accepting her fate. Darkness was falling. From nowhere Medwin leapt from the bushes to her aid, protectively nudging the zombies away.

Then she remembered her talisman, and urgently grasped her arm, lighting it up.

Within seconds she was at the Coliseum gate in a heap on the floor, Guardians running towards her.

CHAPTER NINE

A Hobgoblin's Home

White curtains slid apart on the pole they hung down from, as Charlotte sat up from the hospital bed.

Asphyxiated with agitation, she knew the time had come for the painful process of redressing the wound on her arm. Charlotte trembled as the medicinal liquid touched the tear; she was sure the damage would leave a scar in the shape of her creepy skull-like attacker's claw.

Once again, the nurse syringed a translucent fluid to keep her from bleeding, then wrapped her arm in bandages. To Charlotte's relief, came the sound of her good friend Abacus Creedy walking up the corridor.

'Is she in this one?' he asked a nurse, opening the wrong curtain. 'Oh! Excuse me,' he said as a bare-bottomed Troll objected to the intrusion.

'She's two further along!' ordered the matron sternly.

The pacing of giant feet gave way to the bolting open of the curtains.

'Ah, there you are!' he beamed, rushing inside quickly. Under his arm he was carrying a cage wrapped in brown paper. 'How are you doing, Charlotte?' he asked her, as the nurse left the cubicle. 'I hear you had a run-in with the Shee?'

'Is that what those monsters were?' she eagerly responded, knowing it was time to express some of her concerns. 'Abacus, I keep sleepwalking; I don't know how I ended up in that forest; one minute I was standing in my chamber, the next I was under attack.'

'I am sure that it was the Obelisk that transported you there,' he said. 'You're going to need a way to store it safely when you are not using it. Combined with your telepathic ability, it is a recipe for danger on your part, because you can activate it using your subconscious mind.'

'How do you know all of this?' she asked him, curious as to why he'd never mentioned this before.

He took from his neck a small black pouch, removing from it his very own red pyramid.

'Because I am one of the seven bearers,' he said, whispering secretively and smiling.

Charlotte was amazed and leapt up to hug him; now she finally had someone to answer some of her questions. 'Why didn't you say something sooner?' was the first of many to come.

'I had to clear it with the others first,' he said. 'They all know that our missing bearer has arrived, but obviously they don't know who it is at the moment as we are not allowed to reveal identities.' Abacus put his Obelisk back into the pouch and stowed it away. 'Only they can reveal themselves to you,' he continued. 'It's the law, I am afraid.'

He then looked at her awkwardly, as though he wanted to ask her something but felt a little out of his comfort zone. 'I've been up here a few times,' he began. 'And noticed Lauraus hiding behind the curtain.'

Charlotte paused for a moment and scratched the back

of her head, pondering how best to approach the question she knew was coming.

'I hope you don't mind my asking, but is there something going on with the both of you?'

'I'm not really sure,' she replied, trying to hide her flushing. 'Has he been here a lot, then?'

'I came once before while you were sleeping. I was sure I saw someone leaning over you, touching your face, but when I came through the curtain he'd disappeared.'

Charlotte felt mortified, and at that moment rather hoped she hadn't been snoring; her face went even redder as she screwed up her mouth, feeling a little embarrassed.

'Yes, well, you might want to tell him to be more careful – the royal crest stamped into his shoes gives him away a bit.'

Abacus quickly changed the subject which left Charlotte a little relieved. Placing the cage onto her lap, he then said, 'I got you a little somethin'.'

'A present for me?' she said, ripping off the brown paper. 'Oh, Abacus, you shouldn't have … oh!'

Underneath the wrappings, inside the cage was a green slug covered in horns.

'What is it?' she asked, trying not to look disappointed.

'It's a horned splat,' he said, looking pleased with himself.

Charlotte lent a little closer. Abacus threw a small booklet onto the bed, titled *How to Care for Your Minibeast.*

Inside were instructions about their preferred diet and exercise routine; Charlotte was quite amused to see that it was lengthy, and detailed how they would make a friendly pet, were good at listening and how they would glow orange on your birthday.

'I know the child's birthday,' Abacus advised her. 'When the splat glows orange I want you to come and tell me. If you are indeed Nelphinie's daughter, we'll know soon enough.'

Charlotte leapt from the bed for a second time, squeezing him around the middle. 'Thank you, Abacus, I love it!'

Just then Frugal and Mandy came wandering through the draped material.

'Alright,' said Frugal, glancing at the splat and licking his lips.

'No, Frugal,' said Charlotte, lifting the cage away. 'It's a present ... and I need it.'

'Oh ... OK ... here, we bought you some chocolates,' he said, handing her a purple box. 'They're from England, apparently.'

'How are you doing?' asked Mandy. 'They say you were attacked by the Shee.'

'Indeed she was,' said Abacus with worry in his voice. 'Had it not been for Medwin, I doubt she'd be here.'

'Who's Medwin?' Frugal asked, his eyes still firmly fixed on Charlotte's present.

'Medwin is Nelphinie's horse.'

Charlotte looked up with interest, as this had never been discussed before.

'He seems to be rather overprotective of young Charlotte,' he continued. 'It would appear that your friend may very well possess some qualities that the horse finds similar to his previous owner.'

'Woah, that's awesome,' said Frugal. 'Take me for a ride one day, yeah? I've never ridden a flying horse before.'

Mandy also looked impressed, but didn't say anything.

Charlotte didn't feel she needed to ask any more questions about Medwin, as she'd already seen his story unfold in her dream.

'Why is Lauraus hanging around in the corridor?' asked Mandy changing the subject entirely. 'Are you two an item or something?'

There it was again, that dreaded question. As all three of them looked at her in expectation of an answer, she pulled her sheets up protectively to her shoulders. 'Nothing's been discussed.'

Frugal looked most shocked of all; he clearly hadn't anticipated this response.

'Excuse me for a moment,' said Charlotte, getting up from the bed and rushing into the hall, her long white gown swaying behind her as she picked up her pace.

Standing at the bottom of the corridor, looking out of the stained-glass windows, was the fit physique of a man wearing a flowing white T-shirt that shimmered in the wind. Enraptured by the colourful light, this was the man she was most eager to meet that day, the man she had come to have feelings for.

He looked up at her with striking eyes, an air of guilt consuming them. He appeared to be extremely worried about her and had found it very difficult to stay away. Rushing to take her into his arms, he picked her up and swung her around then kissed her softly.

It was some time before they broke apart. It was a big moment for them both which left them shaking.

Charlotte revealed her bandage. 'It won't heal,' she said. 'I'm going to be scarred.'

Lauraus hit the wall, leaving a dent in the bricks which crumbled to the floor. 'It's my fault,' he cried out angrily. 'They want you because of me.'

Charlotte gently lifted his arm away from his head and led him to the windowsill.

'I have something for you,' he said, pulling out a double-banded ring that split into two and was thicker on one side.

Charlotte gasped, unsure of what was happening.

'It's not that sort of ring,' he said, laughing, having found her response rather funny. 'When the stone turns black, it warns of imminent danger.'

He placed it on her finger, which she held out in front of her; the stone changed from iridescent pearl to scarlet the moment it touched her skin. He smiled, as though the colour meant something, or gave some insight into the way she was feeling.

'I also want to ask that you don't date anyone else; that is, of course if you feel the same as me.'

Charlotte nodded; that went without saying for her. She instantly became connected to the way his body was feeling. She could feel his pores opening with desire and sweat running down his body, having never felt this physically drawn to someone before.

This new-found awareness of the emotion he felt for her made her feel the same way. Charlotte needn't be a telepath to know what he was feeling; she could see it in his eyes.

They kissed slowly under the coloured glass, enraptured by recently disturbed dust particles that were floating in the light.

'Guess that answers our question, then,' chirped Abacus from the shadows.

Frugal and Mandy looked at each other, shrugging.

#

Charlotte and Lauraus spent the next few weeks inseparable, and it became the talk of the Coliseum. Both Frugal and Mandy spent much more time with each other than with her, and were quite understanding, always in the background somewhere. Sinope was seething that the two made no attempt to cover up their relationship and she made frequent attempts to go out of her way to pass them and make them feel uncomfortable.

Those that chose to celebrate the festive period were given optional holiday provisions. Holidays of all faiths were privately celebrated away from the Coliseum, except for Hallows' Eve, which in Avaland was a national holiday.

Frugal's parents had invited Aphra and Walter to join them in Christmas celebration and they were quick to take them up on the offer, eager to visit Avaland for the first time. Though they didn't celebrate it themselves, Frugal's parents, Knave and Kindra, had arranged everything for the day down to the last personalised Christmas cracker. And for a further present, the gift of transportation, Monty Huck had turned out to be a useful fellow to know.

Charlotte had arrived the night before to help them decorate a sawn-off tree from Goblin Woods with all manner of trinkets they had collected over the years, and a few extra that Frugal had charmed up from thin air. They'd spent the morning cozied up in the miniature living room beside the crackling fire, wrapping the last of the presents with newspaper.

Charlotte heard a loud crash from outside, then came the sound of Walter swearing.

'They're here,' she said, getting up quickly, leaving the last unwrapped present to unravel.

They had just made it into the hallway when there was a knock at the door.

'Welcome,' said Knave, pulling the creaky wood aside.

'Thank you,' said Aphra politely, followed by a gruff appreciation from Walter. 'Er, yes, yes, thanks a lot.'

The living room was extremely close to the front door, so they were quickly overcome with a blast of warm air and the sweet smell of mulled wine.

The Christmas tree was sparkling with a multitude of glints and glitters. 'Not bad for beginners, eh?' said Fuzz in admiration, having noticed it catch their eyes.

'I quite like this tradition of yours, we should do this next year,' said Fungus, glugging on a cold beer (something he wasn't normally allowed to do).

'I'm just going to go outside and check on Monty and the dragon,' said Knave, leaving them standing on the rug.

'Our darling girl,' said Aphra, opening her arms for Charlotte to fill. Walter wrapped the length of his around them both, also extremely pleased to see her.

The door behind them slammed. 'Monty has other matters to attend to, so he won't be stopping,' said Knave, opening a bottle of sherry on the sideboard. 'He told me he'd be back for you tomorrow.'

Walter didn't look so pleased about that; in fact he looked quite positively terrified, and took a large swig of his sherry.

Before long they were sitting comfortably, enjoying Christmas day in a Hobgoblin's home, and Walter was recounting his favourite Christmas day stories, one of which was about some of Aphra's most famous Christmas turkeys.

'... ruddy thing had peacock feathers sticking out of it!' He laughed uncontrollably. 'I said to the Mrs, how on earth am I supposed to eat that! I'd never seen anything like it in all my days.' Walter shook his head, dropping a little sherry onto the carpet. Before he could finish his sentence, Walter was interrupted. 'Oh, hello dear …' He smiled awkwardly.

Aphra was scowling at him from behind the pantry door; she must have left the kitchen to start setting the dining room table.

'I was just telling Knave here what an inventive cook you are.'

'I heard,' she snapped wildly.

Walter stuck out his bottom lip; he knew he was in trouble. He then proceeded to follow her round the dining room showering her in compliments and kisses until she was laughing again. As soon as she smiled, he knew he was off the hook and sank straight back to his chair, refilling his glass.

Knave chuckled, then got up to follow Charlotte into the hall.

She was staring at a book she had just pulled from the bookshelf, one she had recently borrowed from the library herself but which had a different front cover. On the reverse of this book was the crystal-clear face of Kristoffer Enoch; a face she had already seen in a vision. On one of his wrists was the same gold band she had been trying to remove her whole life, minus the addition of her talisman. Charlotte's heart leapt inside as she realised that there was more to the bracelet than she had originally realised.

'Can you tell me about him?' she asked, casually flicking through the familiar pages.

'He's a historian; there is a reason I have a particular interest in him,' said Knave, taking a pouch from around his neck.

Charlotte gasped for something to say as he drew from it a glowing green Obelisk. 'You're one of the bearers,' she said, shocked, yet pleased to meet another.

'I plan to hand mine down to Frugal, as Nelphinie did to you.' Knave looked at her with sadness in his eyes. 'I too believe you to be her lost daughter; I think we all do.'

'The others?' she asked, keenly interested in anything he had to say about them.

'I'm afraid I cannot tell you more,' he humbly replied. 'It is up to the bearer to reveal themselves, but then you've got close ties to three of us now so you're almost halfway there.'

'Three?' she asked, searching her head for clarity. 'No, I've only been introduced to you and Abacus.'

'Oh, I thought that you and Lauraus were dating one another?'

Charlotte looked at him with blank awkwardness. 'You mean to say that Lauraus is a bearer?'

Knave looked worried, putting his hands up to his face. 'I've said too much. I thought you already knew.'

'It's OK,' she assured him. 'I won't say anything.'

Knave nodded, biting the corner of his lip in the hope that this wouldn't come back on him.

'There is something else,' he said as way of a warning. 'One of the bearers – though I can't tell you who it is – is not one of us.'

Knave looked as though he wanted to tell her more but to do so she knew would be against the law. 'You must never hand yours willingly over, for there are those that wish to use them for ill will.'

'What do they do?' she asked. 'Mine just glows when I need to read something, and transports me to places I don't want to go.'

'Have faith in your Obelisk. I cannot tell you the path it has in store for you, for they each have a different purpose.' Knave reached up to the top of the bookshelf and pulled down a black box. 'Now, this is neither the time nor the place for this conversation. Shall we not lighten the mood a little?'

Inside the box were a dozen or so whiskey chocolates. He nudged them towards her to offer one.

'No, thank you,' she said as Kindra came flying past with the hoover, wearing a plastic floral apron. If Charlotte was being honest, Kindra didn't look that much different to Knave, except she had curly brown hair and bright lipstick.

'Dinner will be ready in ten minutes,' Kindra informed them, and so it was – spit-roast goose.

Seated around a large mahogany table, the two families indulged in Christmas dinner with all the trimmings.

'Fuzz, pass the tatties,' requested Fungus, filling his plate with boiled eggs – the only thing at the table that didn't belong there. Frugal dug into an oversized bowl of Brussel sprouts (something he had never tried before).

'I hope it's to your liking,' said Kindra kindly, delicately chinking her knife and fork together on the plate.

'We had to go to England to get the seeds,' Fuzz informed them, pointing to a vegetable patch through the garden window. 'We needed to help them along a bit with magic, but I think you'll agree they are really rather good.'

'Oh yes, that reminds me,' interrupted Walter with some urgency. 'Caught the culprit! I know who's been stealing my cabbages! Only that ruddy menace next door.'

Charlotte had forgotten all about the existence of Beatrice until now.

'Thank you for my birthday present,' he continued. 'It strung her up by the ears, it did. Had to hide the knapweed in the basement; the damn neighbours phoned the police,' he grumbled, adding a few words under the cover of his tickling moustache.

'Anyway, cheers!' he said, raising his glass. 'To Avaland.'

Everyone stood and graciously toasted to his words.

'TO AVALAND.'

They had barely sat back down when there was a knock at the door.

'Oh yes, I almost forgot!' said Knave, jumping from his seat 'I hope you don't mind but I invited a friend of ours to join us.'

Fuzz and Fungus jumped up to the window, fighting over each other to get a better look.

'It's not …!' said Fungus.

'I think you'll find it is!' corrected Fuzz.

Charlotte considered Frugal's muddled expression. 'Who is it?' she whispered.

'Take a seat,' said Knave, pointing to the empty carver chair next to Charlotte as Lauraus stepped into the room.

Charlotte got to her feet and gave him a kiss on the lips. Walter looked most confused by this.

'I brought a bottle of mead with me,' Lauraus then said, unwillingly pulling his mouth away. 'I heard it is the finest; I wouldn't know myself as I don't drink.'

'Thank you,' said Knave, waving the bottle at Walter, who followed him into the kitchen.

Aphra looked at Charlotte. 'Is this him?'

Charlotte nodded, hoping Lauraus wouldn't notice, but he did and it left her feeling a little shy. 'I'd like to introduce my ...' But Charlotte stumbled on her words, looking him in the eye; of course, they hadn't discussed that yet.

'I'm Charlotte's boyfriend,' said Lauraus, finishing her sentence.

Aphra looked impressed. 'Charmed.' She said letting him kiss her hand.

Walter came scurrying in holding a tray of glasses with ice.

'This is Charlotte's boyfriend.'

Walter looked shocked, dropping one of the glasses on the floor, but he didn't appear to be totally disapproving. He reluctantly shook Lauraus's hand, then remained very quiet in the corner for several minutes.

'How is your father?' asked Knave, trying to break some of the tension.

'He is well, thank you,' said Lauraus. 'I did tell him I was coming; he is of course very grateful to you for your assistance in the matter of ...'

'It is always my pleasure,' assured Knave.

'Of course,' he responded in gentlemanlike diplomacy, turning to Charlotte in turn. 'I wonder if I might have a word in private?' he asked, extending his hand.

Walter looked disgruntled; he clearly did not like the fact that she had a boyfriend, but she was sure his anger was nothing to do with Lauraus personally. He shook his head to order that she not leave the table with Lauraus, but Charlotte ignored him.

The couple went into the garden, which Fuzz and Fungus were still staring at through the window. Kindra pulled the curtains across and, judging by the howls that came from that direction, she had just told them both off.

'There is something I need to say to you,' he said, looking her in the eyes so closely she could have been mistaken for thinking he was about to kiss her.

'It's OK,' she replied, taking the Obelisk from her pocket.

'You already know?' he said, looking at her in shock.

'I had a hunch.' She smiled, referring to her telepathy.

He then turned away. 'News of our courtship is spreading,' he told her, 'and I forever fear for your safety. I wish to offer you the protection of the Crown.'

Charlotte felt worried for a moment; could dating Lauraus really become that dangerous?

'At the Coliseum, you will of course not require this kind of protection.'

It did worry her that she was going to require minders, but at the same time she was appreciative that Lauraus cared enough about her to provide them.

He drew from a pouch around his neck a blue Obelisk. This was the one that had once belonged to Kristoffer Enoch. Both Obelisks began to drift up into the air, encircling them with light, and he took her into his arms and kissed her passionately, their bodies in an embrace. Both equally drawn to one another, they did not immediately notice their surroundings change to one more in line with their stream of consciousness.

They kissed above the ocean, then with a clear summer's sky; as they held each other tight, he was kissing her neck when they realised they were in a meadow that stretched out as far as the eye could see.

He laid her to the ground, where they continued to share one another.

There they stayed for some time, until darkness drew in and he was forced to pull away, mainly for her safety.

'Take us back,' he commanded the Obelisks, holding her hands tightly above her head.

The garden appeared, and the clock read the same time as the moment they had left. Lauraus smiled and led her back to the door.

He reluctantly left that evening, but assured her that she was safe; everywhere she travelled now she would be protected.

Watching him ride away from the kitchen window, his riders to his side, sadness filled her as she realised she wouldn't see him now until the New Year.

'So did you snog him, then?' joked Frugal playfully.

Charlotte whipped him with the tea towel. 'None of your business,' she laughed.

The washing-up seemed to go on for ages; the food had stuck to the pans and they were struggling to get it off. They were about halfway through when they started to regret offering. The adults were laughing merrily in the living room, sounding a little drunk and disorderly.

'Pass me that stack of plates over there,' said Frugal, pointing to the table with a bubbly spatula.

Charlotte was heaving the dishes to the kitchen sink when, without warning, she was punched in the chest; she dropped the plates, spitting blood onto the kitchen floor.

The vision of a dimly lit room overcame her, and a shattered mirror directly opposite revealed Antonious Draconi's beaten face. He was involved in some sort of brawl, and heavily outnumbered.

Then she was inside his body, looking out through his eyes. Facing a man, holding a broken glass bottle, he felt numb. *It's just another scar*, he thought to himself. *I want the pain.*

Charlotte looked away, unable to watch the bottle strike.

'What is it?' Frugal shouted out, seeing her become more distressed.

'Antonious,' she cried, a tear of blood falling down her cheek. 'Antonious is being attacked.'

The adults ran into the room and Knave seized her by the arm urgently. 'What is it, Charlotte?' he asked with panic in his tone.

'Antonious is being attacked,' she cried. 'He's in a tavern somewhere, he's not even fighting back.'

Aphra and Walter looked at each other with puzzled expressions because they didn't know who Antonious was.

Knave assured her that he would look into it right away, and helped her to her feet.

'Let me look at the wound, dear,' Kindra said, lifting Charlotte's T-shirt. Beneath was a fist-shaped bruise.

'I think she may have a broken a rib,' said Aphra.

'We need to get her back to the Coliseum,' instructed Knave cautiously. 'They can get her injuries looked at over there.'

And for Charlotte Christmas was drawn to an abrupt close.

CHAPTER TEN

LEPRECHAUN TERRITORY

New Year's Day had finally arrived, and with it the introduction of her practical assessment.

But first she needed to report to Abacus. *He must have returned from his Christmas celebrations by now!* Charlotte said to herself impatiently, having already visited his quarters five times since her return. She had not been able to get Antonious off her mind, and was worried about him.

Running through the corridor with no regard for the rules, she headed straight past his door to the hall where she suspected he'd be sitting eating breakfast. Correct in her calculation, she found him sitting with Magnus and Topaz, who were unwrapping their gifts.

As she approached the table, Topaz pulled out a mug from brown packaging. It had a black patch over a body builder's undergarments; she seemed confused as to what it did when you filled it with tea.

Magnus opened his decorated box to find a small tub of lip buffer. He complained loudly, reading from the label: 'To scrub away those crusty years of neglect!' Magnus screwed up his face, blood boiling beneath his skin, clearly having taken offence to his present. 'I'll have you know, I'm rather popular with the ladies.'

Charlotte doubted that, bolting past to interrupt Abacus Creedy's horsey laugh.

'Heheeee haahaaaa, oh Charlotte, I've already given you your present now, there's nothing else in the bag fur ye I'm afraid.'

'How's Antonious?' she said sharply, practically jumping down his throat.

Abacus jolted backwards; she must have caught him off guard.

'Antonious is fine,' he replied with appreciation for her worry. 'Just drinking too much; Sarah's death hit him hard.'

'It was just a squabble,' butted in Magnus, still flushed in the cheeks. He always relished an opportunity to put Charlotte wrong. 'A brawl to Antonious is just a bit of practice for physical combat, he loves a bit of trouble.'

Abacus looked annoyed. 'Oh, would ye shut yer face, ye skittery yelp. You're not helping.'

'I don't think that's right, Magnus!' said Topaz, stepping in furiously. 'He has just lost the woman he loves, and anyway he's far from a troublemaker.'

Stalling, Charlotte wanted to say she felt more concerned with his emotional well-being than his physical health, but decided to leave the conversation there.

'Whilst yer here, I have been informed to notify you that an audience with Sir Gualish Knight has been requested.' Abacus pulled a note from his pocket and gave it to her.

Charlotte had almost forgotten that there was another member of Quartz Clear. Sir Gualish was the only member of Quartz Clear she had yet to meet.

'Get some sausages down yer, and I'll take ye to go meet

him after breakfast.'

Charlotte ate quietly at the table, her thoughts still with Antonious. The sadness was overwhelming, putting her off her food. As she battled with spoonfuls of cornflakes, Charlotte wondered if that was how he was feeling at that particular moment in time.

'Sir Gualish Knight's preferred meeting place is the Labyrinth,' said Abacus when she'd taken her last bite. 'We'll just pop in there quickly now, I know ye have a busy day ahead of ye.'

'Do we have time before the test starts?' she questioned, looking up at the clock above the top table, afraid they might overrun.

'Nah, we have plenty of time,' Abacus replied, short of giving her a full answer.

On the way, Abacus greeted several people but was careful not to start up a conversation, something she knew was difficult for him to do.

Once inside, they adjusted to their new surroundings. Feign Forest was windier than she was used to, and always in the season of autumn; the Labyrinth must have been undergoing some changes in preparation for what was to come.

A ghostly steed – a semi-transparent half-armoured horse – was waiting beside an old tree. To its side was a man of no living form, who appeared to be only a walking talking suit of armour. Spotting Charlotte through invisible eyes, he marched over, his silver suit clattering as he strode.

'Salutations,' said the echoing helmet. 'It is with great regret that I have not had the chance to meet you sooner. Unfortunately my present duties reside away from the

Coliseum. Hie thee hither.'

Charlotte didn't know what this meant, but he started walking so she followed. A drift of leaves blew away from the ground, beneath was a disc made of gold. It had systems of tubing that drew the eye, twisting prettily from the circumference to equally spaced hollows.

Sir Gualish Knight took no notice of its presence, forcing Charlotte to speak up.

'What is it?' she asked, attempting to read the illuminated words.

'The wheel of spirit,' he simply replied. 'You can't read it because it's written in Latin.'

Charlotte bent down and caressed the gold with the tips of her fingers. 'What does it do?'

'It initiates the Golden Dawn,' he said, his words muffled by the reverberating armour, before going on to explain, 'Hundreds of years ago, Goblins successfully activated the wheel. The Pixies never recovered from the losses. Neither did the trees.'

Sir Gualish held out a plated hand, catching a withered leaf falling from above.

Abacus Creedy rested himself against the knot of a trunk and beheld the curious look in Charlotte's eyes. 'If you're wondering what it does, why don't ye take a look for yourself?'

Charlotte waded through the leaves to the place where he was resting. There were indents in the bark where an axe had gouged them out. She stroked the outline of one with her finger; it was hot, so she quickly pulled it away.

This time, resting her full palm, she ignored the burning.

She was overcome with the distorted picture of a

retracting blade as one barbaric massacre was revealed; Pixies desperately fled their homes, attempting to hide their children, only to be halted by menacing Goblin faces laughing in the midst of hair-raising screams.

The sundial was spinning to her side, a rainbow of cloud turning the ground to gold, spreading through the trees and eventually reaching the luscious green leaves, which were stained with Pixie blood.

Charlotte pulled her hand away, unable to watch any more. 'Why?' she demanded with distress, calling for an explanation.

'Goblin scripture depicts the Pixie as their arch enemy, worthy of slaughter,' Abacus explained. 'Sadly, nothing can be done short of eradicating all Goblins that choose to impose it.'

Muffled talking came from behind them. At once Charlotte recognised Magnus Fillius's croaky laugh, but was surprised to see Lauraus turning the corner.

Behind them ambled Knave, sympathetically; he kept turning back to Antonious, who was hopelessly dragging his feet along the ground.

Abacus looked shocked. Antonious was clearly the last person he had expected to see.

Still bearing a fresh wound to the face, Antonious stood back quietly.

'I see we have all arrived safely,' greeted Sir Gualish Knight. 'I assume you have all met your newest member; of course, it has been some time since the stones were reunited.'

'So this is the new bearer,' rattled Magnus, surprised, cornflakes still in his beard.

Lauraus broke free of the conversation he was having

with Magnus and stood confidently, attempting to tease Charlotte with his seductive stare, but her eyes were glued to Antonious. Looking a little put out by her reaction, he nervously ran his fingers through his hair.

Sir Gualish Knight continued to press on with his agenda for their meeting. 'It is because of our new proximity to each other that it is imperative we meet today. The fact we are all together for the first time in two hundred years makes us vulnerable to attack. It is vital that we all know the facts so that we can avoid unwanted activation of the wheel, something that has been prophesied to occur in your lifetimes.'

Lauraus looked at the sundial with fixed eyes. He leant down and touched the inscription with mysteriousness in his glare. 'I take it this is what they used to negate the Golden Dawn.' Disgusted by the very sight of it, he turned away.

'There is another time it's been used,' added Proteus, nudging Magnus's other leg, urging him to speak up.

'Indeed,' said the hooded figure. 'The wheel of spirit was also the birthplace of each of the stones. It is on this sundial that the first seven were sacrificed and their blood encapsulated into the Obelisks, giving them eternal life.'

Charlotte gasped. 'You mean to say the spirits inside were once living breathing souls?'

'That is correct; they are also prisoners of their own existence. As you know, there is a seventh stone, a final Obelisk that completes the sundial's requirement, which does not belong to one of us. Without it the wheel of spirit cannot be triggered. It is known to many as the Chaste Stone.'

Magnus jiggled his bottom lip wanting to say more but Sir Gualish Knight interrupted holding up his gauntlet. 'Will you finally let them reunite?'

The five took out theirs and threw them upward. Instead of falling they floated in mid-air. Charlotte's was delayed, as she took the lead from the others.

Ascending together, the Obelisks spun in a cylindrical motion. For a moment the sundial was lit up like a rainbow. The Obelisks slowed to a stop entirely before falling back into their palms.

Sir Gualish Knight rolled up his visor. 'I apologise that our time is brief. I will call on you again at the earliest opportunity. You are dismissed.'

'Right you are, then,' said Magnus, unrolling his carpet and flying off so quickly he knocked off Abacus Creedy's hat.

Charlotte looked back to Antonious; she wanted to see if he was OK, but Lauraus ushered her away enviously. He led her out the long way round, so she didn't have time to say goodbye. They exited through a trapdoor burrowed into the ground, which led out to the courtyard by the Labyrinth.

The area was empty, which pleased Lauraus because this gave them time for smooching. Charlotte was happy to oblige; that was until Sinope arrived with her friends.

'Oh shit,' cussed Charlotte awkwardly. They both stood uncomfortably, waiting for someone to break the silence.

Thankfully they were soon joined by Frugal. 'Where have you been? I've been looking everywhere for you,' he said impatiently.

Sinope stared at Charlotte threateningly, eavesdropping on their conversation. 'I've been with Lauraus,' Charlotte said, trying to hide behind him.

Frugal acknowledged her with a sarcastic flick of the head. 'Oh, right.'

The courtyard filled with young Gladiators waiting with nervous faces, too anxious to talk to their peers. Then with one swoop, Erebus Quarus landed in front of the Labyrinth doors, which opened the moment his feet touched the ground.

Extending a feathery arm, he held up a medallion for all to see; it was twice the size of a Ruby. 'Each of these represents one of the elements,' he said. 'Therefore every task has been designed to reflect that in some way.'

As he spun the coin in his fingertips, each element was shown in turn. 'Remember that each task has been designed by the master of the territory in which they reside, and they are aware of your presence. Once you have passed the test, you will be presented with the next clue describing the location of the following task. I will of course provide you with the first.'

Erebus flicked the coin into the air, where it disappeared entirely. He then produced a scroll, reading it aloud.

Abandon all hope ye who enter here,
Danger hidden in plain sight.
You'll find me at the finish line,
Succeeding every storm with light.

'What is that supposed to mean?' squinted Frugal, trying to figure out the riddle.

Lauraus kissed Charlotte on the cheek. 'Hopefully I'll see you in there,' he said, running off with London. '*Benediximus*!'

It took Charlotte a moment to decipher what he meant.

'It means good luck,' said Mandy, appearing from thin air and taking a notebook from her satchel, then scribbling down the clue. By the time she had stowed away her pencil, most of the candidates had entered.

'Right then, shall we get going?' said Frugal, keen to hurry them along.

'Hurry up, then!' gabbled Erebus, impatient of their dawdling.

Inside, darkness befell them. A torch burst into flame, giving them light, but dimming before the next. There was only one way to go, so they followed the path laid out for them. The walls were made of dirt; on closer inspection, it appeared to be a tunnel that had been burrowed into the ground.

Suddenly sunlight sliced through the air, casting them from the shadows. They were no longer in a tunnel, but crossing a balcony. Along one side were pictures of dragons; the other side was draped in vines.

Frugal took one of the grapes and popped it into his mouth. 'Yuck, it's sweet,' he said, spitting it over the side.

The squashed grape plunged into a river, where hefty rocks interrupted the intense flowing water. Giant lily pads were skimming the surface like curled-up boats.

'Charlotte, look, there's you!' Frugal pointed towards one that was racing down the rapids, London steering with a stalk.

'It must be an intersection of time,' Mandy informed them, hanging over the edge of the balcony to get a better look.

Next Lauraus jetted passed with Valentine, her face distorted by the airstream. Mandy turned and sighed, resting her back on the ledge.

'What is it?' asked Frugal, troubled by her reaction.

'I think we're going to be broken up,' she told him, looking down towards the floor.

'What makes you say that?' pressed Frugal without distress.

Charlotte knelt down beside them to see what they were talking about. 'No one else is coming,' she observed. 'I'm pretty sure they've all passed.'

'Mandy thinks we are all going to be broken up,' he repeated, not nearly as upset about it as she was.

'I didn't see us back there, Frugal, did you?' Mandy reached into her bag and held out two scrolls. 'So I think it might be a good time to give you these.'

Mandy handed them each a rolled-up piece of parchment. 'If we do get separated at least we'll be prepared.'

'What are they?' asked Charlotte unravelling the crinkled paper, identifying an island arranged in a pattern of small pieces of stone.

'Maps!' reported Frugal, answering the question for her. 'This is the mosaic of Avaland that's on the atrium floor.'

'I took a photograph when no one was looking then had it blown up; I thought it might come in useful.' Mandy bowed her head in shame. 'I got told off for it actually, the flash set off some of the Guardians but it was worth it and I'd do it again.'

Mandy had even gone to the trouble of labelling the compass points. They both thanked her, putting the scrolls away into their satchels.

As they proceeded across the bridge, Mandy administered a swift change of subject. 'So I take it you and Lauraus are a couple now then?'

'Yeah, I guess so,' Charlotte replied, more at ease to discuss it than before. Holding out her hand, she showed them the ring that he had given her.

'Wow,' said Frugal, amazed. 'A real mood ring. They're really expensive!'

'Hmm,' said Mandy, looking into it. 'What does blue mean?'

'I don't know, actually,' admitted Charlotte for the first time. 'He didn't tell me what the colours meant.'

Mandy gave a cunning smile. 'I bet he knows what the colours mean.'

Charlotte blushed; why hadn't she thought of this? It was totally outrageous that he could read her mood but she couldn't decipher his. This was something she was going to have to rectify the next time she saw him. 'All I know is, it turns black when one of us is in danger.'

Mandy bowed her head and looked away. 'Just be careful. Lauraus must have a motive for wanting to give it to you, I bet it's because of Sinope's father, I expect he is angry about your relationship.'

'It's only a present.' defended Frugal.

Mandy pressed her lips together then bellowed, 'I'm only warning her!'

As they came to the end of the path, they were struck in awe as it opened out on to clouds. Deep steel greys and blues led them down from the heavens as they descended one colossal step at a time.

'Wow!' gasped Mandy. 'It's beautiful, isn't it? I feel like I'm flying.'

They took care not to slip over the edge, and the thick fog eventually gave rise to warmer air.

'I bet it's a long way down from here,' said Frugal peering over the edge.

Mandy pointed to a crossway that was almost completely

hidden by the atmosphere. 'We're not going that way,' she said in a domineering manner. 'I'm pretty sure we need to go through that archway.'

Charlotte hadn't noticed it until Mandy pointed it out, and by the surprised look on his face neither had Frugal.

Heading straight for the open door, Mandy turned and called out behind her, 'Are you coming, then?'

Frugal clenched his teeth. 'What's the matter with her today?' he said under his breath. 'If she bosses us around one more time I'll push her off, then she can go join someone else's team.'

Charlotte giggled but lapsed into silence the moment Mandy raised her eyebrows.

Standing stubbornly, Frugal refused to budge. 'Don't we need to continue down these steps to get a bit closer to the ground?' he argued.

Maybe it was the Labyrinth bringing it out in her, but it was becoming clearer that Mandy liked to get her own way in a test environment.

'Shall we just leave her to it and go this way?' whispered Frugal resentfully.

'We'll let her get her own way this time,' said Charlotte, in an attempt to keep the peace. 'But if she continues I'll say something.'

Frugal reluctantly picked up his feet. 'I still think we need to get a bit closer,' he mumbled, Charlotte following behind him.

On entry, the door disappeared behind them. Drab terracotta walls reminded Charlotte of a place she'd gone on holiday, but this was no vacation. Meandering staircases one after another proceeded in unnatural directions; on some levels it was daytime, on others night, and even the seasons had changed.

Frugal kept looking at his watch. He tapped a finger on the clock face to show Charlotte that fifteen minutes had passed.

'I think we're lost,' he said, halting to gather some clarity.

He then pulled out his map, but Mandy snatched it from his grip. 'That's not going to help us here!'

'What's the matter with you today?' he snapped angrily. 'If you're going to keep being like this I'm going off on my own.'

'I'm sorry,' she said clasping her face with both palms, letting out an almighty cry.

Both Charlotte and Frugal became instantly concerned; they had never seen her like this before.

'What's the matter?' said Charlotte, trying to reassure her with a hug.

Mandy took her hands away and pulled a newspaper cutting from her back pocket. Uncrumpling it, Frugal began to read the front page. '*Nicholas Zain incarcerated for false allegations.*' Frugal's bottom lip dropped and he froze, so Charlotte took the paper from him and continued reading.

'Much-loved conspiracy theorist Nicholas Zain has today had his much-anticipated book, The Duplicity of Truth, *retracted from publication after concerns were raised about its legitimacy in relation to previously unknown investigations. A number of false allegations regarding high-ranking officials were referred to as fact. Zain stated that inquiries into criminal cases were sometimes relaxed and in rare cases halted entirely in the interest of national security. The book has also received*

widespread criticism on its standpoint, many concluding the findings offensive. Nobody from the Coliseum was available for comment on the matter.'

Frugal took the paper away from Charlotte, wanting to read it himself.

'Why didn't you say something sooner?' asked Charlotte.

'I was too embarrassed,' she said, blowing her nose anxiously. 'But everyone else knows, they've been staring at me all day. The allegations are false, by the way. I mean how on earth can you be arrested for telling the truth?'

Frugal looked suddenly guilty for being so short with her up until now. 'What happened?'

Mandy had another blow into her handkerchief. 'Can you remember me telling you that some of my father's latest investigations had brought the family unwanted attention? Well, he stumbled on some suspicious activities that weren't meant to be discovered. He reported them in his latest book. The book has since been discredited and stripped from the shelves; now he's been arrested for high treason.'

Frugal glowered, open-mouthed with astonishment. 'What, Orobus Pluto has had him arrested?'

'No, it wasn't Orobus,' she replied. 'I asked him today, he told me it was out of his hands.'

Charlotte felt confused. 'But I thought only elected officials could make those kinds of decisions?'

Mandy wiped one of her eyes with the only remaining patch of cloth that hadn't been used. 'Not in Avaland,' she said, stowing the newspaper clipping away. Taking a deep breath, she stood up straight. 'Anyway, I need to put it out of my mind; this is neither the time nor the place.'

Frugal patted her on the shoulder. 'Look, if you need to talk about things ...'

'It's fine!' she snapped, lifting a hand to her brow, obviously overwhelmed by it all. 'I just need to distract myself with what's going on right now.' And just like that the subject was dropped.

Frugal lifted his head to take a better look at their surroundings. By the time he'd lowered his neck, he was smiling. 'Look up there,' he said. 'We're upside down.'

Both Mandy and Charlotte looked up to the green sky. 'Hold on,' said Mandy, scratching her face. 'That's grass.'

'Then that's where we need to go,' stated Charlotte, nodding to Frugal with acknowledgement of his discovery.

Mandy gave her an annoyed look at this obvious statement. 'But how do we get there?'

Frugal had an idea so quickly interjected. 'I say we keep going until we find a place closer to the ground.'

Mandy scrunched the corner of her lips as she always did when she was brimming with the process of thought.

'I've got an idea.' Pacing backwards until her back hit the wall, Mandy took a run-up and leapt onto an alternative flight of stairs.

Both Charlotte and Frugal looked at each other with surprise; they hadn't been expecting that.

Frugal went first, trying not to look down because he was afraid of heights. Charlotte apprehensively followed. Mandy had been right; it led to a much clearer path down. The trio had finally reached a place low enough for them to jump when Mandy started to pull a rope from her satchel.

'What are you doing?' said Frugal. 'Just jump, we're inside the Labyrinth, remember? It's a soft landing in here.'

'Oh, yeah,' said Mandy, pulling back the zip.

'I'll go first,' instructed Frugal, much more confidently.

Charlotte followed, landing perfectly, realising the Labyrinth had been rigged to work in her favour. Frugal watched Mandy spring from the ledge. 'See, that would have hurt in the real world,' he said as she settled.

But Charlotte wasn't listening; she was too busy exploring the emerging piazza.

What had only moments ago been lawn was slowly transforming to patio. Along the furthermost wall were three doors, and in front four statues.

'That wasn't here a minute ago,' fretted Frugal, puzzled by the altering surroundings.

Freshly made footprints were vanishing before them; apparently, someone else had been here and had also decided to jump.

'Lomax has been here,' identified Frugal, inspecting two oversized foot shapes with fat toes. 'It couldn't have been Grendel, his feet are twice that size.'

Mandy nodded in agreement. 'It's difficult to tell who the others belong to, because they're wearing shoes.'

Frugal looked up to the sky, then adjusted the dial on his watch, making the hands turn anticlockwise with velocity. 'We have five hours of daylight left,' he said. 'I've set a timer; we want to finish before the creepy crawlies come out.'

Joining Mandy to examine the map, Frugal tried to help her determine their location. But Charlotte was more interested in taking a look around. The enclosure was paved with rocks sliced to polished precision. Statues were commonplace inside the Coliseum, normally of Roman spirits; most would glare down on you with such vigour you could be forgiven for mistaking them for being alive. Whilst Frugal and Mandy discussed which way to go, Charlotte took some time to study the details of the four here.

The first she recognised to be Jupiter, king of the spirits. Beneath him was a woman made of stone; she was climbing out of one of the paving slabs, carved to give the illusion of water. The rock bore a name, identifying her as the spirit Venus. Frugal came over and joined her, having lost interest in being told he was wrong about every suggestion he'd made.

'Why is he holding his you-know-what like that?' asked Charlotte, referring to another, an emaciated male, angry and carrying a newborn child over his shoulder.

'That's the spirit of Saturn,' Frugal explained. 'He's Jupiter's father. Saturn devoured all of Jupiter's brothers at birth. There was supposedly a prophecy that one of his sons would dethrone him.'

'That's awful,' gasped Charlotte, horrified.

Frugal held one finger to his lips as though concerned that the sculptures could hear their conversation.

'Luckily for us, Jupiter escaped,' he whispered. 'That's him he's carrying.'

'But that doesn't explain why he's holding his … you know?' Charlotte nudged her eyes towards the withered man's groin.

Frugal raised his volume again. 'Saturn was later castrated by Jupiter and his testicles thrown into the sea. Venus, the spirit of love, was born of them.'

Charlotte walked over to the remaining statue and put her hands on its shoulders. 'So what about this one?' she asked curiously.

Frugal looked puzzled. 'I don't know what the wizard Merlin's doing here?' he questioned, presuming it to be out of place. 'He has nothing to do with the others.'

Charlotte couldn't help feeling that this was the clue they were looking for. Frugal also eyed it suspiciously, similarly concluding something to be amiss.

She diverted her attention to the direction of the bearded fellow's arm, which pointed in the direction of a badly hung outdoor painting.

Wandering over to that section of the wall, she took a further look.

'A waterfall ...' said Frugal, peering over her head. 'And a rainbow.'

'Right, that settles it then!' called out Mandy, arguing with herself. Glaring up, she realised that nobody was listening. 'What are you doing over there?'

'Charlotte's found a clue,' he told her.

Mandy shrugged off the point Frugal was trying to convey. 'We are wasting time,' she declared. 'Quite clearly there are three doorways over there; we need to go through the one on the far right because that one has the eye of enlightenment on the top.'

Just then, chatter came from behind that very door. It opened wide as it swung on its hinges, letting out a small group of people. Among them were London and Lauraus, who were also arguing.

'So what do we do now?' bellowed Lomax, looking irritable. 'We've tried every door.'

'Maybe we've missed something,' reflected Valentine calmly. 'Should we go back?'

Mandy screwed up her face, put out to have been proved wrong so quickly.

'Hidden in plain sight,' gasped Frugal excitedly. 'The first part of the riddle states this very thing, it says the clue is "hidden". "Plain sight" is referring to the view of the statue, in this case Merlin.'

'What are you doing?' asked Valentine, coming over to join them. She gave the boys an irritable shake of the head, tiring of their quarrelsome company.

'It's not much better over here,' joked Charlotte, rolling her eyes, leaving Mandy a little taken back.

'Let's just call it passion,' kidded Lauraus light-heartedly, amazed they had picked up on something he hadn't noticed before. 'I've been training for this for years, and I wouldn't have spotted that.'

'Charlotte found it,' said Frugal, trying to highlight her ability. Lauraus gave her an impressed trout-like smile. Charlotte blinked, because he looked stupid.

'It's a painting of a rainbow,' he then said, bending down to take a closer look.

'I bet there's a pot of gold at the other end of that rainbow,' added London, who had since followed. He grinned like a Cheshire cat, blinding them with his pearly whites.

Lomax cleaned his dirty paws under the water dripping from Venus's statue.

'Don't do that!' scolded Valentine. 'Have some respect!'

'I don't give a shit!' he merely replied, accidently on purpose wiping his muddy foot on Venus's face and laughing.

Lauraus ran his hands along the painting's frame. 'There's a breeze,' he advised, pulling the mount, which gave a slight resistance. An unbricked hole was revealed, enough to fit a person at a push.

'I guess it's this way, then,' said London, poking his head through to the other side. 'Leprechaun Territory,' he reported when his face rematerialised.

'How is Lomax going to get through?' asked Valentine, turning back to catch him drawing a muddy penis on Saturn's forehead. 'STOP IT, LOMAX!' she shouted.

'I think I might stay behind,' he teased sarcastically, because he didn't like being told what to do. As he flicked the remaining mud to the ground, Valentine gave him her best angry girlfriend stare and he quickly recanted his statement.

'Don't worry about me,' he said. 'I'll get through alright!'

Alleviated of her worry, she shadowed her teammates to the other side. Charlotte was the last to pursue.

They stepped out onto a grassy knoll, where a cliff face bore a rickety old bridge. Ahead lay fields of green and, swinging about in the wind, a creaky old sign told them to beware.

Bricks flew past in all directions as Lomax burst through like a rhinoceros. 'Told you I'd get through!' he gloated.

Frugal picked up one of the bricks that had almost hit him in the head and threw it aside with annoyance. Valentine gave her man a brash smile of admiration as he joined the rest of the group.

The bridge swayed loosely in the wind, looking more dangerous with each passing second. All of them waited for someone to volunteer to go first.

Frugal was the first to speak. 'We should go in weight order,' he suggested, clasping his mouth, suddenly realising that he was the lightest. Wishing he hadn't said anything at all, he delicately placed his big toe on the bridge and nudged it down to check its stability.

He then took a deep breath and began to cross, gripping hold of the sides as tightly as his hands would allow. The others looked on in breathless silence, waiting for the bridge to collapse.

By the time he had gotten to the halfway point, he had frozen completely. Turning, he gave Charlotte a panic-stricken 'help me' look.

Lomax nervously tried to break the unbearable quiet. 'I wish Erebus was here,' he said, concerned by the unfolding situation.

'He wouldn't be able to carry you anyway,' responded Valentine with hilarity, finding his nerves endearing. Nobody else found it funny. This was apparently a serious matter and there was no time for laughing.

'Hold on to the sides and don't look down,' instructed Lauraus unhelpfully, because that was exactly what Frugal was doing.

Suddenly a gust of wind swayed the bridge upside down, making Frugal scream loudly. This gave him the motivation he'd needed, mustering up the courage to continue. Making it across the second half much faster, Frugal fell to his shaking knees, taking a moment to pull himself together.

'Right, now for the girls,' ordered Lauraus, throwing a grapple across the gorge. 'Frugal!' he shouted. 'Make it secure!'

Frugal steadied his quaking legs and withdrew from the ground. Tugging on the rope, he yelled back, 'Secure!' his voice still wobbling.

Charlotte was the last of the females to traverse the overpass, the tightrope taut above her head. She had never been anywhere so high or unsteady, and she made it across with a new-found sympathy for Frugal because she wouldn't have liked to have been the guinea pig on this one either.

London was next, sideways stepping across, much like the girls, but posing as he went. Because he was concentrating on looking handsome instead of what he was doing, one of the planks snapped beneath his body weight, making him lose his footing.

'AHHH!' London was hanging on the rope in mid-air, but with a quick swing his balance was restored. He managed to get past but looked rather embarrassed.

Lauraus, however, now had to face a hole in the centre of the bridge.

'Guess you were right about all those bedtime push-ups,' London taunted impishly. Lauraus stuck his middle finger up. It must have been a personal joke.

Eventually reaching the centre, Lauraus sent a lasso to the branch of a close-by tree and swung over.

Now for the problem of Lomax. The sarcastic grin was well wiped from his face, but he didn't falter, only mocked with his usual lightheartedness, 'If it can take the weight of all you fatties, I'll be fine! Here goes,' he whispered, kissing the talisman around his neck.

Thundering across with no care for the delicate wood planks beneath his paws, he shouted, 'WOO HOO!' like an adrenaline junkie, jumping before the bridge gave way.

London gave him a pat on the back as he walked towards them. 'Awesome, you and I are going to get on just fine.'

Ahead of them stood nothing but meadow for as far as the eye could see. As they took their first steps, a yellow trumpeted flower blew. 'Forewarn horn,' Charlotte said, recognising it straight away. 'It warns the Leprechauns that we're coming,' she told them, surprised to see that she was the only one that knew this.

The further into the pastures they went, the longer the grass became until they were completely hidden from view.

London was sweating nervously. 'So, what are we likely to be dealing with here?' he asked casually.

'The usual Leprechaun tricks,' answered Lauraus much more enthusiastically. 'In addition to knapweed and scalopendra.'

London faltered, his spine shuddering. 'I hate spiders.'

Valentine corrected him, unperturbed. 'Technically, scalopendra is a plant, not a spider.'

Charlotte had never heard of it, but had to admit it sounded intimidating. She crumpled up her forehead, trying to imagine what a spider plant could look like.

Valentine saw this and responded with an explanation. 'Scalopendra is a bulbous plant; they are like arachnids but rooted into the ground, and are a common menace guarding the Leprechaun community.'

Charlotte scanned her surroundings cautiously; she didn't like spiders either.

'Well, you're going to have to get used to it in this job,' Lomax advised his new pal. 'Cause they're everywhere.'

London straightened his shoulders in an attempt to hide his phobia. 'I'm not scared!' he hooted. 'I'm just finding out for the others.'

Lauraus also had some good advice for his teammates. 'If anyone sees a Leprechaun, don't attack it, you'll make it mad. They won't hurt us too much if we don't give them reason to.'

So far things had gone without event, but the mood in the group was low. The further they walked, the longer the grass became, looking like some kind of transdimensional woodland. Charlotte imagined it as being how an insect would view the world. Marshy ground concealed the decaying of oversized leaves blown in by the winds of Feign Forest.

The more the sunlight receded, the colder it became, until they were so far into the undergrowth they could no longer see the sky.

'What's the plan again?' enquired Lomax, slipping on gummy leaves stuck between his toes.

'You asked me that thirty seconds ago,' said Lauraus sharply.

'No I didn't!' he retorted with fixed eyes.

Valentine took his furry hand. 'Yes you did, Lomax, because I heard it.'

Lomax looked worried; Charlotte could tell he couldn't remember and knew Valentine wouldn't mislead him. She hadn't heard him ask either, which worried her, because she usually had such strong senses.

'OK,' said Lauraus worried. 'We are getting confused – another Leprechaun trick. We need to tie ourselves together. We don't want anyone getting lost out here.'

High-pitched cheerful laughter came from the bushes, encircling them before disappearing.

'They know we're here,' said Lauraus boldly, looking the least subdued.

Keeping their backs together, they formed a circle, weapons at the ready.

'Don't attack!' insisted Lauraus. 'We'll fail the challenge quicker than you can blink.'

Valentine interrupted, 'But we can't just let them attack us.'

'That is an order!' he exploded, like Charlotte had never seen him do before. 'I told you, they won't harm us unless we give them reason to.'

Valentine gave him an evil look; she clearly didn't like being spoken to in this way, but followed his instruction, retracting her claws.

The group stayed in their formation, letting the minutes pass, convinced something was about to happen. But it didn't. An eerie silence filled the air, and you didn't need a sixth sense to feel it.

Without warning, London was swept away from beneath, hitting his head on the ground and losing consciousness. Because they were tied together, each team member was swept out behind him. They were being dragged by their feet at an alarming rate, deeper into Leprechaun Territory. Lomax tried to grab a tree but missed by inches.

'Not yet,' insisted Lauraus. 'Whatever is pulling him will not relent just because we are holding the other end.'

London was starting to come to. 'Something's got my leg!' He panicked, trying to take out his sword, but he couldn't free it from the harness in motion.

Lomax was trying to slow down the momentum by digging his heels into the ground, but he couldn't slow them enough to prevent London's fate.

Then something very ugly burrowed out of the ground, giving him a fright. A giant bulb with hundreds of eyes and spindly legs was trying to pull London into its hairy mouth. Chattering yellow pointed teeth made an unpleasant rattlesnake noise, adding to the tension.

Charlotte was starting to see that London's fierce exterior

was a bit of a façade; the mask he wore to impress the ladies was not a true depiction of his stamina.

But Lauraus seemed to care for him a great deal, having taken London's hand and pierced a dagger into the mud, but it wouldn't hold for long.

'Shit, Lauraus, don't you let me go. I'm not up for being that thing's dinner.'

'It's not the swallowing part you need to worry about,' Lauraus struggled to reply. 'Their teeth only scratch the skin; you can rip your way out with your bare hands.'

'Why are they dangerous, then?' shouted Lomax, still bearing most of the weight.

'Their venom releases a narcotic into the bloodstream.'

The plant opened its smelly mouth, and out came a long thin tongue, licking London's face. When its saliva went into his mouth, he started to sob. 'I don't want to go in there, Lauraus,' he wailed loudly.

Lomax tried not to laugh; he hadn't expected this reaction at all.

Lauraus looked at his friend sympathetically. 'I'm going to have to let you go.'

London shook his head. 'No, no … don't let me go, you can do it! I believe in you.'

Lauraus let go of his hand. London was pulled involuntarily inside; the plant broke several of its teeth, which were not designed for chomping humans.

Releasing the dagger, Lauraus cut the rope that was binding them together.

The bulbous head blinked all of its eyes repeatedly in a single moment of ecstasy, before shutting them entirely and letting out a gassy belch, discharging narcotic fumes.

'It stinks,' shouted London. 'Get me out of here!'

Giggles came from the surrounding bushes as the smell of rotten eggs filled the vicinity. The scalopendra was preparing its vines to burrow back under the ground. But Lauraus kept his word, fearlessly running over to London's aid.

He ripped the creature open with his bare hands, ignoring the merciless screams. Moments later he pulled London free from the carcass, where he fell to the ground in an unconscious heap.

In an act of true brotherly love, Lauraus repeatedly smacked him in the face until he let out a groan. 'He's alright!' he said, relieved. 'Well, sort of.'

London threw up on his own face, then started singing what Charlotte could only assume was an Avalonian nursery rhyme.

Lomax found this funny. 'It's alright, mate, we won't tell anyone your little secret.' Picking London up, Lomax then flung him over his shoulder. 'Which way are we going now?'

Frugal took out his map and compass. 'North-east is that way.' He pointed, taking the lead.

They vacated Leprechaun Territory quietly, their encounter with the bulbous plant leaving them shaky. Before long the grass was getting shorter again and they could see the sky as they came to the other side of the glade.

Breathing a sigh of relief, the Werewolf rested a snoring London on the short grass.

Valentine whined irritably, 'I can't believe we've been through all of that and we still don't have the element.'

'Listen,' interrupted Frugal, holding out his ear. 'Can you hear water?'

Glancing skyward, Charlotte noticed a rainbow in the sunlit sky. 'The moisture from the waterfall is hitting the sunlight.'

'Of course,' said Mandy, bringing to mind part of the riddle. 'Succeeding every storm with light.'

'Oi, London, wake up now, you can walk this bit.' Lomax said this mainly for his own amusement, tickling London's nose with his feathery tail.

London snorted then shimmied to his feet. He stood upright for a few seconds before landing flat on his face. Lauraus turned bright red with strain as he lifted him from the ground; not an easy task because they were both the same size.

As the waterfall appeared on the horizon, momentum built in the group providing them with a well-needed burst of energy.

The first thing Charlotte noticed was that the water was behaving differently here. Instead of flowing down to a bubbling rock pool, the water was flowing upwards. This must have been the Irish Waterfall that Briony Picket, the owner of the plant shop in Prince Street, had been talking about.

Lauraus put London down, then took off his shirt. 'Here, can you hold this?' he asked, making Charlotte blush.

Walking over, Lauraus cast an eye over the flowing stream, diving from the edge and disappearing from view. When he rematerialised, his forearm was stretched into the air, holding a bronze coin. Lauraus had found the medallion.

'Which element is it?' called out Mandy, elated, as he swam back through the current.

Lauraus climbed out of the water, his arms trembling with fatigue. 'Earth,' he reported, handing it to her so that he could put on his shirt.

Everybody cheered, glad to have finally completed the mission. Charlotte doubted that anybody had expected it to be quite so exhausting, finally understanding why there was a month between exercises.

London put his hand down his trousers and scratched his backside, oblivious to anything that was going on around him.

'This is going to be more fun than I thought,' jittered Lomax, giving the impression that he liked London a lot more now than when they'd entered.

An ornately framed door appeared, bearing the words *Magnum Opus*. Opening by itself, the courtyard floor was revealed.

Charlotte became confused by the unfamiliar language. 'What does "magnum opus" mean?' she asked Frugal naively.

'Great work,' he said plainly, stepping over London and leaving straight away.

Mandy and Valentine were also keen to get to their sleeping chambers, but Lomax held back to offer a hand.

But he needn't have, because Charlotte and Lauraus had commandeered London, lifting his arms and wrapping them round their shoulders. 'Come on, we'd better get him to the sanatorium, then to the Roman baths, I think,' he said, giving her a wink.

CHAPTER ELEVEN

Mermaid Cove

The route through Leprechaun Territory` had been a big insight for Charlotte, who decided the best approach from now on was to expect the unexpected.

Still surprised she had come out of the task relatively unscathed, the next few weeks were spent learning everything there was to know about the world she had become a part of. On a normal evening, you would find her immersed in books from the library or training for ever-increasing amounts of time inside the armoury.

She had been finding it difficult to sleep, so when Frugal arrived during the early hours that morning, the face that greeted him was grumpy and bouffant-haired. Unbothered by the lack of a warm reception, he burst through the darkness and started jumping on her bed.

The purring Grimmelkin shot under the mattress, irritably wagging its tail.

'How could you honestly have this much energy?' she yawned, snuggling a neatly drawn blanket beneath her chin. Charlotte laid sleepily on the bed beneath his hopping feet. She was too tired to be concerned with the mud beneath his toenails.

'There's something I've come to tell you,' he said with wide helpful eyes.

'Frugal, it's five-thirty in the morning. I don't normally get up for at least another hour – can't we discuss this later?'

'No, it can't wait,' insisted Frugal, examining her chamber. He then unreservedly changed the subject. 'Your room's awful by the way, you really need to change it. Why on earth would you choose this colour scheme when you can have anything you want?'

Charlotte hastily peeled open her eyes because she heard a loud ripping sound. Frugal had pulled off a bit of border from her wall that needed repasting. 'It looks like a technicoloured bomb went off!' he snorted.

You could always rely on Frugal to tell the truth at just the wrong moment. He was often embarrassingly frank, but Charlotte knew him well enough to realise that he wasn't intending to be rude, even if she hadn't had a cup of coffee yet. It was, after all, the Hobgoblin way to always tell the truth.

'Is that crochet?' he said, picking up her childhood teddy bear by its poorly stitched leg. Charlotte snatched it back defensively.

Sitting on the bed, he then checked the firmness of the mattress. Charlotte dusted down George the bear and put him back on her dressing table, then thought about what Frugal was trying to say.

'You mean I can have any bedroom I want?' she asked, feeling lifted from her mood.

'Absolutely. I changed mine the moment I got here.'

'But how is that even possible?' she wondered aloud.

'Can't you remember me telling you that the Coliseum is built on an unlimited source of magic? It's something to do with the volcano – instead of erupting, it radiates alchemy. They say Jupiter himself bestowed the enchantment.'

'This place gets more amazing by the day!' she praised, slipping a pair of jeans on and tucking in her nightdress.

'It sure does. I guess there's no time like the present.' Putting his big green hands over Charlotte's eyes, Frugal cleared his throat. 'Right, now think of something you want inside.'

Charlotte sniggered, sounding a bit like a choking pig.

'What's so funny?' he objected, taking his hands away as though she'd offended him.

'Nothing ...' she recanted, trying to withdraw the image of Lauraus wrapped in nothing but a towel. The vision drifted back into the void, allowing her to conjure up some of the most elaborate things she had yet to encounter. Her mind's eye flowed to red silk draping from the ceiling, a closet full of clothes and maybe even a chandelier or two?

The reverberation of hammering heralded more clattering as furniture scraped across the floor. 'That's some imagination you've got,' revealed Frugal, lifting away his hands.

What could only be described as complete shock consumed her as a very different bedchamber burst into view, presenting itself as a scarlet boudoir with a silk-draped divan taking centre stage. Shagpile carpet led to a closet with its own en-suite bathroom, and the ceilings were adorned with candlelit chandeliers.

Considering she had been so annoyed with Frugal moments ago, it could be fair to say her mood had improved tremendously.

'You don't even need to do your own housekeeping,' he continued. 'You just ask your room to be tidy before you enter. I can't believe you've been here all this time and you didn't know any of this.'

'Nobody told me,' she defended herself, expanding her evaluation. 'Does that mean you can do it anywhere in the Coliseum then?'

'Within reason, yeah,' he replied. 'There are some things you can't do, for example use the alchemy for anything negative, violent or harmful to anyone's well-being.'

The Grimmelkin dashed from under the bed and leapt into Charlotte's arms, reminding her that this had not been the original reason for Frugal's visit. 'What was it you wanted to tell me anyway?' she wondered, petting the cat's bottle-green chin.

'Huh? Oh right, course.' Frugal opened his hands, magically manifesting a large hardback from his empty palms. He dropped the book on the bed because it was heavy. 'I think I've found something you might find interesting.'

Turning the pages, Frugal tried not to dislodge the parchment that was coming free of the binding. Opening out on to a list, he began to descend it with his index finger. It was of surnames beginning with the letter E.

'They're grave numbers,' he said, indicating her to read. 'Can you remember the number you found inscribed on the wall downstairs?'

Charlotte pulled the book closer.

Kristoffer Enoch, mausoleum no. 1776

The grave number had been scratched out and replaced with the number *2036*.

'They must have changed it at the last minute,' he said. 'Not normal practice but I thought I should bring it to your attention.'

Shockwaves filled her with astonishment as she considered everything this could mean. Why had Kristoffer Enoch been pictured so clearly wearing the bracelet she could not remove? And was she going to find the answer on his tombstone? Every part of her was coaxing her to investigate.

Frugal closed the cover hard, releasing a scattering of dust that collected as a film on top of her sheets. 'He wants us to go there, I reckon.'

Charlotte continued to analyse the situation, becoming doubtful that they would find anything.

'That's what I thought,' wondered Frugal hopelessly, 'but I think we should check it out anyway. Maybe your abilities could pick up on something they missed?'

She knew Frugal was right. It couldn't hurt to draw their own conclusion on things and she had more of a reason to investigate it than anyone.

Charlotte flicked her hair back and tied it into a ponytail before rushing out of the door. Like a veil of windborne seeds, they sped down the spiralling staircase and passed the canteen.

Frugal rubbed his aggravated belly. 'It can smell the sausages,' he dribbled. But there was no time for breakfast, not if they wanted to be back for the Labyrinth by twelve.

Early morning would be the perfect time to slip out unnoticed. Or so she thought.

Clanking suits of armour strode through the atrium on their way back from morning patrols. Their assertive strides temporarily obstructed the view long enough for her to reposition herself behind a pillar, chest panting.

Frugal recognised her urgency and copied her. 'What's going on?' he whispered, clueless to what had provoked her reaction.

But his ears quickly realised the reason, as they pointed to the other side of the pillar.

Conversing in Latin with some air of secrecy were Zavantus Lavlock and Sinope Blatio: the two people at the Coliseum that liked her the least. Having come to trust her instincts, they were once again persuading her to be unseen by the enigmatic pair.

First came the insidious tongue of Zavantus. '… It is a disgrace to the Dominions of Avaland that such shame has been brought upon its king.' Saliva spat from his mouth with hatred. 'Let me assure you, Miss Blatio, the Heraldry of Elders will not rest until the prince is brought to account for his actions.'

To Charlotte's surprise, Sinope did not seem consoled by his spiteful words.

'Thank you for your concern, Zavantus … and for the backing of the Heraldry, but I can assure you that the matter is in hand; there is no reason for anyone to get involved.'

Zavantus gave Sinope a cold and unconvincing smile before bowing his head and slowly trotting off. When he had gone, Charlotte heard Sinope gasp out, loosening to a faint sob.

Charlotte felt shock at Sinope's reaction, becoming aware in that instant that Sinope wished her and Lauraus no harm. Was this a glance through her normal hard exterior? Could it be possible that Sinope was in love with Lauraus? Charlotte was beginning to wonder whether Lauraus was being entirely honest about their relationship.

Sinope pulled herself together because a group of Goblins were approaching. In an instant, her sadness became an unprecedented expression of strength. She marched away resolutely, her shoulders back proudly.

Charlotte, on the other hand, was a heap on the floor, having been overcome by this new insight.

'What are you thinking?' asked Frugal, once Sinope was out of sight.

Charlotte's eyes shifted side to side, still deep in thought.

'You can't let her destroy what you and Lauraus have.'

'But what do we have, Frugal? He told me nothing had ever happened with him and Sinope. That's clearly not true.' Her fluttering jitters turned to rage. She stood up stubbornly, no longer desiring to see her boyfriend's lying face.

'Do you want to do this another time?' Frugal asked, picking up on the boiling blush beneath her skin.

Charlotte shook it off. 'No, of course not. Come on, let's go!' Straining a pretend smile, Charlotte attempted to put Frugal at ease; she would deal with Lauraus later.

Heading to the Coliseum boundary, they encircled the grounds. It took some time for her to speak again.

'I don't think Lauraus has been being totally honest about his relationship with Sinope being just a betrothal.'

'How do you mean?' Frugal flushed nervously.

Charlotte traversed the lava drawbridge first. 'I mean, I suspect they both had a relationship.' She looked to Frugal for an answer. 'Did they?'

Frugal wiggled his toes nervously through the short blades of grass; it was obvious he didn't want to answer the question. 'It's not for me to say, but I was always under the impression that they were dating. They were really young, and I never saw them kiss or anything, so it doesn't really count, does it?'

Charlotte stopped just short of a privet maze made of trimmed bushes. 'It does to me,' she said, looking like she was trying not to cry.

Frugal rested his hand on her shoulder. 'They were betrothed since they were babies, their fathers used to be friends, then Sinope's father changed so they drifted apart.'

'What do you mean he changed?'

Frugal looked around to see if anyone was listening, then ushered her to walk on. 'His political views became less ethical, and his company more difficult.'

Charlotte looked at him with disbelief.

'The king doesn't want any association.'

'What are you talking about, Frugal? I don't understand what you're trying to say.'

'The same people that have Mandy's father in custody are the ones the king wants no association with. He cares only for the people. There is unsaid fear for his safety, because you do not cross them; if you do you usually pay with your life. That's the way it works here. Sinope's father is one of them. Once you cross one you cross them all.'

'Can't he just leave?' asked Charlotte with great inexperience.

A shake of the head told her she wasn't understanding the point he was trying to make.

'He couldn't leave even if he wanted to, because the Heraldry of the Elders manipulate you by threatening the ones you love. You see, Sinope is the victim here really, but you can also understand why Lauraus doesn't want any part of it.'

The grass was getting longer the further off the beaten track they travelled. At the bottom of the mountain Charlotte could see the flickering lamp posts in Prince Street.

Frugal went on with his pecking order lesson. 'The official records say that Orobus Pluto is the elected leader, but it's a lie, everybody knows it and nobody's prepared to do anything about it.'

'Poor Sinope,' said Charlotte, feeling guilty for making a serious error of judgement. 'She must be terrified.'

His frowning façade suggested that Frugal did not seem to share Charlotte's sympathies. 'I wouldn't feel that sorry for her,' he said coldly. 'There's another reason Lauraus doesn't want to be with her. He probably would have tried to protect her had she not been so …'

Frugal pulled a widened face as he'd already said too much, but Charlotte urged him to continue.

'She can be cruel, she finds other people's misfortunes humorous and she's also a bit of a snob. Lauraus doesn't like that. I know Lauraus is really taken with you, please don't be too hard on him; there are reasons behind all of this, albeit closely guarded ones.'

Charlotte ran her fingers through her ponytail, took a deep breath and decided to let go of her hostility.

The sun was rising now. 'We're here,' declared Frugal, entering the grassy overgrowth.

Tall stalks whipped the skin as they pushed their way out on to a narrow track alongside a cliff face. Even though the sun had risen, the cliffs cast a shadow over them, blocking out the light. The air was colder here too, making it difficult to shake off the feeling that someone was watching.

'Don't worry about that uneasy reflex,' advised Frugal. 'Everyone gets it here. It's the ghosts that cause it.'

Surprisingly, that didn't make Charlotte feel any better, but she reminded herself that ghosts were the souls of the dead and often meant no harm.

As the smog cleared, a thousand stone tombs were revealed.

It was eerily quiet, with nothing but the sound of crows. 'No one ever comes here,' Frugal told her.

A dozen or so birds flew into the sky as she passed them. The narrow gravel path skimmed the edge of a gargantuan mountain cast with monumental doors, each individually decorated with gargoyles in elaborately patterned pewter.

The path ahead became narrower, making the quarry appear steeper with each passing step. Charlotte tried not to look over the ledge … one steep fall would surely end your life. To make matters worse, Frugal kept leaping backwards as fog uncovered creepy faces; for a moment she wondered whether they would reach the right tomb at all. Until …

'Mausoleum number 2036,' Frugal called.

There it was, a small monument in comparison to the others. Imprinted upon a small plinth were words Charlotte recognised to be Latin.

Hic latet secretum non erit ei

Frugal took out a handful of butterfly candles and translated, 'Here lies the secret forbidden to be told.'

The flaming wings lit a disc-shaped door made of stone on which an obituary had been carved; a note to any onlooker about Kristoffer's legacy.

Frugal read it clearly. *Kristoffer Enoch, Founder of the Theory of the First Seven, The Isle of Apples, and elected apparel for the Amulet of Armistice.*

There were two engraved statues either side of the words, one a female, a tear falling from her cheek and another of a small boy looking up towards his crying mother, offering a hand of support. In the young boy's cupped grip were what looked like marbles.

Charlotte bent down to take a closer look. 'Oh my,' she said, making one roll across the rocky muscle of the boy's thumb. 'They're secrets.'

Frugal couldn't believe it either. 'If one of them is meant for you, it will glow,' he advised. In the same moment, the marble fell to the ground.

Without warning, the mausoleum door rolled, making the glass ball shine. Frugal looked at her open-mouthed; he couldn't believe what he was seeing. Kristoffer Enoch himself had created a memory explicitly for her.

Shuffling his feet uneasily, Frugal mustered up the courage to speak. 'I'm not going to follow you in there. Hobgoblin culture deems it an act of disrespect to disturb the dead.'

'You're not meant to,' she acknowledged before declaring, 'I think I'm meant to go in there alone.'

Hesitating, Frugal looked sceptical. 'How do you know that?' he catechised.

Charlotte held up her wrist, exposing the bracelet. 'He had one of these, remember?'

Having weighed up the argument, Frugal agreed then turned to guard the door. 'I'll be right here if you need me,' he promised. The stone disc rolled shut between them, leaving her standing inside a hollow grave, dark and barren.

Then from nowhere torches burst into flame as Kristoffer Enoch entered.

Crackling firelight lit his dripping sweat; he looked panicked and withdrawn. Slipping a book from beneath his cloak, he wiped the dirty cover with his sleeve, then dislodged a brick from a wall in the corner of the room. Stuffing it in, he sealed it with a magical wave of his hand. Taking a deep breath, Kristoffer accepted his fate by resting his fingers on his head and bending down to the ground to surrender.

With only moments to spare, two armoured soldiers entered behind him, then savagely beat him to death with their batons.

Charlotte looked away; the helpless look in Kristoffer's eyes was too much for her to bear.

Without warning, a mist rose from his body, producing an ethereal shadow in the form of his younger self. Kristoffer stood over his lifeless body, overwhelmed by this violent end.

The soldiers seized his right arm and cut with such disregard for his dignity, but when the bracelet sank into his skin they shrieked like juveniles.

Communicating with each other in Latin, their voices became more desperate as they ransacked his treasures, searching for something. Showing no interest in Kristoffer's worldly possessions, the men did not appear to be thieves.

Soon realising he wasn't alone, the ghost lurched sideways, apparently spooked by Charlotte's attendance. A satisfied smile pursed the corner of his lips when he realised that she was wearing the bracelet. Slowly dissipating into a cloudy web of vapour, his floating soul departed as energy and light.

'It's empty?' came Frugal's voice behind the now open door, bringing her back from Kristoffer Enoch's memory, her eyes stinging from the sudden burst of sunlight. 'Is that his skeleton?' he asked, looking down towards the place Kristoffer's body had lain seconds ago. 'They could have given him a better burial than that.'

'He was murdered,' she told him. 'He had treasures too but his tomb must have been raided.' Charlotte glanced outside to check they were alone. ‘Frugal, that book thingy you did earlier … with magic? Can you do it again?’

‘Yeah, I think so,’ he loftily supposed. ‘Why, what have you found?’

Charlotte didn’t answer. ‘Will it be safe there?’ she whispered. ‘Where does it go?’

‘I store it in my subconscious. No one can get to it but me.’

Drifting to the corner, she tried to dislodge one of the bricks, but it didn’t budge until Frugal intervened from outside with a magical wave of the hand. A nook behind the wall revealed a vault dug into the earth; inside was the same book Kristoffer had put there, only undisturbed for centuries.

The cover was embossed with the image of an eye inside a gold pyramid. In her hands was Kristoffer Enoch’s very own copy of his *Life and Legacy.* A quick scan through the stiff pages told her that this copy was different to the others, because it had been scribbled with notes and annotated with symbols.

Frugal looked terrified as he held it in his palms; he didn’t seem to want to touch it at all. ‘Do you know how much trouble I could get into for carrying this?’

‘Please, Frugal,’ she urged him.

‘You owe me one,’ he said with trembling hands, taking the book into himself without further argument. ‘Right, now let’s get out of here!’

Sealing up the hole, Charlotte and Frugal left the tomb. Frugal’s legs jammed, sending him skidding on the cliff face. Frozen with fear, he stood in awe at the sight ahead. Gliding barefoot was the ashen ghost of who was unmistakably Sarah Sanctamoni. Heading for her own mausoleum, Sanctamoni’s tresses flowed out behind her, her white dress cascading in the wind.

'Quick Frugal, run! Maybe we can catch her.'

'Maybe I don't want to catch her,' Frugal argued.

By the time they had reached the other side, Sanctamoni had vanished.

'Damn it,' said Charlotte, slamming her fist on the obituary. Crunching her knuckles, she tried to pull open the door.

'Are you mad?' protested Frugal, out of breath. 'There's a dead body in there!'

Standing back, Charlotte studied the memorial.

Sarah Sanctamoni, 1982–2015, loving daughter to Miriam and Paul, younger sister to Madeline and wife to Antonious.

Charlotte was taken aback. 'I didn't know they were married.'

'What?' grumbled Frugal, vacantly mumbling to himself.

'Sanctamoni and Antonious were married,' she repeated. Frugal stood up and reread the headstone.

'Well, that explains it then,' he said.

'Explains what?' Charlotte interrogated inquisitively.

'Why they were always arguing.'

#

Back inside the Coliseum, the clock tower chimed twelve times. Frugal shook his watch, waving his wrist. 'Oh crap, you're kidding me. Bloody thing's not working.'

Had Charlotte not been so against violence, a kick up the arse would have surely been on the agenda. Deciding there was no time for that now, they raced the halls, prompting an older and much frailer Guardian to shuffle out of the way. 'No running in the lobby!' he objected.

'Sorry!' shouted Frugal behind him. A quick slide across the freshly polished floor revealed the Labyrinth doors open and an irritable-looking Lauraus pacing the empty room. 'Where have you two been?' he nagged, tapping his timepiece; they were fifteen minutes late. 'We nearly had to go in without you.'

'Sorry!' they apologised together. Then Charlotte remembered Lauraus was the one that should be apologising.

'Can we go now!' snapped Valentine, making no attempt to hide her dismay as she approached the Labyrinth doors, taking note of those famous Avalonian words: *Benediximus*.

They immediately found sand beneath their feet and a white grainy shoreline as far as the eye could see. Clear blue water glistened, the soothing sound of waves giving them a false sense of serenity. Skeletal bones crashed against rocks, bringing back the cold hard reality that danger was most definitely forthcoming.

A hawk hovered in the scorching sky, circling hooting seagulls, flustered because they might just be its next meal. But the majestic bird of prey had another purpose. It dropped a scroll from its grasp, thus delivering the next clue. Lomax reached out to catch it, then unravelled the parchment.

Buccaneers are welcome here,
Come listen to our song.
You'll find the booty and our beauty
Where the absent-minded long.

'Good stuff,' he cheered, winding it up again. 'Bit clearer than the last one.'

London pulled out both pockets, his face plummeting with shame as he declared, 'I've forgotten my polypus pearl.'

Lauraus turned to him in disbelief; then blinked owlishly. 'I expect you were befuddled to leave it behind.' Standing straight, Lauraus assumed a regal pose. 'That means this test mostly relies on you, my friend.' Tapping London twice on the shoulder, he walked away.

'That's great!' London picked up a rock and threw it into the water impatiently. 'Why is the Labyrinth always picking on me?'

'Maybe it doesn't like pretty boys,' teased Lomax, cocking his head and arching a sly brow. Valentine air-punched him, showing a small hint of admiration with the ripple of an upturned lip.

Charlotte sympathised with London; after all, he had also drawn the shortest straw in the last task, spending nearly a week in the sanatorium afterwards.

Lauraus didn't look quite so sympathetic. 'I know it all seems a bit unfair, but think of it like … the Labyrinth believes in your higher calling. It must see great strength in you, as do I!'

'You're so full of shit, Lauraus,' bantered London. 'But for now, it's the best I have, so I'll take it.' He pulled out his sword virtuously. 'Follow me, everybody!'

The pep talk now over, London rolled up his sleeves and led the way.

Lauraus rushed off ahead to join him. 'Mate, I know you're keen and everything, but I think we should slow down and make a plan.'

Passing an anchor the size of a ship, they bore right to a bay walled with rocks.

'No need for a plan,' said London, arriving at a cave. 'I will storm the vicinity and slay the beast.'

Lauraus stopped and rubbed his temples before facepalming. He then turned back to the others. 'Keep your polypus pearls close,' he insisted. 'Whatever is in here likes to eat people.'

Cracks through white rocks lit the floor, and dust swept across the ground, blown by an airstream coming from the other side. Suddenly an awful screeching filled their ears.

But London's reaction was bold; he looked to the path with crinkled eyelids.

'What's happened to him?' spluttered Lomax, shocked by this sudden act of bravery. 'Did he eat the heart of a lion for breakfast?'

'No …' said Lauraus, twisting a lacklustre smile. 'I think it's more like he has a point to prove.'

Lomax concealed a coy snort. 'Awesome, I can't wait for that!'

'What's that beautiful music?' London called out, taking no notice of the shattering bones beneath his chalky boots.

They all stared at each other; obviously London was hearing something different to them.

'Ouch!' Without warning, Frugal took off from the ground and stumbled towards Charlotte. 'Whoa, something sharp just pinched my leg.'

'Don't be stupid, Frugal,' patronised Valentine. 'There's nothing in here, I have twenty-twenty vision and I can't see anything … oh!' Valentine stumbled on her words as a skeletal hand burst through the sand, trying to escape.

'Come on,' said Charlotte, still startled. 'We'd better keep moving.'

With bated breath, they loomed closer to their doom, keeping a tighter formation than before.

Lauraus halted abruptly. 'I don't know what's going to happen to you in there without your pearl, so I'm fastening this rope to your belt; I can't lose my right-hand man.'

Bewitched but fighting it valiantly, London looked worryingly dazed but agreed with a dizzy waggle of the tongue. 'Bah …'

Lauraus knelt to the ground and crumbled a piece of bone between his fingers. 'These once belonged to sailors,' he said, a bold guess as to what was facing them beyond the cavern.

Lomax's face dropped, enlightened by this assumption. Peering through a gap in the rocks, Frugal looked spooked. 'Mermaids!'

London dribbled. 'Mermaids!' he boomed, boss-eyed. 'That's a good one.'

'I'm with Lauraus on this one,' said Valentine, becoming annoyed with her boyfriend's curiosity at the gap between the rocks. 'Abacus warned us about them.'

London stood up and puffed out his chest, determined to be the first to enter. Speeding off blindly, the group had no choice but to follow. At the cave's edge, spectrums of colour came from the bottom of a lagoon, like an underwater rainbow. Falling water hit giant pebbles; these stepping stones provided them with an undesirable path through fallen blossom.

A dozen or so unclothed women were singing, with hair varying in sequence – red, orange, yellow, green, blue, indigo and violet – and fish tails of silver and pearl. Surprised at their beauty, and how much they resembled humans, Charlotte could instantly see why they were so dangerous to men.

Ladies' man London was being tested to the limit as merwomen splashed about giggling flirtatiously. He was failing on an epic scale.

With no regard for his personal safety, London plunged into the water and strode to the female he found the most beautiful, then told her that he thought she was so. He cocked his head towards the scarlet vixen, and she licked her lips in what he supposed was a display of sexual attraction. Out came his well-known cheesy grin. Each gave the other a look of love at first sight.

Lauraus buried his face in his hands as though he had seen this many times, then started tugging him back on the rope like a naughty dog. As London was pulled back to the edge of the pool, his arms and legs drifted out in front of him, his face like mush.

A young flaxen-haired girl picked a flower from the water's edge and handed it to Charlotte in a show of friendship.

'Thank you,' she said, putting it behind her ear.

Lauraus stared at her with captivation in his eyes, momentarily distracted from the task.

When a petite lilac-haired female swam to Lomax, Valentine was provoked into reaction. 'This is stupid,' she said, scornful with jealousy. Positioning herself on one of the pebbles, she transformed to a black panther, then roared.

The beautiful women split from their skins, hissing and shrieking. Their beautiful faces had screwed up into ugly ones, with piercing red eyes and fish-like mouths. The green sharp-toothed creatures then set upon them all.

'See, they're nothing but monsters,' thundered Valentine, pleased to see that Lomax was coming to his senses.

But London did not waver. He made his way back to his beloved, unable to resist any longer. 'Not to me,' he shouted, taking the bulging-eyed fiend in his clutches and sticking his tongue down her throat.

Valentine screwed up her face in disgust.

As his chosen regrew her skin, she caught the attention of the siren in charge. 'Sister, he lies,' the head siren screeched in a shrill tone, leaping to cut London's throat with her fingernails, but to everyone's amazement the redhead turned to protect him.

Grabbing his belt, she pulled him underwater for protection. The swirling of red fibres faded with distance, leaving ripples in the water.

'No!' shouted Lauraus, pulling on the rope, but it had been detached.

Lauraus urgently cast aside his sword then dived in after him. When he didn't come back up, Charlotte's heart sank. Something must have happened; had he also failed the assessment?

The hideous creatures had them surrounded, giving them no choice but to fend for themselves. With their two strongest team members gone and no plan, things weren't looking good.

The odious fangs let off an unpleasant smell. Charlotte gagged as the spewing gas blinded them in a mist of emerald fog. The remaining group fell back to the rocks in an attempt to establish the best formation they could muster before an eerie silence befell them. The team remained unified in an unprecedented show of strength, ready to play a game of death.

'Where have they gone?' bellowed an elfish wisp from somewhere close by.

'Is that you next to me, Frugal, mate?' came a disoriented grumble.

'Of course it's me, Lomax, isn't gonna be one of the girls, is it?'

'Will you two stop arguing!' spat Valentine. 'You're giving away our positions.'

'Oh yeah, I'll move,' mumbled Frugal. 'Wait, what's that sound?'

Dragging noises began drawing in from the direction of the cave, the chattering of bones were coming their way.

'I hope that's not what I think it is,' contemplated Charlotte, her stare trailing through the emerald smog to a pair of malicious red eyes.

Valentine had spotted them too; she was fixed upon the siren with her spine arched and fur standing up on end, the occasional wave of a tail displaying the hatred within.

Leaping forward, the monster took Valentine by her long and spindly whiskers, but an upwards strike of the jaw finished it with a frail snap of the siren's neck.

The sea nymphs appeared to want rid of the panther first, relentlessly attacking from all directions. A momentous fight ensued as they picked off the vile temptresses one by one.

Valentine climbed out of the water, forced to continue as a human. A flick of the hands saw her long claws retracted. A spiralling airborne kick disabled two in one attempt before she landed elegantly on one knee.

Lomax took his captivated eyes away, receiving a bite to the arm. He seized the she-beast, ripping it apart with his bare hands.

Behind them were hundreds of skeletons coming their way, prompting Charlotte to take out her daggers.

'You can't kill them,' yelled Frugal, bridging the gap between them with a lengthy jump, turning another to ice in mid-air.

'What should we do?' Charlotte faltered, having never come across zombie skeletons in any of the books she'd been reading.

Frugal lifted both of his arms, clenching his fists around the bendy branch of a willow that he had summoned. 'We need to bind them,' he then said, handing a rope to her.

'Watch out,' screamed Frugal as one of the sirens crept up on Charlotte like a crocodile.

Charlotte clumsily let go of her daggers, unintentionally cutting the creature in half. The daggers came back to her covered in slippery gunge. 'Shit,' she cussed, flicking goo from her fingers.

The remaining few sirens were becoming quickly outnumbered so they surrendered to the water. The dead sailors were coming to finish the job now anyway.

Charlotte tried to tie the reeds to each of the dagger ends, but had cut her hands to shreds with every attempt so far; the slime was making it slippery too, so she leant to the water to wash them.

Valentine seized one of the aerial vines and used it to cross to the opposite side of the pool like a trapeze artist. She couldn't leave Frugal to face the skeletons alone. Lomax proudly followed his girl.

'Well, I guess that's us out too then!' Lomax accepted, looking tired as he got into stance. Frugal and Valentine were equally exhausted and ready for the fight to be finished.

Finally, Charlotte managed to secure the vines. She pulled the daggers to her side and took a deep breath, letting go of them with clear mindful instruction.

The advancing corpses were instantly pulled back from where they stood, so quickly their limbs didn't even touch the ground, and they found themselves spine-bound to the cave wall.

'Finish them, Frugal,' she shouted out, mind racing because the binding wouldn't hold them long.

'With pleasure,' said Frugal, stepping out with a ball of white fire in hand. He blew the hypnotic flames towards the skeletons, turning the bones to ashes where they stood.

When it was over, Charlotte recalled the daggers, placing them in the scabbards to her side.

'Hey, Frugal, why didn't you do that anyway?' Lomax questioned, regaining his normal relaxed posture.

'Because I can't control where it goes once I let it go, I don't wanna be responsible for any of you failing your assessment. Besides, I would only use it under strict conditions in a real-life situation anyways.'

'You should have used it,' complained Lomax. 'Then only some of us would be out instead of all of us.'

'That's not fair, Lomax,' quarrelled Valentine. 'You can't make that judgement for everyone.'

'It's OK, Valentine,' interrupted Frugal. 'Because when Lomax can turn skeletons to ashes, he can make that judgement for himself …'

The arguing continued, but Charlotte had zoned out because she had noticed a faint sobbing coming from a blossom-filled rock pool.

The teenage mergirl who had given Charlotte the flower cowered, frightened, in the corner sure she was going to be attacked.

'It's OK,' Charlotte said softly. 'I'm not going to hurt you.'

Valentine licked her lips for the taste of mermaid blood, but Charlotte stood in her path protectively. 'No,' she ordered. 'She is different to the others.'

Valentine nodded, then took her place at Lomax's side.

Charlotte turned to the yellow-haired maiden. 'We are looking for the medallion, do you know where it is?'

'It is already yours,' she gently advised, returning gracefully to the teary waters.

'What did she mean by that?' snarled Lomax, annoyed that Charlotte had let her get away.

For a few seconds the lake was still, then bubbles came to the surface, popping with a thin veil of green blood. Charlotte panicked; had something gone wrong? 'Lauraus,' she screeched, relieved to find him and London ripping through the water, and carrying the second silver elemental medallion.

Lauraus unblocked London's airway and he started coughing. Watching, Lomax noticed that London was covered from head to toe in green slime. 'Where's all that come from?' he asked, handing London his scarf to wipe it away.

'London just bargained with the merqueen,' said Lauraus. 'She tried to go back on her word.'

'Wow,' Lomax gulped, looking impressed. 'I guess you really do have some moves.'

At that moment a door appeared, ornate gold and emblazoned with the familiar words *Magnum Opus.*

Lauraus helped his friend out of the pea-green water. 'Come on, mate, let's get you back up to the sanatorium. I expect they've still got your get-well-soon cards somewhere.'

As London turned back, he stared upon the face of the redhead that had helped him, his face filling with sorrow. As they took one last look at each other, she seemed genuinely sad to see him go, a tear falling down her cheek. She swam down, her sobs echoing through the water until she was out of sight.

CHAPTER TWELVE

GREGORY'S GORGE

It had been a long and frosty winter, but spring had finally arrived. Charlotte had been waking to the sound of birds for days now, reminding her that she hadn't left the Coliseum properly for months.

Pulling aside her chamber rug and lifting the floorboard, she took out Kristoffer Enoch's very own copy of his *Life and Legacy*, emerging through the atrium door ten minutes later to the sweet smell of fresh rain.

Rising temperatures meant that Guardians were congregating outside the walls more frequently and, with so many interesting places to visit, Charlotte took some time to explore.

She nervously crossed magma bridge to a less crowded part of the grounds, but realised she must have made a wrong turn when she came out on to hundreds of small grassy mounds with windows. When something small and grey opened one of them, then growled, she turned back, mistakenly going even further in the wrong direction. She stumbled across a much smaller bridge, but it seemed equally secure enough to cross so went to see what was on the other side.

The winding path led to an overgrown meadow; the overlooking wall had no windows meaning that she must have been at the back of the Coliseum. Hidden behind an ocean of bluebells was a small courtyard that she'd never noticed before. There were no windows looking on to it and, judging by the overgrown hedges, nobody else seemed to care that it was there. This, she decided, would be a perfect spot for a bit of private reading.

Taking the book from her bag, she quickly peered up through a small gap in the flowers to check that nobody was coming.

She had been analysing this section of the book for days. The difficulty had been that some of the pages had faded over time, making it barely legible.

The place had been marked out by a triangular symbol inside the margins; contained within the pyramid was a drawn-in eye. Charlotte was able to determine that this represented one of the Obelisks and the eye was supposed to be the soul that lived inside. A few pages before had a clearly printed and still decipherable title, so she knew she was reading a continuation of 'The Legend of the First Seven' that wasn't in the modern copy of his life's account.

Heed with warning: to deter trespassers, the fury of he be cast on any man that dare to seek that sacred tree, said to contain the power of the almighty himself. The warning received no pardon; not even his sons and daughters dare quench their curiosity. Except for one, the youngest of his brood, who never cared for rules.

The faceless tree would whisper, frightening the child, but the more familiar the soft voice became the more it was trusted, until one day the golden fruit was harvested. The moment it touched her lips, poison consumed her heart, but she did not die, only grew more captivated by the tree.

A decade passed by. In those passing years, Lilith would slip away unnoticed whilst her brothers and sisters guarded the wheel of spirit.

And on the twelfth night, she was stunned to find another snacking on the fruit. A fight erupted between the pair, but his strength was no match for her. Because he was attracted to her a deal was struck, that they would both eat from the tree without conflict.

Every night she returned as she had before, and for a long time neither spoke until the hidden attraction could be concealed no more. Eventually falling in love, the couple found it too hard to bear; they did not want to be parted another night longer.

Out of desperation, Lilith decided to ask her father if they could marry then the separation would no longer be essential. But Jupiter was enraged. He had ordered that she never go forth to that sacred place and, as punishment, Jupiter instead met him that night and murdered him.

For forty days and forty nights Lilith grieved for the man she had come to love, then on that eve she was sent back to be with her brothers and sisters.

Except something had changed inside. With a vengeful heart she slipped poison into their wine whilst they were sleeping, then the next day bound them each to the sundial, sacrificing their bodies to the end of days.

As golden rain poured down from the heavens, Jupiter rose from a cloud of thunder, discovering the sundial's breach as the Golden Dawn was unleashed upon his people. His sons and daughters had failed him. The end of days was taking place without his authority.

Outraged, Jupiter strode down from his vaporous pedestal, and stormed the Isle of Apples like a beast to the flame, but found each of his beloved children fastened to the spinning wheel, blood emptied from their lifeless bodies. Their souls had been cast forth to the stones that had been sent to protect them.

He looked to his only remaining child for an answer, to find hatred glint her eyes. Lilith struck a dagger to her heart in an attempt to flee the imminent wrath of her father. A seventh stone appeared as the ritual was unintentionally repeated.

Jupiter halted the wheel with a strike of his thunderbolt, then cast it to the other direction, reversing the act, but it was too late for his sons and daughters; and the stones vanished before his eyes.

Consumed with grief, Jupiter ordered the sundial destroyed. But no one could destroy it, not even himself. In desperation he approached his only remaining counsel, a lonesome old hag that lived in an isolated part of Feign Forest. Such a meagre counsel for a spirit almighty, but a true seer and worker of the divine.

'The dial cannot be destroyed without the stones, for where there is a beginning there must always be an end. But …' The hag plucked a hair from Jupiter's head and turned it to a snake in the blink of an eye as it coiled around, turning gold and plated.

'This Amulet of Armistice will keep your subjects safe should the wheel be reactivated. Only the one that wears this talisman can bring forth equilibrium.'

Jupiter took the band with an oversized finger, but no sooner had he touched it than it disappeared. 'Where has it gone?' he ordered, but the hag simply smiled. 'To begin its purpose.'

'And what of the stones?'

'They have been given existence eternally. Their purpose has been justified, because the sundial can no longer be activated without them. But there is one.' The old hag cast one of her eyes into her peppery cauldron, allowing Jupiter to see the truth inside the water. He stared upon the face of his youngest daughter with regret in his eyes. 'What have I created?'

Upon return, Jupiter ordered a plaque be placed upon the tree of golden apples, to honour his brave sons and daughters, enchanted to remain forever.

By chance, some thousands of years on, a charlatan came by that garden. Hung upon the branch of the tree was a golden bracelet that looked to be valuable. After feasting on golden fruits he took it back to his village. He began to notice voiceless whispers; he had been gifted with the ability to hear people's thoughts. He could have sold the bracelet for two pieces of gold but instead decided that he could make more gold by using its power.

So that night he took his place at the poker table. Simply by shutting his eyes he was able to see the cards in reverse and made more than the bracelet's worth in one night.

As time passed by his lucky streak brought him a lot of unwanted attention and one day he bragged of his changing fortune whilst intoxicated with mead. An angry Cyclops ordered he remove the band or he would take his life. The charlatan had made more than enough gold; it wasn't worth dying over, so he tried to remove it but it would not come off.

He was not a rich man for much longer. His executioner intent on taking his prize, but in the charlatan's death the bracelet vanished, succeeding to the next chosen and leaving the Cyclops bewildered.

Closing the book, she laid it gently on her lap. She had scanned the pages many times but only here did it refer to an Amulet of Armistice. It was the only reference in any book, for that matter; the library had no record of such an object either. Sighing in frustration, she knew she should be pleased because she was one step closer to finding out about the band, but in reality she was still so far from the truth. She was correct in her theory that the band had been deliberately put there, and that it had chosen her itself.

Redirecting the natural view of her eyes towards the graveyard, she noticed a man wearing a grey fur cloak that trailed in the wind. Beneath the hood were those unmistakable wolf eyes. Antonious had returned.

Upon her return from the Labyrinth last month, she had scrawled a poorly written scroll to him, telling him about her and Frugal's encounter with Sanctamoni's ghost.

She had received an instantaneous reply in the form of an aggressive order, demanding that she and Frugal tell no one what they saw. She had been wondering for weeks whether she had done the right thing by not mentioning it to Abacus.

Charlotte jumped to her feet to shout out to Antonious, but she needn't have bothered because he was just as keen to see her as she was to see him.

He placed an index finger over his lips, taking her elbow then pulling her behind the wall, out of sight and earshot of anyone else.

'Did you tell anyone you saw Sarah?' he barked, glowering into her eyes.

'No,' she responded. 'You asked me not to.'

Antonious exhaled in one sharp breath, then relaxed his

shoulders. He turned and looked away, but Charlotte sensed he had been impressed by her loyalty.

'Why don't you want me to say anything, Antonious?'

'Because I saw her,' he said with a glimmer of hope in his eyes. He quickly returned to his usual brutal behaviour. 'I don't want anyone to frighten her away.'

Charlotte could understand; there must have been half of Avaland that desired to speak with her, even as a ghost. Because Antonious was a friend, she agreed; anyway, this arrangement could also work in her favour. She continued with the conversation.

'So, I take it you're back now, then?' she asked, breaking the subject a bit.

'I don't have to be!' he snapped aggressively, but Charlotte was starting to understand him; he couldn't help himself, it was the dog in him.

'Antonious, I wonder if I might ask you something? But I, like you, would also require your discretion.'

Antonious gave her a shady glance of suspicion. He didn't say a word, but the answer was in his eyes.

'What is the Amulet of Armistice?'

He raised his eyebrows, suggesting that he didn't feel comfortable with the question, but he didn't really have a choice after Charlotte had agreed to keep his secret. 'It is an enchanted band, handed down through death, but it always cherry-picks its next minder.'

'Is the minder destined to become part of the Golden Dawn?' she asked, still needing clarification.

Antonious lowered his face. 'Yes, to become the shield, built to deter the end of days.'

Charlotte couldn't believe what she was hearing. 'If it's so important then why can't I find it in any of the books?'

As he shook his head, Charlotte saw Antonious smile for the first time. 'The books were destroyed a long time ago, along with all their references, including those that were living. Not even the soldiers that destroyed them were kept alive. Why do you even ask these questions, Charlotte?'

For a moment she wondered whether to tell him, but knew he wouldn't say anything, because she knew how much he loved Sarah.

Holding up her arm, she took down her sleeve and looked up at him. 'Because I am the shield.'

Antonious looked closer. Taking her arm, he held up the band, unable to believe what he was seeing. It twisted on her arm like a snake, then glimmered in the sunlight.

Without warning, a black-haired fellow walked up to join them, removing his hat to greet them. 'Ah, there you are, my old chap,' he greeted. 'How on Saturn's castrated testicles are you?'

Charlotte politely smiled at the middle-aged gent but didn't engage.

'Fine,' barked Antonious, much more like his usual self, before walking off abruptly.

The man nodded nervously. 'Great, wonderful!'

People skills were not Antonious Draconi's greatest asset, but luckily everyone here knew it so didn't take any offence.

The gentleman bowed to Charlotte, then put his hat back on his head before vacating.

#

Part three of the assessment was upon them. Frugal rubbed his hands together in the cold nervously and Mandy wiped the smears on her sceptre, but Charlotte felt more ready than she'd ever been.

Once again, Lauraus directed the group. 'I've been speaking to some of the others,' he said. 'They've reported numerous losses, which means we are in the lead, but it also means we should expect new arrivals because we are the only original team to remain complete.'

Frugal and Mandy stared at each other. They already knew that they were going to be the first ones to be separated from the rest of the group because they had been the only ones absent from the lily pads on the first day of this assessment.

With little or no idea of what to expect, they confronted the Labyrinth doors for the third time. The only complete group in their year.

Charlotte was expecting the tasks to get harder, so held her hands ready to draw her daggers at a moment's notice.

Their background changed once again. Like a watercolour painting in the rain, a new set of surroundings came into view. Parallel hedges ran alongside them, so tall it was difficult to see the snowy sky. Charlotte pulled her coat in closer on herself, then zipped it up to her chin. The group then paused to take warmer clothes from their satchels, all except Lomax, who was already wearing his very own fur coat.

London pressed a tiny button on his chest and his whole body was enveloped by an inflatable suit. 'What on earth are you wearing?' sniggered Lomax with a snarky smile.

But London didn't hear him from beneath what looked like a blow-up deep-sea diver's outfit, so Lauraus answered for him.

'It's one of his latest contracts,' said Lauraus. 'He's modelling a new range of aerobic wear.'

Because the path was difficult to see in the blizzard, Charlotte took out her butterfly candles and let them go so they could fly out ahead of the group. They silently made their way down the path with great difficulty, but found themselves at another set of parallel hedges going in the other direction.

Continuing the path for some distance, they once again found themselves at another set of twinned hedges.

'We're in a maze,' croaked Valentine, her throat as cold as ice.

'Have we missed the scroll?' cautioned London from inside his inflatable bodywarmer. Like a giant marshmallow, he attempted to point out behind him into nothingness. 'Should we go back?'

'No,' stepped in Charlotte, her eyes a glimmer of white. 'The reason we haven't seen the scroll is because we are supposed to find our way out first.'

For two hours they tried to navigate their way through in an unrelenting blizzard. They were cold, hungry and morale in the group was getting low.

After making no real progress, Mandy appeared to have found something in the snow. Sticking out a woolly glove, she halted everyone in their tracks. Valentine was starting to get irritable, so pushed her way to the front. 'What is it?' she hissed.

'Look,' she said, pointing a finger to the ground. 'There are footprints in the snow, we're going around in circles.'

Lauraus marched to the front to inspect the footprints. It was unmistakably them, unless there was another marshmallow with legs wandering about the maze.

'We are playing this maze at its own game; we need to look at it from a new angle.' No sooner had he muttered his last words than Valentine leapt behind him and extended her claws to the verge so that she could climb the hedgerow one paw at a time until she'd reached the top.

She wobbled with the wind, her ears tensed and resting flat against her head as she was hit by each oncoming bullet of snow. Eyes hard and focused she carried out her directive to obtain an aerial perspective; once she had done so, she leapt down and transformed back into the warrior woman they knew so well.

'It's maze for as far as the eye can see,' she said. 'There's no way we're getting out.'

Another attempt by Lomax was futile; he ran at the bushes with all his might, but they were too strong to break through.

Lauraus rested his chin to his palm and looked thoughtful. 'If we can't go sideways or up, then maybe we need to go …' Cupping his gloves, he began to dig out the snow beneath him.

Lomax attempted a joke. 'If you find any chicken drumsticks down there, mate, can you let me know?'

No one suspected for one second he would find anything, so they were surprised when he began to remove bricks from the path. They were loose and came away easily, and when a hole was revealed, the rest of the group started to dig with their hands.

Together they made a hole large enough to climb through.

'I never would have thought of that,' declared Lomax with a sideways tilt of the head as he questioned whether or not he could fit through.

Charlotte poked her head through the gap first, to take a look at what was on the other side.

It was an upside-down hut with windows. Inside, there was a fireplace on the ceiling with roaring flames.

'What's down there?' asked Lauraus, but Charlotte ignored him so she could warm her face a little longer.

She jumped down, legs first, falling upwards onto the ceiling beside the hole. Disoriented, it took a moment for her eyes to adjust. It hadn't been the room that was upside down, it had been her.

Lauraus came flying through the air, only to land directly next to her with a confused shake of the head. The others followed one at a time; Lomax was the last to burst through, leaving a trail of debris because he was correct, he did not fit through the hole that they had made, his large frame making it much bigger.

'That was weird,' said Lomax, wiping away the dust and getting to his paws.

They were not in an upside-down room after all, they had just entered it through the ceiling. On a wooden table beside the fireplace was a long, unravelled piece of parchment.

'The clue!' exclaimed Mandy. Taking it at once, she cleared her throat.

Some think I'm a monster,
Some give me wide berth.
Bring forth metamorphosis,
Create my rebirth.

'Well, that's not easy, is it?' complained Valentine. '*Some think I'm a monster, create my rebirth*? What on earth is that supposed to mean?'

Mandy disagreed entirely. 'There aren't many monsters that undergo the process of metamorphosis. It's obvious that it's talking about a cockatrice.'

'What's a cockatrice?' asked Charlotte, certain she'd never heard of one before.

'They are more commonly known as nightingales. Half dragon, half phoenix, they are not born of nature; you can only create them with a spell.'

'Look where we are, guys,' said Lomax, opening the door. 'I've seen this hut before; I always wondered what it was doing here.'

Lauraus and London marched over to the door to take a look outside. They found themselves on a very small island at the point where three rivers met.

'Look on the door,' said Valentine. 'It's a picture of a cockatrice, I guess you were right then, Mandy.'

They followed Lomax outside whilst he looked for a way to cross the river. 'It's too deep to cross here, we will drown.'

London studied the direction of the flowing water. 'We need to get to Gregory's Gorge.'

'To bring forth metamorphosis,' said Frugal, 'we need a dragon's egg.'

'But we don't just need a dragon's egg, Frugal,' argued Valentine. 'We need all sorts of things to turn a dragon into a cockatrice. Not just that they are deadly; it could be dangerous.'

'Not in here it won't be,' stated London, who had since removed and stowed away his deep-sea diving outfit. Considering London had been singled out in the last two challenges, Valentine couldn't really complain.

'Berth is a cave; that's where the mightiest dragons live,' continued London with the investigation, unperturbed.

Frugal looked nervous. He liked eggs but he could say with unequivocal certainty that he didn't like dragon eggs.

'I know where we are!' said Mandy, looking at the map. 'Dead man's triangle.'

'Why is it called dead man's triangle?' asked Charlotte nervously.

'Because there is no way out,' determined Lauraus with a hastening remark.

'No way out, my arse,' broke in London, striding out confidently to the rescue. 'I used to ride the lily pads here when I was a boy,' he said cheerfully. 'Lauraus, you did it too, once –remember?'

'Was that the time I fell off and broke my arm and my father wouldn't let me see you again for two years?' said Lauraus, punching London's aloft-clenched fist. 'We'll go in pairs.'

Mandy held up her copy of the map to the light. 'This is where the three main Avalonian rivers meet; according to this map, downstream will take us to Gregory's Gorge.'

Lauraus put everyone in pairs apart from Lomax.

But London helpfully stepped in. 'Lomax, you're too heavy to be paired with anyone, in fact I wouldn't be surprised if you sink.' London patted him on the back. 'But good luck.'

Lomax screwed up his chin. 'Speak for yourself,' he said. 'Can I borrow your stupid outfit just in case?'

London turned his head and leapt onto a lily pad. 'It wouldn't fit you, you're too fat!'

Without thinking, Charlotte jumped on to join him, almost slipping, but London grabbed her hand and pulled her back up. 'Be careful,' he said. 'They're a bit slimy.' London held the stalk out in front of him to steer as they cascaded down the rapids with speed.

Lauraus tightened his lips with shock because he'd assumed that they were going together, but Valentine boarded the next giant leaf with him.

Lomax took a nervous run-up, landing so centrally that water burst up from the edges and showered him like a wet dog. He trailed behind them, spiralling out of control and much slower.

Mandy and Frugal waited on the embankment for the next lily pad to pass, but one did not come. The others had almost turned a meandering bank when they were finally able to board.

'There's my house!' Charlotte heard Frugal screaming way off in the distance 'Mum! Dad!'

Lauraus shouted back across the water. 'Mandy! Tell him to sit down, he could fall in.'

Charlotte could just about make out Frugal, with Mandy pulling him ruthlessly back to safety.

'The downstream rivers lead to the sea,' London shouted into her ear. 'We need to get to the coast; that's where we will find the right kind of dragon.'

Straight ahead, the land started to rip apart, causing a rush of water to form another river. 'Veer right,' shouted London. 'The Labyrinth is trying to separate us.'

The first two lily pads managed to pass quite safely, but Charlotte couldn't help feeling that in the case of Lomax it was just luck that allowed him to pass safely, because he was still spinning out of control, and probably hadn't even noticed the landslide. As she looked back in sadness, Mandy and Frugal got caught up in the current as she had expected they would, and both drifted away with the tidal wave.

Charlotte could only watch on helplessly as London took them in the opposite direction. Something she knew Lauraus wouldn't have done, which made her instantly regret not sharing with him.

Lauraus saw the panicked look on her face and tried to speed towards her. 'They'll be OK!' he said with assurance in his voice. 'The Labyrinth wants to separate us now, it's been doing it to other groups.'

'We've been lucky to make it this far together,' London said, trying to reassure her further.

The river meandered through valleys and mountains. Leaves fell from Feign Forest to their heads. Lomax had regained some control of his lily pad, but his dignity had gone right out of the window.

The flow of the river slowed to almost a stop, held back because leaves had scattered on the water so deeply they were unable to move. All of the boys reached up to snap branches from the trees and propelled the lily pads forward, using them as rowing oars.

The sun was setting in the sky; although Charlotte had no desire to be trapped in Feign Forest at nightfall, she couldn't help but appreciate the beautiful sunset. She looked back at Valentine and Lauraus. They appeared to be talking about something in quite some depth, and she wondered what the topic might be.

'You've come along really well, Charlotte,' said London. 'I must admit when you first came I thought you would be completely useless; but I have to say, you've exceeded my expectations.'

'Thanks,' said Charlotte irritably.

By the looks of things, Lomax was getting sick of being by himself so had meandered to the bank and climbed up the mud. The leaves were like quicksand but somehow he managed to stumble up to the top. 'Any closer to the ocean from here and we'll go over that waterfall.' He pointed in the distance beyond the trees.

'It's not far from here,' said Lauraus, helping Valentine onto the embankment.

Charlotte wasn't quite as lucky as Valentine; London didn't help her at all and she fell straight into the marsh.

Having been a tomboy, she had lots of experience in getting covered with mud, but this was horrible because the mud was smelly.

As nightfall descended they waded through the leaves onto the cliffs; Lauraus lagged behind to make sure she was safe, but kept trying not to laugh because now she was covered in leaves that had stuck to the mud.

The sun was setting through the valley and it was beautiful.

'I think we should have a break,' said Lauraus, trying not to sound pushy. 'Charlotte needs a wash, if we take her into the gorge like that she'll be eaten within minutes.'

Everyone nodded in agreement and went their separate ways. London, who was the only one there that was single, went off alone.

Lauraus brushed his hand up against Charlotte affectionately and she turned to face him, but he did not kiss her; he threw her backwards into the water. Because she hadn't been expecting it, she inhaled some liquid down the wrong hole, but by the time she'd risen to the top she realised he was in there with her too.

It was becoming usual practice for them to say what they needed with their eyes. He leant her up against the rock and kissed her. There they stayed until the sun had set completely.

It was completely dark, apart from a light that was glowing under the water. She stopped kissing him to check it out. 'It's the coral,' said Lauraus, who was just as mesmerised. 'It's luminescent.'

Something swam out of the coral towards her, making her jolt back.

'It's OK, it's only the fish,' he continued. 'Everything living glows in the dark here.'

'Right, I've had enough of sitting on my own now,' complained London, appearing from the rocks. 'Where is everybody? Oi, knock it off you two, you're starting to make me feel left out, what with those two over there as well.' London pointed his thumb over his shoulder.

Lomax and Valentine were flirting; he pulled her behind the rock out of view, probably to kiss her.

'You got your snog last time,' joked Lauraus. London laughed and left them a bit longer.

Lauraus helped Charlotte out of the water, and guarded a cave so she could slip behind the rocks to get changed into her spare clothes.

'We need to move forward quickly from here,' said Lauraus with directness as she slipped out again. 'Any lingering and we could be hunted. Dragons are renowned for it.'

They jumped through the rocks with a spring in their step. There was a natural pathway through that took them to different heights. The river flowed alongside as total darkness fell upon them and their surroundings started to change.

A narrow valley appeared between the mountains; a steep rocky wall made up of natural pockets of sediment in which birds were nesting.

They were getting tired, so decided to stop here to rest, just at the point that the birds were starting to become small luminous dragons. It was a spectacular sight; nothing but darkness against the multicoloured patterns of fish and glowing dragons of every colour. Diving from the cliff face in search of meat, several plunged headfirst into the water, capturing fish before soaring back into the sky.

Charlotte was feeling excited. This was like nothing she'd experienced; she felt like she was on another planet. Even some of the plants were insect-like and glowing. A flower opened its petals and sneezed glowing pollen into the air, which unravelled into little flies.

Running and hiding behind rocks was hard; Lomax couldn't help being so large, but it was proving an obstacle, so they decided a change of tactic and entered the ravine.

Dragons dived into the water to hunt the opalescent fish that swam beneath. Coral lit up in shades of pink when they entered, which helped them see where they were going.

'Don't worry,' said Lauraus. 'You're safe, the dragons here are only interested in the fish; it's the bigger ones we need to watch out for.'

'Can't we just take one of these dragon eggs?' asked Lomax, starting to notice their increasing size.

'No, it won't work,' said Lauraus. 'The egg needs to be at least thirty centimetres in length.'

'Good job Frugal's not here,' joked Lomax. 'He would have gorged on all the eggs.'

Nobody laughed at Lomax's rubbish joke.

'Is it me or are they starting to look more carnivorous now?' asked Valentine urgently.

Diving softly beneath the water, they swam to the shoreline, coming up into a pebble gully. From here you could see the ocean. Silently crossing the natural pathway through the rocks, they found themselves looking out up to the furthest cliff face, home to what looked like hundreds of dinosaurs with wings. The ground shook when they left their nests to hunt.

Albeit scared half to death, Charlotte was equally as fascinated. It was amazing to see how many different species there were. Some looked friendlier than others, because they had longer necks and rounder faces. The flat teeth probably meant they were herbivores. But even the friendlier ones were massive and could easily crush you.

'We need to find the biggest carnivore here,' said Lauraus earnestly.

'Fuck off, mate,' cussed Lomax loudly. 'You are having a laugh, aren't you?'

'No, he's serious,' joked London.

'I'll just distract it for you, shall I?' continued Lomax. 'Why don't I just go out there and start doing the hokey-cokey?'

'The what?' grimaced Valentine in a rasping tone.

'I don't know what that is,' chirped Lauraus vaguely. 'But that's a bloody good idea.'

So five absolutely terrified friends climbed the cliffs in moonlight. The only thing they had in their favour was that they blended in to the cliffs. They didn't speak to each other for fear of drawing attention to themselves. The plan was simple. Steal an egg from an empty nest and get back over the cliff top as quickly as possible.

Knowing no real harm could come to her made her feel a little braver than she would have felt normally under the same circumstances, but then this situation was far from normal. Adrenaline had taken over, which was noticeable to the others because she was climbing much faster than them. Lack of being able to communicate was becoming detrimental to their progress and it was becoming clearer that she was going to have to take the lead on this one.

Finally finding an empty nest, she swung on a vine and landed inside; she was much further ahead than the others. She crammed a freckled egg into her satchel and swung it onto her shoulder.

Again she climbed the vine, and she thought she'd done it when to her horror a dark pink dragon with four blue stripes across its nose flew back into the nest just inches from her. Frozen with fear, she hoped it wouldn't notice the missing egg and for a few seconds it didn't.

Valentine was above her now, urging her to pass up the satchel, but beneath them the dragon stirred, having now realised that one of its eggs was gone.

Tugging on the top strap, Valentine pulled the bag upwards and Charlotte released the clip to detach it from her body. To her horror, the release of the clip made a loud sound – *click* – and the dragon looked straight up towards her.

Jumping at her, the beast snapped towards her legs. Valentine made it over with the egg but Charlotte was still in mid-air, hanging from a vine with no escape.

The boys quickly started to provide a distraction. Lauraus stabbed the dragon in the foot. 'Leave my girlfriend alone, you monster!' But it didn't listen, just tossed him out to sea with one kick.

The dragon then picked up Lomax by his satchel and threw him out towards Lauraus. Charlotte climbed the vine and she was almost at the top, but she couldn't get over the edge and she didn't have her tools to help because Valentine had her bag.

London boldly drew his sword and confronted the dragon in a final attempt to make sure Charlotte made it over the top. As London was trying to think of something noble to say, the dragon's wing knocked him sideways over the cliff and headfirst into the water with the other two.

A hand finally came out from over the cliff top and gratefully Charlotte took it. Whilst watching the boys drift out to sea, she was pulled to safety.

'Thanks,' she said, her heart sinking at once because standing before her was not Valentine but Sinope.

CHAPTER THIRTEEN

APOLLO'S FOUNTAIN

Charlotte had spent an entire month preparing for the oncoming test, but the recent encounters with Sinope were leaving her increasingly uncomfortable. To create a cockatrice was one of the most difficult pieces of magic one could perform and to do it with such a negative atmosphere between team members made it all the harder.

Sinope refused to talk to her about anything other than the task at hand, which in some ways Charlotte respected, because the approach was professional.

Thankfully Valentine was around to help ease some of the tension, but cracking jokes was not something she was very good at and made for some interesting dirty looks coming from Sinope's way.

The main event was drawing closer and, so far, they had found the majority of ingredients that they needed to perform the looming spell. A very old dusty hardback on the topmost shelf at the back of the library saw them hidden away for hours with nothing but butterfly candles for light, scribbling down a complete set of instructions copied word for word.

The list of ingredients proved even trickier to get hold of, but after rallying around for weeks in Prince Street and a little help from Sinope's father, they were almost prepared.

Valentine had been sent to collect the last item on the list, mail-ordered in from a little apothecary in Bulgaria. Mail-ordered items were delivered to the village, so Charlotte and Sinope were alone together for the first time, on a back table in the dimly lit library early that morning.

Sinope recounted her list of instructions as she had done so every breakfast time for the last few weeks, so they were completely embedded in their minds.

Arms folded, Sinope tilted her head to the notebook she had scribbled with comments. At the top of the page was the clue they had been given but not read out on the occasion of the last test.

The Talisman of fire you seek,
a fourth and final round.
Come gather and infuse my steep
to galvanise my sound.

'So, this is the only instruction we could find about how to do that,' said Sinope, reading from her notes. '*Galvanisation of the songbird infusion heated to the second degree. Of fountain water it is thought that the more that is given, sufficiently more one will flourish. Saith the deadly nightshade, bruised and heated in the water when drank, kernels in the throat. To such a pinch of each powder initiates hath charm to rouse.*'

Charlotte stared at her with confusion, trying to remember the things they'd gone over last time. 'So it's basically saying, the potion needs to be hot but not boiling.'

Sinope rubbed her temples. 'The infusion mustn't let out one bubble; if it does the whole thing is ruined and we probably won't have time to start again. Then we've failed.'

'Right!' nodded Charlotte. 'No bubbles, got it! It's a good job we are going over all of this because I find it very difficult to understand.'

'Maybe Valentine should brew the potion,' said Sinope, letting out a harsh breath.

'Why don't you do it instead?' argued Charlotte. 'You're the one that seems to know everything.'

This presented Sinope with an opportunity to raise her voice. 'I can't do it because I need to prepare the ingredients!'

A Cyclops on the next table slammed his fist into the book he was reading. 'SHH!'

Sinope pulled a bug-eyed face at him then continued to read the instructions from her pad. *Enchanted water as desired. One handful of deadly nightshade, bruised. One ladle of frogspawn. Liver of toad...*

Charlotte bowed her head awkwardly. 'Don't you think we should talk things through before we go in there?'

'Talk about what!' yelled Sinope, giving her a mirthless laugh. 'How you stole my fiancé? Yeah, sure, Charlotte, tell me the details, I'd love to hear it!'

Obviously, Charlotte was not going to do that so she backed into her chair quietly.

'*Ten milligrams of cornium concordium,* Valentine's picking that up as we speak.'

'You speak, you mean,' squabbled Charlotte, but Sinope ignored her.

'*One pinch each of: powdered dittany, red Pixie dust or periculam powder. Warning: potion recommended for butterflies, birds, dragons or humans only. Do not use with bats, sylphs or any breed of phoenix.* So, as we've agreed, you're mixing the potion. I will prepare the ingredients and Valentine can deal with the dragon.' Sinope then pointed a finger at her aggressively. 'One spill and the whole thing is messed up,' she snapped as though expecting that to occur.

Charlotte's mind, however, was on other things, and seeing as though Sinope insisted on talking to her like this, she mirrored her aggression. 'Lauraus told me you two don't get on. Don't you want to marry someone you love?'

Sinope screwed up her face and leant closer, with clenched teeth. 'What do you know about it, anyway? I wouldn't expect Charlotte Crump to understand anything about duty. We were betrothed! Do you know how humiliating this has all been for me? Thank Jupiter no one outside the Coliseum knows anything. I mean, what are they all going to say when they find out?' Sinope turned her face away to hide a tear, making Charlotte feel guilty. They weren't getting anywhere anyway, so she decided to drop the conversation entirely. Yet another glimpse through Sinope's hard shell left her feeling regretful that she'd not handled things differently. Maybe she and Lauraus had started their relationship too soon.

Sinope slammed her book shut and stormed off, leaving Charlotte alone in a room full of blinking eyes and dusty shadows. The friendly fellow that had interrupted her conversation with Antonious scribbled something in his notebook and shook his head disapprovingly.

As she ventured through the passageways in pursuit of food, Charlotte knew she had to keep an open mind and not feel too guilty. Frugal had warned her about how manipulative Sinope could be. Nerves had been affecting her appetite lately, and she knew she needed to keep her strength up with the next task so close by.

She caught sight of Antonious at the top of the corridor, but when he recognised her he began walking in the opposite direction. She knew he'd been avoiding her for fear of having any awkward discussions. She called out his name, but he ignored her. Charlotte wondered why she'd expected him to turn back; she knew they weren't great friends, why would he care about her?

Out of nowhere, a pair of green hands reached across her eyes. She really hoped it was Frugal; she needed to see a friendly face right now.

'Alright?' came the unambiguous voice. 'Where are you off to?'

'I'm grabbing some breakfast,' she told him, pursing a bottom lip. 'You coming?'

Frugal pulled out his hardboiled-egg-stuffed pockets. 'Nah, I've already been. Got an appointment with Gamelyn. Are you OK, Sinope's not giving you a hard time, is she? She just barged into me and didn't apologise.'

Putting his arm around her shoulder, Frugal walked her to the hall. 'You look terrible,' he said. 'Whatever she's saying, don't listen to her. Honestly, she's a complete cow and everyone knows it.'

Charlotte laughed, but she knew deep down Sinope had a right to be angry. 'She hasn't done anything wrong though Frugal, I think she might still like him, you know.'

Frugal blew a big raspberry. 'Yeah, right, she doesn't like anyone but herself.'

Charlotte attempted to change the subject. 'How are the preparations going for the next task?'

Frugal and Mandy had already recounted their last adventure inside the Labyrinth. Apparently, they had drifted for miles down that watery channel with no control and gaining momentum the further they went. It ended with a brief encounter with Sinope's friends that sent Frugal into hysterics with the memory of it. The lily pad had barged into a Troll on a cliff top. The impact had repelled them back to safety, but unfortunately the Troll was knocked off with the medallion.

'It's a nightmare,' he giggled. 'None of Sinope's friends like us.' Frugal leant in closer to whisper. 'Listen, we overheard them talking to each other. Apparently Sinope just disappeared in the middle of the task. I reckon she bailed on them to find you and Lauraus; I mean, everyone knew you two were on the same team.'

But Charlotte wasn't convinced. She knew Frugal didn't like Sinope, so she preferred to keep an open mind.

Frugal popped a boiled egg into his mouth and mumbled, 'Anyway, I'd better go, see you in a bit.'

As Charlotte entered the hall the room fell silent, making the hairs on the back of her neck stand on end. What was moments ago loud chatter fell to a deafening silence in which you could hear a penny drop.

Reaching the table where Quartz Clear were sitting, she looked to them with concern. 'What's going on?' she asked.

Magnus threw her the paper and Topaz fidgeted awkwardly in her chair. 'The king's placed a notice,' she explained.

Charlotte edged the paper towards herself and opened it.

BY PROCLAMATION OF THE KING

I hereby remove the former decree and declare that the formal decision has been made to annul the betrothal of marriage between Prince Lauraus Balthazar and Miss Sinope Blatio. This act has been approved by the great council with the seal of the realm, and with the final consent of the king.

Charlotte sat in horror at what she was reading. Why hadn't she been warned about this? She began to read the article beneath.

Rumours circulating the Coliseum reveal that the young prince may have engaged in an unlawful affair with a fellow associate at the Coliseum whilst legally betrothed; if our sources are correct this would be illegal under Avalonian law and justice could be sought through the Court of Verderers if Miss Blatio chooses to seek it. Nobody was available to comment for the press.

Although no official statement has been made on the matter, the young prince was overheard telling friends he'd rather marry a goldfish …

'I can't read any more,' said Charlotte feeling even more light-headed. Topaz came over and gave her a hug.

Chatter had started back up again but fell just as silent when Sinope entered. Snatching the paper from one of her friends, her stomach concaved as though wounded by the words. Looking like she wanted to sink into the wall, she abruptly turned and swept herself away.

Charlotte couldn't help but feel extremely sorry for her; nobody had warned her either. Scraping her chair backwards,

Charlotte trailed behind Sinope, calling out her name. But she didn't turn around. 'I didn't know!' Charlotte shouted, halting at the bottom of the atrium staircase.

Blood boiling, rage consumed her, prompting the ruthless hunt for Lauraus to begin.

She knew exactly where he'd be – the same place he was at this time every morning. At the end of the silver corridor, the place he always hung around with his juvenile supporters.

She found him spinning a ball on his finger and joking with London along with a few more of their friends.

Charlotte pushed his chest back into the wall. 'How could you do that?' she shouted, noticing one of Sinope's mates come out from her room.

By the look on his face, he knew exactly what she was talking about.

'You didn't warn her. Or me for that matter!'

His friends looked shocked by her intervention; he was, after all, royalty.

'How could you be so cruel? Is that how I'm going to get treated too?'

Lauraus grabbed her arm softly and attempted to pull her in for a hug to calm her, but she broke free of his grasp, then backed away. 'We're finished,' she said turning to the double doors and pushing them both away.

Normally he would have come after her, but she realised he didn't want to look stupid in front of his mates. One fleeting look as she turned the corner did nothing to reassure him. Perhaps he was more bothered than he appeared at first glance.

#

Charlotte decided not to leave her room for the next few hours. She had never felt so upset before. Things were going to be awkward inside the Labyrinth anyway, but now it was going to be impossible. In Charlotte's mind, this challenge was going to be a complete disaster; the whole group had been torn apart. But she knew she needed to channel this negativity into something positive, so she stood, repeatedly practising the draw of her daggers to perfection.

When she got bored of that she moved on to the manipulation of butterfly candles. A momentary reflection made her realise how far she'd come in the past few months. The growth that she had undergone was quite amazing. If she could transform to the degree that she already had, then surely she would be able to get through today somehow.

Sitting on her bed, legs crossed, Charlotte read over her own set of instructions, going over them several times. It was then that she noticed Kristoffer Enoch's book poking out from her bag, almost like it wanted to be picked up.

Deciding to give it a scan, she wanted to see if she'd missed anything jumbled up among the pages. Most of the book was talking about his adventures and life experiences, but occasionally those encounters led on to different pieces of information that were of use to her. For a moment she didn't think she was going to find anything new, but another drawn-in triangle caught her attention. It was coming from underneath a section where two pages had been stuck together that she hadn't noticed before.

Ripping them carefully apart, she tried not to tear the parchment. When fully separated, she was amazed at what she'd found. On the top innermost page was a diagram of the wheel of spirit, in various stages of the process of activation.

The first diagram showed dense gold elevated from the ground in the form of a ring. Inside was a disc also made of gold, but the directions showed the inner part to spin, activated by a lever on the side.

The next diagram showed six pairs of cuffs for the hands and feet of sacrifices, beneath systems of tubes that collected blood to be carried to the centre through motion.

When she saw how the blood was harvested she closed the book abruptly and threw it at the wall, unable to read the grotesque description.

The harrowing images haunted her thoughts. 'Is this disgusting ritual my destiny?' she shouted, tears streaming down her face. 'This is what I've been chosen for?' Charlotte broke down into floods of tears, crying on her bed. She'd never felt so alone.

A light tapping sound came from behind her chamber door. 'Charlotte, it's me, Topaz. I've come to see if you're OK.'

Panicked, Charlotte got up from her bed and quickly picked up the book, hiding it beneath the loose floorboard underneath her rug. She opened the door with puffy eyes and a red face because her tears had reacted with her skin as they always did when she cried.

Topaz immediately knew she'd been upset and came in to hug her. The albino Elf smiled sympathetically as Charlotte wept helplessly in her arms. 'It's OK, we've all been there. Boys can be right gits sometimes.'

Topaz pulled a wrapped bacon roll from her pocket. 'Here, have this, it will make you feel better.'

'Thanks,' Charlotte said, resting it on the table to tie back her hair.

'Abacus was going to come up here, but I told him this was more of a girl thing.'

Charlotte laughed. The thought of Abacus trying to make her feel better about a guy would have been quite funny. It might have even cheered her up a bit. Even though she was pleased to see Topaz, she would have quite liked to have discussed what she'd just seen in Kristoffer's autobiography. But she couldn't discuss anything she had just found with Topaz, because she wasn't one of the Last Seven.

'Listen, you've a lot going on right now, but you don't need to worry because you've always got us. I know that's not really much of a consolation, because Magnus can be a bit of a pain in the arse, and sometimes Antonious can be a bit grumpy, but you know, we're a good bunch and we'll always look after you. They're all really worried about you down there.'

'Everyone here at the Coliseum understands why Lauraus wouldn't want to be with Sinope, given the circumstances. They understand better than you think they do. Besides, so what if they don't? This is about you and Lauraus, not them.'

'Not any more,' said Charlotte sadly. 'I broke up with him.'

'Oh, I'm sorry, I didn't know.'

'It's OK, it's the right thing to do. To be honest I'm more worried about Sinope at the moment. I have to go up there now and we're on the same team.'

Topaz rubbed her arm affectionately. 'I'll walk you up there.'

Charlotte wanted to say thank you but instead nodded, grabbing her satchel. She had no strength, and didn't know how she was going to get through. But she knew that somehow, she had to. Somehow, she had to carry on.

Having Topaz at her side made her realise that there were people here that cared about her. That gave her the courage she needed to continue. As they silently set off for the Labyrinth, she recognised the feeling of defeat. There was no way she was going to make it. Even though she doubted she would graduate, Avaland was her home now, and later, when she was feeling strong again, she would think of a way to return, with Aphra and Walter too. One last shot, and she was going to give it everything she had. With no strength, Charlotte pushed aside the doors, Topaz by her side. She would have felt quite scared had Topaz not been there.

'If you need me I'm in room 404, OK?'

'Thank you,' said Charlotte, appreciative to an extent that Topaz could not understand. 'And for the breakfast.'

'Lunch,' she joked, lingering by the door.

'You alright, mate?' said Valentine, taking over from Topaz as though it had been previously discussed. 'I heard what happened.'

But Charlotte didn't want to talk about it, especially here because Lauraus was looking over in an attempt to overhear their conversation. 'Where's Sinope?' she asked, looking behind her. 'Do you think she'll turn up?'

'I dunno,' said Valentine. 'I wouldn't blame her if she didn't.'

Valentine realised what she'd said the moment it left her lips. 'I can't believe you have either. That came out wrong, sorry.'

'Don't worry about it,' said Charlotte, sure that it was a genuine mistake.

Sinope marched through the Labyrinth doors with seconds to spare. Charlotte couldn't help but admire her, because it was a very professional thing to do. Not just that, but she and Valentine wouldn't have been able to complete the task without her. They were a team now, after all.

Sinope made no eye contact. 'Come on, let's get this over with.'

They walked through the door, not uttering a single word. The courtyard floor distorted in a flash to the forest floor in autumn. They were back.

Beside the door was the hatched shell of the dragon. 'Where's it gone?' snapped Sinope in an instant of hesitation.

Valentine scanned the woodland with perfect precision. 'It's over there,' she gasped, relieved. 'Munching on bushes.'

Sinope stormed away tutting impatiently because the journey to Apollo's Fountain was a long way from here and they needed to get going quickly. 'Don't let it eat too much. Dragon growth is accelerated with the consumption of food.'

Valentine spotted an area where there were lots of flies and took off to investigate. 'It's a dead rat.' Charlotte was surprised to see her pick it up and spear it with a stick. 'Here, baby dragon,' she said, waving it around to spread its scent.

The blue reptile ran towards her, wagging its bright pink tail. He had caught a squirrel and had brought it with him to share. Valentine patted him on the head. 'You have it, little buddy.'

'Aww, it's so cute,' said Charlotte, stroking its chin.

'You won't be saying that in an hour,' retorted Sinope sharply. 'By then it'll be huge. Are you two coming or not?'

Valentine followed, trailing the dead rat on a stick behind her. The baby dragon flapped its tiny wings, snapping its jaws every few steps. It appeared to be very hungry and hunting anything it could find as they walked.

Gregory's Gorge was far behind them, and the leaves in Feign Forest were deeper than Charlotte had ever seen them, sometimes coming to her waist. It was colder here too; steam protruded from her mouth with every breath as she waded through. Somehow the baby dragon came out of the leaves much bigger than it had gone in, and it had found a grass snake beneath the foliage. It was growing at an alarming rate, making Valentine become more anxious.

To make matters worse, it began to lose interest in the rat, stopping to eat shrubs and branches, with a couple of unfortunate rabbits along the way.

When its tongue pulled in a blackberry bush, Valentine started to worry. 'Are we nearly there yet? I don't think I'm going to be able to hold him much longer.'

Sinope pulled out her map. 'It should be on the other side of this bridge,' she instructed, peering at the frozen lake beneath with difficulty, because thick fog was rising from it.

The familiar angelic singing met Charlotte's ears once again. She had heard this the last time she'd come to the fountain, when she first met Arafolle, then again with Frugal and Mandy at the Wirral. 'It is, I can hear it,' she said.

Both girls gave each other a look of confusion.

'What do you mean, you can hear the fountain?' said Sinope, looking at her the most oddly of all.

The bridge opened out on to the large white fountain. The stone had been carved with magnificent detail and writing in Latin adorned the surface, though she did not have time to decipher it right now. Beside it was a crackling fire, heating a very large black cauldron.

Sinope began to transfer some of the water from the fountain to it. The moment the liquid touched the pan at the bottom, it sizzled. 'Keep filling it,' she then ordered. 'Charlotte, you need to stir to regulate the temperature as we discussed.'

Valentine threw the rat on a stick into the cauldron and the now elephant-sized dragon jumped in after it. Then she began to obey Sinope's directions.

Sinope approached the table, where tools were laid out and extra ingredients were stacked in jars should they choose to use them. Taking her place at the table, she began to prepare the potion.

'Won't the dragon escape?' asked Charlotte, surprised to see how calm it was in the water, waiting to be turned to dragon soup.

'No, heat sends them to sleep.'

The dragon burped dead rat wind, making Charlotte retch, then rolled up into a ball to get some sleep above the fire. The three girls silently brewed a potion in the moonlight.

Apart from the dragon's increasing size, the test had so far gone without any complications and at the rate that Sinope was carving up all of the ingredients they'd be done in no time.

'Here, take these!' said Valentine, handing Charlotte a pair of earplugs.

'What are they for?'

'The cockatrice cry is deadly; it can kill if you're too close by.'

Charlotte put the earplugs in her pocket because she didn't need them yet.

'Keep stirring,' snapped Sinope as she tossed in buds of deadly nightshade one at a time. The moment they hit the concoction it turned a thick glittery purple colour.

'Wow,' said Charlotte, amazed at what she was seeing take place in the cooking pot.

Sinope seemed particularly adept at making potions. She steamed through the cutting of the toad liver with fine chef-like precision, then put a pinch of all the bottled powders into the smooth fluid. Next she measured out ten milligrams of *cornium concordium* and scattered it about the basin.

'Stir it smoother,' she complained. 'That's too fast.'

It was much harder than it looked stirring round a sleeping dragon, but Charlotte did as Sinope ordered.

'One pinch each of powdered dittany, red Pixie dust and periculam powder,' she said aloud to herself, adding them to the pot. 'And that's it! Now we keep stirring.'

Sinope budged Charlotte out of the way and took over, so Charlotte went and stood back with Valentine, who rolled her eyes to the back of her head. She too was becoming impatient with being spoken to like rubbish.

'Why isn't it working!' Sinope grimaced, fuzzy-haired, as the cauldron emitted another plume of rat breath before tickling the air with cold gold flames.

Metamorphosis was upon them, turning the young scaly lizard wings into luminescent feathers. The creature then let out an almighty cry, using its vocal cords for the first time, but it had not yet left the cauldron, which protected them from the effects.

'Put your earplugs in,' shouted Valentine urgently, noticing that Charlotte had not yet done so.

The cauldron broke in two, revealing the giant songbird, the nightingale extending its wings for the first time. The dragon itself knew there was something different because it studied the feathers with its scaly beak.

'It's beautiful,' said Charlotte, only able to hear her own internal voice.

It approached the three girls who stood in awe for a moment, forgetting all the trouble that had led up to this point.

The nightingale coughed up something that fell to the ground: the fourth and final medallion, the element of fire.

The cockatrice looked up to the moonlight, glowing against the stars, and leapt into the sky, eventually disappearing behind the canvas of autumn trees.

As soon as Valentine picked up the coin, the door appeared emblazoned with the words, *Magnum Opus*. 'We did it!' She and Charlotte celebrated in a hug. 'Come on, let's get out of here.'

Valentine led the way, disappearing through the exit. But Sinope pushed ahead. She turned to block Charlotte's path, her expression changing to one of revenge.

A sharp pain caught Charlotte's breath, and she looked down. Sinope had pierced a knife straight into her heart, but instead of death she landed on the familiar mahogany floor. Standing to her feet, she realised she was in the Labyrinth garden.

Valentine came through the doors. 'How did you get here before me?' she said, confused. Turning around to face Sinope, her eyes widened with anger. 'What have you done?'

Charlotte got up from the ground, her talisman glowing around her arm. She ran to Sinope, screaming. 'You bitch!' Pushing her back she grasped her shoulders.

But Sinope fought back, disengaging Charlotte's limbs with a twist of the forearms. 'Did you think I would just let this go?' She smiled, narrow-eyed.

'I earned my way out fair and square,' said Charlotte, pushing Sinope once again.

Sinope screamed at her, nose to nose. 'You earned nothing but punishment. Someone had to make you pay.'

Seconds later they were on the ground, striking each other, but they were equals when it came to the strength of their bodies, so neither managed to overcome the other.

Then Erebus came flying over and separated them. 'Both of you to Orobus Pluto's office, now!'

'What happened?' said Valentine, following Charlotte into the corridor with extreme alarm. 'Why did you materialise outside the doors?'

'Sinope stabbed me so I would be disqualified from the challenge.'

Valentine looked shocked that Sinope could do something so unethical. 'I'm sorry, I should have stayed in there with you.' In a display of support, Valentine accompanied Charlotte to Orobus Pluto's office.

At the end of the atrium, two suits of armour guarded the tower. They crossed their axes, denying them entry to the stone spiral staircase that lead to the door.

Gargoyles stared down on them with such malice that their ugly shrivelled-up skin made their eyes bulge. Their pointed teeth just added to the girls' fear.

For a moment, Charlotte could have sworn one of them had moved, then its stone mouth shifted aside. 'Name.'

Taken aback, because she had never seen anything made of stone talk before, she said, 'Charlotte Crump and Sinope Blatio.'

The gargoyle looked down at each of them in turn. 'Purpose?'

'We have been sent here by Erebus Quarus,' Charlotte replied.

The rocky monster head looked on with suspicion. 'The reason for your visit?'

'Fighting!' bellowed Sinope, scornfully crossing her arms with a lack of concern.

Puffing out his cheeks, the gargoyle gave them several gasps of disbelief, followed by an assault of hissing and spitting noises. Clearly, he had his own opinions on the matter but did not have the authority to express them. Eventually he said. 'You may pass.'

'I'll wait for you,' affirmed Valentine, in a protective display of loyalty.

'No, it's fine,' Charlotte replied. 'I'll catch up with you later.'

Valentine reluctantly backed away from the passage, leaving them alone to climb the tower.

At the very top of the spiral staircase stood a door with a tiny window beside it. A dead plant sat on the windowsill. When Charlotte tapped the iron door handle, the smile was soon wiped from Sinope's face as she thought of the consequences for her actions.

The door opened inwardly, revealing a very small dark green office with a domed ceiling. Across it was an elaborately drawn map of Avaland, with strategic pins to represent each of the Talisman groups on duty. The plain walls showed no sign of sentiment or loved ones in the form of pictures. Filing cabinets were backed against them, so crammed with papers that some of the drawers wouldn't shut.

Additional papers were piled high on the desk. Sitting behind it was Orobus Pluto.

With skin as pale as snow, his hair neatly slicked back with gel, he rigidly squared his shoulders, resuming his authority. 'There's no need to tell me the reason for your visit; I have just received a scroll from Erebus.'

His eyes flashed with some kind of psychic capability. Then he gritted his teeth in a toothy rage, revealing a pair of pointed fangs. His irritable growl left Charlotte immensely frightened, but even though Orobus was clearly a Vampire, she didn't get the impression that he intended to hurt them.

Sinope, however, didn't know this and was quaking in her furry boots.

The room fell silent with nothing but the sound of quill to parchment as Orobus wrote Erebus Quarus a scroll in response. As he finished his final sentence, Charlotte noticed the papers spread out over his desk. He had appeared to be evaluating the Bedweguar family tree.

Was that the man she'd seen fighting with Sanctamoni in Maisie's Woods?

Orobus appeared to slither to his feet as his long black cape dragged behind the desk. He noticed Charlotte glance at the papers, so covered them with a few scattered books.

Finished with the scroll, he rolled it up and cast it into the fire, where it presumably flew up the chimney and back to Erebus with instructions.

He then spoke sharply with an unyielding stare. 'This isn't the start I was hoping for. You do both know that we do not accept fighting among colleagues?'

Sinope waited for Charlotte to justify her actions but was surprised when she didn't defend herself. She turned to look at her for the first time that day.

'Is there something wrong, Miss Blatio?'

'No, sir,' she replied, staring back to face him in a regimented stance.

'Good. Now, please do enlighten me as to why you think you have the right to be fighting on my grounds? Do you believe that you above all others are exceptions to the rules?'

Charlotte could hear Sinope's thoughts. Again, she was waiting for Charlotte to tell him the truth, but she didn't.

'It was over a boy,' Charlotte told him. 'It won't happen again.'

She knew Sinope was confused as to why Charlotte had attempted to protect her.

'I'm glad to hear it. I do not tolerate violence inside these walls. If I see you in my office again for this, there will be consequences. You are dismissed.'

'Yes, sir!' said both girls at the same time.

Orobus assumed a faltering smile then sat back down to his desk and resumed shuffling his papers. He coughed. 'Ahem. Before you leave, Miss Crump, I would like to have a private word if I may. Miss Blatio, please close the door on your way out.'

Charlotte turned to acknowledge his command. Orobus pulled down his glasses to scan the door before he spoke. 'I think it would be a wise decision for you not to travel for a while, nor go too far beyond these walls.'

Charlotte was overwhelmed by this very odd request, but he did appear to have some genuine concern for her safety. She was about to ask him why when the door behind her was tapped three times. A most convenient interruption for Orobus who looked as though he didn't want to explain the reason behind his requirement. He cast an eye to the door; whoever was on the other side had alarmed him. Charlotte became aware that Orobus could see through the door, making her wonder whether he himself possessed some sort of extrasensory ability.

His nose wrinkled as he breathed out, nostrils flaring. 'Don't you think it's strange that whenever something significant happens surrounding Sinope, that message gets out so quickly?'

Charlotte wondered if he was trying to warn her of a spy but didn't ask him to confirm.

Again there were three taps at the door.

'I want you to go straight back to your chamber and you're not to leave it until the morning. OK, Charlotte?'

'Yes, sir.'

Orobus opened the door to a tanned, white-haired gentleman dressed in a pinstriped tailored suit. His hands were covered by a pair of thick leather gloves that were clutching a crook-necked cane. 'Ah, Orobus, I was beginning to think you were ignoring me.' The man gave Charlotte a look of pure hatred before stepping into the office, and Charlotte exited.

The door closed behind them and for a couple of moments she could make out a few muffled words of what he was saying. 'I hear my daughter has been attacked. I do hope that the culprit has been dealt with appropriately.'

Charlotte felt spooked. Sinope's father sounded cruel.

Withdrawing from the tower and passing the hall, she journeyed straight to her quarters as directed, but in the distance she saw Lauraus, falling half asleep on the topmost step.

As soon as she came into view, he roused and ran to her. 'I heard what happened,' he said. 'I've been looking everywhere for you, and come to see if you're OK.'

Charlotte stood silent, wondering what to say. Her head was telling her to make him go, but her heart was saying she didn't want to be alone. 'Orobus Pluto's ordered me back to my chamber straight away,' she said. 'Sinope's father is here, he's very angry.'

'Word gets around in this place fast, doesn't it? OK, I'll come with you.'

He took her hand and led her through the bronze doors. 'You don't have to do this alone,' he reassured her. 'You are with me now. And I won't let anything happen to you.'

Charlotte couldn't help but feel comforted by his words. She unlocked her door, wishing for it to be tidy when they entered. And just like that the housekeeping was done.

Placing her keys on the table, she dimmed the lights and removed her jacket.

'I like your room,' he said, pulling her in towards him. She couldn't resist him any longer, and technically she wasn't breaking any of Orobus Pluto's rules.

CHAPTER FOURTEEN

A Place With No Time

Charlotte had been working to the point of exhaustion for months now. First training in physical combat and now in preparation for her imminent written exam. Everyone else appeared to have the advantage once again. Because they were born and grew up here, most of the questions in the practice papers were just in-built information for them. But for Charlotte, a mountain of what should have been general knowledge had taken over her life in the past weeks.

As of yet, no final decision had been made with regard to her early exit from the Labyrinth, which just added to the stress she was under. So, when she'd flicked to the next page of her diary, the thirteenth of May, she found it stamped with an official order that said *Rest day*. She'd decided to start it with a well-deserved lie-in, something she hadn't been able to do for almost a year now.

She had awoken that morning to an orange shimmer that lit the dust coming from her almost-drawn curtains. The glow hadn't been coming from outside, but from the early Christmas present Abacus had given her inside the sanatorium.

The horned splat throbbed in its cage, oozing an orange glowing gunge, its spongy horns pulsing. It was an unsettling sight. At first, she thought there might be something wrong with it, but then she remembered a colour key in the pamphlet. Luckily, she'd had the foresight not to move it too far. Pulling it free from under the cage, she wondered if this meant what she suspected, but restrained her excitement in case she was wrong.

The gunge could be used in special circumstances as a form of pest control, or if you had an infestation concerning flatulating cabbages.

Horned splats preferred a diet of leaves, grubs and worms; it went on to caution against feeding them egg sandwiches drenched in ginger beer, because they explode. They liked to be talked to and sung to at night, and here it was … glow orange on your birthday.

Charlotte almost swallowed her own heart. Today was her real birthday. She'd never known the actual date because she'd been abandoned as a toddler. Aphra and Walter had given her the same birthday as their favourite person in the entire world, the Queen of England.

In a panicked fluster, Charlotte threw on the clothes she'd been wearing the night before. Scooping up some of the gunge into an old pot of moisturiser, she stormed out of her room, kicking a parcel on the ground beside her door. Charlotte picked it up and opened it. Folded neatly inside was a glittery bodysuit. It was translucent white to the skin and soft but sparkling like diamonds. She had never seen anything so beautiful. Charlotte searched inside the parcel for a note. But there was nothing. Hanging it inside her wardrobe, she set off on her quest to find Abacus.

No one was sitting at Quartz Clear's round table by the time she arrived, so she quickly checked the canteen.

Launching herself the wrong way through the queue, Charlotte became the focus of a few impatient tuts but she didn't care, because she found Topaz at the end of the line, who she was sure she would have missed had she gone the right way around.

'Have you seen Abacus?' she said, walking backwards with the line. 'I need to speak with him, it's urgent.'

Topaz lowered her tray, ready to engage in the emergency at a second's notice. 'He said something about spending the day in the arboretum,' she told her. 'Why, what's the matter?'

Charlotte didn't want to answer the question, she was keen to get going. 'Mmm hmm. Where's the arboretum?'

'Follow the atrium corridor to the end and take the third passage to the right – it'll bring you out to the potters' sheds, you'll see it from there. I can take you there if you like? Is there something wrong?'

'No,' said Charlotte, eager to get going. 'I'll find it. There's nothing wrong, I just found out it's my birthday. If you see him can you tell him?'

Topaz raised a brow, possibly wondering how that could be considered urgent. 'Yeah, sure. If I see him, I'll tell him. Happy birthday!'

Charlotte pushed through the oncomers. 'Thanks, Topaz,' she said, vacating the canteen.

Normally she would have hung around, but she really needed to see Abacus as soon as possible and knew Topaz wouldn't take offence.

Setting off through the atrium, she skidded past the third passage to the right on the freshly polished floor, which turned out to be a small dark alley. The only light came from cracks under the wall, where the bricks had worn. If anybody had been coming from the other side, she wouldn't have seen them. But it turned out that nobody did. Probably for this very reason. A small wooden door opened out on to the potters' shed.

The aroma hit her before the light did; thousands of flowers in the sweet fragrance of bloom. The enormous shed was made from mostly blossom trees, with planked wood running around through the gaps. There was no roof, but the pink blossom kept it sheltered and steadied the temperature, allowing the plants to grow. Something so simple, but beautiful.

Some of the Gnomes saw her struggling to climb down because the door was high up and had no stairs.

They greeted her with surprised faces, because no one often came that way. 'Can you tell me where the arboretum is?' she asked.

'Past the greenhouse to the left,' piped one in a high-pitched voice.

The dry gravel path beneath her feet was covered in pruned stems, freshly cut from pot plants which the Gnomes crafted on wooden tables. Charlotte lingered, enjoying watching them at work.

Eventually coming to the end, she held open the door for another who was struggling inside with a container almost the same size as himself. 'All it needs is a bit of enchanted water, that'll soon perk it up a bit,' he said, nudging the wilting leaves out of his face with his nose.

Charlotte picked it up for him and carried it to the table. The greenhouse was crammed with an array of plants she was unable to identify, placed there because it was not their time to be brought outside. She knew that the arboretum was on the other side of this glass shed.

A valley of dirt-filled tree roots made up a set of steps that led down to a small indoor lake surrounded by an abundance of trees with pale blue leaves. The water inside the lake was glistening a clear blue. This is where she found Abacus Creedy, pouring a watering can and talking to himself and humming. 'Ahh, Charlotte, I had a feeling I might see you today. I'm afraid you've caught me carrying out one of my favourite pastimes. The demands of the job mean I don't often get to do any gardening for myself.'

Abacus led her over to the bench where a prickly mole popped up from the soil. Abacus picked up a knobbly branch and tried to hit it but missed. 'Ruddy thing's getting on my tod, but it's OK, I've loaded the soil with a sleeping agent.' The mole came up in a different spot, then burrowed beneath again after deciding it was in the wrong place.

'I planted this one myself a few years ago,' he then said, stroking a miniature tree with tiny pink buds. 'She's coming along nicely now, I think you'd agree. Very rare, I collected the seed myself from a valley in Leprechaun Territory. Quite similar to the bonsai, but this one delivers a scent that reminds me of my late wife. She wore perfume like this; the flowers are almost as beautiful as she was, and they change colour with time.'

Abacus looked at the plant with admiration. Charlotte had never heard him talk about his wife before; she could understand his sense of loss and why he chose to come here. Perhaps it was a way he could remember her.

'Tricky to take care of,' he went on, 'but very rewarding to see it in different stages of its life cycle. Only needs watering three times a year. I brush it with the water from the lake. Pure liquid crystal.' Abacus tapped his nose. 'My little secret.

I've since adopted some of its neighbours, they also get a little bit of extra treatment from time to time.'

'It's beautiful, Abacus.' Abacus stood back to appreciate it in all its glory, nodding in agreement. 'It's really special here,' said Charlotte. 'If I'd known it was here I would have visited it ages ago.'

Abacus beamed a wide and appreciative smile. 'I know, right. But don't you go telling no one it's here. No one seems to be interested in plants and I'd like to keep it that way!' He then reached into his brown leather bag. 'So, I believe a happy birthday is in order,' he said, pulling out a brown-wrapped parcel tied with string.

Charlotte took the tub of gunge from her pocket, afraid she might have spilled some inside.

'And this is your birth certificate,' he said, handing her a rolled piece of parchment tied with the same string.

Because she'd started opening the present first, she continued. Pulling aside the paper, a framed photograph of a beautiful woman was revealed. She had the same vivid blue eyes as Charlotte but long brown hair. The person on the other side of the camera must have said something funny because she was laughing against a backdrop of snowy woodland.

'Your mother couldn't have been much older than you in that picture,' he said, choking on his words, suggesting that he too might shed a tear. 'I'm only sorry she's no longer with us to give it to you herself.'

A tear fell down Charlotte's cheek onto the glass and she hugged the frame. Nothing had ever meant so much as this gift. She wrapped her arms around Abacus Creedy's middle, causing his eyes to let out a watery twinkle too. Abacus could see how touched she was to receive his gift. Is this why he had led her to this place? So they could share in their sense of loss together?

Charlotte knew what she must ask next, but her lips didn't want to move to the question. Taking a deep breath, she asked, 'How did she die?'

Abacus must have known she was going to ask this, but he still appeared to be uncomfortable providing her with the answer. He re-handed her the rolled-up piece of paper. 'I can only tell ye what everyone else knows, I'm afraid.'

Charlotte unravelled her birth certificate. At the top was the name Charlotte Rose.

After all these years, she finally knew her real name. More tears flooded from her eyes in a brief overwhelming moment. She read on. Beneath her own were the names of her parents.

Her mother's, Nelphinie Elizabeth Rose. Occupation: Guardian of Avaland.

And her father's name, Montague Nigel Wigburt Hobkins. Occupation: Fine shoemaker.

Charlotte couldn't believe what she was holding. In her hands was the answer to the biggest question she'd had her whole life. The names of her parents. 'Do you know if my father is …?'

'Still alive?' said Abacus, continuing her sentence. 'I'm afraid he too is presumed dead.' Abacus regretfully gave her a brief explanation. 'He went missing when your mum was pregnant with you, ye see. She was heartbroken. There had been signs of a disturbance in his shop when he had been working late one evening.'

Charlotte put her hands to her face to hide her pain behind them.

'I'm afraid all ye grandparents have since passed on.'

She now understood herself to have not one living relative. But then she had come to accept this anyway.

'The shoemaker's still exists on Prince Street,' he then said in an attempt to raise her mood a little. 'But has since taken on new ownership.'

Charlotte struggled a smile and nodded. After all, she had never really expected to find any of her relatives. She was just pleased to know who they were.

She then remembered something she'd asked at the beginning of the conversation. 'You didn't answer my question, Abacus,' she said politely, 'when I asked you how my mother died?'

Abacus made an uncomfortable noise. Probably because he took no pleasure in providing her with the answer. He blinked his eyes slowly, because it was so difficult to say. 'Your mother was murdered, Charlotte. By Mizaldus, her non-identical twin sister, the only family you have left alive.'

The shock hit her hard like a thousand knives to her chest, her heart leaping to her throat. Mizaldus was the woman who'd chased her on the bridge inside the Labyrinth.

She knew Abacus was finding this very difficult, but he continued to fill the deafening silence. 'That was why I was so surprised when you told me you'd seen her. You see, Mizaldus is a very wanted criminal. There is a large bounty on her head, and rightfully so.'

Putting fingers to her scalp, she wanted to tear her skin with her fingernails, the pain was so severe. She had been so excited to find out her real birthday, and now she just wanted to crawl into a hole somewhere and never wake up.

'I'm sorry, Abacus, but I'm going to have to go,' she said,

rolling up her birth certificate and re-tying the string. 'Thank you for my presents, they mean a lot to me.'

'I'm sorry I don't have better news,' he said with a guilty stare. He must have previously predicted that she'd feel this way, because he went on to say, 'I rearranged your diary so that you can have a few days off to yourself, and I will see t' it that nobody disturbs you.'

Charlotte silently agreed.

'I can walk you back to the Coliseum, if you like. I will just pack my things.'

'No, it's OK, if it's alright with you, I'd like to be alone.'

'Of course,' said Abacus, pained to see her so upset. She was glad to see that he took no offence to her request. Leaving the tub of orange goo on the bench where she had been sitting, she struggled to a stand and silently walked away.

#

It took three days in bed before she was able to contemplate facing the world. The first day she had spent crying in its entirety. The picture rested against her pillow.

Every couple of hours, Lauraus had knocked on the door, but she didn't answer. Her friends too, taking it in turns to leave food outside her chamber door before clearing away the previous meal.

An invitation had also been pushed under the doorframe. The envelope had a large picture of an armoured gentleman riding a chariot. She had been invited to watch the Gladiators perform in a theatre which was somewhere inside Feign Forest. But she knew she wouldn't attend. She had been advised not to leave the grounds by Orobus Pluto. Charlotte became suspicious of the invitation. There was no note to say whom it was from.

Suddenly the door banged with a fist five times, making her jump. 'It's Antonious, if you don't answer this door I'm bashing it down! I'm starting to think something's happened to you! I need to know if anything has.' She then heard a small bump which she could only assume was his head. 'Just say it hasn't and I'll go,' he repeated in a softer tone.

Charlotte was very surprised to hear Antonious sounding so protective. Even if he was shouting, she was still very touched by his appearance outside her chamber.

'I'm fine,' she shouted. 'I'll be down to dinner in a minute.' Next came a growl, but it faded down the corridor. Charlotte couldn't help but laugh.

She'd needed to be alone, but she finally felt strong enough to get outside. She had come to the conclusion that nothing had really changed. She wasn't expecting to graduate so from now on she was just going to make the most of being here. No more crying; today, she wanted to smile.

Neatly placing the photograph of her mother on the dressing table, she placed her rolled-up birth certificate alongside it.

It was time to see her friends.

Charlotte left her room with the intention of having a very large meal. In fact, there was little room left on the table for everyone else by the time she'd got out of the canteen. Her place was piled high with toast, cereal, sausages, eggs, French stick, fruit and juice.

'Hungry?' joked Topaz, pleased to see her finally eating.

Antonious moved from the seat he was sitting in to be near her, acting a little more sympathetically than before. He seemed to perhaps understand that they both shared a sense of grief.

'It's OK,' she said to him. 'You don't need to worry, it's the way I always deal with things. I am going to be happy today. I have decided.'

'Glad to see you're feeling better,' said Abacus, pointing to the fruit juice on the table to check he could have some before pouring the carton. He then patted her on the shoulder. 'Good girl.'

'Where's Magnus?' she then asked, noticing his empty chair and reaching over to take one of his unread newspapers from the table.

Antonious spoke with a mouth full of raw steak. 'He got hit on patrol.'

Charlotte almost choked on a bit of the sausage and egg she was chewing. 'Is he OK?'

'No, he's in a bad way,' said Abacus, rolling into laughter. 'They say he might never talk again.'

Antonious stopped what he was doing, a hint of a smile suggesting that he too found this funny. Abacus Creedy's laughter was contagious around the table, and everyone was trying not to laugh at Magnus's misfortune.

'What happened?' asked Charlotte with much more concern.

Thankfully Topaz was there to fill her in on that, because the other two seemed to have lost their words. 'He's fine, Charlotte, don't worry,' she said. 'We were out on patrol in Feign Forest and his iron tongue slipped out again.'

'What did he say?' asked Charlotte, buttering her toast.

Topaz folded the newspaper and put it on the table. 'He called the head Pixie a plant pot, so she bound his lips together with an everlasting binding charm.' Abacus and Antonious snorted so she gave them a stern look before continuing. 'He looks so uncomfortable, bless him, I went up to the sanatorium to see him yesterday. Thank goodness he has Proteus with him to communicate, 'cause his body language can sometimes be a bit on the aggressive side.'

Antonious, pushed his plate to the centre of the table because he'd finished.

'You two should go visit him. They were playing poker on the hospital bed when I went up there this morning. They have to keep hiding it from the matron because it's against the rules and she's threatened him with a warning already.'

Abacus chortled a candid hoot. 'Cor, he could chat the hind leg off of a dog that one, but then again, Magnus never really has been one to follow the rules. Can you remember that time he made Ira a Valentine's card and posted it through the wrong letter box? I don't think the Colonel ever got over it.'

'Sir Colonel Fortesque?' asked Charlotte, squirting ketchup on her fried eggs.

'Yes,' Abacus continued. 'And he signed it with several kisses, not that there's anything wrong with it o' course, it was just funny 'cause he thought Magnus fancied him, still does actually.'

Charlotte smiled for the first time in days, then wondered something. 'How is sending someone a Valentine's card not abiding by the rules?'

'Valentine's cards are not allowed here at the Coliseum,' explained Topaz. 'Under strict regulation. Absolutely no traditions are to be practised here other than in your own chamber.'

Abacus interrupted. 'Except of course Hallows' Eve, which is a celebration of our unity, and a commemoration of diversity.'

Charlotte picked up the paper to glance at her horoscope for the first time. Belief in the stars was very prevalent in Avaland and she finally knew her star sign was Taurus.

Abacus then went on to interrupt himself, something important jumping into his mind. 'Oh yeah, Charlotte, I almost forgot to say. A decision has been reached regarding that shameful incident in the Labyrinth.'

'Hmm?' droned Charlotte, her ears perking up her head enough to put down the paper.

'Orobus has decided to pass ye on your practical assessment. Sinope's been given your fate instead. Which means today is your final examination.'

Charlotte jumped up and cheered. This was obviously not normal practice here because everyone at the surrounding tables stopped what they were doing and looked at her. She then slumped back to her chair. 'Hold on, did you say the examination is today?'

But nobody acknowledged her last uttered words.

'I can't believe that Sinope girl thought that she'd get away with it in the first place,' bellowed Abacus.

Topaz nudged him with her foot under the table, then whispered, 'Careful, Abacus, Sinope's right behind you.'

'Is she now,' he raved, turning his chair loudly to stare at the back of her head. 'Well, maybe sh' needs to hear it!'

Sinope sank her head towards the table, ostensibly embarrassed as Abacus continued to glare at her with bulging eyes.

Charlotte sat silently at the table with increasingly sweaty palms. How could she have been so stupid and not remembered the test was today? She hadn't revised for days. It was no one's fault but her own, so she didn't mention it at the table again.

She'd had enough food now. 'If anyone wants to finish it, help yourselves.'

Topaz directed her next question to Antonious. 'Right, well, what's on the agenda for us three tonight, then?'

'Orobus wants us to do a sweep of the Red Forest. Apparently, the Green Queen has been spotted there a few times over the last couple of months.'

'Who's the Green Queen?' asked Charlotte, sugaring her tea.

'Her real name is Diane the Huntress. She's married to the king's brother. They call her the Green Queen because she's known for her jealous rages. She's currently public enemy number one on our most wanted list,' explained Topaz, handing Charlotte the milk sachets.

'Why, what's she done?'

'She turned the king's brother into a pig after she caught him having an affair. He's still missing. If you ask me, their relationship was a stupid idea from the start, everyone knew it wouldn't last with them two.'

'Thanks for that, Topaz,' said Abacus, suddenly sounding much more like their superior. 'You will be sure to keep a lid on those opinions when we get into the forest, won't you?'

Topaz gave him an 'I suppose' shove of the shoulders before checking the hall clock. 'Right, well, I'm gonna make my way up there; I need to stop at the reception desk before we head off. I haven't written Magnus's incident down in the register yet and if Orobus spots it I could get into trouble. Good luck with your examination today, Charlotte.'

'Yes, Charlotte,' said Abacus, also getting up from the table. '*Benediximus*.'

Charlotte watched Topaz and Abacus leave the hall together whilst she finished her drink. When she turned back, Antonious was staring at her intently. He did not move a muscle for a whole minute, making Charlotte feel extremely awkward. 'Well, I guess I'll see you later then,' she said, departing a bit earlier than she'd planned.

'I'm on patrol till the morning so you won't.'

'OK, well, I guess that's an improvement,' she said, leaving the table to meet Frugal and Mandy in the atrium.

Someone female called out her name from behind. It was Sinope. For a moment she wondered whether to stop, but she did.

Sinope caught up to her, looking somewhat ill at ease. The words she spoke were even more discomforted. 'I owe you an apology.'

At first Charlotte wondered whether she'd heard her properly, but when Sinope went on she realised that she had.

'My friend Sonique told me she saw you standing up for me, the day it all happened. And then there's that thing you did in Orobus Pluto's office. I know it didn't work but you still didn't tell him.'

Charlotte couldn't believe what she was hearing.

'Why did you do that, by the way?' Sinope then asked, unable to figure Charlotte's motive.

'Because I don't want to be your enemy any more.'

Sinope evaluated her reply. 'I told my father to stay out of my business. I also told him that this is all my fault. He knows that I'm seeing a boy in my Talisman group now too.' Sinope lifted her hand to a red mark on her cheek, making Charlotte feel sorry for her. 'Nothing I ever do pleases him anyway. The Coliseum is my home now, so I don't have to live by his rules any more.'

Charlotte sensed rebellion in her, something she couldn't help but admire; she knew how scary Sinope's father was.

'The reason I wanted to talk to you is because I was hoping that, maybe, one day … we could put all this behind us?'

Charlotte blinked a confident smile. 'Yes, I'd like that, Sinope,' she said, relieved.

Behind her, Frugal had just left the hall and he came storming up behind belligerently. He must have thought that Sinope was trying to bully her again.

Sinope anxiously twisted the ring on her finger; it was clear that she felt awkward having an audience.

'She's not giving you grief, is she?' Frugal bellowed defiantly, making others stare.

Sinope looked away submissively. 'Anyway. I'd better go. Good luck with your exam.'

'Did I just hear that right?' said Frugal, wagging his ears and raising one eyebrow. 'Did Sinope just wish you good luck?' He put his hands over his ears then tucked them under his chin, astonished. 'I've never heard anything like that come out of her mouth before.'

'Wait up,' called Mandy, catching them up. 'You're going the wrong way. We don't have to wait half an hour anymore. Apparently Erebus is letting some of us in early. Come on, it's down here on the left, I checked out the location earlier.'

Mandy stepped ahead and led the way. 'Oh good,' she said. 'No one's in there yet.' Breathing a sigh of relief. A queue was forming outside a pair of whited-out revolving doors. A rope had been attached to two poles to block the path, currently denying them entry.

'You look exhausted,' said Charlotte, mirroring yet another of Mandy's contagious yawns.

Mandy ran her fingers through her recently braided hair, resting it in front of her shoulder. 'They've finally released my dad, but the court case has been appealed.'

Charlotte could hear sadness in Mandy's voice so put her arms around her and gave her a big squeeze. 'We hope it goes OK. Don't we, Frugal?'

'Yeah, we do, there's plenty of room for everyone at the top. His book was his own creative expression and he's right to stand by his work.'

Mandy mustered a hesitant smile, then continued to stare into nothingness.

The examination room door began to revolve, eventually letting out Erebus Quarus, his wings tucked neatly to his sides. He unclipped the rope before speaking.

'For most of you today, this will be your final examination. Part of your responsibility as a Guardian is to maintain the Coliseum's values throughout your duties and beyond. That is what we will be testing your knowledge on today. General knowledge of law is paramount to the position. And even more paramount is that you understand the vast number of diverse cultures with whom we share our world. The slightest error could start a war. It is imperative that you understand everything there is to know as a mark of respect; this will always be well favoured, even in the most difficult of circumstances that present themselves, and in most cases can lead to mutual cooperation. Only then can we move forward past our differences.

'It is our ability to come together in a display of unity that is the beauty and the test of our world. Because choice is our greatest weapon, to choose to handle our conflicts by peaceful means rather than to destroy innocent lives. It is this act that is the true show of strength. Evolving past our adversaries by choosing to understand them rather than to fight.' Erebus looked pained with the conflicts of the world he shared. He looked through the crowd to the faces that would one day take over the responsibility of creating a world at peace, clearly defining the Coliseum's vision for the future. 'May I remind you all that there is no speaking during the assessment under any circumstances, under strict expulsion. *Benediximus* to all.'

Sinope joined the back of the queue with her new boyfriend; this must have been the reason that she had gone a different way to them in the atrium. He was tall, handsome, and both he and Sinope shared similar eyes. He kissed her passionately goodbye, making Lauraus stare.

'Hey that's K.C. from Tiger's Eye,' said Frugal. 'Well, hopefully she'll get off your case a bit now then, hey?'

Sinope looked back at K.C from over her shoulder whilst fluttering her eyelashes, she then joined her smirking friends at the front.

The line got shorter as people walked through the rotating door one compartment at a time.

Then it was Charlotte's turn to enter. She followed the circle, coming out behind an entirely different person. Behind her, Frugal had also disappeared, replaced instead with a goatee-jowled boy wearing what looked to be a pair of high-waisted breeches, with an upturned collar and ruffled cravat. It was immediately apparent to Charlotte that he appeared to come from an entirely different period.

She found herself inside a hall full of hundreds of thousands of ticking clocks, all showing different times. Rows upon rows of old-fashioned wooden school desks, complete with ink and quills, lined the room, most of which were slightly different shapes and sizes.

The calendar on the front desk kept flicking to different dates by itself as they entered.

Sitting at the top desk was an elderly grey-haired gentleman with a big beard and a round gold eyepiece. He was handing out test sheets to the approaching undergraduates.

Charlotte collected her sheet of paper and sat at one of the desks in the corner of the room. Beneath the lid of her desk was an answer sheet, with multiple choice options that you had to circle to indicate the answer you had chosen.

On a blackboard at the front written in chalk was the word *silence.* Underneath it stated the maximum time allowance for the test was thirty minutes.

The examiner hit the desk with an oversized mallet to indicate they could start and the room filled with the sound of paper being turned over.

Avalonian Law

Please circle the three unaccepted laws of Avaland.

Charlotte dipped the quill into the ink and scratched her answer on the parchment, circling *to Assassinate, to Heckle* and *to Pilfer.*

Please indicate offence urgency levels one, two and three.

Once again Charlotte marked the paper:

Level one – Accidental – no harm intended.

Level two – Intent to harm – immediate arrest, to be brought before legal judiciary.

Level three – Attempted murder – immediate arrest, to be brought before legal judiciary; worthy of banishment.

The test went on to discuss the traditions and practices of separate cultures.

Name two Fairy customs that must be avoided.

Charlotte circled the following texts from the sheet:

Fairy rings – do not engage in the dance.

Fairy feasts – do not eat or drink.

The test took twenty-five minutes to complete, allowing her five minutes at the end to check over her questions. Placing her quill back into the ink pot, she got up and handed her answer sheet to the examiner, feeling confident that she had answered all of the questions correctly.

Turning to leave the room, Charlotte took one last look around; this place was special beyond measure, something she knew she would never experience again.

It was then that she noticed a young blonde at one of the tables who looked familiar to her. Her heart skipped a beat as she realised that the young woman was in fact someone she knew. Sitting there, quill in hand, nervously scratching at the parchment, was a shaking Sanctamoni, albeit much younger than the one she was used to.

The ghostly sight sent shivers down her spine as Charlotte reflected on Sanctamoni's pale blue lips and lifeless face. She couldn't bear to walk past and say nothing to warn her.

'Sanctamoni,' she called out, making her look up, but Sarah did not recognise her. Of course, she wouldn't have done.

'You there! Stop talking!' shouted the examiner, hammering his mallet repeatedly on the desk but Charlotte ignored him.

'I'm a friend of Antonious,' she said urgently, because the security guard was already coming her way. 'The day you see my face, you will be in great danger. I found your body by the River of Colours. Bedweguar is going to kill you.'

The security guard grabbed her by both arms and began pulling her to the door. 'Your husband Antonious is heartbroken,' she continued to call out. 'He keeps going to your mausoleum to see your ghost.'

Charlotte was forced through the revolving door with only enough time to catch a glimpse of the shock written on Sanctamoni's face.

Banging on the whited-out window, she tried to push back the door, but her strength was feeble against the rotation inside. There was so much more she still needed to say. Cast forcefully out to the corridor, she went around again but the room was filled with different examinees than before. Another attempt saw her knock aside a short boy with curly brown hair. For a moment she thought she'd seen Kristoffer Enoch himself, but it was Sanctamoni she was looking for. The boy looked at her from behind wide eyes, too shocked to speak.

'You again,' said the security guard, pushing her back inside the door. 'I thought you'd been expelled.'

Coming out, shaking with the fear of expulsion, she picked up her feet. Time seemed to slow down as she ran through the corridors, searching all of the rooms.

In the atrium she saw the Colonel and grabbed him by both arms. 'Have you seen Antonious?'

'Why yes, young … er …? Sorry, my dear, I seem to have forgotten your name?'

'Where is he?' she said, panicked to the core. She knew she was being rude, but she had to find him straight away.

'Why, there – he is over there.' The Colonel pointed, eager to escape her clutches.

Letting go, she pivoted on the spot and headed straight for Antonious. He could tell there was something wrong by the speed in her step. 'I saw her,' she said, grabbing his robe. 'I saw Sanctamoni.'

In an instant they were joined by several guards and Antonious stood in front to protect her from their grasp. Others began to look towards the disturbance. Abacus forcefully pushed the guards aside. 'Tear your hole off the haggart. I will accompany her to Orobus Pluto's office straight away.'

Antonious growled at them, making them shudder back. 'We will take her.'

The gargoyles had already commanded the suits of armour to let aside the axes, allowing them entry to the tower steps.

'Don't worry about it, Charlotte,' said Abacus in a much more serious tone than she was used to. 'We'll deal with this.'

When they arrived at the top, Orobus Pluto's office door was open.

Knave, Magnus and Proteus were already waiting with him.

'It's written tightly in the rules; to go against them would be political suicide,' Orobus ordered as though arguing with an old friend. 'Charlotte may well have altered the course of history down there, not to mention the examiner is very strict and insists upon it.'

Knave looked up at him and spoke clearly. 'But ultimately the decision does lie with you, Orobus. You know very well she is a member of the Last Seven. You need her here as much as we do.'

Charlotte was shocked to hear that Orobus was fully aware of their existence.

He looked Charlotte's way. 'You have put me in a very difficult position, young lady. Back in my office twice in as many months.'

'You know very well why she did this, Orobus!' Abacus reminded him. 'And it wasn't for her own personal gain. We all have the same goal here, remember. I can assure you that you are going to need this girl around in the future.'

Orobus looked Charlotte's way, as though he knew this to be true.

The door slammed aside as Lauraus hurried up the stairs, panting. 'I got the call – where's Charlotte?' Lauraus ran over to take her into his arms, but she did not require his affection. She was strong enough to stand alone now.

Magnus updated him, though still struggling to speak as he did so. 'Charlotte here is about to be expelled. She warned Sanctamoni about her murder and gave her the approximate date of her death.'

Antonious stood by her defiantly, growing increasingly agitated by their lack of sympathy towards his wife's death. For a moment she heard his thoughts. He wondered if she truly had changed the course of history.

'I don't understand how this is a bad thing?' questioned Lauraus. 'Don't worry, Charlotte, my father will get you out of this. Is that why Sinope's father's outside with the elders?' said Lauraus. 'I couldn't identify which ones because their faces were hooded by black cloaks.'

Everybody fell silent. Orobus went even whiter if that was at all possible. 'What did you say, boy?'

'How do the elders even know this quickly?' questioned Magnus.

'The gargoyles won't let them through because they don't have an appointment.'

'Right, everybody out … I need to deal with this.'

Orobus confronted Charlotte. 'Because of the presence of the elders, I now have to make a decision quickly. Your test paper was completed and handed back to the examiner, I am protecting your expulsion on those grounds. But I am going out on a limb to do it; there are those that are pushing for your exclusion.'

Orobus turned defiantly. 'Besides, if the elders don't like it they will have to rewrite the rule book a little better.' He turned to the Last Seven. 'You know what to do. Lauraus, you go the front way if you please, seeing as they saw you enter.'

Lauraus reluctantly did as he was told.

Magnus gave the next instruction. 'Right then – level nine, the laundry. Proteus, I believe a little demonstration is in order.' Magnus gave Charlotte a little wink.

'I thought you'd never ask,' said the wooden leg, giving a wiggling jump into his hand. Apparently, he was not a wooden leg at all but a magic wand.

Abacus took out his blood-red Obelisk and nodded towards Charlotte to take out hers. Those that hadn't done so already took out their Obelisks and threw them into the air. They spun, levitating just in front of them.

Abacus waved his palm in a circular motion underneath it and the others did the same.

'And yours, Charlotte,' Abacus instructed, maintaining a steady hand.

Charlotte copied the movement with her palm; the energy tickled her hand.

The room blushed with colour, forming a rainbow that Charlotte alone spun within.

They materialised in the centre of a room that was draped with linen. The Obelisks spun in the centre, flooding the room with colour. A breeze came through the window, blowing the sheets to the side. Abacus pulled down a few of them to clear an area.

'We should be OK from here. The Elders only ever hang around the bottom three levels. And they never linger for long; you should be safe making your way back from here.'

Magnus and Abacus put away their Obelisks and exited through the laundry door, relieved to have been able to help in some way.

'I'm awful sorry I have to leave you, Charlotte, but I'm supposed to be retired,' said Knave with apprehension in his voice. 'If anyone sees me wandering about they'll know something's up.'

He pulled out his Obelisk and held it upright in his palm, making it spin. Knave then disappeared with the light. Charlotte just made out the faint outline of a room behind him.

Antonious lingered behind to talk to her. 'I won't let anyone punish you for what you did today. No one has ever done anything like that before, for me, and I'll never forget it.'

'Antonious,' came a voice from behind one of the sheets, which pulled away revealing the teary-eyed face of Sarah Sanctamoni. Antonious plunged towards her in disbelief. Charlotte could feel him. The energy inside took Charlotte's breath away. She had indeed changed the course of history. The sheets continued to blow around them as a breeze came through an open window. His Obelisk danced with light, and they were enveloped by white linen as they kissed beneath it. Charlotte's senses tingled as she walked to the door, aware that they would spend the rest of that night together.

CHAPTER FIFTEEN

THE MASQUERADE BALL

Charlotte and Lauraus had been inseparable for months. Fawning adoration consumed the Coliseum air. For love was not just upon them but others too. Sinope had long forgotten about her spat with Lauraus; instead, romance had been well and truly kindled in the arms of her new boyfriend, K.C.

And Antonious had rarely left Sanctamoni's side, seemingly afraid to lose her again.

Although an uproar had ensued, with an attempt to overturn Orobus Pluto's decision, Antonious couldn't thank Charlotte enough for what she had done. Though Sarah herself spoke little to her, she could see how happy they were to finally be together again.

'You alright?' greeted London, stuffing his hand into his pocket and giving a vicious yank. 'Lauraus asked me to give this to you,' he said with an uncomfortable wrinkled nose. 'I think it's a love letter. He told me to make you open it outside; he's such a nob.'

Charlotte giggled and lifted the envelope. As she did, a hundred glittery kisses exploded around her.

The note inside read: *Meet me at the wishing well.*

'Where is the wishing well?' she asked London, who was flicking glittery kisses from his shoulders.

'It's over there,' he said, pointing to the end of the lawn. 'Where Feign Forest meets the viaduct.'

'Thanks,' she said. 'Who are you going to the ball with, anyway?'

'A few girls,' he said simply. 'I couldn't make up my mind which one to take. I like them all.'

Charlotte coughed. 'Erm, I'm not sure that's going to go down too well, London. You may want to rethink that one.'

London laughed. 'Nah, they love it.'

'Well, I suppose I'd better go, then,' said Charlotte, pursing her lips into a coy smile and shaking her head with amusement.

London peeled himself away from the wall he'd been leaning against with a cocky smile. 'Yeah, I'll see you later.'

Charlotte glided across the lawn, feeling warm and hazy. Was she falling in love?

Reaching the edge of the grounds, Charlotte peered over. Beneath was a bridge composed of several arches between tall towers, not that dissimilar to the Coliseum itself. It had been sunken into the edge, hidden from view because the steps sloped beneath the horizon.

Underneath the pillars was a hot lake that spat out boiling water from geysers. On the other side of this lake was a small well. She saw Lauraus there, throwing a coin into the water, his eyes closed. Perhaps he was making a wish. Leaves rained down over him from what must have been the entrance to Feign Forest.

Charlotte took care as she crossed the bridge, because there was nothing to hold as she descended. 'You won't fall,' shouted Lauraus, having spotted her. 'The viaduct has an imperceptible fence. Nobody from outside can reach us.'

He took her hand to help her down the last few steps and then kissed it softly, making the ring he'd given her blush blood red. He smiled as if that meant something.

Charlotte checked out the colour of his, which glistened deep cerise.

'What does pink mean?' she asked, watching him blush.

Lauraus hooked a brow. 'Maybe the rings were a bad idea.' He grinned playfully.

Nothing could be more perfect than this moment. She didn't want to be anywhere but here with him right now.

He led her to the well and took out one gold Sunstone. 'Make a wish,' he said, putting it in her palm and closing her fingers around it.

Charlotte looked to the viaduct, then inside the well, her hair blowing in the wind.

'I've never seen anything so beautiful,' he said, kissing her neck. Charlotte wished this moment could last forever. Unintentionally casting the coin into the well, she turned to Lauraus and put her arm around him, and they both leaned into a kiss.

A sudden short breeze came their way; it was followed by a quick squeal and a long whine. 'Medwin!' Charlotte called out to the beautiful palomino, who tucked in his wings. The horse then began to clean his feathers.

'Wow,' said Lauraus. 'That's quite a horse; they are very rare.'

'He's my friend,' she told him. 'He saved me; he must want to meet you.'

Charlotte rubbed Medwin's neck affectionately. He nudged his nose at Lauraus to collect water from the well.

'Here, boy!' he said, allowing Medwin to lower his long pink tongue into the bucket.

When almost all the water had gone, Medwin butted Lauraus's chest and gave him a big long sniff.

'He likes you,' said Charlotte, watching him trot back into the forest and spread his wings to the sky.

Charlotte finally heard her coin hit the bottom of the well. 'That's deep,' she said, looking in. 'What did you wish for?'

Lauraus stood confidently to face her. 'That you would go to the ball with me?' he asked nervously, sweeping his hair aside. 'I was gonna ask you sooner, but I'm not used to all of this boyfriend stuff.'

Charlotte smirked light-heartedly. 'I'd assumed we were going together anyway.'

'Of course,' smiled Lauraus with flushed cheeks.

#

It was another week before Charlotte was hit with the sobering thought: what on earth was she going to wear?

She had never been to a ball, and she certainly didn't know anything about dresses. Not just that, but she was going with a prince. She couldn't just turn up wearing any old thing.

She approached Mandy for some guidance; perhaps she could point her in the right direction. But when she arrived, Mandy was already speaking with someone. A male.

He kissed her on the hand before walking off. 'Who's that?' asked Charlotte, pleased to see her looking much happier than she had in a while.

'That's Barry Chapman,' she replied. 'We're going to the ball.'

'Awesome,' said Charlotte. 'Fancy going shopping with me? I need your help to pick out something to wear.'

'I'll come shopping,' interrupted Frugal. 'I've gotta find me a new jacket 'cause I've got a date.'

Charlotte and Mandy were pleased to hear this. 'Who are you going to the ball with?' they asked nosily.

Pricking up his ears, he coughed nervously 'Goatish,' he said.

'Goatish the Goblin?' said Mandy. 'But that's a … Oh …'

'Right, shall we go now then?' interjected Charlotte.

'No, I can't go today,' said Frugal. 'I have to wait until Thursday. It's unlucky for Hobgoblins to go jacket shopping on any day other than a Thursday.'

Charlotte couldn't help suspecting that Thursday would be a little bit late. 'But that's the day of the ball,' she said.

Mandy cut in with a wary reminder. 'Anyway, you're not allowed to leave the Coliseum, remember?'

'Orobus didn't say I wasn't allowed, he just recommended that I didn't. Anyway, I can't just show up in my jeans and T-shirt, can I? I'm going with a prince.'

She couldn't leave it all to the last minute; that would just make her anxious with worry and she was sure by then that all the best dresses would be gone. If they hadn't already.

Lunchtime would be the perfect time to slip away. She stood in her room, slipped the Obelisk into her hand and threw it into the air. It levitated as before. This would be the first time she had used it without supervision. But then, how hard could it be?

The Obelisk began to glow. 'Take me to Prince Street.' As the room filled with exuberant white light, within the light shadowy outline, a new blurry set of surroundings came to be. Beneath her feet appeared a brick path. And when the light faded she was in Prince Street. Nobody was around because the weather was dismal; it was supposed to be a summer's day, but rain persistently poured. A flash of light signified the beginning of a thunderstorm. Charlotte stuffed the Obelisk into her pocket. Running to the path, she took shelter beneath the canopy of a burgundy shop window.

Hoping it to be a dress shop, she was met with shock to find the words *Felix Fergal's Fine Shoes.* Charlotte was so overcome she thought that she might cry. She looked on as the apron-dressed senior crafted at his bench in the place where her father had once stood.

Charlotte smiled; in some way, seeing the old man at work brought her peace inside. It was time to move on. She knew she must not linger. Across the way, a shop called Madame Bella's Boutique caught her attention.

In the window was a mask made of the same lacy material as her new bodysuit; this gave her an idea.

The doorbell rang as she entered, the overwhelming scent of heavy perfume inflaming her nostrils, so pungent her eyes began to sting.

Charlotte took the mask from the mannequin head. As she did so, it glistened with fine threaded detail. The price tag was high, but she knew it was worth it.

The iridescent mask attached to her skin, gleaming opalescent with the dust of diamonds.

Looking around for someone to pay, she called out to the back room. 'Hello!'

But nobody came. Deciding to wait around, she explored the room with her eyes. It was dark, with hot pink walls, and dried rose petals were scattered about the place.

On an elaborate dressing table sat a bone china teapot with cups and saucers. Behind it was a large, elaborate gold-framed mirror. Above her head was a red stained-glass dome, raining rose petals that disappeared before they hit eye level.

Even though she had been expecting someone, it came to her as a bit of a surprise to see the short buxom blonde come out of the mirror towards her.

'I am Madame Bella,' said the pair of thirty-something red lips, 'and this is my boutique.'

Charlotte moved her head hurriedly as a perfume bottle flew in her direction and squirted her in the face.

'Not in the eyes,' commanded Bella, giving it a flick into the wall with her hand. 'Take a seat, my dear,' she said, pushing Charlotte into the dressing-table chair.

'Oh, I don't want my hair and make-up doing, I just came for the mask,' explained Charlotte, who hated anything girly.

'Nonsense; you have your ball, yes?'

'I do but it's not today.'

'Well then, I will give you a tonic. I have no appointments for the rest of the day and far be it from me to say that all the other young ladies will be having their hair done for the evening. I will do your hair for the ball and you can tell all of your friends where you had it done. Agreed?'

'What's a tonic?'

'You have it done, and I bottle it. When you uncork the bottle, it applies itself with no effort.'

Charlotte couldn't help but admit that that sounded like a really good idea; besides, she would like to see how that worked. 'Well, maybe a little hair and make-up couldn't hurt,' she eventually agreed, taking a seat.

Straps came up from the corners of the chair to hold Charlotte down, making her regret her decision immediately.

Bella dropped her scissors on the floor. 'My goodness, I'm all fingers and thumbs today.'

To her horror, Bella then cut off her entire ponytail.

'Ahh!' Charlotte shrieked in panic. She suddenly realised why the shop was so empty, because Madame Bella was beyond any doubt the craziest person she had ever met.

'I call this one our twenty-four-hour cut, because the hair grows back while you're sleeping. Relax,' said Bella, admiring her work. 'Rest yourself for all that dancing.'

Charlotte found it rather difficult to relax and had no intention of resting; she was too busy trying to escape the chair. 'You've cut off all my hair!' she screeched in distress.

'I thought short hair would look nice with the mask; put it up to your face.'

'But I didn't ask for that,' argued Charlotte.

'Ah-ah-ahh, Madame Bella knows best.'

After flouncing about in front of the mirror and applying all manner of things to Charlotte's face, Madame Bella spun the chair around so she could see her reflection.

With platinum-blonde hair and bright red lips, Charlotte stared into the mirror. It did look pretty tomboy-ish; a look she kind of liked.

'There's no need to re-apply the make-up,' said Bella, commanding her tools back into her case with a wave of the hand. 'It will set for twelve hours.'

Charlotte pivoted her head around to check the angles. 'You did say that my hair will grow back in twenty-four hours, didn't you?'

'Yes,' Madame Bella said, grabbing an opaque blue glass vial from the cupboard and drawing it to Charlotte's face. Her new hair and make-up simply slid off her skin into a smoke that was corked inside the bottle. 'Or apply as desired. Simply hold the bottle to your face and your old look will return.'

'Well, as long as it grows back, I suppose.'

She wasn't sure whether to pay Madame Bella or not, but decided to take extra money from her purse and put it on the counter.

With a polite show of gratitude, she eagerly left the boutique, with absolute certainty she would never visit it again. Running to the adjacent alley, she took the Obelisk from her pocket and spoke the words, 'My chamber, the Coliseum.'

Within moments she had returned. Her job was done, even if it hadn't been as quick and painless as she had hoped.

#

The week passed quickly, and the time had finally come to do the one thing she hated most. Be girly.

She slipped on her bodysuit and uncorked the bottle, effortlessly ready within minutes. Now for the mask. Once it was applied to her face, she looked very different indeed. The short haircut actually worked with the mask, giving her a cool edge as she elegantly glistened with diamonds.

She could hear Guardians in the corridor, laughing excitedly as the door was knocked four times. The time was seven o'clock and Lauraus had come to meet her.

Charlotte nervously stepped outside, sure to shut the door quickly so he didn't see the mess in her bedroom.

Lauraus had to look twice to check that it was her before he leant in for a kiss. 'You've cut your hair,' he said, wide eyed.

'Don't worry, it only lasts for twenty-four hours.'

He glided up the stairs like a phantom, wearing a sweeping gold-clasped cloak and mask.

They stood beneath the clock tower, awaiting the signal of a half-hour chime. The light of the full moon shone upon them as they awaited the beginning of this most peculiar charade.

As soon as the chime struck, an orchestra began to play, but this was not like any music Charlotte had ever heard before. It was strange and odd in melody.

Lauraus took her hand with his white glove and lifted it to the air. He led her to the balcony so together they could see the passers-by roll through. Fog filled the grounds, coming from the direction of Feign Forest, and behind came the masked figures of Guardians of all shapes and sizes. Every movement was slow and exaggerated as they danced with eerie unison to the music. The men wore elaborate dress and the women mostly long dresses with feather attire.

Zombies burst from the ground and ghosts came out from the fog to join in the celebrations for the night. In the courtyard beneath, candles randomly appeared and pumpkins floated like balloons, lit to highlight their scary faces. Statues came to life, miming on their pedestals.

Lauraus led her down the polished staircase to where candles were burning upside down on the ceilings. A tiny jester almost knocked her excitedly, descending the staircase at the same time.

Two groups of Vampires were missing from the reflection of the mirror adjacent to them. She turned to check where they had gone; one bowed, removing his feathered hat.

The double doors opened and Lauraus raised their arms as he led her inside.

Acrobats on the ceiling dropped glitter to the polished floors where hundreds were joining in perfectly timed pirouettes, dancing in figures of eight. Two-faced masks bore six legs, these child-sized people dancing twistedly on raised platforms where pointy-hatted waiters handed out drinks on unicycles. At the back of the room danced a man on stilts with a single red rose in his mouth, waiting for his date for the night.

The orchestra was made up of self-playing instruments, a Goblin conductor waving his baton.

The younger ones were mostly having great fun, but the older generation appeared to be taking the celebrations more seriously. A wooden-legged man tapped his stump, enjoying the music in his pirate hat, drinking what looked like straight whiskey.

Twirling dresses filled the room as Lauraus led Charlotte to dance. One of the wonderful things was that nobody knew who they were. Masked, they danced a passionate waltz beneath the candelabras. Charlotte wrapped the inside of her leg around his groin, which he seemed to appreciate, and he bent her back towards the floor, kissing her neck.

They spun on the dancefloor until they could take no more oddness, and gently retired outside to a fountain lit by fireflies. Both removed their masks and continued to slow-dance to the sound of flowing water, the music quietly playing in the distance.

'There you both are!' barked Antonious, ruining everything entirely. 'I've been looking for you both everywhere, there's an urgent meeting downstairs.'

Whatever the meeting was about must have been important because Antonious rushed off ahead. Lauraus and Charlotte followed behind, running side by side, taking care not to crash into the masked partygoers coming down the hall in the other direction.

Antonious checked the corner to see if anyone was coming, then led them into a blackened corridor that lit when they entered. The torches revealed a square burgundy room, hung with the finest wallpaper. 'No one ever comes here,' he eventually said.

Charlotte began to inspect sets of ornamental marble pillars equally distributed around the room. Each had a portrait of a different male grasping a trophy. 'What is this place?' she asked, studying the same fine trophies sitting upon the pillars.

'The Hall of Triumph,' said Lauraus. 'This is where all the Elders sit upon their thrones. That's why no one ever comes here; they can never be elected out and nobody likes it.'

'But isn't that illegal?' enquired Charlotte, calling for an answer.

Lauraus thought how best to reply. 'Not if you're the one that makes the laws,' he said.

Antonious grumbled, then tapped his right foot heavily on the ground four times. 'Come quickly,' he ordered.

Without any warning, a trapdoor opened beneath them, lowering them down so quickly they might has well have jumped.

'This is the secret room,' Antonious informed them, leading them through a dark narrow hall.

They came out into a great shadowy room filled with junk that had been placed about with no care, nor recently dusted, leaving a grey powdery film. Above a chest of drawers sat a pile of books that looked as though they hadn't been moved for at least a century. On a badly hung shelf stood a mannequin's head with an elaborately feathered hat that would have probably made a nice museum exhibit before the head had been caved in with a carelessly placed walking stick.

'The office,' grumbled Antonious, forcefully opening the door. Inside was a desk that Abacus sat behind. The room had five more chairs leant up against the walls at various places around the small room. Magnus and Knave stood up to greet them.

Old framed photographs and newspaper cuttings hung on the walls and behind the desk was an elaborately painted tree. Every branch represented one of the Obelisks, each stem providing a neatly written name. Abacus noticed her looking. 'This is the tree of bearers. You and Lauraus are our newest additions. Take this as an official welcome to the team.' He pointed to the remaining seats to indicate they sit. 'I'm just sorry we can't start with better news.'

Knave stood up to take the briefing over from Abacus Creedy. 'Orobus Pluto secretly interviewed Sarah yesterday. It was confirmed that she was ordered to break into Orobus Pluto's office and locate the vault number for the Dagger of Thor. The claims you made against Bedweguar were also confirmed to be true, thus concluding that the alibi provided by Quentin Blatio was false and fraudulently provided. He has since been remanded and is awaiting trial. Second to that, she also confirmed that the Elders were responsible for her murder. Obviously, this places her in further danger, so Orobus has taken her to a safe house. There is something else,' he said reluctantly.

Abacus this time directed his words to Charlotte. 'The reason for her death is because she did not comply with her orders. Her orders to kill you, Charlotte. They must have seen it as a great opportunity to take the dagger, and place the blame on her shoulders.'

Knave rested against the table with his arms crossed. 'Except you put a stop to that too! We believe they are wary of you, Charlotte.'

Abacus interrupted Knave; he could see that Charlotte was getting anxious. 'It is with regret that I have to request the support of the Last Seven tonight.'

Lauraus took Charlotte's hand protectively. 'Why?' he asked, restlessly shuffling about in his chair.

'Quentin has escaped the holding cells this evening.'

'That's impossible!' snarled Antonious from behind narrow lips. 'Someone must have freed him.'

'He was last seen entering the Labyrinth,' continued Abacus, a whipped-in cheek suggesting that he wordlessly agreed.

Wrenching a hand to her chest, panic consumed her. 'Sinope's in the Labyrinth! She wasn't allowed to the ball because she hadn't graduated yet. I spoke to her this morning.'

'Sinope's in the Labyrinth alone?' questioned Lauraus surprised. 'I thought everyone had graduated now.'

'They have,' replied Charlotte. 'Sinope's the only one left, she has to do the challenges alone.'

Lauraus bowed his head. Was she sensing that he felt sorry for Sinope?

Abacus continued to sway his eyes with thought. 'I'm sure she'll be fine. If we see her we shall tell her to evacuate; I don't expect he has any intention of hurting his own daughter. Try not to worry, Charlotte.'

Charlotte was going to find that difficult, especially after seeing the bruise Sinope's father had recently left on her cheek, so decided to make finding her a priority.

'We should scan from four corners to the centre in groups, leaving behind a trail of knapweed,' said Antonious, logically. 'Then we can literally drive him out until he's trapped.'

'Sounds like a good plan.'

But where are we gonna get knapweed seeds at this hour?' argued Magnus, his wooden leg detaching itself to speak at the table.

'We have plenty o' those,' said Proteus, throwing up six and giving himself a little shake to let out a yellow stream. 'Just blow on 'em to rouse everlasting giant knapweed.'

'Won't this hurt Sinope?' interjected Charlotte with alarm.

Magnus pulled back his wand and readapted it to his knee. 'No, she's in the Labyrinth, remember?'

Charlotte picked up the larvae and put it in her pocket, then joined the others in taking out their Obelisks. Each colour lifted from the palm and spun, cascading them with light. Red, yellow, green and blue, then black and quartz added to the rainbow.

'Charlotte and Lauraus, you go together,' came their final instruction in Abacus Creedy's voice from behind a dim orange glow. 'Call us if you find anything.'

Soon the secret room had vanished, and they were surrounded by the night sky. A rainbow of light traversed the clouds before separating to the compass points.

They came to a halt at the furthest reaches of Avaland along a wall of barbed wire fencing that Charlotte recognised from the warm-up exercise with Gallore Knatterjack.

Charlotte opened her mouth to speak. 'This is where the spiders are,' she said.

Lauraus bit his bottom lip nervously. 'That's right, and it's where Feign Forest meets the banished lands. So we should block this off.'

Taking out his larvae, he squeezed it into a coffee bean shape and blew, causing a whirlwind of seeds that grew into enormous fast-growing leafless bushes. They thrashed around, violently twisting into malformed shapes.

Charlotte shut her eyes and also propelled a gust of seeds that transformed to worms then coiled into twiggy snakes, slithering among the foliage. They both ran quickly to escape the weeds' clutches, high-jumping fallen hedgerows blocked by the path of scurrying spiders twice their size.

'We need to be off the ground,' shouted Lauraus with panting breaths.

Shutting her eyelids, unsure it would work, Charlotte clearly expressed a word from the eye of her mind. 'Medwin.'

Lauraus spun his Obelisk into the surrounding breeze, instructing Charlotte to do the same. The butterfly candles showed them the danger of lurking spiders encircling them. Together they leapt towards the light, instantly taking off into the night sky once again and scanning the depths beneath then beyond.

Something was flying towards them, difficult to make out in the night sky, but the closer it came the more she realised that this creature was not the winged Pegasus she had called, but none other than a cockatrice, and it was headed straight for them.

'Cover your ears,' came the intense stammer of her boyfriend's words, but it was too late, the cry disabling her from the light. Falling into clouds she came to a halt somewhere in the sky. A rising white mist surrounded her entirely making it difficult to see. Startled, Charlotte lost her focus, 'Lauraus!' she shouted in panic, but no reply came. 'Lauraus!' she shouted again, fearing the worst.

Someone was approaching in the distance, but the closer she came Charlotte realised that the figure walking towards her was female, in a white flowing gown. For a moment she thought it might have been the lady of the lake, but it was a different woman similar in age with brown hair pinned neatly to her scalp; dressed in fine gold jewellery, but naturally so.

Stumbling to her feet, Charlotte clutched her hands near the daggers, ready to draw. 'Who are you?' she called out suspiciously, ready to trust no one.

As she spoke Charlotte, noticed blood dripping from both the woman's wrists, leaving a trail behind her.

'My name is Athene.' She spoke softly, yet with cold confidence.

Charlotte still didn't let down her guard; this answer did nothing to prove that she was safe. 'Where am I?'

Athene spoke with distant unfeeling. 'You are inside the Obelisk.'

Realising that she was talking with the deity that Sir Gualish Knight had been speaking of, she lowered her daggers.

Charlotte looked upon Athene's wrists, still dripping from the ritual. 'I'm sorry for what happened to you,' she said.

With an icy emotionless drone, the deity glided towards her. 'My sister trapped me here a long time ago; I get few visitors and regularly change hands.' Athene looked away, presumably too hurt by the memory of loneliness to continue. But the bracelet caught her eye. 'My father created that,' she said, refocusing her stare then again to Charlotte. 'It is a shame that it was too late for my brothers and I.'

Charlotte swallowed her fear. 'Do I await the same fate?' she asked, hoping for a less frosty response, but none was given.

'Sooner than you might think,' she merely replied. 'Such a cruel world, yet there are many out there that believe themselves moral, only to be caught up in such mindless murder. Especially here where the biggest monsters wear masks. At least the true pretend to be nothing other than they are.'

'Are you talking about Mizaldus?' asked Charlotte, confused about what she was trying to say.

'Especially Mizaldus, but not in the way you might think. Nelphinie fought her entire adult life trying to free her sister, something she died for in the end.'

'I don't understand what you mean. What was my mum trying to free her from?'

'The curse,' she snarled with cold-hearted flair. 'Does nobody know that Mizaldus is not acting of her own free will? She has never been. The seventh Chaste Stone is the one responsible for all of this.'

Charlotte couldn't believe what she was hearing; the only relative she still had alive was not acting of her own free will and nobody knew this. 'The soul inside the seventh Obelisk is the girl in the legend of the Isle of Apples?'

'That's right. She was very upset when her fiancé was killed, naturally so, but the tree twisted her. She now cares for nothing but mindless murder, but even still she does so wearing a mask. Only cowards wear a mask. There is only one way to break the curse for Mizaldus. The stone must be destroyed, and the sundial.'

Charlotte knew that this was impossible, because nobody had ever achieved it before.

'It can only be destroyed when it's at its most vulnerable,' Athene continued. 'The sundial is only weak enough to be penetrated when it has been activated.'

But to activate it would be suicide and mass murder, because it could unleash the Golden Dawn, ending all life in Avaland as they knew it.

Athene soared above her, encircling her in shadow. 'I suspect in some way Mizaldus might just be in there somewhere,' she said, tapping her forehead. 'Don't you think it's strange that the very weapon that could end it all is solely in the possession of the person that wants to destroy it?'

'And what of my father, do you know anything about him?'

The deity looked at her without speaking, still spinning in the light before sinking down slowly. 'Only that he was never found. They were very in love. He was not a fighter; your mother loved that about him. She found him funny too. I would often hear her laughter echoing through the glass. Nelphinie endlessly searched the farthest reaches of Avaland looking for him, whilst heavily pregnant. In the end she settled in the Wirral. I think it's important to tell you that your mother would never have chosen this fate for you. She would never have wanted you to be next in line for the band.'

Charlotte smiled timidly. It was so nice to hear some word of her parents, and of a time that they were happy together.

Athene turned to sail among the clouds; it was then that Charlotte remembered she hadn't asked the most important question. 'How do I activate the band?' she shouted out.

'I do not know, but when the time is right you will know what to do,' came the resounding echo of her voice.

Fog lifted then consumed the air until she could no longer see. Charlotte chased Athene through the cold mist. 'Wait, I still have questions.' But the deity had gone.

The ground changed to crispy ice that became slippery and soggy to the touch. Snow pummelled her shoulders with such velocity that she knew she needed to find shelter, but there was none to be seen. Whilst desperately searching for somewhere out of the cold, she walked into something hard. She stopped to see what it was. A quick scrape away of the snow revealed bark. She had found a tree. The entrance to a wood, in fact. Her senses became numbed, unable to see where she was going. 'Lauraus!' she yelled out.

But once again there was no reply. She listened intently for some clue to direct her to shelter, because her senses had been dulled by her lack of ability to see.

For a moment she thought she'd heard a baby's scream, halting her in her tracks. There it was again, it was a baby screaming. Charlotte urgently ran towards the cries. 'I'm coming. Stay where you are!'

As the crying grew louder she knew the child to be nearby, eventually finding a peach blanket in the snow. Just beyond it, cowering in a bush, was a crying toddler, screaming helplessly for her mother.

Charlotte picked her up and cuddled her in, picking up the blankets and wrapping them around. 'It's alright,' she said, stroking her thick curly hair and rocking her from side to side. 'I'll help you find your mummy, but we'll have to wait until the storm calms down a bit, OK? Then we'll look for her together.'

The terrified little girl must have decided that Charlotte's face didn't look too scary so took comfort in the safety of Charlotte's presence, eventually calming her weeping entirely.

Charlotte reached down into her satchel to take out as many butterfly candles as she could find, then threw them aside to light them. They flapped about, struggling through the windy blizzard before settling on the tree branches above, providing them with a little extra warmth. Charlotte held the girl under her chin, who had since fallen into an exhausted sleep.

At long last the snow began to subside beyond the trees, as did her lack of visibility. The Obelisk must have fallen from her pocket because it was lying beside her thigh, so Charlotte picked it up to put it in there again, but it was already in there. She carefully retracted the other with her hand whilst balancing the child on her chest, unable to understand how she could now have two Obelisks.

Charlotte rested it on the blankets, curiously looking on at the bruised toddler in her arms. For a moment she wondered – but then it couldn't be.

Noticing the gleam of a gold fleck piercing through the snow, she traced her finger to investigate, pulling out a locket. Prising it open with one hand, she found an engraved picture inside. Her heart in her mouth, she looked on with astonishment at the faces of her parents.

Picking up the girl's left arm was the only confirmation she needed, the two bracelets sparkling together in recognition of their meeting.

Unable to hold back the tears any longer, she knew how scared the little girl must have been, because she had felt that fear her entire life. Charlotte attempted to fill the child with love, something she had never cared to do for herself until now. A moment so sacred, that she had never experienced before. 'Everything's going to be OK,' she whispered into her ear, unable to contain the emotion.

She knew then that she would never let anyone hurt her again. She stood against anyone who dare hurt this defenceless child, ready to face anyone who dared to try. Because she wasn't helpless any more; she was strong. Life had made her that way.

The sun was starting to rise and the cursing in the distance told her that Aphra and Walter were nearby. Oh, how she longed to see them, but she knew she mustn't interfere.

Again she heard Walter's goat-like moans; he must have fallen on the ice. They were not far now, so she lay the toddler to the ground as warmly as she could before she had to leave, making her way back into the snow. But fog enveloped her once again until she no longer had the ability to see.

CHAPTER SIXTEEN

THE GOLDEN DAWN

As though waking from a dream, Charlotte's lashes flickered open to the light. She felt at peace, filled with a new understanding of self-love. She turned her head to the side; her ability to see was poor. It took some time to pinpoint her location beyond the muffled talking. A far-sighted blur distorted her timeless reality.

Aware enough for now, she tried to move her arm to stand but it had been bound to the gold surface on which she was lying. Her other arm too. The shock roused her entirely as she realised she had been constrained. Bound to the wheel, spinning in the sunlight.

She pulled on the clasps holding her wrists in place above her head, noticing Antonious at her side.

'Transfigure,' ordered Abacus with unprecedented urgency in his tone.

'I can't,' Antonious barked back with passionate rage. 'I'm trying to – the sundial has taken my power!'

'Mine too,' shouted Knave, rattling his cuffs. 'Check the encasing for a way out.'

'Proteus has gone,' screamed out Magnus, who recognised his inefficiency to help.

Charlotte knew that if Antonious couldn't break free of the clasps with brute strength then none of them were going to be able to, so began to look for another solution.

Smoothing her fingers across the gold, she tried to find a way to unlock them, noticing Lauraus to her right, trying to slip his hand through the bracket. He looked at her with a brief flash of guilt, because he was unable to protect her.

Soon came the high-pitched sound of a woman laughing. 'Look at them, trying to escape like rats.' More mirth came from the shadows, hilarity as a group of men watched their struggle to survive.

The black-cloaked, evil-eyed figure of a woman joined them in the spiral, taking her place by their feet, her long cloak twirling in the airstream.

She placed the seventh slightly bigger gold Obelisk into its central connection. It fitted together with exact accuracy, lighting up a system of tubes beneath. The prism then sent a beam of light into the sky forming rich clouds above their heads. A thunderstorm began to rouse and golden rain fell from the sky. The droplets coated anything they touched, twisting into gold-plated ornaments. Only the area around the wheel of spirit seemed to be immune, protected by an invisible force field of some kind.

The revolving was getting faster, Mizaldus's cloak spinning out to momentarily block Charlotte's view. When she reappeared, Mizaldus had pulled from her clasp dozens of live coiling snakes attached to what looked like a precisely sharpened blade.

'The Dagger of Thor!' shouted Magnus. 'She has the dagger.'

Antonious thrashed about violently, breaking part of the chains' encasing.

'I think I'll start with the handsome one.'

Charlotte thought she'd meant Lauraus, but was surprised to see that she in fact meant Antonious. She teased him, wrapping her thighs around him. 'Be still.'

Beneath them, a system of tubes filled with harvested blood and it looked as though it was leading to the central-most disc. She came to the awful conclusion that he was being sacrificed, and this was the ritual she'd read about in Kristoffer Enoch's book.

Then Charlotte remembered the bracelet. She looked up to her right arm, ready for vengeance, hoping for some solution.

As Mizaldus held the dagger to his throat, dozens of venomous snakes hissed ferociously in Antonious's face, but he growled back even more fiercely.

The bracelet began to unravel of its own accord. Charlotte had been unable to remove it herself for this many years; apparently it had been awaiting this very instance. She wished that it would untie faster; she could not bear to watch her friend butchered by her side.

Antonious didn't once flinch as he stared into the eyes of Mizaldus, burgundy being sucked into the tubes.

Then a set of pins came up from beneath, piercing their skin, the blood adding to the flow. Around them twitched the shadows of hooded figures. They spoke in Latin, but Charlotte found it difficult to understand the words. She recognised one of the voices as the father of Sinope. Quentin Blatio.

Finally, the bracelet came away, enabling her to move freely through the clasps because it was enchanted to do so.

Mizaldus rose to join her. Smiling menacingly as she spoke from behind psychopathic eyes, she walked towards her.

Charlotte stood to face her worst nightmare, the love still in her heart. She had seen her own beginning and now she would see her end at the hands of the one who had murdered her mother.

The Elders began to chant, perhaps casting some kind of spell, but they did not engage, believing Mizaldus capable of rectifying this situation.

Pain suddenly soared through Charlotte's head. The humming was rendering her immobile. Again, a searing pain throbbed through her entire body, causing her to fall to her knees.

'Let's help it all along, shall we,' cackled Mizaldus with a malicious smile.

'No!' screamed Lauraus, writhing with stricken panic, desperately trying to break free.

Mizaldus let go of the dagger and it slithered towards Charlotte, injecting poison with each of its bites, a black ink beneath her skin.

Charlotte was unable to move as the poison spread around her body. Mizaldus now decided her unworthy of her attention and cast her aside. Black blood filled the tubes where her torso lay. She could no longer hear the screams of her friends, nor could she hear the cackling of Mizaldus.

Mindful of only herself, Charlotte emptied her thoughts into a trance-like state. The vison of that little girl she'd sworn to protect came to mind. *I will never let anyone hurt you again,* came the recollection.

Pain scathing her entire body, she retained her focus, knowing she would only have an instant to carry out her promise. Ignoring the resting urges of her body Charlotte crawled to her knees. The pain had numbed her so much already she could no longer feel the snake bites. Grabbing the dagger Charlotte pierced the centremost stone with the tip of the blade, penetrating the gold with rotting poison. The stone had been compromised.

Mizaldus froze, slanting her arms and tilting her neck to the heavens into a merciless scream. Her body split three times, lifting up into black smoke, and when it had cleared only one was left, huddling to the floor and weeping.

The sundial finally started to surrender before turning the wheel in the opposite direction and replenishing the blood to its victims. The Obelisks now seemed to gain some of their power and were fighting the direction of the spin. Once revitalised, the clasps retracted, allowing them free.

One of the hooded figures said something Charlotte did not understand in Latin. They then began to leave, calmly walking back to the shadows before disappearing entirely. Most of the Last Seven chased after them, but Charlotte was helpless on the ground, unable to assist further.

'What are you doing, Mizaldus?' snapped Quentin with bad-tempered embarrassment. 'Get up! Finish her off!'

But Mizaldus didn't move from the spot where she was kneeling.

'Fine I'll do it myself,' he snapped, pulling out a blade, but a masked saviour pulled him back from the dial. Quentin stuck the blade through their chest for inconveniencing him, then pulled away the mask. His face dropped from an expression of satisfaction to great pain as he watched his only daughter, Sinope, fall silently to the ground. His hands began to tremble as he held her up to him, rocking. 'I'm sorry … I'm so sorry.' But Sinope lay lifeless beside him, already passed.

Quentin abandoned her lifeless body for now, replacing his grip on the blade that had just killed his daughter. He took to the sundial to kill the one he believed responsible for his daughter's death.

The Last Seven looked back in horror; they had assumed the grief of losing his daughter would have disabled him, but they were wrong. How could they have been so stupid?

Quentin held the dagger to Charlotte's neck, with a satisfied look of menace in his smile.

But to Charlotte's amazement a blow cast him up into the air and onto the ground beneath. 'No one hurts my niece,' came the voice of Mizaldus, clutching Charlotte to her side.

Suddenly Charlotte was thrust up over the shoulder of Antonious and could just make out the trees as she watched his calves run through the leaves of the forest, with nothing but the sound of his panting breath.

CHAPTER SEVENTEEN

The Grandiflora

Cast into water, her breath was stolen as she sank unresponsively to the bottom. What should have been the nethermost base of the fountain gave rise to fresh waters, coming out to a pool on the other side of the water's surface. This must have still been Apollo's Fountain, but the other side, because it was an exact replica.

Charlotte felt herself being dragged up the steps and laid upon the stone courtyard floor. Ringing reverberated from the walls as water trickled, evaporating the poison from beneath her skin, subdued by her lifeless soul, so close to death.

The sound faded and soft singing filled its place, but it wasn't coming from anywhere nearby. For a moment Charlotte wondered if she was dead and hearing angels. But she sat up, aware that her body had been drained of the poison running through her veins and she felt very different indeed.

Somehow her senses had been enhanced; she could see with crystal-clear precision. She watched a hummingbird drink nectar from the corner of her eye with such clarity it made her gasp. She took raindrops to her lips from a white lily that had grown towards the pool, and she drank the liquid, watching a crimson beetle scurry across her hand. As it did she could hear the fast beating of its tiny heart. It tickled so she giggled, able to hear its tiny footsteps scurry away.

In her mind she saw white flowers that adorned the vine-covered walls, only to confirm them a moment later with the turn of her head. Clear spiders of all shapes and sizes scuttled from their webs to meet their new guest.

Something around her neck was humming. She lifted her hands to find a necklace. The locket of her mother and father. But hadn't that only been a memory?

Her mind gifted a new picture in slow motion; a female running her fingers through the water. 'Isn't everything beautiful when you're shown it from a new perspective?' came the voice, making Charlotte turn her head. Water droplets fell from her fingers to her naked body, long red hair covering her modesty.

Charlotte noticed spiders upturned on the ground, filled with the poison, having sacrificed their lives for her by sucking out the toxins.

She looked upon the woman's bulging green eyes. 'I'm sorry about the spiders,' she said with weakness in her voice, having made it back from what should have been certain death.

The woman must have been able to hear her thoughts because she added further to what Charlotte had been thinking. 'You would not have made it back at all had you not been wearing the armour the Eringi spiders provided,' she teased, resting her chin to a concaved shoulder. 'I have been watching over you,' she said softly, staring with grief at the two upturned spiders that had just given their lives.

She seemed to have great love for them, as though they were her friends. 'I am the Grandiflora. You currently reside in the Wirral, your birthplace. Which is why you can make it through the fountain.'

'You are the woman in the reflection,' said Charlotte, recognising her at once. 'You gave me my talisman through the water … and again in the lake, you warned me about Mizaldus.'

The Grandiflora dipped her toes into the water. Charlotte saw that it was reflecting these very images to her. 'Yes, Charlotte, that's right. I have been watching over you for a long time.'

Charlotte looked down to her forearm noticing that only her talisman remained there. 'Where has the amulet gone?'

'It has fulfilled its purpose' said the Grandiflora plainly. 'The wheel of spirit has been destroyed so it is no longer needed.'

Four palm-sized spiders climbed her thighs then began the job of repairing her body suit. 'You gave me the bodysuit on my birthday,' she said recognising the thread to be the same.

The Grandiflora sat by the fountain holding her knees to her bare chest. 'It is Eringi-made, a very rare gift, I fear you may not have still been here had they not granted it.'

Charlotte felt indebted to the spiders as she watched them shimmy down her chest and pluck the armour's fibres to check for weaknesses. 'The soul inside my Obelisk told me that Mizaldus has not been acting of her own free will,' questioned Charlotte, realising that she did not have the pyramid in her possession anymore. 'Is that true?'

'It is, Mizaldus has been the victim of a cruel possession that has caused her to do a great many things that she would not normally have done. But I suspect that she manipulated the thoughts of Lilith to collect the Dagger of Thor in the first place. It was probably the only defence she had. That Lilith could hear her thoughts and she must have cleverly used that to her advantage.'

'But I don't understand how the Obelisks were created in the first place,' said Charlotte, confused because there had been no mention of it in any of the texts.

'The Obelisks were originally created by Jupiter to allow his sons and daughters a means to travel at the speed of thought.'

Charlotte held the locket around her neck, reflecting on the pain of being an orphan and feeling of closure that embracing her younger self had brought her. 'Even time travel?' she asked wondering if that was how it had been achievable.

The Grandiflora creased a brow. 'It is possible, but rare,' she said curiously.

Charlotte opened the locket. 'I saw myself as a toddler, I was alone in the woods before Aphra and Walter found me. I accidently took this locket, there's a picture of my mum and dad inside.'

Sweeping her hair aside the woman gazed over Charlotte's shoulder to look upon the long narrow face of her father. 'I bet he looks a lot older than that now.'

Turning her head in disbelief a burst of excitement filled Charlotte's chest. 'You mean he's still alive?'

Looking upward from the corner of her eye the Grandiflora took a moment before answering. 'I believe so yes. I told your mother the same thing, before she died of course. It gave her hope I think, but, if he is still alive there is only one that would know his whereabouts and I'm not too sure whether she would provide it, especially, now she's been arrested.'

Excitement quickly turned to guilt as she thought of Sinope. She must have followed the Elders out of the Labyrinth to try to protect her. 'But Quentin Blatio tried to kill me and Mizaldus protected me from him, doesn't that prove her innocence?'

'I'm afraid that will make no difference,' said the Grandiflora. 'She is a wanted criminal, having committed a number of crimes.'

Charlotte glanced inside the pool. She could see Antonious searching the water with his arms on the other side. Lauraus dived in panic-stricken, exploring the hard bottom of the pool. The Grandiflora noticed this too and frowned sorrowfully because she knew it was time for Charlotte to go. 'You know you can always write to me?' she suggested hopefully.

'I will,' said Charlotte. 'And thank you for everything.'

The time had come to descend the steps back into the water. Taking one last glance at the red head she began lowering herself down.

The Grandiflora nodded and gave a broken smile before Charlotte disappeared under the surface.

#

Upon return to the Coliseum, I graduated with honours.

Lauraus and I were naturally upset; he didn't want to marry Sinope, but he certainly hadn't wished her dead. Especially at the hands of her own father. It's so awful.

Quentin was arrested, and banished by direct order of the Court of Verderers, never to return.

Mandy has been dating the same boy for almost two months and Antonious has since made a full recovery, reunited with Sarah that very night. My friend Frugal and the Goblin had had a huge argument at the ball; it turned out the Goblin didn't like eggs, something Frugal could never learn to accept.

And Lauraus and I, well, let's just say things couldn't be better. He'll be round in a minute. I'm going to meet him now.

'Come on, Charlotte!' shouted Walter up the staircase. 'Your boyfriend will be here in a minute.'

Charlotte rolled up the parchment, and wrote the name *Grandiflora*. The second she let go, the scroll disappeared up the chimney.

She ran down the stairs, grabbing one of her coats from the railing before vacating through the front door.

Walter mumbled something like 'Young love,' before returning to the only job he had been given to tend to in the kitchen, mashing the Brussel sprouts.

She made it just in time to see the number four bus coming up the road and halting on the corner of Hoddinott's Bluff. She still didn't know why he insisted on taking it, but he said he wanted to do things properly, whatever that meant.

As the doors opened, the bus driver gave him a confused glance because he was wearing his full armour and his sword was at his side for the occasion. A mark of respect in Avaland.

'Will you be requiring anything else, your excellency?' said the wartiest man Charlotte had ever seen. The bus driver extended a blank wide-eyed stare.

'No, Feebes, that will be all, thank you,' said Lauraus. 'You may make your way back to the castle.'

Feebes bowed several times whilst walking backwards to the back seat. 'Your majesty,' he chirped.

Lauraus descended the steps with vigour, his cloak flowing behind him valiantly. The driver rolled his eyes and shut the doors before driving off again, Feebes waving royally from the back window.

'Oh great,' said Charlotte, realising that Constance and Beatrice were headed straight for them. She had warned Lauraus about these two in a scroll before he had arrived. Lauraus turned with surprise to see that Charlotte had been so intimidated by a pair of human girls with no weapons.

'Is this your freaky boyfriend?' Beatrice spat hastening a guess.

Constance laughed then snorted. 'Nice outfit!'

Lauraus stood in astonishment, shocked at how a person could be so rude. 'Look here, you,' he said. 'I'll have you know that I'm a prince.'

Both girls burst out in fits of laughter, hardly able to contain themselves.

'Just ignore them,' said Charlotte, pulling him hurriedly across the road.

'Got any money for me?' Beatrice smirked, putting her hand in Charlotte's pocket. 'None?' she said, pulling out a bottle of Hairy Ears, Nose and Toes Tonic.

'But that old bag's always giving her money,' said Constance, snatching the bottle from Beatrice. 'What's this?'

Constance held the bottle and squinted. They watched in horror as hairs sprouted from the tips of their fingers and glided up their arms.

Charlotte thought back to where the bottle could have come from, then remembered seeing London at the apothecary.

The apologetic look he had given her must have been because he had hidden this bottle inside her jacket so his lady friend didn't see it. Because she hadn't worn the coat since, it had been in there all these months without her realising.

Lauraus looked on, delighted, as the pair got a taste of their own medicine, even if it had been unintentional. The two girls ran off screaming. Charlotte wrapped the bottle up in an old tissue and threw it into a nearby bin so nobody else could get hurt.

Lauraus looked at her, confused. 'Why do you have a bottle of Hairy Ears, Nose and Toes Tonic in your jacket pocket?' he asked, leaning in for a kiss.

'I'll explain later,' she said, with absolutely no intention of doing so at all.